BY THE TIME YOU READ THIS, I'LL BE DEAD.
This isn't Jackie. It's her son Wade.
She doesn't know where I am.
She doesn't even know I can get on her FB
page, so don't ask her. This isn't her fault.
I am not her fault. I wish I could tell you
the truth of what happened,
but it's not my truth to tell . . .

"*If I Die Tonight* continues Alison Gaylin's
winning streak with its timely, twisty, and utterly human
take on the way we live (and die) today."
—LAURA LIPPMAN

"Alison Gaylin is at the very top of her game,
crafting exhilarating and audacious crime novels that are
both rich in character and rivetingly told."
—MEGAN ABBOTT, Edgar Award–winning
author of *You Will Know Me*

"This is mind-blowing suspense from an exceptional writer."
—ALEX MARWOOD, *USA Today* bestselling
author of *The Darkest Secret*

"Alison Gaylin is a great storyteller."
—MARK BILLINGHAM, author of *Love Like Blood*

If I Die Tonight

Also by Alison Gaylin

What Remains of Me
Trashed
Heartless
Reality Ends Here

the Brenna Spector series
And She Was
Into the Dark
Stay With Me

Samantha Leiffer novels
Hide Your Eyes
You Kill Me

If I Die Tonight

A Novel

ALISON GAYLIN

wm

WILLIAM MORROW

An Imprint of HarperCollins*Publishers*

P.S.™ is a trademark of HarperCollins Publishers.

HarperCollins books may be purchased for educational, business, or sales promotional use. For information, please email the Special Markets Department at SPsales@harpercollins.com.

FIRST EDITION

Designed by Diahann Sturge

Title page and chapter opener art © dimitris_k/shutterstock, inc.

Library of Congress Cataloging-in-Publication Data has been applied for.

ISBN 978-0-06-264109-0 (paperback)
ISBN 978-0-06-264110-6 (library edition)

18 19 20 21 22   LSC   10 9 8 7 6 5 4 3 2 1

For Marissa.
You make me proud every day.

If I Die Tonight

Prologue

From the Facebook page of Jacqueline Merrick Reed.

October 24 at 2:45 AM

By the time you read this, I'll be dead.

This isn't Jackie. It's her son Wade. She doesn't know where I am. She doesn't even know I can get on her FB page, so don't ask her. This isn't her fault. I am not her fault.

I am writing to tell my mom and Connor that I'm sorry. I never meant to hurt anyone. I wish I could tell you the truth of what happened, but it's not my truth to tell. And anyway, it doesn't matter. What matters, what I want you both to know, is that I love you. Don't feel sad. Everything you did was the right thing to do. I'm sorry for those things I said to you, Connor. I didn't mean any of it.

Funny, I'm thinking about you right now, Connor. How you used to follow me around all the time when you were a little kid. How you used to copy everything I did. You probably don't remember this but when you were about four, I taught you the middle finger, and you did it to that mean babysitter we had. What was her name, Mom? Loretta? Lurleen? Anyway, Whatever-her-name-was had some crap reality show on the TV. *Real Housewives of the Seventh Circle of Hell.* She wouldn't let us watch the Mets game and called us nasty little brats and told us we had no business talking at all because children should be seen and not heard. Whatever the hell that's supposed to mean.

So, Connor gets off the couch, walks up to Lurleen, and flips her the bird. He was so little, he needed two hands to do it. He used the left hand to hold down the fingers on the right. Do you remember this, Mom? Because I'm pretty sure she ratted us out without explaining the context of forcing us to watch her crap TV show. You were so mad, we didn't get dessert for two weeks.

I remember thinking how unfair the whole thing was and how quick grown-ups were to believe the lies of other grown-ups, especially when it came to their own kids. But looking back on it now, all I can rememberis how red Loretta's face got and how hard we both laughed, even with her shrieking at us. It was one of those moments. My English teacher Mrs. Crawford called them memory gifts. You kep them in a special part of your brain and you kind of wrap them up to preserve them and tie them with a ribbon so when you need them hwen you're feeling reallybad you can unwrap them and you remember all the details and feel the moment all over again. So thanks for that memory gift, buddy. It's making me smile now.

I'm all alone here right now, unless you count the ghost lol. I'm writing this just after taking the pills, but I won't post it until I start to really feel them. According to what I read, death comes pretty soon after that.

So I'm typing extra fast. Sorry about typos.

This will probably make a lot of you very happy. Good. For anybody who might be sad, sorry. But you know what? Stuff happens. Things go wrong. And the more you stick around, the wronger they get. I know I'm just 17. But I think of what life would be like if I wasn't here. I think of the way things could have gone without me in the picture, how much better it would be. And then I know. I'm sure of it. I've lived too long already.

👍 1,043 people like this

One

Five days earlier

In bed late at night with her laptop, Jackie Reed sometimes forgot there were others in the house. That's how quiet it was here, with these hushed boys of hers, always with their heads down, with their shuffling footsteps and their padded sneakers, their muttered greetings, their doors closing behind them.

When did kids get to be so quiet? When she was their age—well, Wade's age anyway—Jackie clomped around in her Doc Martens and slammed doors. She'd blast her albums loud as they'd go—Violent Femmes and Siouxsie and Scraping Foetus off the Wheel—edging up the volume until her bones vibrated with the bass, the drums, flailing around her room, dancing as hard as she could with her parents pounding on the walls, begging her to turn it down.

Please, Jacqueline, I can't hear myself think!

Looking back on it now, she saw it as a rite of passage, the same one her mother had gone through with her Elvis and her Lesley

Gore, and her grandmother too, no doubt, cranking the Mario Lanza as though she were the only person who mattered in the cramped Brooklyn walk-up where she grew up.

There was such power in loud music, such teenage energy and rebellion and soaring possibility. Who'd have thought, back then, that it would all go extinct within just one generation? These days, teens plugged themselves into devices, headphone wires spooling out of their ears like antennae. They kept their music to themselves, kept everything to themselves, and their devices and the friends they talked to on those devices, all of whom you couldn't hear, couldn't see unless you swiped their phones away midconversation to read the screen and who wanted to do that? Who wanted to be *that mom*?

They shut you out. Your children shut you out of their heads, their lives. And that was a form of rebellion so much more chilling than blasting music or yelling. They made it so you couldn't know them anymore. They made it so you couldn't help.

Just yesterday, she'd been making breakfast when Wade's phone had gone off like a bomb on the kitchen counter. That incoming text tone of his, literally *like a bomb,* the sound of an explosion. *When and why did he download that?* Jackie had nearly jumped out of her skin, spattering bacon grease, hand pressed to her heart . . .

The phone's case was missing—an accident waiting to happen, the latest broken screen of so many broken screens in this house. Why didn't her boys take better care of their things?

Moving it back from the edge of the counter, Jackie had looked. The text had been from someone he'd nicknamed simply "T": *Leave me alone.*

The gut punch of those words, the intimacy of the single initial. *Who was this person? A girl? How could she say that to*

Wade? What has he done? All those questions looping through her mind. And here, a day later, Jackie still didn't know the answer to a single one of them.

Once Wade had retrieved his phone and left for school, she'd checked his long-abandoned Facebook page for cryptic posts from friends with *T* names and dusted his room for evidence of a girlfriend—but not too deeply. She couldn't bear to hack his laptop or go through his drawers. She wasn't *that mom.*

Casually, in the car on the way to his guitar lesson, she'd asked Connor, "Do you know if Wade has been fighting with any of his friends?"

Connor had shaken his head and replied quietly, saying it to the car floor in his cracking, changing thirteen-year-old voice, "I don't really know too many of Wade's friends, Mom."

Jackie sighed. She and Wade needed to talk. But not now. It was nearly midnight, and his third and final chance at the SATs was tomorrow and he needed his sleep. Wade was looking so tired lately, she wondered if he ever really slept at all.

Jackie felt a chill at her back, cold night air pressing against her bedroom window, against the thin walls, creeping through cracks in the plaster. Her house was so drafty, even now in mid-October. She hated thinking about what the winter would be like. A lifetime ago, Jackie had lived in sunny Southern California. The Hollywood Experiment, she and her ex-husband, Bill, had called it, when they were still young and childless—not even married yet, Bill with his screenplay, Jackie with her half-finished novel, driving out to L.A. to follow their dreams. It had only lasted a year, the Hollywood Experiment coming to a crashing close when Jackie had gotten pregnant with Wade and they'd moved back to Havenkill, where they both were assured real jobs. But what a warm year it had been, in every way. Those breath-hot Santa Ana

winds on the back of her neck, the camellias blooming bright, all
the way into Christmas. In twelve months, Jackie hadn't needed
to unpack a single pair of socks and they'd slept nude, crisp sheets
against their skin . . .

Jackie pulled the comforter tighter around her and focused on
her laptop screen—the scrolling Facebook feed with its lurid shots
of five-star dinners, vacations in St. Bart's, Miami, the Mexican
Riviera, perfect cocktails brightened up with exotically named
filters. Perpetua, Valencia, Clarendon.

So many selfies too. One caught Jackie's eye: her friend Helen
Davies, who worked with her at the Potter Bloom real estate
agency and had gone to high school with her thirty years ago
in this very town. Helen with her chunky gold earrings and her
Mona Lisa smile, head tilted down, ducking the camera in the
same way Jackie did, that middle-aged female way, hoping for
low light. But Helen looked so much livelier than Jackie, so much
more satisfied, her peachy-skinned, seventeen-year-old daughter,
Stacy, thrust in front of her like the lovely feature she was.

Girls' day in the city, the caption read. *Shopping at Saks!*

Jackie looked at Stacy's bright smile and felt a stab of jealousy.
Did they know their children better than she did, these mothers
of daughters? Were they as happy as they looked?

Stupid question. Nobody was as happy as they looked on
Facebook—even Jackie knew that. She reached for her glass
of Chardonnay and took a long swallow, feeling the comforting tartness of it at the back of her tongue, the warmth as it
slid down her throat. She glanced down at the corner of the
screen: 11:27 PM. Time to sleep. Or try to. Why did her brain
do this to her every night? She'd wander through her whole day
exhausted, and then as soon as it was time to go to bed, all of
the worries and misgivings she'd successfully buried during the

past sixteen hours would pop out of their shallow graves, one by one, and parade through her brain, keeping her awake. Memories too. Like the time she was showing her very first house and the couple got the time wrong and she wound up half an hour late at Wade's preschool to find him sitting on the bench in the parking lot, his little face pinched red, teacher dabbing at his tears.

Mommy, where were you? Did you forget about me?

Jackie slid open her nightstand drawer, found her bottle of Xanax. She took half a pill—just half, washed down with the rest of the Chardonnay. By the time she'd quit out of Facebook, closed the laptop screen, and flicked off her light, her breathing had slowed and she felt herself sinking into a velvety half sleep, her muscles relaxing. Jackie closed her eyes and drifted off, drowsy and warm with the knowledge that everything in life was temporary, life included. And really, when it all came down to it, nothing was worth the effort it took to worry.

A SOUND JOLTED Jackie awake; she wasn't sure what. She'd been dreaming she was in a rowboat in the middle of choppy waters and the oars wouldn't reach, and when she woke, she felt queasy from something, either from the dream or the Chardonnay. It took her several seconds to blink the cobwebs out of her brain and focus on the sound, which was coming from across the hall—a scuffling, the clink of metal. She reached for her phone; *911,* she thought. *Call 911. No. No, breathe first. Listen. Could be the wind. Could be anything.*

Jackie breathed. Three deep breaths, what Helen called cleansing breaths, Helen and her yoga classes, out with the bad energy, in with the good. She tried to focus on the scuffling, really hear it. She exhaled again, hard, air tumbling out of her. Listened.

Arnie. Connor's pet hamster, racing around his cage. Nocturnal or not, that animal slept all the time . . . *What woke him up?*

From down the hall, near the front door, Jackie heard the creak of floorboards. A thump. She bolted up to sitting. Looked at the digital clock on her nightstand: 1:48 AM.

Heart pounding up into her throat, Jackie grabbed her phone, crept toward the bedroom door, bare feet on the hardwood floor, heel to toe, heel to toe, breath soft and shallow, arms straight out like a tightrope walker . . . *Don't make a sound.*

She pressed 911 on her phone, her finger hovering over the send button. If she saw anything, anyone . . . She cracked the door. *Don't hurt my boys,* she thought. As though they were smaller than she was. *You hurt my boys, I'll kill you.*

Jackie peered into the darkened hallway.

Behind Connor's closed door, Arnie squeaked and shuffled in his cage.

Jackie kept a baseball bat by her bedroom door. Left over from Wade's long-forgotten Little League days. She took the bat in hand, the cool metal against her palm calming her.

She moved into the hallway. "Hello," she said. "Anyone there?"

Jackie flipped the hall light on. She glided across the hall to Connor's room, bat and phone in the same hand. With the other, she cracked the door. The room was warm, pitch-dark, heavy with the sound of her son's sleep-breathing, Arnie's insistent squeaks. Her eyes adjusted. No one in here but the two of them.

She lowered the bat, her heartbeat slowing as the last shards of sleep fell away and everything grew clear. *Okay,* she thought. *This is what's going on.* She backed out of Connor's room. Softly closed his door.

Wade's door was ajar, and she knew without looking that the bed would be empty, that the thumps she'd heard earlier had been the sound of someone leaving the house, not breaking in. From where she was standing, she could see him through the long window next to the front door, the shadow of him in the porch light. A few steps closer and she saw him in full. Wade. His back to the house, the glow of his cigarette. Watching the stars. *When did he get so tall?*

Jackie should stop him, she knew. He needed to sleep. He shouldn't be smoking. She knew all of that. But she couldn't.

Let him have this.

Jackie slipped back into her own room, slid open her nightstand drawer, and took the other half of the Xanax, this time with nothing. She pulled the comforter up to her chin and closed her eyes, waiting for the calm. As she started to drift, she found herself thinking of Wade. How smiley and talkative he'd been when he was little, so eager to please. He was different now. A different boy, a sad boy . . .

No, *sad* was the wrong word. Sad was something she understood.

PEARL MAZE WAS on the phone with the drunk's wife when the rain started.

"I'm sorry, ma'am," Pearl was saying, eyes on the drunk, headache starting to blossom. "But we can't just hold him here indefinitely."

"Isn't that what they're for?" the wife said. "Holding cells? I mean, Jesus. It's nearly three in the morning. Why should I have to suffer for his idiocy?"

"We don't have a holding cell, ma'am," she said. "We're too small for a holding cell. We just have a holding bench."

The drunk was cuffed to the bench. His head lolled to one side and his eyes were half closed and his mouth open, drool trickling out the side of his clean-shaven face and into the collar of his pink-and-white-striped oxford cloth shirt. The drunk did have a name, though Pearl didn't see the point in remembering it, him losing consciousness and all. She'd typed it into the computer and fingerprinted him after Tally and Udel had brought him in, kicking and screaming that he'd committed no crime, that he hadn't been driving, he'd been enjoying the evening for chrissakes and looking up at the stars and what the hell did they mean, disturbing the peace, disturbing the peace was his God-given right as an American, you're all worse than my wife, you know that?

The drunk wasn't from around here—he was visiting from New York City. A leaf peeper, staying at the Pine Hollow B & B with his incredibly put-out-sounding wife. Pearl was over and done with the both of them. *Go back to New York City. I'll pay for your train tickets.* The whole booking room stunk of him now—whiskey and stale cigarettes and whatever else he'd rolled around in between consuming eleven Jamesons and a beer chaser at the Red Door Tavern and sitting cross-legged in the middle of Merchant Street, yelling obscenities at the flashing traffic light. The smell wasn't doing anything to relieve her headache. Pearl shut her eyes and squeezed the bridge of her nose. She needed a glass of water, two cups of coffee, three Advil.

"All right, fine," said the wife. "I'll be right over."

"Thank you." Pearl hung up. *Thank you, Jesus.*

The drunk said, "She coming?"

Pearl nodded.

He nodded back at her. Then he leaned over and threw up all over the booking-room floor.

"Beautiful." Pearl jumped up from the desk and hurried into the break room to get paper towels and water and away from the drunk. That was when the sky opened up. *Could this night get any better?*

"What happened in there?" Bobby Udel said it as though he couldn't care less. He said everything as though he couldn't care less. Udel was one of the younger officers, about Pearl's age. Nice enough, she guessed, but to her mind he was suspiciously mellow for a cop. He'd grown up in this town. Maybe that had something to do with it.

Pearl looked at him—those watery blue eyes, that weak, little boy's chin. Cradling a mug with a map of New York State on it in smooth cherubic hands. She felt old enough to be his mother. "You don't want to know."

He chuckled. "Jim Beam tossed his cookies, huh?"

Pearl found a bucket and started to fill it in the sink. "Jim Beam," she said. "That's a good one." She grabbed a glass out of one of the cupboards, held it under the running faucet, and gulped it down. The rain drummed on the roof. It made her heart pound. *Any day now,* she thought. *Any day the roof will cave in . . .*

Pearl had known about the structural damage since she took this job. All the cops joked about it because what else are you going to do? In keeping with the rest of Havenkill, which was more often than not referred to as Historic Havenkill, it was a charming building to look at—bright blue shutters, brass door knocker. Window boxes even, as ridiculous as that may sound. But it was also condemned. A lovely shell of a place, falling apart for years, though Hurricane Irene had pounded the final nail into its coffin. "The Death Trap," the sergeant called the station. "The Busted Bunker." The hardwood floors buckled and popped; wind whistled through gaps in the doorjambs. And on rainy nights like this, the ceilings bled out in dozens of places. Pearl could see a spot now, right at the center of the break room, dripping angrily, water spattering on the floor. Less than two weeks, and the Havenkill PD would break ground on a new station, Pearl and her fellow officers moving into a double-wide in the new parking lot. Closer quarters, but much safer ones, especially considering the nasty winter the weather people kept predicting. *Keep it together, Busted Bunker . . . Just nine and a half more days . . .*

A gust of wind knocked into the side of the building, the rain thudding now. Hammering. She ripped off a swath of paper towels, grabbed the full bucket, a bottle of Murphy oil soap, a mop out of the janitor's closet. *The puke is fixable. Focus on that.*

"Need any help?" Udel said in his halfhearted way. Pearl shook her head. As she headed down the hall on her way back into the booking room, she was certain she could hear the creak of shingles detaching.

The drunk was slumped on the bench, snoring. Holding her breath, Pearl poured some of the water from the bucket onto the mess he'd made, and followed it up with a few squirts of cleaner. It roused him a little. "You don't know," he murmured at her.

"Huh?"

His eyes opened. "You're young," he said. "Just a kid. You don't know yet how pointless life is."

She stared at him for a few seconds, remembering his name. "You're wrong about that, Mr. Fletcher."

"Shit," he said, not to Pearl but at the explosion of noise—a furious pounding on the front door and then the buzzer, someone leaning on it so hard it was as though they wanted to break it.

"That doesn't sound like your wife, does it?"

He shook his head.

Pearl rushed toward the door, Udel, Tally, and then the sergeant leaving his office, moving in front of Pearl, pressing the intercom and trying to talk to her, the woman on the other side of the door, trying to calm her as she half screamed, half cried like women never did on the quiet streets of this historic Hudson Valley town. "Please, ma'am," the sergeant said. "We are going to let you in."

But she didn't seem to hear. "An accident." That was all she kept saying, over and over again, even after he opened the door for her and she fell through it—makeup smeared, weeping in her bright red raincoat and rainbow-dyed hair, wet as something dredged up from the river. "There's been an accident."

"MOM?" CONNOR CALLED out from the kitchen.

Jackie couldn't answer. She was in Wade's doorway, eyes fixed on his empty bed.

"Mom!"

Jackie swallowed hard and made her way into the kitchen. It smelled of the coffee she'd set to brew last night.

"Can you take me to Noah's house?" Connor said it around a mouthful of cereal. He was sitting at the kitchen table, back turned to her, eating fast. "I'm gonna be late."

Jackie said, "I thought Wade was taking you."

"I . . . He said he didn't have time."

"He said that."

"Yes."

"This morning."

"Yes, Mom."

"It's ten." She said it slowly, staring at the back of his head. "Why didn't he have time? The SATs don't start till eleven thirty."

Connor shrugged elaborately. "How do I know? I just need a ride." The word *ride* pitched up an octave. The back of his neck flushed red. Poor kid, voice constantly betraying him. Puberty was cruel, and for Connor, it often proved a lie detector, his voice cracking more than usual during those still-rare attempts to be deceitful.

"Connor."

"Yeah?"

"Did Wade come home last night?"

"What?" A thin squeak.

"It's a simple question."

"Mom, if I don't leave for Noah's, like, now, we won't have enough time to work on our science project."

"Did you see him?" Jackie said. "Did you see your brother this morning?"

"Yeah, of course I did." He said it quietly, carefully. "He was leaving when I got up."

"Look at me."

Connor turned around. He blinked those bright blue eyes at her, his father's eyes. "Mom," he said. "Are you okay?"

Jackie swallowed. *No,* she wanted to say. *I'm not okay. I used to know you guys so well I could read your thoughts, and now it's as though every day, every minute even, I know you less. You're turning into strangers.*

You're turning into men.

She looked at the half-empty coffeepot, the demolished bowl of cereal placed next to the sink, unemptied, unwashed, a few stray Cheerios swimming in puddled milk. Wade never washed out his cereal bowls. Connor did. Wade drank coffee. Connor did not. Wade had been here this morning, she decided. Last night, he'd had his moment on the front step with his cigarette and the stars, and then he'd come back inside. He'd gone back to bed, gotten up this morning, and left early, for whatever reason. Connor wasn't lying. Connor didn't lie. Not about anything big, anyway.

"Mom?"

"I'm fine."

"You sure?"

She cleared her throat. "Maybe after I get home from work, you and Wade and I can do something."

Connor looked at her as though she'd just sprouted a third eye. "Umm."

"Maybe go out to dinner. See a movie? Talk?"

He blinked at her again. "Sure," he managed after a drawn-out pause during which they both locked eyes, a type of standoff.

Jackie smiled. It was natural, she knew, this aching feeling, this growing divide between the boys she raised and herself. All those books she used to read, the shrink she used to go to, all of them told her that as a single mother of sons she needed to maintain distance, to teach them to stand on their own early, lest they grow up too dependent on her, too possessive. Nobody liked a mama's boy. But still, that didn't make it any easier, your baby wincing at the thought of spending time with you.

"Go get your stuff, and I'll take you to Noah's."

Connor propelled himself out of the room.

Jackie went to the sink, spilled the milk and cereal out of Wade's bowl and rinsed it, thinking about all the times she'd yelled at him to rinse his bowl, how carefully she'd explained to him that if he didn't wash it out right away, the cereal would crust on and never come off, no matter how many times she put it through the washer. She'd shown him the evidence: the scarred, ruined bowls, cereal remnants clinging to the sides like cement. Wade would nod at her, that dyed black hair of his flopping into his eyes, but it never sunk in. Or maybe he ignored her on purpose, the same way, without warning, he'd blackened the sandy-blond hair that used to match her own. The way he'd taken his phone the day before yesterday, checking his texts without looking at her. And how he'd said, "See you later, Mom," in that calm, unreadable voice, without making eye contact, without looking at her at all.

It was normal, the way the boys treated her, the way they made her feel. Growing up was hard, and parents bore the brunt of it, mothers especially. Mothers of teenage sons.

It is normal, she thought. *Isn't it?* And then the doorbell rang. The police.

Two

I didn't lie." Connor Reed thought the sentence so hard that he actually said it out loud, and even then, he was so deep inside his own head that he didn't realize he'd said it until his friend Noah gave him a funny look and said, "Umm . . . What?"

"Nothing."

Noah frowned at him. Went back to cutting leaves in half. For their science project, they were supposed to figure out how caffeine affects the structural matter of plants, and so they'd taken some leaves from Noah's mom's ficus tree, Noah cutting them in half as Connor crushed caffeine tablets with a Smucker's jar. Once they were done, they'd stir the crushed tablets into six different beakers of water, the ratio of caffeine to water less and less, the final one caffeine-free. Then they'd drop the leaves in and observe them for six days. Connor was trying to work fast. Noah had the newest version of Skylanders. Connor had wanted to play it for months and that's what they planned to do, once the leaves were in the beakers. But all he could think of was the weird conversation he'd had with his mom this morning, and then the cops showing up at his house . . .

He hadn't lied to anybody.

"Dude, that's plenty crushed," Noah said.

Connor looked up at him and then down at the kitchen table. He put the jar down. What was left of the pills was now a thin coat of dust.

"You okay?"

"I told you I'm fine."

"No you didn't."

Noah's kitchen smelled of burned cookies and Play-Doh. His three little sisters had been in here this morning, messing up the whole room, when Connor had arrived. Even though Noah's mom had made them clean it all up before shooing them out, the smell still hung in the air. Made it feel like preschool in here, which was sad in a way Connor couldn't quite put his finger on.

"Sorry, Noah. I'm fine. Just . . . you know . . ."

"Nervous about the project?"

Man, Noah was a dork. "Yeah," Connor said. "That's exactly it."

Noah smiled, not catching the sarcasm, of course. He had a mouth full of metal that he kept free of food by brushing probably fifty times a day. "We'll ace it," he said. The braces gave him a lisp.

Noah had been Connor's best friend since before kindergarten, but lately that seemed to be changing. A year ago, six months ago even, he would have told Noah everything about last night. Everything he remembered, anyway. He'd have told him what he'd said to his mom and the cops and then he would have asked if Noah thought it was a lie. But he couldn't. Not anymore. He felt weird around Noah lately—as though they were in two different cars, with Connor speeding ahead and Noah just watching him out the window, smiling that big, dorky smile of his, getting smaller and smaller in the rearview. "Sometimes, we outgrow our friends. It's nobody's fault. It just happens." Connor's mom had said that to him once, a long time ago. She was right, but he hated remembering that now. It was the last thing he needed, hearing Mom's voice in his head. *You didn't lie to her.* "I'll start filling the beakers," he said.

As he headed over to the sink the image flashed in his mind: Wade in his room. Had to be close to four in the morning—Connor hadn't looked at the clock. The wet smell coming off of him, mud and sweat. Wade's shadowed face. Hair dripping, which made Connor realize it was raining before he'd heard that crash of thunder, like everything in the world exploding to bits. For a few seconds, in the lightning flash, Connor had seen his brother's eyes. *I can trust you, right, buddy? You won't say anything?*

This morning, when Connor had awoken, he'd thought maybe it had all been a dream. But then he'd seen the drips of water on his floor. A muddy footprint. He'd walked down the hall, poked his head in Wade's room. It had been empty. *You didn't lie. You did see Wade this morning. What you didn't say was that it was very early in the morning when you saw him, before the sun came up. But that's just leaving stuff out. It isn't lying.*

Connor half filled the first beaker of water, shook in three teaspoons full of caffeine dust, then set it back in its holder. "Hey, Noah?"

"Yeah?"

"Did the police come by your house today?"

"What? No. What are you talking about?"

Connor filled another beaker, measured out two and a half teaspoons. "I guess some kid got hit by a car," he said.

"What?"

"Some kid," he tried again, thoughts returning to the cop at his door, the gun in his holster that Connor had tried to avoid staring at. A real gun. *It happened just a few blocks from here,* the cop had said. *Wondered if you saw or heard anything last night. Anything unusual . . .* "Like a hit-and-run or something."

Noah gaped at him. Why did he always breathe through his mouth like that?

"They were canvassing the area." Connor wasn't sure exactly what that meant. But that's what the cop had said, as though they were covering their entire street with a giant canvas, blocking out the sun, smothering everybody.

"What kid?" Noah said.

"They didn't tell us."

"Did the kid die?"

Connor exhaled hard. "The cop told my mom he's in critical condition."

"Wow. So . . ."

"Yeah?"

"It happened in your area."

"*Yeah?*"

"You live in a high-crime area now. I probably shouldn't go to your house anymore. Like . . . you should just come here from now on."

Connor turned. Stared at him, but he wouldn't look back. Noah had found a stray piece of his sisters' Play-Doh and was rolling it between his fingers, his whole face focused on it, as though it were some great archaeological find.

"What are you talking about?"

"Nothing. Just. I mean come on. They were canvassing your area."

"You don't even know what that means."

Noah put the Play-Doh down on the table, now a perfectly round ball, slick from his sweaty hands. "Okay. Look," he said. "It's your brother."

Connor dropped the beaker he was holding. It landed in the sink, smashing to bits.

"Oh man, Mrs. Briggs is going to make us pay for that."

"What about my brother? What are you talking about?"

"Just some stuff I heard."

"*What?*"

"Jeez, Connor. That's school property. Those beakers probably cost a ton. My dad's going to—"

"What did you hear?"

Noah let out a heavy sigh, his braces whistling from it. "Mason Marx said he worships the devil."

He stared at him. "*What?*"

"That cat. The one that went missing a few weeks ago? All those pictures on the telephone poles?"

"I can't even believe this. Mason Marx is a total moron. We both know—"

"He said Wade sacrificed it."

"And you believed him? Mason Marx? That douche-nozzle?"

Noah shrugged. "Mason isn't the only one who says stuff like that about Wade. And, you know . . . better to be safe."

Connor moved away from the sink, muscles tensing. "You're supposed to be my best friend," he said. "If someone said crap like that about one of your sisters, I'd stick up for her."

Noah took a step forward. "My sisters aren't freak-show rejects who smell like ass."

"Apologize."

"You're the one who broke school property!"

"Apologize for saying that about my brother."

Noah stared at him. "Seriously?"

Connor stared back, waiting.

"Since when did you become Weird Wade's big defender?"

Something happened in Connor's head, like a door slamming hard. Every muscle in his body tensed up and his face grew hotter, electric sparks in his veins, pushing him forward, lifting him.

Noah sighed. "Okay. Whatever," he said. "I'm sorry I said that about your weird-assed brother."

And then Connor was on Noah, chair toppling to the tile floor, tile slamming into his knees, with Noah beneath him, covering his eyes, Connor punching and punching even though Noah wasn't fighting back—why wasn't he fighting back?—just yelling and crying and covering his eyes, Connor pulled tight like a rubber band about to break, fists slamming into Noah's soft baby skin and hating him so much, hating every part of him, never wanting to stop.

"YOU WANT TO tell me what happened?" Jackie said.

Connor said nothing. He hadn't said a word since she'd arrived at the Westons' with her heart in her throat, Cindy Weston icing her son Noah's black eye and looking at Jackie in a way that stopped her short of speaking too. She'd grabbed Connor's arm and yanked him out the door, her fingers so tight on his skin, she may have left marks. "What the hell," Jackie said in the car outside their house. "What the hell, Connor?"

Again, nothing.

"*Answer me!*"

"I don't know, Mom." He said it so quietly she could barely hear him. "He just . . . Noah just . . . I don't know."

They'd met the Westons at Connor's preschool, *they* being Jackie and Bill, her then-husband, the boys' then-father. It had been maybe a few weeks after their kids had started there. Orientation night, where they were served cookies and punch in the big playroom, the children's art tacked on the walls, and parents milling about awkwardly in their hello-my-name-is stickers, longing for wine. "Noah can't stop talking about Connor," Cindy had said back then, her grin wide and genuine—the mirror image of her son's—and Jackie had felt her shoulders relax almost instantly. She'd assumed they'd be great friends, the four of them. She'd envisioned family get-togethers and barbecues at each other's houses, double-date nights with a shared babysitter. As they chatted about their favorite restaurants in town, she'd allowed herself to picture the Reeds and the Westons out at one of them, or maybe even a concert up in Albany, tossing back beers and taking a hired car home for a splurge. Of course, none of that had ever happened. Bill had left Jackie before it could. Moved three towns away with that girl of his. The Office Girl, Jackie had called her, perhaps unfairly. She'd been the office *manager*, as Bill himself had pointed out. And she was a woman now. Close to forty. Proud mom to their three little girls . . .

The thing was, Connor had never gotten into a physical fight before; neither of her boys had. Well, maybe a playground scrap here and there. But nothing like this. Over the phone, Cindy had told Jackie, "I may have to take Noah to the hospital," which, okay, was an exaggeration. But Jackie could see how Cindy would have been thinking that way, her son whimpering the way he was as she held the towel full of ice to his eye, Jackie's own son at the other side of the room, staring at the floor with clenched fists and breathing deep, his face purple-red and furious. How could he hurt someone like that?

Jackie started up the car, pulled out of the Westons' driveway. "Noah just what?"

"Huh?"

"Noah. You said, 'He just.' What did he do to make you that angry? How could you . . . Connor, what was running through your mind?"

"Mom."

"That's it? You beat the crap out of your best friend and all you can say is—"

"Mom. Please."

Jackie pulled over to the side of the road. Stopped the car with a screech and shifted back into park. The house she pulled in front of was a tidy ranch house much like Noah's, and she was aware of a dog barking at them from behind the big street-facing window, the curtains moving.

"Who are you, Connor?"

"What?"

"What kind of a person are you turning into?"

Connor stared straight ahead, eyes boring into the glass. She wished she could figure out the look on his face. "We . . . we just got in a fight," he said. "It was no big deal."

"All right," she said, and started up the car. It wasn't all right, of course. Nothing was all right. She'd only said it in order to fill the dead air. "You're going to have to figure out a new science project."

"Mom . . ." Connor was watching her now, tears sliding down his cheeks, lower lip trembling.

She shifted the car back into park, trying to remember the last time she'd seen Connor cry. Over a skinned knee maybe, when he was a little boy. Something inside her started to crumble.

"What?" Jackie said. "What is it? Tell me, Connor. Talk to me."

"I'm . . . I'm sorry."

His face was wet. Jackie pulled him into a hug, and he began to sob, his head on her shoulder. How small he felt in her arms. How helpless. "I'm sorry," he said again and she knew he meant it.

Her thoughts traveled back to earlier this morning, the policeman at their door. A boy was in the hospital, in critical condition. Hit by a stolen car, the policeman had said. He hadn't given details, but she'd felt as though she could see it. A young boy, alone and lost on one of these quiet, dark streets, wheels speeding over him, crushing him, headlights blaring. A stolen car. It hadn't even slowed down.

Could have been one of my own, she'd thought. *That boy. That poor, lost boy.* As she'd spoken to the policeman, she'd squeezed Connor's shoulder tight and fast—the way you do when you're in the dark with someone and you want to make sure the other person is still there.

"It's okay," she whispered now as Connor's sobs subsided. "Everything's going to be okay."

ONCE THEY GOT home, Connor's mom made him call Noah's house and apologize. No one picked up the phone, and he was grateful for that because he really wasn't sorry. If he had to lie, it was easier to do it into somebody's voice mail than with them live and on the other end of the line, breathing at you.

After he was finished leaving the message for Noah, Connor's mom made him write out a formal letter to Noah's parents on the thick, cream-colored stationery she kept in her desk drawer, next to the pile of checkbooks and the half-finished romance novel manuscript she thought Wade and Connor didn't know about. She dictated the letter, Connor writing down the words as neatly as he could. She made him start off with "Dear Mr. and Mrs. Weston," even though he'd been calling them Cindy and Dave since he was five, but he didn't say anything about that. Just wrote

down her words. Somehow, it felt good to do exactly what his
mom told him to do.

Once he was done writing the letter, Connor's mom announced
he was grounded for the next two weeks; then she left the house
to go to work, taking his phone with her.

The house felt quiet with Mom gone. Not a nice quiet either.
That panicky type of quiet that roars in your ears and makes your
heart pound. His room was perfectly still, Arnie asleep in his
cage. Connor took a look at him, made sure he had enough water
and that he was still breathing. Connor had asked his mom for a
rat for his birthday, but rats grossed her out, so he was stuck with
Mr. Narcolepsy here. A hamster's life expectancy—he'd looked it
up—was three years, tops. Why bother living at all if you're going
to spend your entire life sleeping on the floor of a cage?

Connor opened up his laptop, jammed his headphones in his
ears, went onto Spotify, and called up his favorite playlist. "King
Kunta" was playing. He loved that song. "What's the yams?" said
Kendrick Lamar, and then the backup girls repeated the line,
Connor's face twitching into a smile just as it always did when
they said that, a reflex. He'd introduced Noah to "King Kunta" a
few months ago, and Noah loved it too, to the point where he was
always texting *What's the yams* at Connor.

Well, not *always*, Connor supposed. Not anymore.

Connor sighed. Skipped the rest of the song. "Forrest Gump"
by Frank Ocean was next. He could get lost in that one and so
he did, leaning his head back and just listening for a few minutes,
listening and breathing and thinking about how, someday, things
would be normal again. He tried not to think about Wade's face
last night, or the cops on his doorstep, or the kid who got run over
by a stolen car, just half a mile away from their house. Maybe it
wasn't even true, the part about the kid. Maybe the cops were just

trying to catch whoever stole the car, so they made up that a kid was in the hospital in order to scare people into spilling whatever secrets they had. Cops made stuff up all the time, didn't they?

He went onto Facebook and wrote a group message to his friends, letting them know not to text or Snapchat him, his mom had taken away his phone. *No huge deal,* he wrote. *I'll tell you about what happened later.* For a few seconds, Connor thought about including Wade in the message; strange, since he and Wade never texted. Hardly ever talked, really, outside of last night.

When he was a little kid, Connor would spend whole after-noons with Wade, following him around, watching him draw. *Make a spaceship for me,* Connor used to beg him. *Make a monster truck.* And Wade would. He drew anything Connor wanted him to. But sometime around when Connor was in fifth grade, Wade's artwork started getting weirder and Wade started getting weirder too. "He's growing up," Mom would say. But that didn't seem like the right thing to call it.

Connor went ahead and sent the message to his friends. He listened to Frank Ocean sing "I won't forget you" and then wrote a separate message to his brother: *Mom has my phone.* He couldn't think of anything else to say, so he sent it, just like that.

On the other message thread, Connor's friends started reply-ing, asking him what happened, what he'd done to make his mom mad. They weren't trying to be nice; they were just looking for something to talk about. Bored, like they always were. Like everybody in Havenkill was most of the time. He didn't owe them an answer, and anyway, Noah would tell them all soon enough. Noah gossiped like a girl.

Connor was going to close the laptop when another private message came in, this one from his friend Jordan: *Did you hear about Liam Miller?*

Connor typed, *No.*

Liam Miller was a senior. He dated Jordan's older sister, and for that reason alone, Connor knew him well enough to say hi. Once, though, he'd given Connor a ride. It had been raining and Connor had been walking home from soccer practice when Liam pulled up. "Try not to get my car wet," he'd said. A joke, because Liam's car was a real beater. A Ford Taurus from the 1990s with a cracked headlight and a chipping paint job. Liam had stretched a towel over the front passenger seat to make up for the ripped upholstery, and sitting on it, Connor had felt as though any minute he might fall right through to the floor.

They'd driven the whole way to Connor's house in silence, but it hadn't been uncomfortable. The crappy car had made Connor feel more equal than he would have felt if he'd gotten a ride from a different senior. Liam's best friend, Ryan Grant, for instance, drove a sweet red Mustang. And Jordan's sister, Tamara, had a convertible Beetle. Brand-new. Anyway, before he'd let Connor off, Liam had said, "You know what, Reed? You're not a bad kid." And though he hadn't said anything more, Connor had known what he'd meant. *As opposed to your brother.*

Connor had thanked him—for the ride, not the compliment. Though if he was going to be honest, it had been for both. Most of those older kids couldn't see him past the weird specter of Wade, which was why Connor had been walking in the rain for so many blocks in the first place. Before Liam had stopped, at least three seniors had sped by, pretending not to notice him, even when he waved.

Connor stared at the screen. Jordan's reply was such a long time coming. And the longer the screen said that Jordan was typing, the more nervous Connor got. There was a rising feeling inside of him—an actual physical sensation that he couldn't give a name to. *No, no, no,* he told the feeling. *Go away. Stop.*

When Jordan's response appeared, Connor's stomach seized up. His throat felt tight. For several seconds, it was as though he'd forgotten how to breathe. "What took you so long," he whispered finally. Stupidly.

And then he started praying for Liam to come out of his coma.

MAYBE JORDAN WAS wrong. Maybe he was confused. Connor refreshed his feed, though, and the pictures started appearing. Liam and his best friend, Ryan, in their football uniforms. Liam with Jordan's sister, Tamara, at junior prom. Liam with a group of friends, head thrown back, laughing. Liam as a baby. Liam as a little boy, holding a puffy red baseball bat, huge smile on his face. Shared posts, spreading like a rash through his feed. A disease. Connor scrolled down, half reading the words that accompanied the pictures, his head light and fuzzy. He pulled the headphones out, the silence crushing him, blood pounding in his ears. *Praying for you . . . Love you, man . . . You can't read this now but . . . My best friend . . . My cousin . . . Hang in there, hero.*

Connor's gaze rested on the word. *Hero?*

The kitchen phone rang, and Connor went to it. His brother's cell phone number in the caller ID. "Wade?"

"Mom's at work, right?"

"Yeah," Connor said quickly. "Did you hear about Liam Miller?"

Wade breathed, in and out. "The bag in your closet. I need you to get rid of it."

"What?"

"Connor."

"What are you—"

"Just do it. Not in our trash can, though, okay? Walk to the Lukoil. Throw it in their Dumpster."

"What are you talking about?"

"I don't have time for this." Wade's voice sounded tense. Desperate. "I showed you last night. Were you, like . . . were you asleep the whole time? Jesus."

Connor swallowed hard. "I remember a little . . ."

"Never mind. Just . . . just do it. It's in there. The bag. Get rid of it."

"Wade?"

"I have to go."

Connor stared at the phone, his mind wandering back . . . Wade in his room last night, turning to him from the closet: *I can trust you, right, buddy? You won't say anything?* And he could remember nodding, sleep still clinging to him but nodding anyway, thinking, *What is Wade doing in my room?* And then the thunderclap and Wade's eyes on him and, for a few seconds, Connor was five years old again, wanting to follow his older brother anywhere, everywhere . . . "I'll help you," he had said. "I'll do whatever you want."

Connor put the phone back in place, left the kitchen, and walked to his room. As he made for his closet, he heard a scurrying, the squeak of Arnie's hamster wheel. *Awake.* "Whatever you want, Wade," Connor whispered.

Three

They're mysteries," said Helen Davies. "We think we know how they'll turn out, but they're always full of surprises." They were at work, Jackie and Helen, Jackie on floor time as they say in real estate, a somewhat glamorous-sounding way to describe sitting behind a desk and waiting for customers. Helen was early for a client meet. She had a listing up on her computer and she was taking notes on it, scribbling into a small leather-bound notebook and barely paying attention to the conversation Jackie had started, which was about children, of course. Raising them. "Sure, they're open books," she'd said earlier. Helen, who'd never met a metaphor she didn't like. "But you have to consider the genre."

Jackie adjusted the flowers in the vase on her desk—stargazer lilies. The pasty scent was starting to get to her.

Helen said, "Any reason why you asked about Stacy?"

Jackie said, "Um . . ." While she had asked, out of the blue, if Helen's perfect gem of a daughter had ever behaved rebelliously, she was hesitant to say why. Truth was, Jackie hated confessing her troubles to Helen—particularly those having to do with money or child rearing. Not so much because of the way Helen might respond (she wasn't judgmental; her advice was always sound) but because it always pointed up the difference between them, the paths they'd taken since high school: Helen's straight and smooth and perfectly landscaped, Jackie's full of obstructions and detours. *Now who's overdoing it with the metaphors?* "Connor got into a fight," Jackie said.

Helen glanced up from her computer. "What?"

"I know. It's . . . Well . . . talk about surprises, right?"

"Connor? Little Connor? With who?"

"His best friend, Noah. Connor gave him a black eye."

"*Why?*"

"Boys," she said. "Go figure." Jackie turned to her computer, called up the office Web site to check inquiries, but her mind wasn't there. What she was really thinking of was the phone call from Cindy Weston when she was on her way to work. She was remembering seeing Cindy's name on her screen and debating whether or not to answer, scolding herself, *Don't be a coward,* and putting Cindy on speaker because she still couldn't figure out the Bluetooth on the used Subaru she'd bought three months ago so Wade could have her old car.

Cindy's voice. How strangely apologetic it had been.

"Hey, Jackie. Listen. Noah told me what started the fight, and you know I don't condone violence, but of course I can understand why Connor was upset with him . . ."

Jackie said to Helen, "He was sticking up for his brother."

"Connor?" Helen said. "Little Connor was protecting *Wade?* From another thirteen-year-old boy?"

"No," she said. "No, Wade wasn't there. He was . . . Well, his friend said something insulting about Wade."

Helen's face relaxed. "Ah."

"Yes."

"He loves his brother."

"Apparently."

Helen gave Jackie a smile. "You know what? I'd say you raised him right."

Jackie tried to smile back, though she didn't feel like smiling at all. Thirteen-year-olds were saying insulting things about Wade. That was what she'd taken away from the story Cindy had told her. That, and the sweeping desire to blacken Noah Weston's other eye. "You're nice, Helen," she said. "You're so much nicer than me."

Helen went back to the listing. "That's not true," she said, pencil scratching at the paper. "That isn't true at all."

INTERESTING THE WAY nostalgia worked—the way it could lie in wait, lodging itself in something as innocent as a key ring. The key ring was a ceramic calico kitten with moss agate eyes, a pretty little thing that Wade had given Jackie at the end of the summer. "I saw it and thought of you," Wade had said, flush with lawn-mowing money, part of what Jackie had called the Summer of Odd Jobs. She hadn't been sure where it had come from, that sudden desire to mow lawns and clean gutters and help with auto repair for their neighbors. But she had welcomed it without question. The Summer of Odd Jobs had transformed Wade, however briefly, into a boy with a wallet full of cash and a smile on his face, his sandy hair streaked blond by the sun. A normal, happy boy. He would disappear for hours and come home muscled and glowing, passing out gifts and making jokes.

It had been less than two months ago. But reaching into her purse in the office bathroom, going in for her lipstick and finding that key ring instead, Jackie felt as though it could have been years ago, decades. She ran her finger over the carefully painted whiskers. Handmade, Wade had told her. Must have taken somebody a long time.

The door opened and Helen came in, trailing fresh perfume. "The Courtneys changed their minds about the new property. They want to see the house on Riverview again," she said. "I think we may be closing in on an offer." She applied frosty pink lipstick. Smoothed the arch of her brow.

Jackie pulled her lipstick out of her purse and dropped the key ring back in. "Good luck."

Helen's soft eyes sought out Jackie's in the mirror. "Connor is going to be fine," she said. "He's a boy. Boys get into fights. It's the way of the world."

But Jackie wasn't worried about Connor. Connor had never been the problem. "Helen?"

"Yes?"

"Does Stacy ever talk about Wade?"

"Wade?"

"Does she ever tell you things about his friends? Or who he's dating? You know. Gossip?"

"No, honey. Stacy really doesn't gossip about Wade," she said. "Different circles and all."

"Right," Jackie said. Though it didn't used to be that way. Stacy and Wade had been inseparable as children, to the point where she and Helen had once caught them dressed as bride and groom, a lacy pillowcase arranged on Stacy's head like a veil, her stuffed bunny rabbit apparently performing the ceremony. "Remember when they got married?"

"Who?"

"Stacy and Wade. Remember? They were in love when they were little."

Helen removed a piece of folded tissue paper from her purse and gently blotted her lips. "As I recall, Stacy treated him more like a pet," she said. "He let her give him makeovers. I remember trying to get this awful purple eye shadow off of him before you picked him up. He was probably five and it wasn't even for humans—it was from Stacy's doll's makeup kit, full of glitter and epoxy and God knows what else. I was worried he'd have an allergic reaction."

"Love hurts."

Helen grinned. "In the wise words of Nazareth. Yes. It does." She dropped her lipstick back in her purse, gave her reflection the once-over, and fluffed her chestnut hair, diamond earrings sparkling. "Remember when we used to be able to get away with no makeup at all?"

She started to leave, but Jackie put a hand on her arm. "Wade got a text."

"Okay . . ."

"I don't normally look at his phone, but it was in the kitchen and I read it and I found it . . . troubling."

"What did it say?"

"'Leave me alone.'"

"Excuse me?"

"That's what the text said."

"That's all?"

"It was from someone named 'T.' Do you know who that might be? Any girls at the school with *T* names?"

"Listen," Helen said. "'Leave me alone' can mean all sorts of things. Most of them a lot less awful than what you're imagining."

"How do you know what I'm imagining?"

"You're a writer, Jackie. You create these elaborate scenarios in your head, these fictions, when it was probably just some buddy of Wade's telling him to stop being such a wiseass."

Jackie exhaled, her breath shaking. "Thank you."

"For what?"

She forced a smile. "Calling me a writer, for one thing. I haven't written anything since before the boys were born."

"Jackie."

"Yes?"

"He's not a little boy anymore."

"I know that."

"I mean it," she said. "I know it sounds patronizing, but believe me, I have to remind myself the same thing all the time about Stacy. They're not going to let us into their lives as much, but that's normal. Wade's a complicated young man now."

Jackie's face flushed. "Believe me, I know he's complicated."

Helen gave her a probing look. "That's over now," she said. Reading her mind. "He's better. Two years is a long time."

Jackie gritted her teeth. "You know that for a fact, do you? Well, that's a relief."

"I didn't mean it that way."

Jackie remembered a day, must have been around six months ago, before Wade had a car of his own. Helen had been at the school anyway for a PTA meeting and so she'd given Wade a ride home. They hadn't seen Jackie working in the garden, Helen and Wade, yet she'd seen them. Spied on her eldest son and her oldest friend for a full five minutes, their two faces behind the windshield, Wade talking and Helen listening, nodding every so often, her expression so intent and serious, Jackie half expected her to take notes. She hated that feeling of being on the outside looking in, that awful yearning to pound on the glass until it broke so she could hear what her son was saying and know his thoughts. It was the way Jackie almost always felt with Wade, but it had been so much more pronounced in that moment. Jackie's friend giving her son the advice she couldn't. Understanding him as she never would. She felt it again now with Helen scratching open that old wound, no matter how kind her intentions had been. *Two years is a long time. Is it really, Helen? Go fuck yourself.*

"I'm sorry, sweetie," Jackie said finally, a forced lightness in her voice that she hated but couldn't help. "I think I just need more sleep."

JACKIE HAD ONE more hour of floor time left when Helen returned from her showing, a pot of fiery orange mums in her arms. She held it out to her. "Happy fall."

"Oh Helen, they're beautiful," Jackie said. "And mums are my favorite."

"I know."

"You didn't have to—"

"Please," Helen said. "I saw these on my way back and I couldn't resist. I got two pots for myself too."

Jackie leaned into the flowers, inhaling their scent, fresh as an apology. She remembered how she'd snapped at Helen in the bathroom and her face flushed from guilt.

"Do you feel any better?" Helen said.

She nodded.

"He's a good soul," Helen said very quietly. "Both of your sons are."

Jackie wasn't sure she'd ever met anyone as considerate as Helen. "So how did the showing go," she started, but Helen's cell phone chimed, interrupting her.

She glanced at the screen, held up a finger. "Stacy."

It was a short call, Helen saying "Oh my God" and "Okay" a few times and then hanging up, color drained from her face. "I have to take Stacy to the hospital."

"What? Why?"

"One of Stacy's very dear friends, Liam Miller . . . Do you know him?"

"Yes. I know him," said Jackie, though she didn't know Liam Miller so much as remember him—a boy with corn silk hair and sparkling eyes on Wade's Little League team. Liam Miller, who had once helped her wash dishes after Wade's birthday party, when was that? She'd still been married to Bill at the time. Wade's seventh birthday party. *What a sweet little boy* . . . "Is he all right?"

"He's been hit by a car. He's in intensive care."

"Oh," Jackie said, stomach clenching. "That's . . . awful."

"Stacy wants to go to the hospital, but I think I should talk to Sheila and Chris first. Do you?"

"Who?"

"His parents. Liam's parents."

Liam Miller. The boy from this morning, the boy the police were talking about. That poor lost boy. It was Liam. Jackie wanted to ask what he'd been doing out on the street so late, the night before SATs. But that would sound like she was blaming his parents. And it could happen to anyone. Any parent. *Turn your back for one moment.* She thought of Wade standing alone on the front step, cigarette in his hand. Her Wade, awake and outside at that hour, that very late hour . . . And a feeling swept through her—sadness of course, but something else as well, a type of dread she couldn't quite identify, as though the floor beneath her had suddenly turned to glass, thin and untrustworthy. Just about to shatter.

PEARL'S HANDS WERE heavy on the wheel as she drove Amy Nathanson home. She hadn't slept in eighteen hours and she was

exhausted, emotionally and physically, Amy Nathanson the reason, Amy Nathanson the last person in the world Pearl wanted in
the back of her cruiser. But it couldn't be avoided. Nathanson's
car was still missing: an emerald-green 1973 Jaguar "in perfect
condition," referred to by Amy as "her baby," and indeed, she'd
described it with all the loving care one would use in describing
a missing child. She'd asked to be driven home, and the sergeant,
starstruck as he seemed to be, had volunteered Pearl, explaining,
"Amy told me she'd be more comfortable with a woman behind
the wheel."

Pearl sighed. As the only female police officer on the Havenkill force, she had a locker room big enough for eight people all
to herself, complete with a shower of her own. But she also had
to drive Amy Nathanson all the way to Woodstock—a forty-five-
minute ride with a has-been pop singer from the 1980s, who
insisted on playing the role of victim as though she were pulling
for an Oscar. You win some; you lose some.

"You don't know," Amy was saying now. "You just don't understand what a violation it was."

Pearl kept a box of Kleenex in the front seat, which she'd given
to Amy at the beginning of the ride. Amy yanked what had to be
one of the last few tissues out of the box and blew her nose with
it. She'd been crying solidly for the past twelve hours and she had
said the word *violation* so often it could have spawned a drinking
game. "I understand, ma'am," Pearl said.

"I tried to talk to him. The other boy. The one who tried to
get my baby back. I checked his pulse and he was alive, but he
wouldn't speak to me. Wouldn't open his eyes. His back might be
broken."

"Yes, ma'am."

"I didn't have my phone. It was in the Jaguar. I shouted and screamed but no one came so I had to walk. I had to leave him. He'll be okay, won't he?"

"I don't know."

"That . . . that monster drove off with my baby. He was all in black. Black hoodie. Black pants. He was so big and threw me to the ground. He took my purse. My phone. He got in my car. My beautiful leather seats. I had to walk. In the pouring rain. All the way to the station."

"You said that, ma'am. You said all of that, in your report. I took it all down, remember?"

"I remember. I'm just telling you it was—"

"A violation."

"Yes," Amy said. "So do you think you'll be able to find her?"

"Her?"

"Baby."

"We've put out an APB on the car, but stolen cars can be hard to track down, especially if the plates have been changed."

"So what do we do?"

"We hope for the best," Pearl said pointedly. "Just like we're hoping for the best for Liam Miller's recovery."

Pearl waited for Amy to say more, but she didn't. Pearl took a long, deep breath, relieved at the silence in the car. She was over the bridge now, just about twenty minutes from Woodstock. The sky was cloudless—that crisp, true blue that you only see in the fall after a big rain. There was something hopeful in that type of sky. Washed clean, if only for a few hours.

She kept an eye on Amy Nathanson: the vintage raincoat of shiny red vinyl, the rainbow-striped hair. The mascara, like the blood on Lady Macbeth's hands, still staining her face, no matter how much she'd tried to scrub it off in the station bathroom. Some things, Pearl supposed, washed clean easier than others.

Amy wore bright red lipstick, which Pearl assumed was a thirty-year-old trademark. She'd applied and reapplied it so many times since she'd fallen into the station, over so many questions from the sergeant and phone calls to the state police, over a seemingly endless stream of reports to fill out and hospital updates to receive, over so much sobbing and shivering and cups of hot coffee, Pearl fetching towels from the locker room so that Amy could dry her drenched hair, clothes, face.

Hours and hours of tears and worry and still Amy Nathanson's lipstick had stayed perfect. "Aimee En," Sergeant Black had said, sighing at one point, calling her by her stage name. "I saw you at the Palladium, must've been 1988 . . ." Sergeant Black, who had actually asked for her autograph. What a dumb hick move that had been. So embarrassing.

To Pearl's eye, Aimee En was a drama queen, treating the world like a stage, expecting all the misplaced respect that came with celebrity. And yeah, up here in the boondocks, thirty-year-old celebrity still counted. Pearl couldn't help but wonder what Sergeant Black would have said to a woman he'd never seen before, at the Palladium or otherwise, had she shown up at the station at three in the morning with whiskey on her breath, clearly more concerned about a missing car than about the unconscious boy she'd left in the middle of the road.

"Officer Maze." Amy was watching her as well from behind the glass that separated the backseat from the front, making eye contact in the rearview mirror. Pearl wasn't sure for how long, and for a few moments of sleep-deprived panic, she wondered if Amy had been able to read her mind.

"You can call me Pearl, ma'am," she said.

"Pearl. Lovely name."

"Thank you."

"So, Pearl, have you ever killed anyone?"

Pearl turned her gaze to the road. *Wow.* "Small talk, huh?"

"I'm sorry," Amy said. "I just . . . You probably think I'm being overdramatic about the car."

"Well . . ."

"It's not the Jaguar."

"It isn't?"

"Well, not really. It's just that some things are easier to worry about than others."

Several car lengths ahead of them, a red pickup truck was going close to seventy-five in a fifty-five mph zone, though Pearl was neither in the mood nor in the position to give out a ticket. She pressed down on the accelerator anyway, weaving and screeching around other cars until she was right behind the truck, tailing it so closely she was practically in the cargo bed.

"Whoa," Amy said.

"Just teaching a lesson," Pearl said, and within moments, the pickup truck pulled into the right lane, reducing its speed to a crawl. "See?" She let herself smile over that one moment of power. Pearl took satisfaction wherever she could find it.

Amy said, "I don't know what I'm going to do if that boy dies."

Pearl's smile dissolved.

"I don't think I can cope with the guilt."

Pearl reached a stoplight, the word tugging at her. *Guilt.* She turned around, looked directly at Amy through the glass divider. "Why would you feel guilty?" she said. "It wasn't you that ran Liam Miller down."

"No, no. That's true."

"Well then—"

"But my car did. Baby did. I let that piece of shit take Baby away from me. I screamed for help and that other boy . . . Liam . . .

he came running. If I hadn't screamed, he wouldn't have come. Baby wouldn't have run him down."

Pearl nodded slowly, Amy's story playing out in her head, all the flaws in it. *You were stopped at the stop sign on Orchard and Shale. A teenage white boy in a hoodie, a tall, strong boy "hopped up on drugs," and "laughing," reached through your open driver's-side window and grabbed your purse off your lap. You leaped out and fought with him, allowing him to push you to the ground, jump into your unlocked Jaguar, and steal it. But it was freezing cold last night, even before it started raining. What was your driver's-side window doing open? Were you talking to the hopped-up boy? Did you know him? Was there even a boy at all?*

"It's a shame," Pearl said.

"If I'd had a gun. If I'd just had a gun I swear to God I'd have—"

"Left it in the car, probably. Along with your phone."

"Look," she said. "I just want to know if I'll ever be able to close my eyes again without seeing the whole thing happening, over and over."

Pearl pulled onto Route 28 and drove, reading billboards as she passed. Pest control, car insurance, a Halloween haunted house . . .

Amy said, "Please tell me. Have you ever killed anyone?"

Pearl had been asked this question before, more often than not on dates. It came with the job, and she usually said no. But something about the desperation in Amy's voice, or the clarity of the sky, or perhaps simply her own overwhelming exhaustion, made Pearl more truthful than she usually was. "Not that I remember," she said.

"What does that mean?"

Pearl looked once again at Amy, the black mascara stains on her gaunt, sad face, the rainbow bangs limp against her forehead. *She looks doomed,* Pearl thought. Though maybe she was just projecting. "It means that when I close my eyes," she said, "I see nothing."

HAVENKILL HOSPITAL BROUGHT back memories for Jackie, good ones. She'd given birth to both her boys here. But she felt guilty for indulging in those memories now. After all, Liam Miller had probably been born here too, and his life was in the balance. He was the one who needed her thoughts.

The visitors' lot was a long way from the building, and she tried to keep her mind off the past as she walked, her wool coat heavy on her shoulders, the air colder now than it had been earlier, thin and hard to breathe. She found a smoky scent in it—a woodstove burning somewhere, which felt to Jackie like fall and home and warmth. But also like something else. Something sad.

The maternity wing was on the opposite side of the hospital. Liam was in intensive care, which was in the main building. Jackie knew where it was from calling the hospital after she'd done her last hour of floor time, talking with two sets of leaf peepers, and showing one of her listings to a ridiculously pretty male model who'd come here from Belgium and was, as he'd put it in his continental accent, "through with that snake pit called Manhattan." *Real potential,* Jackie would have normally thought. *Rich and ready.* But showing him the house had felt like stalling, the whole afternoon a long-drawn-out preamble to calling the hospital.

"What is the condition of the boy?" Jackie had asked as soon as she'd dropped the model off at his parked rental car and driven off alone. And while the nurse had told her she could only provide that information over the phone for family, she had offered that

Liam Miller had many friends "camped out in the ER waiting room," and she was welcome to do the same. After Jackie had hung up and was on her way to the hospital, it had dawned on her that she'd never given the nurse Liam's name, referring to him only as "the boy." That was how small and safe Havenkill was, how rare it was here for a boy to be in intensive care.

The ER waiting area was down a short hall to the left of the hospital's entrance. Before she even turned the corner, Jackie could sense the crowd inside, the buzz of muffled conversation, the worry among the visitors, which gave off a type of heat. She walked into the waiting room, moved toward the front desk, past all of them—teenagers she'd never seen before huddled together on the bank of chairs against two of the walls, some sitting on the floor, talking to each other in hushed, frightened voices and tapping away at their devices, ignoring the NO CELL PHONES sign on the wall, which bore a picture of an old flip phone with an antenna and didn't relate to them at all.

Who were all these kids? Why didn't she know any of them?

It occurred to her that it had been probably six months since Wade had invited a friend over and even then . . . who had it been? A boy by the name of Rafe Burgess, who had been partners with Wade on a history project. *Such a polite boy,* she had thought. But so stiff too, as though he'd rather be anywhere else. Rafe Burgess had begged off staying for dinner, even though the kids had finished their project exactly at dinnertime and Jackie had made homemade pizza.

"He seems nice," Jackie had tried, after Rafe had left.

But Wade had just rolled his eyes. "The teacher put us together." Rafe Burgess, the last friend Jackie had seen Wade spending any time with—and it had stuck in her mind so deeply, she remembered the kid's first and last name.

Did Wade have any friends at all?

Jackie reached the front desk, corralling her thoughts. The nurse was typing into her computer, but when Jackie tapped on the glass, she looked up.

"I was wondering," Jackie said, "how is Liam Miller doing?"

"He is the same, ma'am."

"Critical?"

"If we have any news from intensive care, we will let all of you know."

Jackie swallowed. "Are his parents around?"

"They're with him, ma'am."

"Oh, yes, of course . . ."

"Intensive care waiting room is reserved for close family. You understand."

"Yes," she said. "Yes, I understand."

The nurse returned to her computer. Jackie backed away from the desk, her gaze traveling around the room, the unfamiliar faces. *Why did I come here?* Before now, she hadn't questioned it. All she'd felt was the need to be here, the need to *know*. But why? Jackie figured it was for the same reason she slowed down at car accidents. Not to stare at the carnage despite that old saw. Not to rubberneck and get some kind of sick thrill. She did it in order to care about what had happened, and she was certain other people felt the same. To make certain that someone else's tragedy didn't go ignored.

Well, Liam wasn't being ignored. There had to be more than fifty people in here—a good percentage of the senior class, all of them waiting for him to wake up and speak. Just to the right of the front desk, a boy and a girl were crouched on the floor, staring into a single screen. There was something heartbreaking about the way they huddled together, coping with a feeling that was too

big for them, too old. The boy looked up at Jackie. Just for a few
seconds, their eyes locked, and Jackie saw in his such despair; the
eyes of someone caught in deep, churning water and knowing
that he was about to drown, that nobody could help . . .

The girl, she realized now, was Stacy.

It had been years since Jackie had seen Helen's daughter outside of a Facebook photo, but still she felt the warmth of recognition. Stacy's hair was the same pale blond as it had been when she
was a little girl, pillowcase veil pinned to her head. Jackie said her
name, and Stacy looked up at her with dull, flat eyes, as though
Jackie were just another screen. *She doesn't remember me*, Jackie
thought, which was more than understandable, given the span of
time—an eternity for a teen.

"Jackie Reed," she said quietly. "Wade's mom."

"I know." Stacy's voice was as flat as her eyes, her face, the
whole of her as close to lifeless as a healthy teenage girl could be.
Numb from worry. That must be it. Poor girl. "You just missed
him," she said.

"Excuse me?"

"Wade. That's why you're here, right, Mrs. Reed? Wade?" She
said Wade's name like it was an embarrassing ailment. The boy's
eyes stayed on the screen, absorbing the light.

"Yes," Jackie said, playing along. "I'm looking for Wade."

"He just left," Stacy said. "My mom showed him out."

"She *showed him out*?" It came out louder than she'd intended.
Jackie glanced around the waiting room, at the downcast eyes and
sidelong exchanges of teenage shock, of dark amusement, hands
thrown over gaping mouths, everyone so studiously not looking at
her. Her face felt hot. Sweat trickled down her rib cage.

Jackie left the waiting room and sprinted down the hall, out
the door, into the parking lot. She could see the car leaving just as

she got there. Wade's car. Her old car—a metallic-green Corolla, dented and distinctive as hell, even from this distance.

"Jackie?" Helen jogged up next to her, cheeks flushed from the cold, shearling coat pulled close to her slim frame. "I didn't know you'd be coming to the hospital."

"What happened with Wade?"

"Huh?"

"Your daughter said you escorted him out of the waiting room."

"Stacy said that?"

Jackie exhaled, condensation puffing from her lips. "Not in those words," she said. "But that's what she meant. What did he do? Why would he need to be escorted out?"

"Stacy is upset. She doesn't know what she's saying," Helen said. "He stopped in very briefly. I wanted to go out anyway for a breath of fresh air, so I walked out with him."

Jackie gave her friend a long look, trying to figure out whether she was being truthful or kind. Helen so frequently went for the latter.

"Look, Wade came here for the same reason I did," Helen said, finally. "The same reason Stacy and all her friends did and the same reason you did, Jackie. One of us has been hurt. He was worried. He wanted to know what was going on. He found out, and then he left."

"Okay," Jackie said, believing. Wanting to believe.

"I'm freezing," Helen said. "You want to go back in? Maybe get a cup of coffee at the cafeteria?"

Jackie pulled the belt on her coat tighter. "I should probably just head home."

"Okay. See you tomorrow?"

Jackie nodded. Helen started to head back in.

"Wait," Jackie said. She reached into her purse, fingers touching the cat key ring as she grabbed her wallet, slipped out a twenty-dollar bill. "Can you buy Liam flowers from Wade, Connor, and me? Something nice from the hospital gift shop?"

"Any preference?"

"Mums if they have them."

Helen smiled. "You got it."

Jackie gave her a quick, tight hug. She jogged back to her car, thinking, as she had earlier, of Wade's birth, only she allowed herself now to really remember it—the thunderstorm lighting up the room, Bill's strong hands on her shoulders, and the Bob Marley tape in the boom box. The breathing and the ice chips and the burning, cooling tears. Bill's smile. The pink sunrise. The exquisitely fragile weight of her newborn son on her chest.

Four

The bag was from Stop & Shop. Wade had probably gotten it out of the kitchen, Connor figured. Mom shopped there all the time. She kept forgetting to bring the canvas bags she'd bought to be environmental, and since Stop & Shop only carried plastic bags, not paper, one of their kitchen drawers was stuffed with them, Mom rationalizing that if they were going to contribute to the destruction of the environment with petroleum products, they should at least try and reuse the bags. The handles were tied tight. The plastic knot pressed into Connor's palm as he left the house with it, locking the door behind him, walking fast and with his head down so as not to be noticed but not really knowing why. Connor was determined not to open the bag and look inside. The less he knew, the less chance he'd tell someone about it. And he couldn't tell anyone. He'd promised Wade.

I can trust you, right, buddy? You won't say anything?

It had taken Connor hours to get himself to open his closet door, to look behind the sneakers and baseball mitts and old textbooks and all the other stuff he kept on the floor of it in order to locate the bag his brother had stashed there last night. The thought of the bag had scared him. He'd imagined a Hefty bag with a head in it, a collection of limbs. Not that Wade was capable of anything like that. It was just the way his voice had sounded over the phone . . .

Connor watched way too many scary movies.

When he'd finally found the bag and taken it out of the closet, Connor had felt kind of stupid. It was small and white and clean. It didn't smell, and it couldn't have weighed more than a few ounces. All this time wasted over a little plastic grocery bag that held . . . what? Something Wade wanted to get rid of. Outside his front gate, Connor jiggled it a little. The thing inside made a *shook-shook* sound.

Whatever. It wasn't a severed head. He'd keep his word and toss it in the Dumpster at the Lukoil station and then he'd go home and play Minecraft and act as though he'd never been outside at all.

Connor shivered. It was so cold, and he had left the house without a coat. Why had he waited so long to do this? It had been much warmer out earlier, and now, because of stupid fall, the day was almost over. Mom would be home soon and so would Wade, and he didn't want to be seen outside by either one of them. *Just get it over with.* He walked faster, the wind biting at his face, the tips of his ears, creeping under the collar of his flannel shirt.

And those leaves. Those dumb, noticeable fall leaves . . . Connor's street was called Maple, and maple trees lined the sidewalks, their leaves now orange, yellow, and red, bright and swirling as cartoon fires. Maple Street was one of Havenkill's poorer streets, the houses dinky ranch homes with postage-stamp lawns. Nobody had a pool or even a garage, but this time of year, it almost looked impressive. Usually Connor didn't think much about the changing leaves. His mom always remarked on them—"Look up from your screens and out the window, boys!"—but Connor would roll his eyes. Changing leaves meant fall, which meant back to school, which meant boring. Everybody knew that. "You just love those leaves because they help you sell houses," Wade had said to Mom once. He hadn't been wrong.

But now the leaves seemed too bright. They were drawing attention to Connor, making his neighbors look up from their screens and out their windows, and then they'd see him, the younger Reed boy, walking without a coat, shaking all over. Would they call each other, wondering what he was up to? Would they ask his mom?

The thing, whatever it was, bounced in the Stop & Shop bag as though it were trying to tell Connor something. *Shook-shook-shook . . . I know the story. Don't you want to look inside, so you can know it too?*

Connor reached the end of his street and crossed onto Orchard, the main road that fed into town. He hugged his shirt tight to his body, his breath coming out in white puffs, the tips of his ears burning now, eyes watering, the thing in the bag *shook-shooking* away.

The Lukoil station was three blocks up and across the street. Connor made a run for it, sprinting with all his might. The sidewalk was so cold he could feel it through the soles of his shoes, but at least this was a way to work off these nerves.

What a day this had been—the police at his door, the fight with Noah, the news about Liam, the phone call from Wade, and now this . . . No. That was wrong. The day hadn't started with the police at his door. It had started with Wade in his room at three in the morning . . .

Shook-shook-shook.

He was sweating, the sweat freezing on his skin, his fingers numb as he clutched the bag. *It's nothing. It's no big deal. Just trash. Taking out Wade's trash.* He rounded the corner and made for the Lukoil station, but he was barely onto the crosswalk before he heard the screech of tires, a horn honking. And then, the blip of a siren.

Connor stopped. His hands shot up, a reflex.

"You're not under arrest," said the cop. She talked to him through an opened window, her hand resting on the door of the cruiser. Her face was shaded by her hat, but he remembered her—one of three police officers who'd come to his school at the end of last year for assembly, the one girl officer, telling the seventh and eighth graders about the dangers of heroin. Connor had been in the front row sitting next to Noah, who, in typical clueless Noah Weston fashion, had remarked, loudly, on the girl officer's hotness. Connor stared back down at the pavement, hoping she didn't recognize him, hating Noah all over again.

"Watch where you're going," the cop said. "The traffic light's green. You could have gotten hit."

"I'm sorry, ma'am," he said. "I mean, officer. I'll be more careful."

"Go back to the curb. Wait for the light to change. Look both ways."

Connor went back to the curb, and she sped off. It wasn't until the police car was gone that he realized his hands were still raised, the bag clutched in one of them like he was a robber from a bank heist movie. He gazed up at the bag. He could see the outline of the object inside—pocket-size and rectangular. *A phone?*

Connor dropped his hands. The light turned red and he hurled himself onto the crosswalk, racing across the street to the Lukoil station without looking both ways. When he reached the Dumpster, he fell against the side of it, wheezing. Connor lifted the lid and threw the bag in fast, listening for the soft thump of its landing over the sound of his own breath.

Done.

For several seconds, he stayed bent over, eyes on the rusted side of the Dumpster, hands gripping his knees. He breathed deep, ten counts in, ten counts out, until the stitch in his side smoothed out and the balled-up tension inside him started to unravel and, finally, he began to feel normal.

He straightened up. Behind him, Connor heard the slam of a car door, then footsteps—boots clicking on the concrete, coming closer. A lump formed in his throat. He thought of that cop again. *Is she back? Did she see?*

But then he heard something that was, in a way, a lot worse: Mom's voice saying his name. Connor straightened up. He gave her a small, idiotic wave he wished he could take back.

She stared at him, looking strange. Like she didn't know what to do any more than Connor did. "What on earth are you doing here?" Mom said.

Connor tried his best to think of a lie.

PEARL'S PHONE JOLTED her awake, the ringtone piercing into a dream that was more memory than imagined: Amy Nathanson falling into the station, mascara running down her face just as it had at 3:00 AM in real life, sopping wet curls clinging to her forehead, yellow and orange, blue, green, and red like a clown. A drowned clown. *"Don't you know who I am?"* Said directly to Pearl with such an odd thing going on in her eyes, almost as though she were daring Pearl to say no.

In real life, Pearl had shaken her head, thinking, *What a weird question*, and *Who cares*, before Sergeant Black had called her by her stage name, mollifying her. But in Pearl's dream, that was all Amy Nathanson had said. *"Don't you know who I am?"* Over and over again, until it sounded like nonsense and Pearl wanted to slap her, to scream at her, to handcuff her to the holding bench and leave her there, alone. *A boy is in the hospital, barely alive, and all you want is to be recognized.* But she couldn't move, couldn't speak. Pearl could never move or speak in her dreams. She wondered if that was normal.

Pearl's ringtone was wind-chimey and placid, but it woke her anyway. She'd only been sleeping for an hour, after all, and she had that weird, sick feeling she got when forced awake, the whole room swimming and the dream still nagging at her, the fog of it in her head like a mild fever.

She ran a hand across her eyes. This was like waking up after a night of drinking, only she was alone in her own apartment with nothing fun to remember or regret. *"You know who I am, Pearl,"* Amy had hissed at the very end of the dream. *"Because it takes a killer to know one."*

Pearl grabbed the phone from her nightstand. Looked at the screen and saw the number moving in and out of focus. Albany area code. Same number she knew from the reverse directory search. She declined the call. Him again. Third time this week. She wondered if maybe this time, he'd leave a message. "Hi, Dad," she whispered.

And now she couldn't sleep.

Pearl struggled out of bed and padded over to the kitchenette in her socks. Her floors were hardwood and freezing. Her apartment was as drafty as every other ancient, cracked structure in Havenkill—but Pearl never wore shoes inside; she couldn't. She lived in a two-story brick complex called the Garden Crest. It was populated almost entirely by senior citizens, and save for the noise of some of the hard-of-hearing residents' very loud TVs, quiet here was enforced. Mrs. Waterford, who lived in the unit downstairs, had once knocked on Pearl's door, complaining about her "clomping around up there in those clompy shoes" and warning Pearl that if she wore shoes indoors again, she'd hear from management. This had been at around 5:00 PM on a Saturday, two days after Pearl had moved in. Her shoes had remained by the front door ever since. Pearl was a uniformed police officer, after all. She knew from authority.

She opened the refrigerator and grabbed a beer, so cold the hand gripping it went numb, and when she popped the top and drank it, she felt frozen inside—the opposite effect of what she'd been going for. Instead of drowsy, she was hyperawake, an image flashing in her brain—Amy Nathanson's two-story Colonial home in Woodstock with its peeling paint and rows of brown weeds so tall they reached halfway up the front door. The shades had been drawn on every single window. A hoarder's house if Pearl had ever seen one—and she had seen one. She'd grown up in one.

Amy had burst out of the cruiser, shedding it like a dead layer of skin or a bad memory, racing up the driveway and around the back of the house, leaving Pearl behind without asking her in. Of course she hadn't asked her in. No one was welcome here, that was clear—not even a gardener or a painter.

Pearl took another swallow of beer. She savored the bitterness of it, and remembered the whiskey scent on Amy's breath in the booking room as she told her about the gig she'd played before the accident. "Club Halifax in Hudson," she'd said. "Ever heard of it?" All those *H*'s toxic with the smell. *Drunk driver,* Pearl had thought then. Still did. Whether or not the carjacking story was true, alcohol had played a role in Amy's decision-making process.

As she headed back to her bedroom, gulping down the rest of

the beer, Pearl tried to figure out how Sergeant Black had been able to ignore the booze on the breath of his idol. She wondered what he would say if he saw that weed-choked house that belonged to Aimee En. Would he ignore that too, or would he think, as Pearl was thinking now, *Something is going on with her. Something sad?*

Trying to sleep again, Pearl flashed on that young boy with his hands in the air, that kid she'd nearly run over when she was coming back from Amy's—oh the irony of that.

Probably on his way to buy cigarettes at the Lukoil, with some ridiculous-looking fake ID in his pocket. Probably had no idea that five blocks away, a boy just a few years older than he had been run down and left for dead by a different car less than twenty-four hours earlier. Run down by Baby. Pearl had driven by the spot where it had happened. She'd seen the yellow tape on the maple trees, the cruiser still blocking off the street, the flashing lights, a few gawkers, kids from the high school she half recognized from community outreach. She'd passed them slowly and she'd thought about that boy, a friend of theirs maybe. A healthy boy, running and then motionless.

In just a few seconds, such awful things can happen.

Pearl's eyes welled up. She felt as though something big and heavy were sitting on her chest. The same thing that had been there for nearly her whole life; sometimes it eased up, but never long enough for her to really breathe deeply. She grabbed her phone and checked her voice mail. Nothing. *Should I have answered for you, Dad? What would you have said to me?*

Pearl needed to sleep, but she couldn't. She so very rarely could.

She opened her hookup app and swiped right on the first douchebag she saw—big ugly tattoo on his neck, tons of product in his hair, ice-blue eyes that were probably contacts. She could practically smell the Axe spray through the screen.

His screen name was HudsonStud, and of course he matched with Pearl. He messaged her exactly the way she knew he would: *S'up?*

She didn't waste time. She messaged him her address, craving him like another beer. *When you get here,* she typed, *leave your shoes by the door.*

"I WAS JUST throwing some stuff out," Connor said.

Jackie looked at him. "At a gas station?"

Connor mumbled something along the lines of wanting to get some fresh air. He had no coat on and he was trembling. His nose was red and his lips were tinged blue. Jackie was terrified he might catch something—pneumonia, hypothermia even. She wanted to put her arms around him, clutch him to her until he was warm, as though he were still a baby and she had no trouble meeting all of his needs. "Get in the car, Connor," she said.

He did. Jackie turned the heat all the way up and they drove home in silence.

HUDSONSTUD WAS A lot shorter than Pearl had expected. She stood eye-to-eye with him when she answered the door—something that, at five feet four inches, she wasn't accustomed to. She may have even looked down on him a little, but once they were in bed and he was on top of her, behind her, beneath her, it didn't really matter. If anything, their closeness in height made for smoother transitions. She liked that he didn't talk during sex, and she was fascinated by the neck tattoo—a fairly intricate drawing of a twisting orange fish, each scale clearly delineated. *It must have hurt,* she kept thinking.

"How long did it take?" she asked as they put their clothes on, backs to each other. "Your tattoo?"

"Three and a half days."

"Kept coming back for more, huh?"

"You make a commitment," he said, "you've got to stick with it."

"Does it mean anything?"

"Nah. I just saw the picture in a book. It made me happy."

"And that was enough for a lifelong commitment?"

"Couldn't think of a better reason."

Pearl turned around and looked at him. He smiled. A kind smile. He was fully dressed now in jeans and a dark blue sweatshirt with no brand logo on it, no words. She hadn't noticed when he'd first come in, but unlike most guys their age from this area, HudsonStud wasn't dressed in a theme: rapper, hipster, deejay douchebag. He was just wearing clothes. "What's your name, anyway?"

"Paul. Yours?"

"Pearl."

"Wow," he said. "Our names are practically anagrams."

Pearl felt herself smiling. "You want a beer?"

"Sure."

He followed her into the kitchen. He didn't sit down. She pulled out two icy bottles and used the opener chained to the fridge to crack off the caps and they both stood there, not talking, taking long, slow gulps.

Pearl was so much thirstier than she'd thought. She closed her eyes and felt the familiar cool slide of the beer, the calming presence of the stranger standing next to her. But after a few blissful moments the calm dissipated and Liam Miller's face eased into her mind. Again.

When she'd first gotten home from Amy's, back when she was

still too keyed up to get into bed, Pearl had googled the name *Liam Miller* plus *Havenkill*. A lot of sports articles from the local weekly had come up—he was quarterback for the high school team, the Havenkill Ravens, and so it hadn't taken her long to find his picture—a boy with pale blond hair and an infectious smile and a face that was so camera-friendly, it looked familiar. At first, Pearl thought he must resemble someone famous, she just couldn't figure out whom. But soon it hit her that she really had met him before.

It had been less than two months ago—the last week in August, when Havenkill was bathed in a heat wave, the air thick with humidity, nighttime just as oppressively hot as day. You couldn't go outside without pouring sweat, and Pearl was taking at least three showers a day in the station locker room. Her uniform was torture. The call had come in at around 10:00 PM—a woman, saying that her neighbors, the Schwartzes, were out of town but she'd heard voices in their yard and suspected a break-in. Pearl had driven over with Ed Tally, an older cop and a war vet. Nice enough guy, but very by-the-book. When they'd gotten to the house—the type of two-story stone home that people describe as "grand" or "gracious"—they'd caught four high school boys outside by the pool. Liam Miller had been in his swim trunks, bouncing on the diving board, some buddy of his ready to capture the moment on his phone. She could still recall the way he'd dived in—the graceful arch of it, the way he'd entered the water like a blade, his hands and feet barely making a ripple. She remembered the expression on his face when he'd come up for air—pure joy, then terror at the sight of Pearl and Tally in their uniforms, approaching. "Oh my gosh," he had said.

Tally had shaken his head. "Rich kids think they're above the law," he'd said. But Pearl had found it hard not to crack a

smile. Liam Miller and his friends had been pool-hopping on a
hot night—which, legal or not, was one of the few things for a
teenager to do in Havenkill during the summer that didn't involve the 4-H Club, drugs, or dressing up like some dork from
the Renaissance.

The way he was acting, though, you'd think he'd blown up a
bank. "I'll never do it again, officer," he had said as his friend with
the phone raised his hands in the air like the kid at the Lukoil
station and the other two boys ran away. "I promise. Just please
don't arrest me. I want to go to college. I want to be a doctor."

Pearl finished her beer. She started to go for another but
stopped herself when she saw that Paul was only halfway through
with his.

"So," he said. "You're a cop?"

"Yep." It was the one piece of true information she listed on
hookup sites; she did it to keep the crazies at bay.

"Ever kill anyone?"

Pearl found herself looking into his eyes, which were a deeper
blue in person than on his profile pic and not, as it turned out,
contacts. Pearl had been right about the Axe spray, but there was
no sticky gel in his hair, and he hadn't asked to use her shower
the way most of these guys did, looking for an excuse to stay. He
seemed decent and normal, which meant she'd never see him
again. And so she saw no reason to lie.

"Yes," she told him. "I killed my mother."

ONCE JACKIE HAD pulled into the driveway, Connor unlocked his
door and started to get out.

"Stop," she said. "Wait."

He looked at her, eyes dry, his gaze direct and unreadable.
"Cindy Weston called," she said.

"Yeah?"

"She told me why you hit Noah, and I think . . . under the circumstances . . ." She opened her glove compartment, removed his
phone, and handed it to him.

He smiled a little. "Thanks, Mom."

"Why didn't you tell me?"

He took a breath, let it out slowly. "I . . . I felt bad for Wade,"
he said. "And you too."

"Me?"

"I mean . . . I know how worried you get about us. You want us
to be happy, Mom."

"Of course I do."

"But . . . I mean . . . That's kind of a lot to expect."

"You can't blame me for that, can you? Wanting you to be
happy?" She ruffled his hair and tried smiling at him. He didn't
smile back.

Once they were both out of the car, Jackie noticed Wade, sitting on the front step. She saw him put out a cigarette but pretended not to see. She'd cross that bridge later, along with the
hospital, the way those kids had looked at her, the way Stacy had
said Wade's name.

Connor headed into the house, brushing past Wade. "I think I
need a hot shower."

"How was the SAT?" Jackie said once he was gone.

"I didn't take it."

"What?"

Wade's head was bowed, so all Jackie could see was messy
dyed hair, skinny legs in faded jeans, letters scrawled on them in
Sharpie. She so very rarely saw his face these days and so she had
to gauge her son's emotions by the state of his hair, his clothes, the
writing on his jeans. *Is that a* T *inside a heart?*

"Wade," she said. "Talk to me. Why didn't you take it?"

He looked up at her and she gasped a little. How pale his face was, how sunken the cheeks. And then she noticed the tears in his eyes. "Oh . . . Oh, honey."

Wade never cried, not since the day his dad had left home—a day of loud, aching sobs and then an announcement: "No one's ever making me cry like that again." And he'd stuck to it. Not a tear out of him until now. "Wade," Jackie said. "Are you upset over what happened to Liam Miller?"

Wade nodded, the movement barely noticeable.

"It's okay." Jackie said it tentatively, like someone defusing a bomb. She wanted to hug Wade so badly, but she wasn't sure it would be welcome or even that he would take it the right way. It had been so long since they'd hugged, after all, and she was afraid he might think she was trying to baby him.

He stood up, ran a sleeve over his eyes. "Thanks, Mom," he said. Jackie remembered Helen telling her why Wade had gone to the hospital. *He was worried. He wanted to know what was going on.* She felt a surge of pride. Wade cared about other people, whether they liked him or not. And that would serve him well, once he busted out of this gossipy, airless little town and found friends who deserved him.

She put a firm hand on his shoulder, the way a father might have done. "Everything's going to be okay," she said. And in that moment, it felt like the truth.

Five

Selected posts from the Facebook page of Liam Miller.

Stacy Davies ▶ Liam Miller

October 20 at 12:45 PM

My mom baked you M&M cookies! Get out of that hospital before I eat them all. I <3 U. Get well soon!

Rafe Burgess ▶ Liam Miller

October 20 at 2:00 PM

Heard what happened. You are a HERO!! Hang in there. Let's do something insane when you wake up. GO RAVENS!

Ryan Grant ▶ Liam Miller

October 20 at 3:58 PM

Hoping and praying, for you, buddy.

    Bobby Udel: ^^^ Like the kid said. ^^^ Get better soon!!!!!!!!

    October 20 at 4:04pm

Tamara Hayes ▶ Liam Miller

October 20 at 4:50 PM

Please post on your page when you feel up to it. We're all worried about you and we just want to know you're okay.

Stacy Davies ▶ Liam Miller

October 21 at 12:37 AM

EVERYBODY IN HAVENKILL PLEASE PRAY FOR LIAM.

👍 320 people like this

October 21 at 9:45 AM

We are deeply sorry to announce that our beautiful son, Liam Franklin Miller, was pronounced dead at 3:30 this morning. We want you all to know that he died as he lived, trying to help another person. Late Friday night a woman's car was stolen. Instead of ignoring her screams, as most boys his age would have done, Liam rushed to the scene and charged straight for the car in an attempt to save it, only to be run down and fatally injured.

We are very grateful to the lovely woman who told us the story, and to all of you for your kind wishes and memories and words of hope for Liam. We can still use them. Perhaps now more than ever.

We are doing all we can to help the police find and capture the monster who killed Liam.

God bless you all,

Sheila and Chris Miller

Six

Last night had been the type of night Jackie hadn't experienced in she didn't know how long: both boys with her at the kitchen table, devouring the lasagna she'd made and talking to each other. Really talking. Connor had mentioned needing to change his science project, and Wade, attentive and bright-eyed, had suggested new ideas. Wade, listening and speaking, participating in a conversation . . . Even Connor had looked surprised.

"Did you know," Wade said as he served scoops of rocky road ice cream, "that yeast breathes?"

"Gross," said Connor.

"It's not gross. It's just alive."

To Jackie, it felt as though Wade's tears that afternoon had brought down a wall that had surrounded him for years. Or at the very least, made a few cracks in it so the three of them could breathe again. Throughout dinner, neither Wade nor Connor had looked at their phones or listened to music. They'd even helped with the dishes. Well, Connor had helped. But Wade had brought his to the sink without being asked. Together, they'd watched a few old episodes of *The Office* on Netflix and then they'd all gone to bed early, Jackie avoiding both Facebook and her bottle of Xanax and drifting off peacefully and naturally with no nightmares, no dreams at all.

She'd slept in a bit, waking up at nine thirty and checking in on her boys to hear both of them sleeping behind closed doors, snoring away just like their father.

Jackie made coffee in silence, forgoing the Hudson Valley cable news station she usually watched in the kitchen on Sunday mornings. When the coffee was done, she poured herself a cup, breathed in the steam of it. And it was only then, as she made her way to the laundry room, warm mug pressed to her palms, that she really *heard* the silence and understood how she'd been avoiding local news, social media, her phone—all links to the suddenly chaotic world outside her house. Jackie saw it now: she had been avoiding Liam Miller. Maybe that's what had led to the previous evening. Maybe her boys had been avoiding Liam too.

She pushed the thought out of her mind. Tabled it, the way she'd table a call from a potential client when she was carpooling or buying groceries. Jackie would come back to the outside world, but for now she was focused on the laundry—the never-ending disappointment of it. The washing machine was filled with damp and wrinkly clothes that smelled vaguely of mildew. Jackie sighed. She'd put these clothes in Friday afternoon before running off to the Leones' closing, asking Connor and Wade to transfer the load to the dryer as soon as it was done. *Thanks, guys.*

As she scooped clothes out of the washer, she heard light footsteps in the kitchen, the sound of the refrigerator opening. One of the boys, awake. She thought about marching whichever one of them it was in here and forcing him to transfer the load, but why bother? It would take longer to nag and criticize than just to do it. She pulled open the dryer door. Then she stepped back, staring.

There were clothes in the dryer.

She put the wet laundry on the folding table and pulled it all out . . . Black hoodie. Black T-shirt. A pair of dark jeans with one of the pockets ripped off. The same clothes Wade had been wearing the night before last, when she'd seen him on the front step.

Why had he run them through the dryer?

In the kitchen, she heard the squeak of a chair. "Wade?"

No answer, and when she returned to the kitchen, she saw Connor, sitting at the kitchen table, staring into his hands, into his phone screen. "Any idea why your brother . . ." She stopped. Connor was looking up at her, phone still clutched in front of him. His jaw was tight, his lower lip trembling so slightly, she doubted anyone other than a mother would notice. "Liam?" she said.

He nodded. Jackie went to him. He didn't start crying until she took him in her arms.

"HE'S GONE," SAID Udel as soon as Pearl emerged from the locker room, showered and blow-dried and in uniform, remnants of beer hangover like cobwebs in her head. "Liam Miller. He's gone."

No . . .

Pearl said nothing. A strong wind barreled past the station, rattling the frail windows. A threat. Pearl remembered Liam's face on that hot summer night, the drops of pool water glistening on his cheeks. *I'll never do it again, officer. I promise.*

Udel was looking at her as though he expected her to say something. What she wanted to tell him was this: *bad things happen and they happen for no reason and there's nothing you can do about it.* Paul had said that to her yesterday after she'd told him about her mother: "You live through those things. That's what you do. You live through more and more of them until you say, 'Okay, I get it.' Then you stop living." Paul was a paramedic as it turned out, so he ought to know.

"We'd better get going," Pearl said. "We'll be late."

"That's all?" Udel said. "That's all you're going to say?"

Sentences flipped through her mind. Apologies, niceties. But what came out was something else Paul had told her: "A word never brought anybody back to life."

AT THE START of each shift, the sergeant met the on-duty officers in the conference room and gave them their assignments. They'd been called beats back in Poughkeepsie, where Pearl had worked before coming here, but in such a small town and with just nine cops counting the sergeant, all of them except the sergeant working part-time, "beats" seemed a little pretentious. During one of her first weeks here in Havenkill, she'd referred to her patrol as "the Orchard Street beat" and the guys had all laughed at her. For weeks, they'd called her Danno after the by-the-book cop from the old TV show *Hawaii Five-0*—a nickname that fortunately didn't stick.

It was generally a pretty laid-back affair, the conference room meeting. But today, there was a pall over the room, a seriousness Pearl could sense as she and Udel approached the door. Inside, it felt almost as if they'd walked into another police station, one with a larger force and regular beats and cops too busy to give each other sarcastic nicknames.

All nine officers were in the room, which was unusual. Sergeant Black stood at the far end, next to a petite woman in a tailored pants suit and a balding, middle-aged man with the type of thick mustache favored by 1970s porn stars and current-day hipsters trying too hard to be ironic.

"I'm sure you've all heard, but the hit-and-run case involving Havenkill High School student Liam Miller has now become a homicide investigation," Sergeant Black said, his eyes fixed on some point over their heads, as though he were reading from a teleprompter. "We will be assisting state police in the investigation. To that end, I'd like to introduce Kendall Wind and Alex Wacksman of the Bureau of Criminal Investigation. Detectives Wind and Wacksman will be working in our area, in and out of the station for the next few weeks at least, if the case isn't solved earlier."

Pearl felt as though she'd walked through some portal and into a different station far from Havenkill, the sergeant body-snatched and replaced by someone who never, in a million years, would have asked a weeping carjacking victim to sign his Burger King bag the way he had with Aimee En the night before last. Even his voice sounded different. Unnaturally deep, like a documentary voice-over. Pearl turned to Udel, hoping to catch his eye. But he stared straight ahead, posture stick straight in a way she'd never seen before—callow, lazy-assed Bobby Udel body-snatched too. As the sergeant continued on with his speech, Pearl's gaze moved up to Udel's face, bright eyes blinking. *Tears.*

Pearl looked away. As Sergeant Black brought them all up-to-date on the specifics of the case—the APB issued for Amy Nathanson's Jaguar, the composite sketch drawn of the alleged assailant, requests on local and statewide news outlets for information leading to a possible arrest—she focused on the female detective, Kendall Wind, who was probably just a few years older than herself, curls tamed into a bun, eyebrows plucked to a perfect arch, full lips pursed and painted a sober burgundy. Doing everything she could to will on an extra ten years, to separate herself that much more from the boy whose death she was investigating.

The boy who died.

The sergeant was giving out the day's assignments. Pearl listened for her name, thinking about Liam again, Liam in the heat of summer, his eyes shining in the garden lights, the same color as the water in the pool. "I'll never do it again," he had said. But Pearl and Tally had called his parents anyway. They'd called the two remaining kids' parents in the hopes of . . . what? Scaring them off pool-hopping forever? The picture-taker's dad had rolled his eyes. "They're just being kids," he'd said. But Liam's parents had been different. "How could you?" his mother had said to him. "Did we raise a criminal?"

It hadn't been Pearl's idea to call them. In fact, when Tally had first insisted on it, she'd pulled him aside. "Hey, who's Danno now?" she had said. A joke. But Tally hadn't found it funny. "Just because you're a rich, white kid from a rich, white town, it doesn't give you extra rights," he'd said. And that had sold her. Pool-hopping in Havenkill translated to breaking and entering in Poughkeepsie. Forget about calling parents. These boys would have been taken in to the station and booked. Pearl had said that to Liam and his friend, whose name had been Ryan, she remembered now. Ryan Grant, a square-jawed kid with the rosiest cheeks—she hadn't been able to tell if that had been from health or humiliation. She'd said it again in front of their parents. Breaking and entering. Taken in and booked. She'd used those exact words.

Did that night change Liam Miller? Did it turn him into the

type of person who was so desperate to do good, he rushed at
speeding stolen cars?

"Maze and Udel," the sergeant said, interrupting her thoughts.
"You'll be patrolling the Kill."

WHEN THE MEETING ended, Pearl hurried ahead and caught up
with Ed Tally. "Hey, Ed," she said.

"Hey."

"You remember Liam Miller, right? From the summer?"

He stopped. She wanted him to say something, or at least look
at her in a way that showed he remembered everything he'd said
on that pool-hopping night and felt some of the guilt she was feeling. "I remember," he said. But his eyes stayed flat as a locked
door, and Pearl wondered if that calm was something that came
with age or from innocence. She envied him both. "Makes me
glad I have daughters, the way boys are," Tally said. "Always getting up to things."

"REPRIEVE," BOBBY UDEL said, once they were in the parking lot,
heading for their patrol car.

"Huh?" said Pearl.

"You said a word never brought anybody back to life. But,
like . . . if you're on death row . . ."

"Ah. I stand corrected."

"You want to drive?"

"Sure."

They got in the car—the same cruiser she'd driven Amy
home in. Pearl started it up, feeling tired, exhausted actually,
the beer headache lingering, Amy's scent still heavy in the air,
hair spray and wet vinyl and pancake makeup, her voice in

Pearl's mind all over again. *I don't know what I'm going to do if that boy dies.*

Udel said, "When you were in Poughkeepsie, did you see this a lot? You know . . ."

"Teen homicides?"

He nodded.

"Not a lot," she said. "But there were a few . . . Gang stuff." She studied his pinched, pained face. "It's never easy."

"I've only known this town," he said. "My whole life. I went to Havenkill High. HCC. The Police Academy up in Albany, but I commuted there from my parents' house. Hell, I went to New York City once, when I was a kid. My mom and dad took me to *The Phantom of the Opera*. Serendipity. FAO freakin' Schwarz. All I wanted to do was come home."

"You like it here."

"I *get* it here," he said. "It's like reading the same book over and over. You know what's going to happen. You know how it ends . . ." His voice cracked.

Pearl looked at him, his eyes clouded, glistening. "Did you know Liam?" she said.

He nodded. "My cousin Ryan is in his class," he said as she pulled out of the space. "They're best friends . . . Were best friends."

"Ryan Grant?"

"Yeah," he said. "How did you know?"

This town. This small, small town. "Just . . . School assembly, I think," she said.

He nodded. A tear spilled down his cheek. Pearl went for the Kleenex box and held it out for him. He grabbed a handful without thanking her and raked it across his eyes. "Don't tell the sergeant I cried."

"Why not?"

"I need to work this case. I'm scared he won't let me if he finds out I have feelings about it."

Pearl stopped the car. Looked at him. "We all have feelings about it."

Udel shook his head. He pulled something out of the pocket of his uniform and handed it to her: a faded picture of three boys, smiling, arms around each other—two in Little League uniforms, the older one at the center, a tall, gawky teenager, making devil horns behind their heads. "Liam's parents gave this to me yesterday. Before he . . . when he was still on life support. They told me we're like family. Ryan and me both."

Pearl studied the photo. The husky, dark-haired boy to the right, those rosy cheeks of his. The boy to the left, white-blond hair sticking out from beneath the blue baseball cap, so much smaller then, but still unmistakable . . . *I'll never do it again, officer.* Small hands clutching the teenage boy's waist, hugging him. "That's you in the middle."

Udel's hands in his lap, clenched into fists. Reddened eyes glaring at the window, acne dotting his cheeks. Same boy as the teenager in the picture, only with the wind knocked out of him. Anger burning in his eyes as though someone had taken his favorite book, the one he'd read over and over, and ripped a page out of it. "My feelings," he said, quietly. "They're different."

"WADE."

It was past 1:00 PM and Wade was still sleeping. Connor stood over him in his darkened bedroom, listening to his heavy snores. It smelled of sweat and stale smoke in here. He wasn't sure what to do. He said his brother's name a little louder, but Wade didn't budge.

"Mom's gone," Connor tried. "She's showing a house."

Still nothing. Maybe Wade was drugged. Connor wondered if he'd taken something.

He flicked on the light switch and stumbled back. Man, Wade's room was a mess. Dirty clothes everywhere, a broken skateboard from probably five years ago, stacks of old comic books, and stupid crap that Wade had found on the street and decided for whatever reason to take home with him (*Why the* FOR SALE *sign? Why the orange safety cones?*). Connor wasn't winning any neatness prizes either, but at least he cared enough to shove most of his crap into his closet. *"Wake up."*

Wade rolled over onto his back and threw an arm over his eyes. "What are you doing in here?"

"He died, Wade."

"Huh?"

"Liam Miller."

"Wait, what?"

"Liam died this morning. Everybody's talking about it."

Wade sat up. Connor's gaze moved from his face to the stack of his drawings peeking out from under the bed. Connor could make out a woman's bare leg, the curve of a breast. It made his breath catch.

"Oh," Wade said. "Wow. That's . . ."

"I know."

"That's awful."

Connor wanted to look at him, to figure out if he really meant what he was saying. Mom said she could always tell if Connor was lying from the sound of his voice, but with Wade it was his eyes. "Those big brown peepers never lie," Mom had once said, which was probably why Wade was always staring at the ground or at his phone. Mom's mistake, showing her hand like that. But it didn't matter anyway, because much as he wanted to look at Wade, Connor couldn't take his eyes off the drawing.

"What are you looking at?"

"Nothing." Finally Connor tore his gaze from the leg. *Is that a bruise or just a shadow?* "I just can't believe Liam's gone," he said. "It isn't fair."

Wade's eyes were downcast, shielded by heavy lids, lashes thick as a girl's. His dyed black hair stuck out at weird angles, and his thin, ropy arms were almost the same color as the white T-shirt he wore, and Connor thought, not for the first time, how weird his brother had become and in such a short time. As if he'd erased his old self and replaced it with one of his freaky drawings. "Nothing's fair." Wade said it to his hands. He picked at a nail.

Connor's gaze returned to the girl's leg, her breast. He thought about Liam again, how his life had ended in a second, but as much as he tried to focus on that, all he wanted to do was to slip the paper out from under Wade's bed, to see the rest of her.

"Connor?"

"Yeah?"

"The bag."

"I got rid of it," he said. "At the Lukoil. Like you told me."

"Look at me."

Connor took a breath, turned to Wade. Put the girl in the drawing out of his mind and took in his brother's face: the eyes like black holes, the purple circles underneath.

"Did you tell Mom?"

"No."

"She saw you there, though, right? She picked you up at the Lukoil. She said she found you by the Dumpster . . ."

"I didn't tell her anything," Connor said. "I swear to God."

A moment passed, a silence thick enough to see. "Thanks, buddy," Wade said finally.

Connor started to leave, but the question came out before he could stop it. "Wade," he said. "Where were you that night?"

"Huh?"

"When you came into my room. When you put the bag in my closet. You were all wet. Where did you come from?"

Wade looked at him. "Nowhere."

"But . . ."

"Just outside. That's all. Having a cigarette."

"At four in the morning?"

"I couldn't sleep. I got caught in the rain."

"It just seemed like you'd . . . been somewhere."

"Connor?"

"Yeah?"

"Do me a favor, okay? Pretend two nights ago never happened."

Connor blinked. "How am I supposed to do that?"

"Never think about it again. Never ask about it again." Wade put a hand on Connor's shoulder. "It was just a dream," he said. "Okay?"

Connor nodded.

"You never saw me. I was never there."

"Okay."

Wade's eyes were like deep, black water. "That's really awful about Liam," he said. "But . . ."

Connor stared at him, wondering how he could possibly finish that sentence. "But what?" he said, finally.

"Nothing. Nobody deserves to die."

Connor started for the door, a feeling inside him like he was in a strange room, talking to someone he'd never met.

BACK IN HIS own room, Connor made sure Arnie had enough
food and water and then he lay down on his bed, closed his eyes,
straining for something nice to think about.

He came up with his fifth birthday. Party at Pizza Haven, that
ice-cream cake from Carvel shaped like a spaceship—a stripe
of vanilla, a stripe of chocolate, crunchy cookie pieces, whipped
cream, and blue and white buttercream icing that he could still
taste if he thought about it hard enough. All Connor's friends
from kindergarten and Noah sitting next to him and Mom looking so happy. He could remember blowing out the candles and his
friends cheering, but most of all Connor could remember Wade
and the present he had given him: a drawing of Buzz Lightyear
he'd made himself. Mom had gotten it framed, and it still hung in
Connor's room over his desk. He opened his eyes and looked at
it—the careful, straight lines, his brother such a good artist, even
at just nine years old, thinking so hard about whatever it was he
chose to draw.

And now . . . *that girl.*

He tried to push her out of his mind, to think of other things—
the fight with Noah, Liam Miller dying, Connor and Wade's long-
gone dad, whose face he could barely remember even though he
supposedly lived just a few towns away. Everyone and everything
that had left his life. But when he closed his eyes, she was all he
could see—the drawing under his brother's bed, the outstretched
leg, the freckles and straining calves, the clipped toenails. The
round breast, row of ribs beneath it.

Connor could tell. He knew. The drawing of that girl wasn't
like Wade's other drawings, where the bodies were so airbrush-
perfect and out of proportion that anybody could see they'd
been copied from comic books or porn sites. This one was different. She would stay in Connor's thoughts. *She,* not *it,* just as if

he'd walked into Wade's room and seen a real naked girl there, hiding under his bed. Because that's what the girl in the drawing was, with her faded tan and her ankle bracelet, puckered skin at the thighs, muscles braced, ready to jump off the paper. *Real*.

Seven

Its real name was Haven Kill; the Kill was just what everyone called the murky body of water at Havenkill's less populated western end, in order to avoid confusion with the town itself, *kill* being Dutch for riverbed. Lots of Hudson River towns were built around kills and were named for them, though this particular kill, Pearl thought, looked awfully stagnant for a riverbed, more like an enormous pond.

She hadn't patrolled the Kill much. Being a newcomer, not to mention female and young, Pearl was, in the sergeant's somewhat old-fashioned mind, better suited to the more populous areas: the shopping district on Orchard, the tree-lined streets surrounding the middle and high schools with their brightly painted Victorian houses and well-kept gardens, just a stone's throw from the park.

The Kill wasn't like the rest of Havenkill. It was more like something out of an old summer-camp slasher movie. Back in the 1970s, the land around the Kill had been designated "forever wild" by the town council in order to stave off what they saw as rampant commercialization in the area, and while indeed there weren't any strip malls here (or in the rest of Havenkill for that matter) there weren't any houses either. Just a few abandoned hunting cabins Ed Gein would have felt at home in. Creepy plant life too: mangy cattails, poison sumac. And crows, dozens of them, screaming from the trees.

"They gossip, you know that?" Udel said as they got out of the car, his voice barely audible over the shrieks. "If somebody's mean to one of them, they tell each other, and then they all gang up. Listen to them. Trash-talking us."

Pearl looked at him. "Were you ever mean to a crow?"

He shrugged. "Probably."

The ground was mucky, tugging at Pearl's boots, and the water was high. The Kill was pretty deep to begin with, but the storm had transformed it. There was a nasty smell to it too—wet moss and sulfur and dying, rotting things. The current churned and the sky was a threatening gray. Kind of a crappy day to go fishing, but there they were, the reason why Pearl and Udel had stopped the car: a leaf peeper, standing thigh-high in the Kill with what had to be his kids, a boy of about twelve and a little girl, maybe five years old, all in fishing vests and wellies and faded, floppy-brimmed hats, looking as though they'd stepped out of an L.L.Bean catalog, only—as Pearl could see as she got closer—Dad was too busy diddling his phone to pay attention to either one of them, and the girl looked miserable.

"How you folks doing?" Udel said it too loudly, a big unnecessary smile on his face and a slight . . . was that a southern accent? Pearl wasn't sure whether he always went all Andy Griffith on civilians when questioning them or if he was simply overcompensating for his grief over Liam. "Catch any big ones?"

"Not yet," said the man.

"I did, Daddy," the little girl said, gravely. "I showed you."

The man gave her a sharp look. "Fish, Emily," he said. "They're asking about fish and you know we haven't caught anything."

He turned to them—thick dark hair, graying at the temples, weathered skin, vacant eyes you might say were twinkling if you weren't all that observant. Phone in his hand, glowing. Pearl figured him for divorced with visitation rights and, from the looks of things, he didn't take advantage of those rights very often.

Pearl said, "Can you show us your license, sir?"

He started to go for his back pocket.

"I don't like fishing," Emily said.

The boy shushed her.

"You might like it," the dad said, between his teeth, "if you gave it half a chance like Holden and me." The little girl said something so softly, Pearl couldn't hear it. She hung her head and stared at the water. *Odd girl out.* Pearl saw her own early childhood in flashing frames: The car pulling up. Aunt Ruth's house looming before her. Her father shapeless, formless. Just a voice, because that was all she could remember of him. "Stop crying. You don't want to hurt Aunt Ruth's feelings." Had he really said that, or were those words something Pearl had created in her mind, along with the crying itself? She couldn't remember what type of car it was or what it had felt like to be dropped off at a stranger's house by a dad who could no longer bear the sight of her. But she always imagined herself crying. And she always imagined him scolding her for it.

The man held out his driver's license.

"Fishing license, sir," Pearl said.

"Fishing license?"

"It's not a traffic stop." Pearl smiled. He didn't smile back.

Udel said, "You need a license to fish here, sir."

"Seriously?"

"You can get one at the town clerk's offices. It's a hop, skip, and a jump."

"I don't get very much time with my kids," the man said. "How about you two just let us stay and—"

"I don't want to stay."

"Emily."

"That isn't an option, sir," Pearl said. "We're being nice not fining you."

"All right," the man said. "As long as you're being *nice.*"

Udel rolled his eyes at Pearl. "Whatever," he whispered, the Andy Griffith act slipping away.

Pearl gave Mr. Phone Diddler a big, fake smile. "I could easily write up a ticket. Comes with a super-duper nice fine."

"We're leaving," the man said. "Holden, Emily. Let's go."

The boy glared at his sister. "Nice going."

They trudged out of the Kill: Dad first, still gaping at his phone, with Holden close behind. Then Emily, dragging her feet, staring down, her father and brother not even glancing back at her, even as she tripped and fell in the shallow water. Pearl helped her up, and when the girl looked at her, she saw tears in her eyes.

"For what it's worth," Pearl said, "I wouldn't want to fish here either."

Emily said nothing.

Pearl tried, "You caught something, huh?"

She nodded slowly.

"A mermaid?"

Emily shook her head. "A cat."

"A cat?"

"Yeah," she said. "You want to see?"

"Emily!" Mr. Phone called out, already nearing his parked car, noticing just now she was gone. Father of the Year.

"I'd love to see the cat," Pearl said.

Emily smiled, finally. "She's really pretty." She dug into the pocket of her fishing vest and pulled something out. "See?" she said, opening her little fist. It was a deco figurine, a silver one.

"She *is* pretty," Pearl said.

"You want to hold her?"

"Sure."

"Emily, we need to leave *now*!"

The crows screamed. *They do know a jerk when they see one.*

Emily placed the cat in Pearl's open palm. She was surprised by the weight of the figurine, but then she took a closer look at it—a shiny silver cat, sleek and leaping. She touched the face, the bared teeth. *A jaguar.* "Hood ornament," Pearl whispered.

"Huh?"

"Where did you find this, honey?"

"Next to that tree." Emily pointed to it—a thick birch about twenty yards away, straining out from the water's edge. *Must have fallen off on its way in.*

Pearl lifted the girl onto the shore and walked over to the tree. She ran her hand down the thick trunk, feeling and then seeing the scrape in it. "Emily," she said. "Can I borrow the cat for just a little while?"

"Will you be nice to her?"

"Promise." She called out to Udel and told him to radio state police, all the while thinking of Amy Nathanson, of her baby's leather seats, soaking in the Kill.

"ARE YOU ALL right?" said Jackie's client, a retired New York City schoolteacher by the name of Inez Ventura.

"Oh yes, of course. I'm just a little . . . I need to get more sleep." Jackie made herself laugh, though there was nothing funny about what she'd said. Inez laughed along, because she was a nice woman.

For easily a minute, Jackie had stood frozen in the laundry room of the eyebrow Colonial she'd been showing Inez, her hand resting on the washer-dryer as though she were taking an oath, staring down through the open dryer lid and thinking of this morning, of Wade's black clothes at the bottom of her own dryer, the rest of the clothes in the washer, untransferred. What with the shock of Liam Miller's death and comforting Connor over it, Jackie had put it out of her mind—Wade's clothes in the dryer, what that could possibly mean. But now it was all she could think about.

Jackie closed the lid. "Washer and dryer are both state-of-the-art," she heard herself say, the sales pitch reanimating her in a way; she made eye contact with Inez while her brain stayed stuck on Wade, her sad-eyed son with his blackened hair, the black clothes in the dryer that would have been so easy to hide had he thought of transferring the other load, blending his own wet clothes in with the others. But no. Teenagers were still children in so many ways, unable to keep anything safe, including their own secrets. *The night before SATs, you went out. You got caught in the rain. You tried to hide it.* "Of course, these appliances come with the house, as do the Sub-Zero fridge, the dual-fuel oversize range . . . Did you notice the details in the kitchen? The subway-tile backsplash?" *The same night someone stole a car and killed one of your classmates with it.*

Vaguely aware of Inez shaking her head no, Jackie said, "Let's go take a closer look then." Jackie led her into the kitchen and then through the rest of the house, walking and talking as though she were moving through a dream. *Where did you go, Wade?* She thought it with every step, the words in her head like a mantra, a prayer, but one she kept shutting out of her mind because of the memories it dredged up from two years ago. Her son missing from home. A stolen car . . . *Where did you go this time, Wade? What are you hiding?*

AFTER SAYING GOOD-BYE to Inez, Jackie called Wade's phone. He answered before she'd solidified in her mind what she was going to say to him, and something about the catch in his voice, the way he said, "Hi, Mom . . ." made her rethink it all.

"You heard about Liam," Jackie said.

"Yeah. Connor told me."

"I'm sorry, honey."

Wade took a deep breath. Then another. She remembered him crying yesterday, how pained he had looked, tears on his face for the first time in years. "Are you . . ."

"No," he said. "I'm not crying."

"It would be okay if you were."

"Mom?"

"Yes, honey?"

"I really don't feel like talking now."

Jackie's turn to breathe. "All right," she said. "I understand." After she ended the call, she said, "Will you ever feel like talking?" To the dashboard. To no one. *Will you ever feel like telling me the truth?*

She called Wade's school and pressed the button for the guidance counselor's office. As directed, she said her name clearly into the voice mail and asked if she could make an appointment, anytime on Monday, to discuss her son Wade. She'd start with the fact he missed the SATs, she figured. If she liked what she heard, she'd take it from there, maybe make an appointment for Wade too.

After she ended the call, Jackie felt better, but only for a few seconds. The guidance counselor would be swamped tomorrow. So many kids trying to cope with the death of their friend and here she was, treating him like her personal therapist. Same way she'd treated his predecessor two years ago. Of course, Ms. Mulroney had asked for that, with all those lengthy after-school meetings, the phone calls when Jackie got home from work, asking not about how Wade was *doing*, but how he was *responding*, as though he were her patient . . .

Jackie sighed. She hated the sound of her own breath—tremulous and fragile. She hated her thoughts, her awful suspicions. *A stolen car. Wade, missing from home.*

She needed to stop thinking.

Jackie was heading north on Orchard, taking the road out of town. She told herself she just needed a drive, some air, time alone, but as she gazed out the window at the row of fiery-leafed maples that lined the wide street, jaw clenched, thoughts full of spikes, she knew where she was going, and it was as though the car were taking her there. As though it had a mind of its own.

IT WAS CALLED Mother Goose's Book Nook, and it was painted pink, with alternating yellow and green shutters, bringing to mind an Easter egg. Jackie had never seen it in person—only in the pages of *Hudson Valley Magazine,* where its owner, Natalie Reed, had been profiled last month.

Natalie Reed, former Office Girl. Now "happily married to Rhinebeck-based attorney Bill Reed and the busy mother of three little girls," as described in the magazine, which failed to mention Bill's *other* family or that, one month before closing on the Book Nook as an "early Christmas present" for his beloved wife, Bill Reed had filed a restraining order against his firstborn son.

He only wanted to talk to you.

Jackie didn't like to think about it. She'd found a way to close a door in her mind on the whole ugly incident, but how could she stop herself now? With Wade sneaking off at night and keeping secrets yet again, it all seemed so horribly, frighteningly relevant.

And you don't care, Bill. You don't give a damn about your son and whether he hurts himself. Or someone else.

Jackie was standing on the sidewalk in front of the store. It was closed—probably so its busy owner could spend some quality time with her family.

She peered through the big window at the space inside— the rows of thin-spined picture books and chunkier tomes for older kids. Fantasy stories for people young enough to believe that anything is possible. The antique brass cash register and the colorfully painted chandelier and the oversize rocking chair, everything so adorable it made Jackie want to gag. What had Natalie called it in the article? Oh, right. "My very own never-never land." Double gag.

A memory wormed its way into her mind: the three of them in the living room when Wade was just about three years old. *SpongeBob SquarePants* on the TV. Wade standing on Bill's feet, hanging on to his daddy's fingers as Bill walked around the room, taking great big strides. Wade beaming up at Bill, the way he always did when he was little, as though the whole world revolved around his father. And laughing. Wade used to have the most wonderful laugh.

Jackie's pulse pounded. She wanted to break the lock, to find a brick and throw it through the window, to pull the books off the shelves, empty the cash register, leave Natalie's never-never land in a shambles and make Bill pay for the damages.

Make Bill pay.

"Excuse me?" The voice came from behind her. Jackie turned and found herself looking straight into the eyes of Natalie Reed. "I had to run out for a few minutes, but I'm just about to open up," Natalie said. "Can I help you with anything?"

Jackie couldn't speak. Her mouth felt dry. Natalie smiled at her. No sign of recognition in her eyes. She wore yoga pants, a hot pink T-shirt that showed off a tan, golden highlights in her red-brown hair. Expensive-looking. She smelled faintly of honey and mint—all-natural shampoo, no doubt—and she had a couple of extra pounds on her. Residual baby fat maybe, but it suited her. She looked healthy and rested. Soft. "Hello, Natalie." She hadn't meant to call her by name.

"Do I know you?"

Jackie looked at her, this smiling woman whom in all honesty she *didn't* know. She'd seen her only once, at one of Bill's office parties, ten, eleven years ago. And if they'd been formally introduced, Jackie didn't remember. *Young,* that's what Jackie had thought back then as she watched Bill keep his distance, the way he so purposefully avoided the girl's steady gaze. *She is so incredibly young.*

What had Jackie been thinking, coming here? What had she imagined she'd accomplish, even if Bill had been here, as she'd hoped he would? He sent money every month. He'd pointed that out to her over the phone during the screaming match they'd had following the restraining order. The last time they'd ever spoken. "I send money every month. If he expects more than that, it's on you, not me." Bill viewed it as a mistake: his marriage to Jackie, the family they'd created together. Natalie was his do-over, and nothing Jackie could say could keep him from looking at things that way. "I know your name," she said, "from the article in *Hudson Valley Magazine.*"

Natalie exhaled. "Oh, yes. I can't believe they gave the store that much space!" She put a key in the front door and pushed it open. "So . . . What can I help you with?"

Jackie backed away, feeling Natalie's kindly business-owner's gaze on her and needing to get home or somewhere else, anywhere but here. *You can't help me with anything,* she wanted to say. But all the time, it was bubbling up inside her, that molten anger. The idea that this woman wouldn't know her. *The idea.* "My name is Jackie Reed," she said.

Something shifted within those crystal eyes, like clouds starting to form. "Excuse me?" Natalie said.

Jackie took a step closer. Looked directly into her eyes and said it, calmly as she could. "I'm the mother of your stepchildren."

IT DIDN'T TAKE long to find Amy Nathanson's car. Deep as the Kill was, especially after the rain, it was still a relatively compact body of water and, judging the point of entry from the scrapes against the tree, divers were able to locate the Jaguar within an hour. A tow truck arrived and cables were attached, and soon it emerged from the depths like a monster, plant life hanging off the rear frame, state troopers and investigators alongside Udel and Pearl, looking on like a rapt audience as the back end of the car emerged to reveal the banged-up body, the smashed rear window. "Poor Baby," said Udel.

"Right? Amy's going to freak out." Pearl's phone buzzed in her pocket. She plucked it out to silence it, expecting Paul, but seeing the Albany number instead. Her father's number. She glanced quickly at Udel, who was moving toward a trooper, answering a question. She declined the call.

"Officer Maze?"

Pearl turned to find Kendall Wind standing on the other side of her. She wondered how long the detective had been there and felt her own heart pounding, as though Kendall Wind would recognize her father's number and know everything that was on her mind. "Yes?"

Wind wore a heavy coat that swallowed up her small frame. Up close, she looked younger, more delicate, but when she shook Pearl's hand, her grip was strong, and there was a hardness to her eyes. "I understand you spoke to Amy Nathanson on the night she came into the station," she said.

"Yes."

"What was your read?"

"Very upset," she said. "And very wet."

"Huh?"

"We had a bad storm that night. She got caught in it."

"Did you find her trustworthy?"

Pearl looked down at the soft ground. "It was hard not to believe her."

"Meaning?"

"Meaning carjacking/hit-and-runs aren't exactly common here, but the story seemed too bizarre *not* to be true. And . . . you know . . . the way she was crying."

"Not for nothing," Kendall Wind said. "But if I ran a boy over and drove away, I'd cry. A lot."

Pearl thought about the whiskey smell on Amy Nathanson's breath and how she'd been the only one to notice it—a similar species, sniffing another out.

"I couldn't find Breathalyzer results in the files," Kendall Wind said, as though she'd been reading her mind.

"Yeah, well . . . When she showed up, there was so much confusion . . ."

Wind smirked. "He's a big fan."

"Excuse me?"

"Sergeant Black. Huge, hopelessly smitten Aimee En super-Stan."

"How do you know that?"

"Who gets an autograph from a potential suspect and frames it a day later?"

"He *framed* the Burger King bag?"

She rolled her eyes. "So now we know why there was no Breathalyzer," she said. "A Burger King bag. Jesus."

Pearl looked at Wind, her cheeks flushing. *She's good.* "Ms. Nathanson did come to the station voluntarily," she said. "We all viewed her as a witness."

"All of you."

"Yes."

"Did she talk about the carjacker a lot?" Wind said. "This . . . hooded teenager?" She may as well have been saying "headless horseman" or "little green man from outer space." So patronizing. Pearl found herself feeling more and more defensive of the sergeant, of their tiny police force with its condemned station house and its holding bench. Of Amy too, as annoying as she was, if only for the fact she hadn't been treated as a suspect. "She gave us a description," Pearl said. "It's in the report."

"Did it strike you as an accurate description?"

"It was okay."

"Just okay?"

"Ms. Nathanson was out of sorts, crying," Pearl said. "She was upset about her car and Liam Miller and I'm sure she'll be able to remember more details about him when you question her."

"Wow," Wind said. "That's interesting."

"What is?"

"You said Amy Nathanson was upset about her car being stolen and Liam Miller being run down."

"Yes . . ."

"Are you aware that you put the car first?"

She is really, really good. "She does love that car."

Kendall Wind raised an eyebrow like Scarlett O'Hara. Pearl had never seen anyone actually do that in real life.

"She was upset about Liam Miller too," Pearl tried, but Kendall Wind wasn't listening. Everyone hears what they want to hear, and she'd already given the detective what she wanted. Pearl took a step away and the mud tugged at her shoes, and she thought, *I stepped in it.* Literally and figuratively.

"Aimee En," Wind mused. "Crying over a car."

A gust of air pushed in off the Kill, so cold it made Pearl's eyes water. She pulled her windbreaker closer, wishing she'd worn her winter jacket and shuddering at the thought of the station, the cracks in the windows, that damaged, trembling roof. "Sometimes," she said, "it's easier to worry about things than people."

Pearl's phone buzzed again, three short blips, signifying she'd received a voice mail. She tried to steady her breath. Her father on her voice mail. Her father talking to her for the first time in twenty-two years. "Black Pearl," Aunt Ruth had called her once, after too many Molsons. "Your father will never speak to you again and can you blame him? Can you blame him, Black Pearl, black-hearted Pearl . . ."

Pearl felt a heat behind her eyes. She shut them for a few seconds, swallowing hard to smooth out the feeling.

"Anyway . . ." Pearl said. But Kendall Wind's hard gaze was no longer on her. The detective watched the Jaguar now as the truck towed it onto the embankment. Pearl watched it too, the lily pads stuck to the chassis, the luxe emerald-green paint job roughened with algae. Pearl thought of Amy Nathanson in her cruiser, the sad squeak in her voice when she'd asked her if she'd ever killed anyone. She remembered what Paul had said, right after she'd told him exactly how she'd killed her mother, and, standing next to this shark-eyed detective, she realized she could easily say the same thing to Amy Nathanson today, whether or not she'd been the one behind the wheel: "Whoa, girl. That's some shit luck you got there."

"She played a gig that night," Pearl said. "Place called Club Halifax—not more than twenty minutes away from where the accident happened."

Wind looked at her. "And?"

"She said she played late for lots of fans," Pearl said, thinking out loud. "She did lots of encores."

"So . . ."

"So," Pearl said. "What if one of those fans wasn't a fan at all? Teenage boys aren't her usual demographic. What if he was at the bar for whatever reason and he saw her as an easy mark, followed her out . . ."

"Followed her in his own car until she was stopped, then ditched his car so that he could come out of nowhere on foot and take hers?"

"It's possible."

"We'll look into it."

"It's as possible as Amy Nathanson pushing her most beloved possession into the Kill."

Wind turned, looked at her. "Good point." She actually sounded impressed.

Pearl felt someone watching her, and when she turned, she saw a kid, half hiding behind a tree, holding up his phone, taking her picture. She glared at him. The phone hand dropped, but she knew there would be more like him—many more, once word got out.

"They have to document everything," Wind said.

Pearl nodded. "I texted a lot as a kid, but the photographing. There's something so creepy-compulsive about it."

"My partner, Detective Wacksman, he blames the Kardashians. He has a theory that they're working for the CIA, purposely normalizing exhibitionism so nobody minds surveillance."

"You guys must have interesting conversations on stakeouts."

"Yep," Wind said. "We took his phone, you know."

Pearl looked at her. "Liam Miller's?"

She nodded.

"It was smashed to bits."

"Have you ever heard of JTAG?"

"Vaguely," Pearl said. The truth. She'd heard it mentioned back in Poughkeepsie—a forensics program of some sort. But beyond that she didn't have a clue what it was.

"They have it at the state lab. Once they de-solder the chip, JTAG can show us everything that was on Liam's phone." She gave Pearl a meaningful look. "Including video."

"You really think he filmed it?"

Wind jammed her hands into her coat pockets, eyes fixed on the ruined car. "You wouldn't believe how many teens have filmed their own deaths."

"So maybe Liam caught the carjacker on video."

"Or whoever ran him over."

"Right," Pearl said, sighing a little. "Whoever ran him over."

"By the way, have you ever seen an Aimee En music video?"

"No . . ."

"There's a bunch up on YouTube," Wind said. "Amy's quite an actress. She cries in almost all of them."

CLUB HALIFAX WAS not, as Pearl had assumed, some hipster para-
dise in the heart of Hudson. Far from the pricey antique stores
and oh-so-chic Manhattan-style restaurants that dominated the
downtown area of this onetime working-class town, the place
where Amy Nathanson had performed was on the outskirts, on
a decidedly off-brand street between a boarded-up bodega and a
check-cashing place that wasn't open today. No leaf peepers here,
that was for sure.

Club Halifax itself was a windowless building that could
have doubled as a porno store. Pink neon letters spelled out the
name of the club in lewd, disco-era script, but the sign wasn't on,
the overflowing Dumpster alongside the club the only real proof
that the place was still in business.

As Pearl pulled up in front of Club Halifax and parked the
cruiser, she tried to imagine a cheering crowd, but the truth was,
she couldn't even imagine people here. The bricks were painted a
charred black, and the whole street had a deserted, creepy feel to
it, as though it had long ago been conquered by zombies.

Pearl got out of the car and headed for the front door, determined to find someone to talk to about Amy. She had to keep it
fast. No one knew she was here. Ostensibly, she was on a coffee
run for the detectives, and the last thing she wanted to do was
make Wacksman and Wind wonder what was taking her so long.

She tried the door. Locked. She pounded on it with the side of
her fist and put her ear up against it, but she heard no movement
inside. "Hello?" she called out. "Police!"

No answer. A car whizzed by and Pearl jumped a little. Until that very moment, there had been no traffic on this street at
all. Pearl moved past the Dumpster, her footsteps echoing as she
curved around to the back of the club, which, interestingly, didn't

look anywhere near as extinct as the front did. There was a parking lot back here, CLUB HALIFAX in shiny red letters on the black brick, two big red doors with a show schedule taped near the place where they met.

There were even windows here, albeit shuttered ones. She pictured those doors flung open, fans pouring out of them and into the parking lot. The way the back of the club must have looked on the cusp of Saturday morning, Aimee En in all her glory in her vinyl jacket, her bright red lipstick, leaning against one of these doors as she signed autographs after a lengthy set.

Aimee En, heading into the parking lot, high from performing and from the lateness of the hour and, yes, maybe a whiskey or two. Not drunk, necessarily. But sloppy, cheerfully oblivious as she slips behind the wheel of her gorgeous car, no idea that she's being watched by a teenage boy, his eyes glued to that sweet, vintage ride . . .

It's possible. Pearl walked up to the red doors, pounded on them for good measure, though she knew there was no one here. No cars in the parking lot, for one thing. For another, the schedule taped to the back door said Club Halifax opened at 6:00 PM. She scanned the big laminated page, the acts announced in a bold font, the same red as the door, each show boxed in shiny gold. Pearl recognized a few—some newer bands, but a lot of oldies with patronizing reminders printed under their names: "70s icon . . . Known for the hit song . . . Formerly of the legendary group . . ."

Pearl's gaze drifted down the list of dates, searching for October 19. She saw the name and reminder right away: "Aimee En, 80s punk/pop goddess."

Not a bad thing to be called a goddess. It made Pearl smile, but only for a second. Once she looked more closely at the date, at everything printed within that gold box, Pearl's smile dissolved. Yes, Amy Nathanson was pitiable. With her weed-choked hoarder's house, her painted face, and her run of bad luck, she was maybe even a little bit heartbreaking. But she was not to be trusted. Not ever again.

Eight

Liam Miller had the same white-blond hair that Amy Nathanson used to have as a little girl. And as she stared at his picture on her laptop screen, published in the online edition of the *Havenkill Journal,* Amy felt a tug in her chest, an ache. She hadn't noticed those flaxen curls two nights ago. All she'd seen was a flash of his face, caught in the glare of her own headlights, his cries drowned out by the screech of her tires . . .

The photo was his senior-class picture: Liam Miller posed against a blue background that matched his eyes and the stripes on his oxford cloth shirt, angled so that he appeared to be gazing at something far away and important.

"Whatcha looking at?" Vic said just as Amy found the headline again: HAVENKILL HS STUDENT DIES FROM HIT-AND-RUN INJURIES.

"Nothing, honey," Amy said, trying to keep it all secret: the held-in tears, the ripping within her heart. "Why don't you go back to sleep?"

"Not sleepy anymore." Vic pushed the button on his bed, bringing him up to sitting.

"You feeling okay?"

"Sure."

Ever since the home health aide had left, Amy had been sitting in Vic's room on the big chair next to his bed with her laptop open, listening to the sound of him sleeping. She did this often. There was something comforting in Vic's deep, even breaths, the creak of the hospital bed as he shifted, the smell of the chemicals keeping him calm and free of pain.

She turned to find him watching her with soft eyes and quickly closed her laptop. "Nice dreams?" she said.

"Meh. How was the gig last night?"

He had asked her the same question when she'd first gotten home yesterday afternoon, and again this morning, when Jacinta had left. She answered the same way: "It was fine."

"Get lucky?"

A panicky feeling swept over Amy. *Don't think*, she told herself. *Don't think.* Until the feeling subsided. "I'd never cheat on you, Vic. You know that."

"See? I'm the lucky one," he said. It was a thirty-year refrain, and it made her sad.

All those times back in the old days, when Vic Iota was the big gun on the L.A. music scene and Amy would look at him—the way his face lit up at the sight of her, the way he'd put out his cigarette when she entered a room. "Secondhand smoke will hurt your beautiful voice," he would say—and Amy would smile, wishing with her whole heart for Vic to always see her this way: young and pristine and perfect.

She'd gotten her wish. Vic saw her the same. He saw everything the same. More than once within the past several weeks, Amy had found him rooting through his closet, looking for his "club clothes." *Where's my leather jacket? I have people to see.*

Belinda and Henry and Exene. Exene would laugh her ass off if she saw me in one of these paper robes. Is this a joke? God, you've got a sick sense of humor. I need my leathers, Amy, where are my leathers?

Had she wished it on him, the dementia? Amy didn't like to think so, what with the way Vic struggled with it when he wasn't feeling his pills, the confusion and fear that would cross his features during those brief moments when he saw things as they really were: the thick dust that coated his massive record collection; the boxes in the dining room, overflowing with thirty- and forty-year-old backstage passes; the concert flyers stacked on his bedroom floor, smelling of mold, yellowed from age and neglect; the weeds climbing up the windows of their onetime party palace. Not to mention Amy herself . . . She had changed so much too.

But Amy saw now how it could be a blessing, the veil in front of his thoughts. In Vic's mind, she had been in New York City two nights ago, playing a sold-out show at Madison Square Garden. He'd never know where she'd really been or what she'd done there or what had happened afterward. He would never know about Liam. Or Baby. The one vestige of her old life she'd managed to hang on to all these years, her only big purchase after her first record hit the charts. Amy had never figured herself as the type of person who'd name a car, but Baby was different. Baby would always be different. Behind the wheel of a shining emerald-green 1973 Jaguar XJ6, the world would always be what it once was—beautiful and full of possibility. She could take Vic to the doctor, stretch him out in the backseat, and he'd inhale the leather and close his eyes and smile. Baby could take anybody back in time.

"My purse and phone got stolen," Amy said.

"What?"

"The police are on it."

"Probably a fan."

She exhaled. "Probably."

"Make sure you cancel your credit cards."

"I did. I'm getting a new license too."

"Babe?"

"Yeah?"

"Did you do something you shouldn't have last night?"

Her heart stopped for a second. *"What?"*

"Did you do coke?"

She exhaled. "No, Vic, of course not."

"Your eyes look puffy. Like you haven't slept." He squinted at her. "Sweetheart, you know what that does to your voice."

"Vic," she said quietly. *I haven't done coke in twenty years.* But she couldn't say it. That would only confuse him. "Vic. I didn't."

There was a knock at the door, an insistent pounding. The doorbell didn't work. Amy knew that, but she'd never thought about fixing it. Outside of the home health aide, Jacinta, who had a key, there was nobody she and Vic needed to open the door for.

"Who's here?" Vic said.

"I'll get it." Amy put a hand on his frail shoulder. "You stay here."

Amy moved into the other room and headed for the door. Through the peephole, she saw a balding middle-aged man in a madras shirt. "Can I help you?" she said through the closed door, only to recognize him as soon as he said his name.

"Hi, Ms. Nathanson. Sergeant Black."

She opened the door. "I'm sorry," she said. "I didn't recognize you without your uniform."

He smiled a little. "I could say the same."

Amy felt her face heat up. She was wearing a pair of baggy

jeans, one of Vic's Ramones T-shirts, her rainbow hair tied back in a ponytail. She wasn't wearing makeup, not even lipstick. Her hand flew up to her face.

"No," he said. "You look terrific." Which made it worse. She knew a lie when she heard one. "You okay?" he said. "You feeling any better?"

Amy backed up enough to let him in. "I'm okay," she said.

"I understand you've heard the news about Liam Miller."

"I . . ."

"Liam's parents. They said you'd contacted them."

"Yes," said Amy, just now realizing. "I sent them a message on Facebook. We're not friends, so I didn't know whether they would even get it, but I felt like I had to say something. I hope that's okay."

Sergeant Black didn't respond right away. He was gaping at the great room, at the stacks of boxes and old newspapers and dusty, broken mementos that Jacinta always said were a firetrap but Amy no longer noticed. They were Vic's things. She was used to them. "We're still kind of moving in," she tried.

He nodded. "Just . . . couple of things. First of all, we think we found your car in the Kill."

Amy stared at him, everything inside her freezing, then starting to crumble. The look on his face. *Don't cry. Imagine how it will look if you cry over a car.* She heard herself say, "Do you think it can be fixed?"

He frowned, and she wished she could suck the words back. "I'm not a mechanic," he said slowly.

"No. No, of course."

"Anyway, the make, model, and license plates match up, but if you want to come with me and identify it . . . Ms. Nathanson? Are you okay?"

Amy realized her eyes were closed. "I'm fine," she said, opening them.

"It's been a rough couple of days," he said. But there was something in his eyes now. A hardness. *I shouldn't have asked about
the car like that. Now he's suspicious. Anybody would be suspicious.* "Ms. Nathanson?"

"Yes?"

"We'll also need you to come by the station."

Her stomach dropped. "Why?"

"State police is handling the case. Detectives have a few questions for you."

"For me?"

"Just a few questions. No big deal."

Amy smoothed a lock of hair behind an ear. She gave him the
Aimee En pout, which was nowhere near as effective without red
lipstick, she knew. His eyes stayed focused on her. "Is that necessary?" she said.

"No big deal," he said again. "It'll only take a few minutes."

"You should be looking for that boy. The one who pushed me
to the ground and—"

"This will help the state police to find him." He gave her a
weak smile. "Officer Maze will be there. I know you like her."

"Babe?" shouted Vic from the bedroom, his voice tremulous.
"Are you still there? You're still here, right?"

"I'm here!" Amy called out. "Don't worry! Stay where you
are!" But she heard movement anyway, the light thud of his feet
on the wood floor, his shuffling footsteps. *No . . .*

Sergeant Black's eyes widened. Amy turned to Vic and saw
him not through her own eyes but through his. "This is Vic Iota,"
she said, calm as she could, gesturing at the frail ghost in the

hospital robe, wispy gray hair wild around his face, the jutting bones, the eyes full of terror, the start of tears. "My manager."

"ARE YOU OKAY?" Helen said through Jackie's Bluetooth as she drove away from Mother Goose's Book Nook. Helen had called about a GoFundMe page one of the moms had made for a football camp scholarship in Liam Miller's memory. "I thought you might be interested in contributing," she had said. But Jackie couldn't get herself to respond. She was still trying to work her mind around what Natalie Reed had said to her: *"What are you doing here? Why are you in New York?"*

"Bill's wife," Jackie said. "She thought the boys and I had moved back to California."

"What? Why?"

"Bill told her."

"He probably was trying to make me feel better." That's what Natalie had said. *"I was so scared."*

"Of what?"

"Of your son. The older one."

Jackie clutched the wheel, heart galloping. A tear trickled down her cheek. "She didn't even know Wade's name." Which was beside the point, she knew. But it's how the mind works. It grasps onto whatever simple complaint it can and holds on for dear life because that's so much easier than facing the real problem . . .

"Why were you scared of him?"

"Wow. I mean . . . He never told you? You don't even know?"

"Jackie." Helen said her name too slowly, too calmly, as though she were talking someone down from a ledge.

"What?"

"Why were you talking to Bill's wife?"

Jackie wondered if there had ever been a question she'd wanted to answer less. She pressed the accelerator. The car surged. "Can we talk about this later, Helen?" she said, without waiting for a response. "I really need to get home."

OPENING THE FRONT door, Jackie couldn't get her hands to stop shaking. Her bag hung against her side, phone burning inside it. As she pushed the door open and walked into the foyer, then the kitchen and toward the hallway that ended in Wade's room, it all played out in her mind for the first time in two years. Her car, missing from its space outside her office. The call to the police. The return call, hours later: "Ma'am. We've located your car in Red Hook . . ." And how her heart had dropped at the sound of the town's name. She hadn't even been able to focus on anything else the officer had said.

"Never mind," Jackie had said when she'd seen Wade standing in front of her in handcuffs. "It was a miscommunication. Of course I won't press charges. He's my son. Are you crazy?"

She'd been slapped with a six-hundred-dollar fine for Wade's underage driving. And then, one week later, the restraining order. "I only wanted to talk to him, Mom. I swear. You have to believe me." She'd believed Wade. Of course she had. Bill was a narcissist who saw no harm in abandoning an entire family, while Wade was a boy. A sensitive boy whose mother, who had given him false hope by teaching him how to drive at fifteen, had just told him she couldn't afford to buy him a car for his sixteenth birthday. A fifteen-and-a-half-year-old boy who was angry and blamed his wealthy father, as any boy would have. Any abandoned boy. It had been a rash act to steal his mother's car, a mistake to want to see his father, but he hadn't meant any harm. She'd believed that, all this time . . . She'd believed Wade.

He only wanted to talk.

"Hi, Mom." Connor's voice followed Jackie, an afterthought as she brushed past him, sitting at the kitchen table, absorbed in his recently returned phone.

Jackie stopped. Looked at him. *You never even knew about the stolen car. You never knew about the restraining order. You were just eleven years old and I saw no reason to tell you.*

"Mom?" Connor said. "Are you okay?"

The second time today someone had asked Jackie that. *No. No, I'm not,* she would have said if she wasn't a person who avoided the truth, hid from it. Turned her sons into liars and worse. "Is Wade in his room?"

"Yeah. I think so . . ."

Jackie couldn't look at Connor anymore. Poor Connor, whom she was bound to ruin too. She turned and left the kitchen, propelling herself down the hall to her son's room, pounding on the door so hard her knuckle hurt from it.

"What?" Wade snapped, and it only made her angrier, the tone of his voice.

She tried the door. It was locked. "Open this door *now.*"

Jackie heard movement, footsteps. Then the door opened, her son peering around it, a sheepish look on his face that made her heart drop. "Hi, Mom," he said. "Is . . . uh . . . is something wrong?"

"I know what you did."

Wade let go of the door. He seemed to shrink before her eyes, the slight tinge of color draining out of his face as he backed up, shaking his head. "What do you mean?"

"You heard me." As Jackie reached into her purse and felt for her phone, she half expected not to find it there, for the messy floor of Wade's room to melt away, Wade along with it, Jackie waking up in a drenching sweat, exposing this entire day for the bad dream it was.

No such luck. Jackie's phone was solid and real and when she called up her recent photos, it responded the way it was supposed to. She closed the bedroom door behind her, took a few steps closer to her son, and watched his face, an expression she'd never seen before—a dawning fear. Or was it guilt? "I spoke to Natalie today."

Wade opened his mouth; then he closed it again. "Wait. Who?"

"Stop playing games," Jackie said, not in her own voice but in the clipped tones of her own mother. "I spoke to Natalie. Your father's wife. She told me what you did."

He stared at her without speaking for several seconds, his face relaxing, color returning to his cheeks. "Why were you talking to *her*?" Same as Helen had said.

"I asked Natalie why she and Bill had seen fit to hurt you so much." Jackie said it firmly, but quietly. She didn't want Connor to overhear. "She took me to her house and she *showed* me, Wade."

"She showed you?"

"She's kept it in a locked drawer all this time. Ever since you broke into their house and taped it to their refrigerator."

"Oh . . ."

Jackie turned the phone around, the picture filling her screen so Wade could see it—the drawing that had made her stop breathing when Natalie had shown it to her. "Bill doesn't know I've kept it, but I have," Natalie had said. "Just in case something happens and I need evidence."

That awful, damning word. *Evidence*. Yet Jackie couldn't get angry at her. She couldn't stand up for her son or get indignant for the way this woman viewed him because she knew that, had she been in Natalie's position, she'd have wanted evidence too.

The photo was of a carefully drawn rendering of Bill, Natalie, and their three daughters, the youngest just a baby, all of them posed and smiling. All with *X*'s for eyes.

"You drew this," Jackie said.

"I copied it," he said. "There was a picture of them in the Red Hook paper. They were at some stupid event."

Jackie's voice started to rise. "I don't care whether you drew it or copied it or carved it out of marble. *Why did you do this?*"

"I was mad."

"Why did you lie to me about it?"

"Probably because I knew you'd be like *this*," he said. "Taking his side. Not standing up for me when I had every right to—"

"Break into your father's house and threaten his family?"

"To be angry. I had every right to be angry. Look, you didn't even know about that drawing. You thought I just wanted to talk to that asshole and you still treated me like I was crazy."

"I did not. I took you seriously and—"

"Oh, come on. What do you call forcing someone to go to an idiot guidance counselor for therapy sessions every day? What do you call listening in on my phone calls and hiding all the freakin' razors in the house and—"

"*Wade.*"

"It was two years ago and *he deserved it*. That whole family deserves it."

Jackie stared at him, at the gleam in his eyes, ugly and proud. She said, *"I am ashamed of you."*

Wade stared at her, the gleam dissolving. His face started to crumple.

She gripped the phone. *Take it back,* a voice inside her said. *Take it back. Tell him you aren't ashamed.*

"I . . . I need to take a walk," Wade said.

As he moved past her and out the bedroom door, Jackie turned and watched him, the way he shuffled down the hallway, drowning in those baggy black jeans, that black hoodie. *Like a child in his father's clothes,* Jackie thought, her heart sinking, breaking. Until she realized that those clothes were the same ones she'd seen in the dryer.

From the kitchen, Jackie heard Connor asking, "Where are you going?"

Wade replied, "Back soon." Which wasn't an answer at all.

STANDING ALONE IN Wade's dark, messy room, Jackie remembered all the promises she'd made while pregnant with him, how she'd vowed not to be the way her own parents had been, dismissive and judgmental and cold. She remembered what Bill had once said when Wade was a baby, still small enough for the bassinet: "At least once a day for the rest of his life, let's tell him he's the greatest."

Was she wrong to be disappointed in her child, when she and Bill had let him down so much themselves? That was the Merrick/ Reed style of parenting, she supposed. Make a series of promises and then successively break every one of them until your kid has no choice but to rely on himself.

Jackie sighed. The room was such a disaster. Dirty clothes everywhere, empty potato chip bags, discarded drawings and things like safety cones and street signs that had no business indoors. Six months ago, Jackie had stopped taking care of the boys' rooms beyond giving them clean sheets, clothes, and linens. And in Wade's case, it showed.

Jackie plucked a shirt off the floor—a yellow dress shirt she didn't remember buying him and couldn't imagine him wearing. Carefully, she buttoned and folded the shirt. Placing it on his unmade bed, she smoothed the front. She felt something in the pocket—a small box—and slipped it out. It was from Kay Jewelers in the Hudson Valley Mall.

She struggled with whether or not to open the box, but only briefly. *Ask Wade a question, he lies. Confront him with the truth, he runs out of the house.* Could have just been an excuse, but that didn't matter. She lifted the lid.

Inside the box was a necklace. It looked expensive. *This explains the Summer of Odd Jobs.* Jackie held it up to the light—a silver chain, a pendant dotted with tiny diamonds, in the shape of the letter *T.*

"Oh . . ." Jackie replaced the necklace very carefully and slipped the box back into the shirt pocket, hating herself for looking, for learning something she couldn't ask about at all.

She left the room quickly. On her way out, she almost stepped on Wade's phone, which lay on the floor plugged into its charger, left behind by its brokenhearted owner in his haste.

AMY SAT IN the back of the cruiser with Officer Maze driving again—curly-haired Officer Maze with the dove-gray eyes, the long eyelashes, and the sharp, no-nonsense jawline. *Tough number,* Amy had thought when she'd first seen Officer Maze at the station, the type who made up for a slight build and a sweet face by carrying herself like someone not to be messed with. Someone a lot like Amy herself used to be when she was young and on her own in Hollywood and wore brass knuckles as an accessory, vials of fake blood dangling from her ears.

"You all right?" said Officer Maze, whose first name, Amy recalled now, was surprisingly delicate and old-fashioned. Pearl.

"I'm as all right as I can be." Amy said it to the gray eyes in the rearview, which were looking at her strangely . . . Or was she being paranoid? "Why do you ask?"

Pearl tilted the mirror briefly, so Amy could catch a glimpse of her own puffy, swollen eyes. Yes, she'd cried at the sight of Baby, but she thought she'd wiped away the evidence.

"It's just been a traumatic day." Amy wished she hadn't seen her face, so tired and crepey in the afternoon light. Old. She needed lipstick, but she hadn't even thought to bring her makeup bag, distracted as she'd been, as she still was, over Vic. Jacinta had assured her she was on her way, but still Amy hated leaving him alone . . . "A traumatic *couple* of days."

"You know," Pearl said, "if there's anything you want to amend on the police report, you can do that with the state detectives."

Amy stared into the mirror. "Why would I want to amend anything?"

"You may have been too tired," she said, "or too traumatized to tell the complete truth."

Amy opened her mouth. Closed it again, her stomach starting to turn.

"I'm just saying that this happens with a lot of victims of violent crime. The first time they talk about it, they don't always get the specifics right."

Amy's shoulders relaxed. *It's just a spiel. Same spiel she gives all witnesses probably. It's not directed at you.* "Okay," she said. "I'll take that under consideration."

They drove in silence away from Baby's resting place—that dank, sulfurous swamp the sergeant had called the Kill. She stared out the window, longing for her phone, her car, the antique compact she kept in her purse, everything she'd taken for granted but never would again. *A clean conscience.* How she wished she could climb into bed with Vic, pop a few of his pills, and watch old music videos and forget what year it was.

The streets here in Havenkill had been made festive for the season, with jack-o'-lanterns and paper skeletons arranged on charming front porches, pots of orange and yellow mums in window boxes, everything well kept and freshly painted and full of cheesy, pumpkin-spice charm.

How she hated this side of the river. *If I hadn't played that gig,* she thought. *If I had just stayed home . . .* "Can you tell me what's going on with the investigation?" she asked. "Have they gotten any leads on the carjacker?"

"I'm not sure," Pearl said. "The detectives would know better."

"How can I help?"

"Ma'am, all I can suggest is that you tell the complete truth."

Again? "Of course I'll tell the truth."

"That's the best advice I can give you," she said. "Don't embellish. Tell the detectives what you remember."

"I wasn't planning on embellishing. Why would you think I—"

"Good. Then everything should be fine, ma'am."

"Should be?"

The car slowed, even though there was no traffic light and they weren't even close to the station. Through her window, Amy saw a police car parked along a side street, yellow crime-scene tape remnants dripping from two trees like tears. *That's where it happened.* The name of the street was Shale. Amy had learned that later, at the police station. But just after Baby had run over that poor boy, she'd seen that street sign in the flash of headlights and misread it as Shame. *Shame Street,* she had thought. *Street of Shame.* And then it had started raining.

Amy watched the group of lookie-loos milling about the crime scene, a few of them using their phones to take pictures, and thought back to the scene at the Kill—all those police officers, probably press too. She'd heard cameras . . . God, why had she cried? *Crying over a car. What must that have looked like?*

At the base of one of the trees was a patch of brightness. Amy looked closer and saw that it was bouquets of flowers, probably a dozen of them, piled on top of each other. *This is where it happened. This will always be where it happened.*

For a second, Amy thought she saw blood on the macadam and her eyes snapped shut, though she knew rationally it had only been a shadow. *Street of Shame.* "Can you drive faster, please?"

The car sped up slightly. When she opened her eyes, Amy saw Pearl watching her through the rearview, peering at her, as though to gauge her response.

"I didn't embellish," Amy said quietly. "I didn't lie."

Nine

Killer car, read the caption on the picture Jordan Snapchatted to Connor. But it was the picture itself Connor couldn't stop staring at—the car that had killed Liam Miller, yanked out of the Kill by its banged-up rear frame, trailing dead cattails with cops clustered around it, taking pictures and collecting samples from this crazy vintage Jaguar as though it were a dead body.

Or a murderer. Which, in a way, it was.

Jordan and this new kid Chris Stapleton from Connor's math class both claimed that some rich old lady from Woodstock had gotten carjacked by a gang member from Poughkeepsie and, when Liam had tried to save her car, the gang member had run him over without even slowing down.

Connor took a picture of himself looking shocked. Captioned it, *Holy shit! Any gang stuff on the car?* Snapchatted it to Jordan, who was there, "at the scene of the crime," as he'd called the Kill, looking for "evidence." Jordan had said he knew "for a fact" that the killer was a drug kingpin from the Crips. But then Connor's friend Malcolm from Little League—whom he'd been texting with at the same time—said that Jordan was full of bull. Malcolm's mom had told him there were no Crips anymore, that the Crips were from the 1990s, and even back then the Crips were from L.A., not Poughkeepsie.

But what did Malcolm and his mom know? They weren't with the police.

Another snap came in from Jordan: a woman in a heavy overcoat standing next to a female cop, their backs to the lens. Jordan had taken it from a weird angle too, off to the side, partly behind a tree . . . The car wasn't in the frame. Connor looked at the photo for a while, trying to figure out what it meant. He cringed. The cop was the same one he'd seen on his way to Lukoil. The one Noah had acted like a dick in front of at assembly. Had to be. He recognized her hair, which was long and curly and pulled back in a ponytail.

He took a snap of himself frowning, then typed in: *Why did you send me that pic?* He sent it and waited.

Connor heard the front door opening, his mom's light footsteps. But he was too absorbed in his phone to turn around. He needed a response from Jordan—something he'd missed in the cop picture, a piece of evidence, something gang-related.

There had to be something. Maybe there weren't Crips around here, but there *were* gangs. Connor knew that much. Just this past summer, there'd been a robbery at the CVS: one of the windows smashed, a cash register emptied, a whole bunch of pills swiped from the pharmacy. The robbers were never captured, but everybody knew it was gang members, come into Havenkill from somewhere else, somewhere dangerous— Albany, Poughkeepsie, a real city. Connor had even heard that there had been gang signs scrawled in bloodred paint on the pharmacy wall.

And so it had to be a gang member who had killed Liam. Because if it wasn't a gang member . . .

He didn't want to complete that thought. It was dumb and paranoid, plus it was all Noah's fault.

Mom brushed past Connor on her way to the hallway. A rush of cold air flew off her, coat waving, boots pounding the floor. It was out of the ordinary and kind of terrifying, the speed of her step, like a runaway train. To slow her down, Connor said hi.

She stopped, turned. Looked at Connor in the weirdest way, as though she was trying to figure out who he was.

"Mom?" he said slowly. "Are you okay?" His phone vibrated—probably a new snap from Jordan, but he ignored it.

Mom said, "Is Wade in his room?"

"Yeah," Connor said. "I think so . . ."

Mom whirled around and headed down the hall and, seconds later, he heard her pounding on Wade's door, so loud it made him want to cover his ears. *What is going on?*

For several seconds he sat frozen, breath held, listening. Wanting and not wanting to hear.

"Open this door *now*," Mom said.

Connor could hear Wade's door opening, Wade's questioning voice, then Mom's, like a baseball bat wrapped in barbed wire. "I know what you did."

Connor held his breath. He heard some muffled words, Wade's door closing. Then silence.

Two years ago, Wade went crazy and stole Mom's car. No one knew that Connor was aware of this, but he was. He'd been in his room and their mom had been out and he'd overheard Wade Skyping with one of his last remaining friends—this kid named Rafe Burgess who at the time was new and would talk to anybody.

A lot of the Skype chat had sounded like bullshit to Connor:

Wade claiming he was going to steal the extra key to Mom's car, drive up to Albany, and buy a gun so he could shoot out the windows of their dad's house. "And too bad if anybody's inside when it happens."

Rafe had replied, "Oh, come on," and Connor had been with him on that thought. Sometimes Wade could be the most dramatic person ever.

But then a couple of days later, Mom's car had gotten stolen . . .

He took out his phone, looked at the new snap from Jordan. Two cops walking, with a weird-looking lady between them. She had on a shiny red coat and her hair was dyed rainbow—a strange contrast to a worn-out, pale face. She reminded Connor of an off-duty clown.

She's the one, the caption read. *She owed the gangsta drug money. He took her car as payback.*

The picture disappeared in seconds, as all Snapchats do. Connor wished he'd screenshotted it so he could have looked at it longer. The woman could have been a druggie. A meth head. She sure looked like one. Connor took another selfie, captioned it, *How do you know? Did the cops say so?* Then he crossed his fingers—literally crossed his fingers and said a little prayer that Jordan would say yes.

From down the hall, he heard his mother's voice, angry and pained. *"Why did you do this?"*

Connor's stomach clenched up. What were they talking about?

Connor's phone vibrated twice: a text. He expected Malcolm again, but when he looked at it, he saw that it was from Jordan.

My sister just texted me. She says the football team is gonna kill whoever did it. Come after him and kill him. They think they can get away with it.

Connor texted back: *Even if it's a whole gang?*

There was a long pause, then another text from Jordan: *The woman with the crazy hair is named Amy. She's from Wood-stock.*

Connor snorted. *Figures.*

Down the hall, Wade was practically shouting. " . . . guidance counselor for therapy sessions every day . . . listening in on my phone calls and hiding all the freakin' razors in the house and—"

"Wade."

Another text came in from Jordan: *So Amy told the cops it was a lone wolf. A weird kid in a hoodie.*

Connor's stomach dropped. He had to type his reply three times, because his fingers were so jittery he kept missing keys, his stupid phone autocorrecting it to nonsense.

Wade's door creaked open. Connor heard his brother say he needed to take a walk. He breathed in deeply, then typed: *But Amy could be lying, right??? She's some druggie from Wood-stock, in deep with some gang. Nobody believes her, right?*

Wade swept into the room, angry-fast like Mom and all in black, a black hoodie . . .

"Where are you going?" Connor asked.

"Back soon."

Wade went out the front door. Connor got up and followed him, slipping out and into the freezing air before Mom could see him, closing the door carefully. "Wait!"

Wade spun around, his face pink and sad, a purple-gray sky behind him. Just 4:00 PM and already the day was caving in. Con-nor hated fall.

"What do you want?" Wade said.

"Tell me what's going on."

"I'm just getting some air."

"Why was Mom so mad at you?"

"I don't know."

"You *know,* Wade. Come on. I heard you guys screaming at each other."

"It was just something stupid I did a couple of years ago, okay? I don't know why she's freaking out all of a sudden but it's nothing for you to worry about."

"I *am* worried."

"Well don't be." He smiled. "Okay, buddy?"

Connor didn't answer right away, and for a while the two of them stood there on the path in front of their house, Wade all in black, that purplish sky haloing his black hair. *A shadow,* Connor thought. *He looks like a shadow.* "Wade."

"Yeah?"

"Did you . . . Did you hear about Liam? About who ran him over?"

Wade shook his head slowly. He took a step back, and Connor remembered the way he'd looked at him back in his room, when he'd asked him to pretend two nights ago never happened. "I didn't hear anything," he said, black eyes aimed at him. "Did you?"

Connor held his gaze as long as he could. "Some people are saying it was gangsters from Poughkeepsie."

"Could have been." Wade put his back to Connor and headed down the path. "You should get back inside," he said as he made for the green Corolla Mom had given him, taking the key out of his pocket and opening the driver's-side door. "It's cold out here."

WADE WAS RIGHT. It was cold. Connor went back in the house. His mom was in the kitchen, talking on her phone. "I don't know," he heard her say. "I just don't know." Which was the theme of everything these days, wasn't it? Nobody knew anything in this house, in this town. Connor grabbed his phone off the kitchen table and pulled his jacket out of the closet. "I have to pick something up at a friend's house. I'll be back soon!" he called out, without waiting for an answer. Once he was back in the cold afternoon, he unlocked his bike and jumped on it, taking off in search of his unknowable brother.

PEARL TOOK AMY into the booking room, where the two state detectives were waiting for them. They exchanged niceties: chatter about the cold weather, Halloween plans, Amy's music career. The man did most of the talking. All of it, actually. "You know, I used to love Dead Enz," he said, name-checking Amy's old backup band the way a true fan would. He looked directly at her as he said it and gave her a dreamy smile, eyes half closed and a little misty, as though he was seeing and remembering her at the same time. She often got this from men of a certain age, the ones old enough to remember her onstage with Dead Enz, wearing nothing but a kilt and electrical tape. You make a strong enough impression your first time out of the gate, with some people it truly can last a lifetime.

"I'm Detective Wacksman, by the way," he said, still with the smile. "Feel free to call me Alex."

"I'm Detective Wind," said the female detective, who was a good two decades younger, probably in diapers at the time Dead Enz split up. No first name for her, apparently.

Amy stuck a hand out. "Nice to meet you," she said. But Detective Wind just nodded at her and Amy had nowhere to put her hand. The room smelled of cleaning fluid, and Detective Wind's mouth refused to lift at the corners and Amy felt like a suspect, queasy and tense.

The booking room. Same place she'd first talked to Pearl and the other officers, with that drunk preppy cuffed to the bench, vomit stains on his oxford cloth shirt, head lolling, asking when "in the gaping depths of hell" his wife was going to get there, over and over again until the poor woman finally arrived. Back then, Amy had thought, *At least I'm not her.* Of course, Liam Miller had still been alive back then, and she'd assumed he'd stay that way. What a difference two days can make if the circumstances are awful enough.

Wacksman said, "Let's go into the interview room, shall we?"

"Interview room?"

"It's where we're conducting all the interviews related to the case while we're here," Wind said, so cold and official, Amy felt as though she were at a press conference. She looked at Pearl, who simply shrugged. She wasn't sure whether the intent of the shrug was to make her feel better or worse, or if there was any intent behind it at all.

"It's just a conference room, ma'am," Pearl said. "There isn't anything to be afraid of."

IT REALLY WAS just a conference room, with a window facing the street, a tree full of golden leaves taking up most of the view, the sky behind it pinkish with the first breath of sunset. Wacksman and Wind sat next to each other at one end of the large table with Amy directly across from them and Pearl standing in the doorway. She would've liked to have had Pearl sitting next to her, the way a lawyer might have been if this were an actual interrogation. Cold as the young officer had been acting lately, Amy still knew and liked her better than either of these detectives: Wind with her sedate clothes and her hard stare and her lack of a first name, Wacksman with his thick mustache that lifted obscenely when he smiled, like a skirt.

This room smelled of the same cleaning fluid as the booking room. It made Amy wonder if they'd scrubbed the whole place down just before she'd come here, so they could lift her fingerprints off the furniture. She breathed in the piney chemical scent, feeling terribly alone. She tried smiling at Wind again, again unsuccessfully.

Wacksman slid a microcassette recorder onto the table. "We're going to be tape-recording you. Is that all right?"

Amy stared at the tiny machine. "Yes," she said. "I guess." He clicked it on and Amy thought of the demo tapes she used to make, the spools turning. "I thought you just tape-record when you're talking to suspects."

Wind smiled for the first time since Amy had met her, but the smile didn't reach her eyes. "No, no," she said. "We do this with important witnesses as well."

Alex Wacksman said, "Can you please state and spell your name?"

She did, and when he asked her to state the date, she did that as well.

"So getting things started, can you tell us what you were doing in Havenkill two nights ago?"

"I was playing a gig."

"Where?" Wind said.

"Club Halifax. In Hudson."

"Right," Wacksman said. "So . . . from the looks of the report, you played a long gig there, after which you left for home. And when you were passing through Havenkill, the carjacker approached."

Amy looked at him. "Yes."

Wind glanced over at Pearl in a way that felt meaningful. Amy turned to look at her. The girl's eyes were fixed not on the detective, but on her. She recalled the way Pearl had acted in the car—the suspicion in her tone, the chill in her eyes through the rearview. *What do you know? What did you tell the detectives?*

"Okay, so can you give us the timing, please?" Wacksman said. "What time did your show end?"

"Around one thirty in the morning." She could feel Pearl's eyes boring into her.

Wind said, "Did you have anything to drink at Club Halifax, before or after your show?"

"No."

"You're positive?"

Amy didn't like this line of questioning. "I was working," she said. "I was singing."

"Were there a lot of people there?"

"Yes."

"Many adoring fans. Autograph seekers."

"Yes." She breathed.

"And you left at one thirty AM. You were heading directly home."

"Yes."

Wind stared at her, saying nothing. Amy stared back. Wacksman coughed. Then Pearl. This may have gone on for around ten or fifteen seconds, or it could have been an hour—Amy wasn't sure. All she knew was the thickness of the silence, the way it roared in her ears. She felt as if she were teetering on the edge of a very sharp cliff.

"Ms. Nathanson," Wacksman said. "We really need you to tell us the truth."

And then she fell. "What, what . . ." she started to stammer. "What makes you think that, that . . ."

"Officer Maze?" Wind said. "Can you please let Ms. Nathanson know what you told us?"

Amy turned to Pearl.

"I warned you in the car," Pearl said quietly. "I told you not to embellish."

"What?"

"You were the opening act."

Amy's mouth felt dry. This wasn't supposed to be happening. She was a witness. *A victim.* "Why are you treating me like this?"

Pearl kept her gaze fixed on Detective Wind. "Doors opened at six PM. The main act was a Psychedelic Furs cover band and they went on at eight."

Amy closed her eyes. "Fine," she said. "Fine. I was the opening act."

"No encores?"

"Does it matter?"

"Yes."

Tears sprung into her eyes. "Why? Why do you need to know? Why are you even bringing it up, other than to humiliate me?"

Wind said, "We're bringing it up, Ms. Nathanson, because of the timeline. We now don't know where you were between eight PM and the time of the accident. We don't know whether you were drinking for hours before you got behind the wheel."

Amy looked at the detective, the ice in her eyes, the sharpness of her jaw that seemed to mirror Pearl's, the two of them brass bookends on either side of her, Wacksman smiling beneath his mustache. She hated it here. "I wasn't drinking."

"Most important, it matters because it means you lied to us," Wind said. "If you lied to us about this show, how do we know whether you were telling us the truth about the boy in the hoodie? Or about Liam Miller rushing to save you?" Her gaze drifted to Pearl, then back to Amy's face. "How do we know you are being truthful about anything that happened that night, other than the one thing you can't lie about: that your car killed a seventeen-year-old boy?"

Amy's mouth felt dry, the cleaning fluid smell pressing in on her. She considered asking to call a lawyer, but then she remembered Liam's parents—the hope they said she'd given them in her private message—and stepped away from that thought. "I'm not a killer," she said. "And I'm not a liar."

"Prove it."

Under the table, her hands clenched into fists. Her fingernails dug into her palms. "I didn't do any encores," she said, that awful night replaying in her head. Such a crap bar it had been, and so loud, the mic fuzzy and people talking over her as she sang. No band. The manager of the place had called just two weeks ago, giving Amy no time to put one together. *Beggars can't be choosers,* she'd thought. *Every comeback has to start somewhere.* And so she'd put on her vintage vinyl minidress and her hot pink go-go boots. She'd colored her hair and slathered on her trademark red lipstick and driven to this club, which smelled of mold and stale smoke and had walls the color of old teeth, no doubt from years of cigarette pollution.

She'd sung with some lousy piano player who doubled as a bartender—some kid who wouldn't have known her from a crack in the tooth-colored wall and who played like both his hands had fallen asleep. "I sounded great." She said it not to Wind and Wacksman, but to Pearl. "That's not an embellishment." She *had* sounded great—the clarity of her head voice, the soul of her belt. She'd been practicing for months, and if anybody in that club had bothered to listen they would have known that.

Wind said, "So did you leave after your set?"

Amy exhaled. "Yes."

"Where were you and what were you doing between when you left Club Halifax and when Liam Miller got hit?"

That was it. The billion-dollar question. She put her hands on the table, her heart-shaped ring glistening. "How does that matter to the investigation?"

Wind said, "Do you really want me to explain to you how it matters?"

If only she hadn't played that gig. If only she hadn't gone out afterward, if she hadn't done what she'd done. If only she had driven home right after the gig, if she hadn't stopped the car until she was back over the bridge where people were decent and kind and didn't get you into situations you had no right to be in. *If only, if only. If only . . .*

Wacksman said, "Ms. Nathanson?"

"I know."

"So, where were you?"

"I played a private show," she said, the words easing out of her. "A house concert."

"Whose house?"

Amy took a breath. Why were they making her relive this? "I played a house concert. I was driving home after it was through and this . . . this monster grabbed my purse and—"

"Let's not get ahead of ourselves," said Detective Wind.

"Why do you care?"

Wind gave her a look.

Amy spun around in her chair and glared at Pearl. "You could have warned me," she said. "You could have told me you knew I hadn't headlined instead of . . . of letting them spring it on me like this."

Pearl's face was calm, unreadable. "Would you like me to leave the room, ma'am?"

"You hate me."

Wacksman said, "Let's walk back a little," and Amy found herself doing that, walking back and living it again—the gig at Club Halifax and what had come after. *It really happened, whether you think about it or not.*

"You played two shows that night?" Wacksman said. "An early show and then a private party."

She looked him in the eye. "The second show," she said, "was for a much smaller audience."

Their house had been lovely. A Tudor with such a large dining room, that stunning chandelier . . .

Wind said, "What songs did you play?"

Amy felt her face flushing. "I don't remember."

"Did you have anything to drink?"

"Excuse me?"

"At the second show," Wacksman chimed in. "Did you drink any alcohol while you were there?" That obscene smile again. "It was a concert at a private home. I'm sure cocktails were served."

"I might have had a little wine."

"Before or after?"

Her face flushed deeper. "What?"

"Did you drink wine before or after the show?"

"Oh. I don't know."

It was Wind's turn now. "How soon did you hit the road," she said, "after you might have had a little wine?"

"Look," Amy said, grateful to change the subject. "I wasn't driving drunk, if that's what you're insinuating."

"Okay," Wind said. "Where exactly was this house party?"

"What difference does that make?"

"The incident occurred close to the corner of Orchard and

Shale. We'd like to determine how long you were on the road before it happened."

Amy chewed on her lip. *They're never going to stop until you tell them the truth.* "It was in Havenkill. I don't remember the address, but I was probably driving for about five minutes when it happened."

Wind said, "That seems odd."

"What does?"

"That you wouldn't know the address of a scheduled gig. I mean . . . not even the street name? Musicians usually keep records of where they're playing." She turned to Wacksman. "Doesn't that strike you as kind of odd?"

"Yes," he said. "Yes, it does strike me as very odd."

Amy gripped the cold metal arms of the office chair she was sitting in. How she hated both of them, these smug, holier-than-thou cops, no different from the ones who used to hassle her outside Hollywood clubs when she was young, demanding her ID, picking through her purse in search of drugs. Only these detectives were picking through her life, weren't they? The ugliest parts of it. "What you're asking about has nothing to do with the creep who took my car."

"I'm sorry, Ms. Nathanson," Wind said. "But it very well might."

Wacksman nodded. "We have to turn over every rock, you know."

Amy looked at Pearl. Her expression was softer now, almost apologetic. "If you just answer their questions, ma'am, they can move along."

Amy asked if she could have a glass of water—a stall tactic. And when Pearl went to get it for her, Amy wondered how she could explain it to them, what had happened after she'd finished her set at Club Halifax. The couple approaching her as she col-

lected her sheet music, shaking out the few sad dollars from the
tip glass on the piano.

Well, actually, the man had been the one to approach her. The
wife just hovered. "I'm a big fan," he had told Amy. And the state
she'd been in, after that set she'd just played . . . It had sounded
so good to her. He'd looked good to her too—the neatly shaved
head, the diamond earring, the cologne that smelled like money,
success. And that word. *Fan* . . . The wife was a lot younger than
he was—plump and nondescript except for her hair, which was
dark and lush and shiny. The entire time they spent together, the
wife had barely said a word.

Pearl returned with a plastic cup filled with water and Amy
downed the whole thing in three long gulps.

"Ms. Nathanson," Wind said, "how many people were at this
house party?"

Amy leveled her eyes at her. "Three," she said, her cheeks
burning. "A husband and wife. And myself."

Wind held her gaze. "How long did you perform?"

"Four hours," she said. "And then they paid me in cash."

A silence fell over the room. Amy glared at the tape recorder
as it immortalized this moment, hating the detectives with every
cell in her body for making her relive that night, the weakness
inside her that had made her go home with that couple, to break
Vic's heart that way. He could never know.

She'd followed the couple's car in Baby. She hadn't paid attention to street signs and addresses, focused as she'd been on
making excuses, telling herself again and again that it was just
another gig, that she was doing it for the money, that she needed
to pay for Vic's health care, and so this was a selfless act, really.
*Imagine that. Trying to soothe your own guilt by saying, "It's
only prostitution."*

But it hadn't been the money that had made her go with them, good as the money was. It had been the word—that one word the man had said to her, with the crowd chanting for the headlining act and her mouth tasting of the expensive whiskey he'd bought her, that Amy had yearned for more than cash. That word . . . *fan*.

She could feel Pearl watching her, and when she turned, Amy saw a strange, soft expression on the girl's face. Understanding or, more likely, pity. Wacksman was looking down at the desk, twisting his wedding ring. But Wind was still with her, her gaze cool and direct.

"Can we please keep this between us?" Amy said.

No one answered right away.

CONNOR TOOK ORCHARD through town as fast as he could, weaving through traffic on his bike, legs pumping, cold air cutting into his lungs. It was easy to pick up speed in fall weather, which made you want to do everything faster anyway, just to keep warm. It didn't take him long to spot Wade's car pulling up to the light on Orchard and Flower, slowing at the yellow and stopping just as it switched to red. For all his weirdness and unpredictability, Wade had always been a surprisingly cautious driver. He'd promised Mom that if she taught him to drive early, he'd never get a ticket, and on that, he'd kept his word.

Connor hung back, keeping several cars between them so as not to be noticed. The sun was setting now. Lights glowed the way they always did at the very start of twilight—streetlights, taillights, traffic lights, as though they'd been shot full of magic for that one hour. Connor balanced on his bike and kept his eyes on Wade's car, the metallic-green paint job glowing too in the pinkish light, like the edge of an oil slick.

When the light changed, Wade pulled into the left lane. He

put his blinker on and slowed down, ready to turn onto the next
street, Jackson Road. Jackson Road was the wealthiest street in
town by far. When Connor was little, Noah's mom, Cindy, used to
take the two of them trick-or-treating on Jackson, and even then,
as a five-year-old, it was easy to tell she just wanted an excuse to
gawk at the houses.

Connor waited for Wade to turn before he made the moves to
do so himself, hanging back long enough so his brother wouldn't
catch him in his rearview.

Once he was finally able to turn on Jackson Road, Connor
didn't spot Wade's car right away. He was afraid he might have
lost him, which was strange, considering the way Wade drove.
Connor stopped pedaling and let himself coast down this quiet
street, admiring the enormous houses—*piles*, his mother called
them—some of them three or even four stories, with chande-
liers sparkling in the windows, front porches and balconies big
enough to hold a set of furniture, tennis courts and fenced-in
pools peeking out from around the backs. And as showy as the
houses were, what impressed Connor even more were the cars in
the driveways—Escalades, BMWs. In front of one house, he even
spotted a Mercedes SLR, the same kind of car Kanye drove, and
he nearly fell off his bike. Mom always told Wade and him not to
be materialistic. "Don't place importance on things you can lose,"
she would say. But that was kind of silly, wasn't it? There wasn't a
thing in the world you couldn't lose.

Connor coasted for another block before he caught sight of
Wade's car again, a few blocks ahead, crawling as though he was
lost.

What are you doing, Wade?

He coasted some more, until he was just about twenty feet
away and watched Wade's Corolla as it pulled in next to the curb

between a Jeep and a Fiat, two of many cars that were parked along that side of the street. *Is he going to a party on Jackson Road? Who would he even know here?*

Connor got off his bike and wheeled it closer. The cars were parked in front of a big brick house with white columns out in front—an actual mansion. The lawn was soft and rippling like a carpet and as green as a lawn could get at this time of year. Potted, sculpted plants lined the path that led up to the front door, each one of them so perfect-looking that it seemed as though they'd just been bought today.

Wade's Corolla was parked now, but he'd yet to get out of it. Connor felt sad looking at the Corolla with its cheesy paint job and the dent in the back. It had never embarrassed him when his mom used to drive it, but it seemed to have deteriorated during Wade's three months of ownership, the dent more noticeable, the color degrading, so out of place on this billion-dollar street. It made Connor wonder who lived here, why they'd invited Wade to this party, if they'd invited him at all.

Connor thought about the picture he'd seen back in Wade's room, the naked girl's leg and breast so real on the paper. Maybe she was the one who had invited him. Maybe she was right there, in that house . . . Connor's face flushed thinking about it. A girl he'd seen naked, at least partly.

He got on his bike and rode across the street and several doors up, where he could get a better view without Wade noticing him. He leaned the bike against a big oak tree—one of many that lined the sidewalk—and slipped behind it, peering around the side. His brother was still in the car. From where he was standing, Connor could see through the Corolla's windows. Wade was stock-still in the front seat, his head turned toward the house. Watching.

What is going on?

The house had a big front porch, and there was a fairly large group of people on it, strange for such a cold day. Everybody wore jeans and sweaters and puffy coats—dressed more for the weather than for a party. The front door was open. From where Connor was standing, he would have heard music if there was any, but all he could hear was the soft hum of voices. A crowded house, but a quiet one.

A sad one.

He couldn't see everybody on the porch, but he could make out a few familiar faces—a hot senior named Stacy Davies and her mom, who was an old friend of Connor's mother and worked at the same real estate place. Mrs. Davies was holding some kind of casserole dish and talking to her husband. Stacy was with another girl who, when Connor looked closer, he recognized as Jordan's sister, Tamara. Liam's girlfriend. Stacy had a hand on Tamara's shoulder, and she seemed to collapse under the weight of it. Still another girl came up to them—a shorter one with red hair—and the three of them hugged so tightly and for so long, it was as though they were holding each other up, each one unable to stand on her own.

Connor felt a tightness in his chest. He knew whose house it was, even before he saw Liam Miller's old beater parked in the driveway.

What are you doing here, Wade? Come on. Drive away. These aren't your friends. Don't embarrass yourself.

Wade started up the car again. He revved the engine loudly, intrusively. Stacy Davies broke away from her friends. She put her hand on her hip and turned toward Wade's car along with Tamara and the red-haired girl, Tamara weeping, the red-haired girl's arm around her shoulders, the two of them leaning against each other like accident victims stumbling away from a crash.

Wade revved the engine again. *Stop it.* Connor cringed. He was watching Stacy, that emotion on her face, the way it wrecked her pretty features.

Stacy headed down the porch steps, then jogged the long slope of lawn, bypassing the path. Before she could reach the car, though, Wade had pulled away from the curb, heading up the street, much faster than usual.

Connor watched Stacy, holding his breath—the way she stood so still at the edge of the lawn, staring after Wade's car in a way that almost made him fear for his brother. *What did you do, Wade?* he kept thinking as he hopped on his bike and pedaled away. *What could you have done to make anybody hate you that much?*

Ten

From Tamara Hayes's Instagram. Selected captions that appeared beside a photo of Liam Miller and Tamara, posted on the afternoon of October 21.

Tamara_Hayes Liam's parents asked me to thank everyone for your kind wishes and to let you know that they will soon be posting details about the funeral. In the meantime, some of you have asked are they seeing visitors. The answer is yes. Liam's friends are welcome to stop by their house later this afternoon. They are taking care of some things now, but will be back by 4. #RIPLiam #love #payingrespects

Ginneeee Love you Tam ☹ </3

PrincessBelle So, so sorry, cuz. He is in heaven now. Xxxooo

StacyDee You guys were beautiful together. I'm so sad.

Tamara_Hayes @StacyDee You coming?

StacyDee @Tamara_Hayes Yes. With my mom and dad.

Tamara_Hayes @StacyDee Good.

Wade.Reed Can anybody come?

StacyDee lol just like the hospital.

Tamara_Hayes Friendly reminder that this is only for people who knew and loved Liam. His parents are very fragile right now, so we want to keep this small.

RG1999 Stay strong, Tam.

Wade.Reed She's not strong. None of you has ever been strong. You spoiled brats. You wear grief like it's the latest fashion. You don't care deeply enough about anything or anyone to really feel the pain of loss. You're liars. Can't wait for the next of you to die.

The last five comments were later deleted.

Eleven

Amy asked if she could take a break. The two state detectives quickly agreed to it, and Pearl left the conference room immediately, bursting out the door as though she'd been held underwater for the past twenty minutes and was finally allowed to come up for air.

Pearl headed into the break room and poured herself a cup of coffee, just to feel the heat of it. She was still cold from the Kill, but also the line of questioning had chilled her, the bizarre turn it had taken. *Four hours with some rich Havenkill couple. For pay.* She leaned over the countertop, clutching the hot mug in her hands, breathing in the steam with her eyes closed and trying not to think about Amy, what had been going through her mind that night. Such desperation . . . *Here I'd thought she'd just stopped at a bar, maybe had a few too many before getting on the road.*

"You okay?" It was one of the newer officers, a gym rat by the name of Mitch Romero whom Pearl didn't know all that well but wouldn't have minded smashing if he wasn't married and didn't work with her and there was no chance she'd ever see him again.

Pearl jumped. "You scared me."

"I'm not that scary, am I?"

She smiled. "Meh."

He gave her a wink—such a flirt. She didn't mind. Pearl took a sip from her mug, winced. The coffee in this station was so bad, she'd started to believe it was some kind of endurance test. "Soylent Green brew," she said.

"Huh?"

"Nothing."

Romero picked up his cup of coffee and moved closer to Pearl, keeping his voice low. "Hey."

"Yeah?"

"You were in there for the questioning?"

She nodded.

"You buy it? That purse-snatching story?"

Pearl could smell the coffee on his breath—no more pleasant there than in her cup, nice as his lips were—and so she took a step back. "That's hard to say." It was the truth. "I want to believe her." Which was the truth too. But.

"I don't know," he said. "The longer I work this job, the harder it is to believe anybody."

Pearl poured a cup of coffee for Amy and stirred some non-dairy creamer into it to cut the tarry taste. "I'm starting to think it might be us," she said. "They see a uniform, all they want to do is lie."

THE CONFERENCE ROOM door was open, Amy sitting at the big table, alone.

Pearl handed her the coffee. "Where did the detectives go?"

"Smoke break," Amy said, which was surprising. Pearl hadn't figured either of them for smokers—especially Kendall Wind.

Pearl sat down at the table, across from Amy, both of them sipping their horrible coffee, simply because it was easier to do that than to talk. "Do you still want me around?" Pearl said, finally. "I don't have to be here. It's really the state detectives who are handling the case."

"Can't stand to be in the same room with me, huh?"

"What? No. Of course not."

"Look," Amy said. "I know I shouldn't have lied about my . . . timeline for the evening. I was hoping I could just keep that secret from my manager and . . ."

"No need to explain."

"I'm telling the truth about the boy."

Pearl watched her face. She wished she was one of those cops who had the utmost confidence in their ability to read people. But she couldn't get herself to feel that way, having been read wrong so many times herself. There was no believing anyone, really. There was only *wanting* to believe them. "Hey," Pearl said. "I'm just a local cop. I'm not involved in the investigation. I'm nobody, far as your case is concerned."

Amy nodded. "That sounds evasive."

"It might be," Pearl said. "But it's also fact."

Amy took a swallow of her coffee and grimaced. "Good coffee."

Pearl gave her a look.

"See? I'm not good at lying." Amy smiled. Honest Amy, who, on the night of the hit-and-run, had claimed to be ten years younger than she actually was. Sergeant Black had found her real age this morning when looking up her driving records, which, by the way, had also included a DUI she'd never mentioned either, even when he'd asked her point-blank. Suffice it to say, the sergeant was no longer quite so much of an Aimee En fan.

"Nobody's perfect," Pearl said. "What gets us in trouble is when we try and pretend we are."

Amy glanced around the room and leaned in very close, her voice low and urgent. "I did a lot of horrible things that night."

"I don't judge."

"No. You don't understand."

"You want to explain?"

"Going home with that couple," she said. "I can't explain why I did that . . . I love Vic. I've never cheated on him before. I don't know what I was thinking. It was like I turned into a different person."

"We've all done things we regret."

"No," she said. "I'm trying to tell you something."

The look in her eyes, like the truth is in there, trying to burst out.

Amy took a breath. "After I left that couple's house, I felt so awful, I needed to numb that feeling. I needed to forget what I'd just done."

"You went for a drink," Pearl said, choosing each word carefully. "You liked the way it made you feel, the alcohol. This whiskey. You liked the way it made you forget. So you wound up drinking too much."

"No." She sighed. "I had a drink or two at their house. Early on. To loosen up. But I didn't get drunk, if that's what you're implying. I'm not really a drinker." Amy picked at a fingernail. "I was fine to drive."

"You can tell me the truth."

"*I am telling you the truth,*" Amy said, her voice rising, getting away from her in a way that felt almost theatrical, that burn in her eyes intensifying. It was powerful, but it was also familiar, and now Pearl realized where she'd seen it before: the "Kill Me with Your Love" video. At the station, waiting for the sergeant and Amy, she'd gone onto YouTube, just as Kendall Wind had suggested.

"Okay," Pearl said, her skepticism returning. "So if you didn't get drunk, how did you numb the feeling?"

She closed her eyes and breathed in deep through her nose like someone meditating. When she spoke again, her voice was calm and quiet. "I was driving. I was crying so hard I could barely see."

"Okay . . ."

"That boy. The one in the hoodie. He shows up out of nowhere."

"At three in the morning? On a residential street?"

"I didn't know what street I was on. I didn't know what time it was. All I know was what he said to me."

"Which was what?"

"He told me he had pills. Oxy. Benzos."

"He said that? How did you hear him?"

"He showed them to me first," she said. "They were in a big Baggie. All these pills, like he was a pharmacy."

Pearl's eyes widened. She leaned in closer, her mind running. "He showed you pills. So you opened the window."

"I already had the window opened a crack. I'm claustrophobic. But I had to open it wider. For the . . . the transaction." Amy played with a ring on her index finger—a big red stone, cut in the shape of a heart. "I'm not into drugs. I'm sober, actually. But sometimes, if I'm having a really bad day, I'll take a few of Vic's pills. Not enough for him to notice. But I wanted something more that night. I wanted . . . I wanted to just go off somewhere and take a whole bunch of them until I blacked out everything I'd done. And I had all this cash. They had paid me in cash."

"You opened your purse to pay him."

She nodded slowly. "That's when he grabbed it," she said. "He just reached through the open window. And then I decided to fight for it . . . for the money I made."

"Was it that important?"

"To me it was."

"Why?"

"Because without that money," she said, "I wouldn't even have an excuse for what I did."

Pearl handed her a Kleenex. A pointless gesture, considering the box was right between them and Amy could reach it just fine. But the look in Amy's eyes . . . It made her feel as though she had to do something.

There had been a break-in at Havenkill's CVS in early August—the only major crime of the summer. Never found out who did it; no IAFIS match for the fingerprints, so it wasn't a known criminal. But pills had been stolen. OxyContin. Xanax. *Could it be?*

"I tried to get my purse back." Amy dabbed at an eye. "That's how he got my car."

Pearl could hear footsteps coming up the hall, along with voices—Wind's voice, then Sergeant Black's. Amy started to shred the tissue, and Pearl watched her hands—the veined twisting fingers. She wanted to believe Amy. But how could she believe such a habitual liar—an actress, who was now giving Pearl the same anguished look that she'd given her leading man in the "Cut Me So Deep" video? "That's a pretty ring," Pearl said.

"Vic got it for me," Amy said. "He gave me two of them, actually—this one's a garnet. The other was a yellow citrine and it was my favorite, but I lost it that night too."

The detectives and sergeant came into the conference room. Pearl stood up and stepped out of the way as Wind and Wacksman took their seats at the table, but Amy's eyes were still on her. "I lost everything that night," Amy said—something any-one would believe. And then she turned her attention to the two detectives. She told them everything she'd told Pearl. Word for word, as though she were reading from a script.

"ARE YOU KIDDING me, Jackie?" said the voice on the other end of her phone. Bill's voice, she realized, but not right away. She hadn't spoken to her ex-husband in so long that it took a little while to add things up in her mind. "Are you kidding me? Going to Natalie's store?"

Jackie thought of Connor, around the house somewhere, lis-tening. She kept her voice calm. "I had questions for her and she answered them. I don't know how she portrayed it to you—"

"She didn't portray anything. She was shaken up. She brought up two years ago. She asked why I'd never told you the reason for the restraining order. It didn't take much figuring out on my part."

"Oh."

"What were you thinking, Jackie?"

Jackie exhaled. "I don't know." She could hear the front door opening behind her. "I just don't know."

Get him off the phone, Jackie thought. *Say what he wants to hear and get rid of him.* And then Connor came bursting in, throwing open the hall closet door, grabbing his phone off the kitchen table, a whir of energy and determination. She held up a hand but Connor didn't see her, immersed as he was in his own thoughts.

Jackie had never realized it before, how protective the self-absorption of children could be. *Not the slightest clue that his father is on the other end of this line.*

"I shouldn't need to tell you," Bill was saying, "but please don't do this again."

Jackie gritted her teeth. *The self-absorption of certain adults, on the other hand, serves no purpose whatsoever.* Connor rushed back out the door, muttering something about picking something up, being back soon . . .

"I don't know why you would do something so blatantly hostile, Jackie," Bill said. "To be honest, I'm shocked."

She said, "Your son is deeply unhappy."

"What?"

"I know you don't think of him that way. But that's what he is. Your son. And he's grown up knowing that his own father wants nothing to do with him."

"Jackie, I don't need to tell you—"

"No. You really don't. You send child support in the amount agreed on. You fulfill your end of the deal. Always have, always will. You don't have custody of Wade and Connor, and so their upbringing is not your responsibility. That *is* what you were going to tell me, right?"

Silence.

"Okay, then. Point well taken," she said. "Welcome to the results."

"Look," Bill said, his voice softer now, "I tried to have a relationship with Wade. I bought Yankees tickets and took him there and he didn't say a word, the entire time. At the end of the day, he said, 'I hate you.' He said he never wanted to see me again."

Jackie's jaw tightened. Her cheeks felt hot. "You're telling me you honored his wishes?"

"He didn't want me around."

"He was *seven years old*, Bill," she said. "What the hell is the matter with you?"

"I . . . Okay, listen. Do you need more money? I'm fine with that. Just let me know how much."

Jackie gripped the phone so hard, the edges dug into her hand. She wanted to throw the phone across the room, to break the glass into a thousand pieces and cut him with it. "Wade is a Mets fan," she said. "He hates the Yankees. He has always hated the Yankees."

She ended the call while Bill was still stammering about money, thinking not of her ex-husband at all but of her older son, of that necklace in Wade's shirt pocket—a gift given back, "T" doubling down on a text telling him to leave her alone. She thought of Wade's clothes in the dryer and the dark, secret side of him she'd never known or understood because, even under the best of circumstances, boys don't show their mothers that side.

Mothers have to go looking for it.

Jackie got up. She headed out of the kitchen and down the hall toward Wade's room. Once she got there, she picked his phone up off the floor and keyed in his pin, which, as she recalled from when she first gave him the phone, was simply his first name. It still worked, and that gave her a weird sense of relief. *He didn't change it.* Jackie went right to the texts.

There were very few of them, and most were to and from herself. She saw a few more from Connor, unanswered, asking him to pick him up from school. Also, an exchange with Rafe from back in April—a back-and-forth about an English assignment. But nothing else. Nothing from any other friends. Nothing at all from "T." *Leave me alone* gone, as though the text had never existed to begin with. *Did he delete more texts than that one?*

She went to his photos, holding her breath as she did it. Hating herself. She was *that mom* now, but she had to be, didn't she?

Jackie exhaled. The photos were mostly landscapes: fall foliage on sloping hills and glowing, oversaturated sunsets that showed

Wade's artist's eye, interspersed with still lifes that were more than a little self-indulgent. The most recent ones had been taken inside his room: a carefully blurred shot of an orange safety cone, the birch tree outside his window, and half of Wade's face, the mouth downturned, the eye sad and searching. She scrolled down, past older pictures: a close-up of a gum wrapper, a dead bird on a lawn, the hallway outside their bedrooms, a colorful shot of cereal in a bowl, drops of milk glistening on Froot Loops.

Why do I let them talk me into buying that sugary cereal? It's so bad for them.

Jackie felt a vague sense of relief. There was loneliness to these pictures, yes. But it was teenage loneliness, familiar and finite— something Wade could look back on and possibly even mock in a few years, when he'd found his way in life and high school was a part of his past.

But one picture made her stop. Amid all the landscapes and sweetly pretentious still lifes was a selfie, taken in front of a mirror. In it, Wade was wearing jeans and no shirt. Jackie hadn't seen him shirtless in years, probably since the last time they went to the public pool, and strangely, he seemed to have shrunk since then. His chest was sunken and pale, his body so thin, he could have been a child.

That's what first caught her eye: Wade's thinness. What surprised her even more, though, was the maturity of the pose. His free hand was hooked into the loop of his jeans—a cheesy stance, tailor-made for *Playgirl* magazine or maybe a bad Tinder profile pic. And the way he was looking at the camera . . .

Whom did he take this picture for? Where was it taken?

It was a room she'd never seen before. Jackie tapped the picture so that it grew bigger, filling the screen, then stretched the image with her fingers so she could pick out details behind him: a pale pink wall, a framed black-and-white photograph of the Eiffel Tower. She brought her fingers together again and stared at her son's face—that unsettling smile.

According to the date at the top of the screen, the selfie had been taken at 2:00 PM on Tuesday, May 15. A school day.

She closed the picture quickly, scrolled up through the other photos, wishing she hadn't ever touched this phone. No mother should ever see her son looking at a camera like that. *What did you expect? He's a teenage boy. These are his private pictures. Better close them fast before you see something a whole lot worse.*

Her gaze returned to the more recent shots, the leaves and sunsets—a quick, necessary palate cleanser for the mind, though she couldn't stop thinking about it. *Whose bathroom was that? What was he doing there when he was supposed to be at school?*

Another photo interrupted Jackie's thoughts—a recent one she couldn't quite make out. It was very dark, speckled with small, glistening shapes. She tapped it, but it made even less sense larger, until she held it out a few inches from her face and tilted her head and the speckles became coherent. Drops of water on glass. The picture had been taken from the inside of a car at night. Jackie was looking at raindrops on the windshield, the dim blur of a streetlight behind them. Heavy rain.

"Oh . . ."

Jackie checked the time when the picture was taken and stopped breathing. Her hands began to shake so much that she dropped the phone and had to pick it up quickly, to make sure she hadn't cracked the glass.

Heavy rain on a windshield. Light shining through. And the time and date listed up top was this past Saturday, at 3:15 AM—the same time that Liam Miller had been hit.

Twelve

The bartender at Club Halifax was wearing flannel Snoopy pajama pants and a skintight tank top with a cannabis-leaf pattern. Yet still she was overdressed for this dismal place, which smelled of mold and decades-old cigarette smoke—an asthma attack waiting to happen. Pearl had driven here right after her shift ended and Amy had called a cab to take her back to Woodstock, walked in, and ordered a Johnnie Walker on the rocks without even thinking first, as though compelled by some unseen force. She told herself it was the need to retrace Amy's steps, to figure out what she was lying about and what she wasn't. Bolstered by the detectives' reaction to her pill story, Amy had provided a much more detailed description of her alleged assailant—a teenage boy with a "loping walk," whatever that was supposed to mean. A boy who, Amy now theorized, could have been stalking her and her car for hours. ("He seemed to know me," she had said, that tragic music-video look in her eyes. "He seemed to know who I was.")

But above that, it was the need to escape. Truth told, Pearl wasn't ready to go back to her lonely apartment with nothing but beer and stale bread in the fridge, the hookup app beckoning and her father's call still waiting on her voice mail, like some burning thing left unattended.

Pearl took a long pull of her drink, the warmth radiating up into her cheeks and bringing an extra feeling of comfort to her off-duty clothes: the soft ripped jeans, the thick socks she wore under her boots, the fisherman's knit sweater that still smelled faintly of Paul's Axe spray. She'd order another after she was done with this one, just enough to get her a little slurry, take the knots out of her neck. Then she'd brave the quiet of the road. She could easily drive home after two Johnnies. Pearl was well aware of her limits.

"You've been working here long?" Pearl asked the bartender, whose name, Joy, didn't fit her facial expression.

"About a year," Joy said.

"You like it?"

She shrugged, which actually seemed like the only polite response to a question like that. Club Halifax was a true pit, made all the more obvious with so few people in here and the lights on too bright—the chipped paint on the walls, the yellowed vinyl floors, riddled with sticky beer stains no one had ever bothered cleaning up. (Man. Pearl hoped it was beer.)

The stage was at the far end of the room and it was tiny. Pearl pictured Amy up there, belting one of her old hits into a cheap, fuzzy mic, feedback all around her. A few tables had been set up in the space between the bar and the stage, and Pearl found herself wondering which one they'd sat at, the couple. If there had really been a couple . . .

Pearl cleared her throat. "Hey, by any chance, were you working the night of the Aimee En show?"

"The who?"

"Aimee En. She has rainbow hair?"

"Oh right. She opened for Ghost In You. Sings like she's got the hiccups."

Pearl took another swallow of whiskey. "That's the one."

"I was working that night," she said. "Why?"

Pearl finished the rest of the glass. "Did she have a big crowd?"

Joy shrugged again and glanced meaningfully at the only other customers—two guys in matching green and blue sweatshirts at the other end of the bar, drinking beers in complete silence. "Bigger than this one."

"Did you see her talking to anybody? After her show?"

"Yeah. There was a couple who got here early. They said they were fans of hers. I remember the dude because he was a really good tipper."

"A couple." *Point goes to Amy.*

"The dude bought her a few drinks. They all left at the same time."

"A few, huh?"

Joy shrugged. "I wasn't counting."

Pearl pushed her glass forward. Without another word, Joy refilled it—a good heavy pour. She took a swallow that was big enough to burn. "Did you happen to notice any teenage boys at the Aimee En show?"

"Teenage boys?" Joy put a hand on her hip, gave Pearl a look like an eye roll waiting to happen. "That's an interesting question, especially considering we don't serve anyone under twenty-one."

"I'm looking for one boy in particular." Pearl took another swallow and then recited Amy's description word for word. "Dark hair that hangs in his face. Pale skin and kind of a wide mouth. He's about six feet tall. Loping walk. And that night, he would have been wearing a black hoodie. "

"You a cop?"

Somehow, Pearl knew that yes was the wrong answer. She played with her drink stirrer, stared into her glass. "He's my little brother," she said.

"Your brother."

"He's been getting in a lot of trouble lately. Trying to head this off at the pass."

Joy sighed heavily. Not buying a word of it. The Sweatshirt Twins started laughing about something and Pearl noticed for the first time how quiet the bar was. No music playing. "Like a library in here," Pearl said. "You got a radio you can turn on?"

"I didn't see your little brother." Joy retreated to the other end of the bar and started wiping it down. Conversation over. *Great job, officer.* Pearl sighed. Whatever. It had been a long shot anyway.

Pearl's phone buzzed in her pocket. She glanced at the screen and saw a new text from Paul: *S'up.*

She thought about texting him back but not for very long. He was somebody she could talk to, which wasn't a good thing. And besides, she didn't feel the slightest bit horny. She sucked on an ice cube. Stared at the voice mail icon with her finger hovering over it, daring herself to tap it.

The phone rang. The finger hit accept before she fully registered the return number—same as the one on voice mail. Her father's number. She wanted to end the call, or at least to say something, but she just sat frozen on the barstool. Unable to do either.

"Is this Pearl?" said the voice on the other end, a male voice. Younger sounding than she'd have thought.

"Yes?"

"Sorry . . . I guess I didn't expect you to pick up."

"Who is this?"

"Did you get the voice mail?"

"No," she said. "I mean, yes. Yes, probably. I haven't checked my voice mail." She winced. This wasn't going well. Music exploded out of the bar's speaker system—Joy's sarcastic delayed response—and it was all she could do not to fall off the chair.

"Am I catching you at a bad time?" said the male voice.

"What? No." Pearl clamped a finger over her ear to shut out the song—"Naked Eye" by Luscious Jackson, one of those melodies that brought her back to being a kid. *The universe does have a sick sense of humor.* She said, "Is this my father?"

"No. It's James."

"Who?"

"James. Your brother."

Pearl's phone felt hot in her hand. She shut her eyes for a few seconds, sorting out her thoughts. She hadn't spoken to her brother since . . . Well, not ever. He'd been a baby when their father had sent her away. "James," she said. And then, "How did you get this number?" Most pointless question ever.

"I called the station. They gave it to me. I'm sorry."

"No," she said. "Don't be, I just . . . James. Wow." The music roared at her. She wanted more whiskey. "Why are you calling?"

"Listen, Pearl," he said. "Dad's sick. We're not sure how long he has."

Pearl opened her mouth. Closed it again.

"He wanted me to tell you. I know this is . . . well, it's weird, I know."

"Yeah."

"Anyway . . . You don't have to. But if you do decide you want to visit, to say good-bye . . . I think he'd like that. You know . . . He said he wants closure."

Pearl gritted her teeth. She listened to Luscious Jackson sing about seeing the falling rain and tried not to hate James for saying what he'd just said. *He doesn't know better. He was only a baby.* "I'll think about it," she said and ended the call quickly.

"Dad," James had called him. As though the man wasn't a stranger.

Joy was back again, looking at Pearl with something that actually approached concern. "Bad phone call?"

Pearl nodded.

"You want another?"

She nodded again.

Joy took her glass, dropped a few more ice cubes into it, and poured her a fresh drink, this time to the brim. Pearl lifted it slowly to her lips so as not to spill any. She drained half of it too quickly, her head swimmy now, vision starting to blur.

"One sec." Joy went back to the end of the bar; then she brought the bottle over. She topped off Pearl's glass, poured a shot for herself. "Cheers." She clinked the shot to Pearl's drink, then downed it.

"Cheers," Pearl repeated, planning on just a sip but gulping too much, again. "Can I ask you something?"

"Sure."

"Who's the stupidest man you've ever met?"

Joy snorted. "Actually, that's quite a contest."

Pearl took another long swallow. "Yeah I know," she said. "But I'm not talking about run-of-the-mill douchebags who . . . like . . . spell wonderful with two *l*'s."

Joy gave her a small, tentative smile. "I dated a guy once who wanted to know how far a drive it was between Miami and Florida."

"That's pretty good."

"Right?" she said. "He also thought Rosetta Stone was a civil rights leader. Thank God he was cute."

"Okay, that is really good."

"Don't judge me."

"Of course not," Pearl said. "But I hate to tell you, I've got you beat."

"No way."

"No, no. I do."

Joy started to pour her more, but Pearl put her hand over the glass. "The thing is, everybody thought this guy was smart. He was a career police officer up in Albany . . . totally respected."

"No kidding."

"I kid you not," Pearl said. She finished most of the glass, Joy's face blurring into two faces, but only briefly. She waited for it to settle back into one before she spoke again. "So this respected officer. What he does is, he leaves his personal firearm out. Doesn't lock it up. Even though he's got a baby and a three-year-old daughter. Jesus, I mean this guy is so dumb he doesn't even *engage the safety*."

"Wow . . ."

"Right? And so his daughter, the little dickens . . . she picks up the gun and she's curious, right? She was always very curious. She's still that way. Can't help herself."

"Oh," Joy said. "Oh no . . ."

"Yep. The little dickens picks it up and she pulls the trigger and she shoots her own mother dead."

Joy stared at her, those seen-it-all eyes going soft.

Pearl lifted the glass to her lips, sucked down the last few drops. "Now, how is that for a stupid, stupid man?"

"It wasn't her fault," Joy said softly. "It wasn't the little girl's fault." Which was the same thing a therapist had once told Pearl. "It wasn't your fault." It hadn't helped. Not with Aunt Ruth's words always in her brain and her father so completely out of her life and that dark voice inside her, telling Pearl that she'd been no good from the start. "Black Pearl." A murderer before she'd been old enough to read.

One of the Sweatshirt Twins said, "Miss! Can we settle up?" But Joy didn't even turn in their direction. She just kept watching Pearl with her head shaking, that infuriatingly sad look in her eyes.

"Anyhoo," Pearl said. "You might have to call me a cab."

Joy exhaled. "Look . . ."

"Yeah?"

"I did see that kid here."

Pearl gaped at her. "What?"

"Your brother or whoever the hell he really is. I saw him here during the Aimee En show."

"You did?"

"First you need to know that I did *not* serve him. He had the crappiest fake ID I've ever seen."

"Fine. I don't care about—"

"Seriously. I remember because he literally tried to change the numbers on his driver's license with a Sharpie."

The room was swimming, some other 1990s pop song— Smashing Pumpkins. Or was it *The* Smashing Pumpkins, she'd never been sure—blasting too loud over the speaker system, scrambling Pearl's thoughts. *Do they mean "smashing" as an adjective or a verb?* She blinked a few times, wishing she could will that third drink back into the glass. "Was he alone?" she stammered. "The boy?"

"I think so," Joy said. "But I also think he might have been planning to meet someone because he kept walking outside into the parking lot. Then coming back in again."

The parking lot. Where Amy left her "baby" . . .

Pearl gripped the bar. Why hadn't she chosen beer instead? She was no good to question anybody right now. But as her aunt Ruth always used to say, "If you can't consume a drink without letting it consume you, you shouldn't be drinking." Boy, talk about a hypocrite. Pearl closed her eyes, collecting her thoughts. *Come on . . . you can do it. Come back to the present.*

"You okay?" Joy said.

And then it came to her. "The driver's license," she said, words still slurring maddeningly, but the idea itself in sharp focus. "You said it was a real one that he'd tried to change himself."

"Yeah, that's right. And apparently, he figured he could pass for twenty-nine." She laughed a little.

"Do you remember the name on it?"

At the end of the bar, one of the Sweatshirt Twins threw some money on the bar, and both of them headed out the door in a huff. "Thanks for the great service!" one of them yelled.

Joy just rolled her eyes. "Weirdly enough, I do," she said. "Well, the first name, anyway, because I called him by it a few times— you know, trying to see whether or not he'd naturally answer to it."

"And did he?"

Joy nodded.

"So," Pearl said. "What name did this twenty-nine-year-old answer to?"

Joy smiled, wide enough to show her teeth this time, the tiny diamond affixed to her front incisor. "Wade," she said. "The kid's name was Wade."

"HI, MOM. I'M at Jordan's," Connor said to his mother's voice mail. "I'm getting a homework assignment. I'll be back soon." He ended the call as he watched Jordan disappear into the spreading darkness, orange reflector glaring at him from the back of his bike.

Connor wasn't at Jordan's. He was on the edge of the Kill, where he'd found Jordan after losing Wade. He'd spoken to him here, both of them hiding from the few cops that remained, both of them shivering from the cold, Jordan telling him what he'd learned through chattering teeth, white puffs escaping his lips with each word. "Dude. Seriously. The detectives were talking. I heard everything."

The last of the police cars had just pulled away, and now Connor stood here alone, hanging on to the cold metal of his bike with Jordan's words swirling through his brain. He wished he'd never left the house.

The sky was a deep purple now, the Kill dark and still as a pool of blood. Once, when he was little, Connor had come here with Wade and a couple of his then-friends. Guys from Little League who rolled their eyes at the thought of the baby brother tagging along. It had been a hot summer night and they'd stayed long past dark in one of the abandoned fishing cabins on the other side of the Kill, the older boys sharing a stolen pack of cigarettes and snickering. They'd told Connor about a sixteen-year-old girl who had escaped to that very shack thirty years ago after slaughtering her entire family. By the light of the full moon, the girl had slit her own throat. They'd pointed at the floorboards, insisting that if Connor looked close enough, he could see traces of the dead girl's blood. "She returns when the moon is full. She comes for more souls. She drags them to hell."

Connor could still remember how he'd trembled at the words

and how small and powerless he'd felt. Like a baby. Like Arnie in his cage.

He'd never felt quite like that again until five minutes ago, when Jordan had told him what he'd learned about the carjacking. And this time, it wasn't just a stupid ghost story. His brother wasn't there to say, "Cut it out, you guys," like he had back then.

This time, his brother was the ghost.

Connor got on his bike and headed back to town, legs working harder than they needed to, sweating into his heavy jacket, the ugly moon lighting his way. Jordan's words floated through his brain: "So listen, just a little while ago, they found her purse with everything in it." When Connor finally reached Orchard, he swung onto the wide street. "See that tree? That's where they found it. One of the guys in uniform. I saw him with the purse. Heard him talk about the wallet." The streetlights stared down at him. He wheezed and lurched, lungs aching from the cold.

"But this is the thing. Whoever took the car and killed Liam. He got rid of everything, the car, the purse, all the lady's money that was in the wallet, which makes me think it's not a gangsta, because then he would have taken the money, right?"

The lights were still on at the Lukoil station. Connor headed fast for the red-and-white sign, without bothering to think of what he'd say if anyone caught him there. "I heard that detective say it, the girl one . . ."

Once he reached the Dumpster, Connor squeezed the brakes and jumped off his bike without making a sound. "She said . . . only thing missing is the phone. The lady's phone. She wanted them to keep looking for it. She wants the divers back in the Kill because the phone is missing. She was on the phone with her boss. I think the boss said it was too much money or something because she was fighting over it, saying there could be pictures on the phone . . ."

Connor clutched the side of the Dumpster, pulling himself up, up, arms aching, cold metal cutting into his palms, rust flaking off of it like bark. Up, until the garbage fumes filled his nose and he wanted to puke, up, until he could finally see over the side . . .

It was empty. Of course it was. Wade must have known the trash would be picked up soon, back when he'd asked Connor to throw out the bag.

But really, it didn't matter. Connor knew. He held it all in his mind—the *shook-shooking* sound as he'd walked to the Lukoil station on his brother's orders, the lightness of the bag and the shape he'd seen when he'd raised his hands in the air—a rectangular shadow through the thin plastic. *A phone.* It was with him, that knowledge, whether he wanted it or not.

Hours after Liam Miller had been hit, Wade had asked Connor to get rid of a phone.

Connor pulled his own phone out of his pocket. For a few moments, he scrolled through his Instagram feed, almost every picture on it a shot of Liam: Liam laughing with his buddies; with Jordan's sister, Tamara, at last year's prom; Liam in his football uniform, the padded shoulders like a costume, as though he'd gotten dressed up as the man he would never be.

Connor needed to get home. It was dark now and he didn't want his mother worried enough to call Jordan's mom and ask where he was. *Connor told me he was getting the homework assignment. Was that a lie?*

Connor's eyes started to well up at the thought of Mom, of all the awful things she didn't know and hopefully never would . . .

He clicked on his texts, wrote a quick one to Noah, then inhaled sharply, the hot air escaping his lips in a puff of white. *I'm sorry I hit you,* he'd typed. And then he sent it. There was nothing else he could safely say.

JACKIE WAS WORRIED the mums might die in the cold. An odd thing to be concerned about at a shrine for a dead boy, but that's the way her mind was working right now, lasering in on small worries, scuttling away from the big ones. The pot was heavy and her back hurt from carrying it these few blocks to get here, to the spot where Liam Miller was hit. But she knew she couldn't come to a shrine empty-handed, and these mums—the glorious orange mums Helen had given her—were all she had.

She'd noticed the shrine driving home this afternoon, but it had been much smaller then—just a few bouquets. Since then, it had grown exponentially. And as she knelt down to place the pot of mums, she took it all in: the bouquets of roses and fresh carnations and Day-Glo gerbera daisies; the stuffed animals and glittering sports trophies; the old photos and high school yearbooks and Mylar balloons; all of it spreading like a rash, like a disease, this overgrown grief, taking over the sidewalk, spilling over the curb, edging into the intersection.

It terrified her.

Jackie didn't want to think about what she'd seen on Wade's phone—though that had been what had brought her here: the vague notion that she might be able to sense her son's energy in this place. Or not. *Please. I don't want to feel it.* She looked up at the streetlamp, wondering if it had been this very light shining through the raindrops in the car photo. Wondering because she had no way of knowing. Even if she asked Wade about the pictures, he probably wouldn't tell the truth. He was a teenager and a boy, and a painfully private one at that. And so all she could do was feel.

No. There had to be an explanation for the photo taken inside the car that didn't involve this intersection, that stolen car, that poor boy, Liam. *Wade might try to scare people, the way he scared his father with his art. But he wouldn't hurt anyone. He couldn't.* She remembered the other picture of him—that look on his face, that boy she'd never seen before. And she repeated the words in her head like a prayer, said them out loud: "Wade wouldn't hurt anyone."

A fat teddy bear glared at her. A football trophy figurine took aim at her with his ball. And Liam Miller's face stared up at her from what she now saw were dozens of photographs, some framed, some scattered: Liam as a child and as a young man, alone and with his friends and . . . God . . . his parents. Handsome, teenage Liam and his parents, standing in front of a Christmas tree. A Christmas card photo, probably from last year. Just the three of them. *Liam was an only child.*

She heard the slam of a car door. "Mom?"

Jackie stood up. Her eyes were blurred from tears and so she blinked them away, blinked all the thoughts out of her mind and walked toward her son, her Wade, standing across the street next to his parked car, arms folded across his chest, his eyes sad and glistening in the light from the streetlamp. "Mom," he said. "What are you doing here?"

"Paying my respects."

"I'm sorry, Mom," he said.

She moved closer to him, thinking, *Tell me.* And then, *Don't tell me.* "Why?" she said.

"I'm sorry for getting so mad. Back at the house."

Without a word, Jackie put her arms around Wade. Through his sweatshirt, she could feel his ribs, his spine. His chin was heavy on her shoulder and he smelled of cigarette smoke and all she wanted to do was protect him, hold him, keep him safe from the world.

"I love you, Mom," he said.

"Me too, honey," Jackie said as a car pulled up next to the shrine. "I love you too."

They stayed like that for a while, Jackie holding her son in her arms with her gaze fixed on that car, on the woman getting out of it and walking to the shrine and dropping to her knees.

"Who is that?" Jackie whispered after they pulled apart, both she and Wade staring at this woman, who looked even sadder and stranger than Wade ever did, rocking on her knees, clutching her stomach, her tangled, rainbow hair glowing in the streetlight as she sobbed.

Thirteen

From a comment thread on the TMZ story: "Aimee En: Hit-and-Run Horror! 80s Pop Star's Jag Implicated in Death of NY Teen . . . She Claims It Was a Carjacking!" (Posted 10/21 at 8:00 PM.)

Babablooney

Crackhead does too much crack and runs over some poor kid. Then makes up a story to cover her tracks. Nothing to see here, folks.

Space Oddity

I agree. The whole story is ridiculous, down to the fact that the supposed purse stealer/carjacker left the purse behind with all her money in it. I call bullshit. This bitch (whoever she is, I've never heard of her) is a murderer.

rc2486

You don't know what happened. Innocent until proven guilty. She could have been carjacked. We weren't there. There is only one truth to this story and that's that Aimee En is FUGLY LOL!!!

Mickey Moose

Excuse me . . . Aimee WHO? This is supposed to be a **celebrity** gossip website. Hello?

Call Me Stupid

What's going on with her hair? Looks like a unicorn threw up on her head.

Gracie

I saw Aimee En at a club back in the 90s. She was so wasted she could barely stand up, she smelled like death, AND she totally threw herself at my boyfriend. Beauty and fame may be fleeting. But hot mess lasts forever.

Fourteen

You worked the CVS robbery, didn't you?" Pearl said to Udel as they drove to Havenkill High for the special assembly. She'd woken up with a rip-roaring hangover this morning, yet still she'd managed to come up with that tidbit in the shower while scrubbing the smell of Club Halifax out of her pores. Lazy Bobby Udel had been on duty the night of the robbery. Pearl hadn't been, but she remembered him bragging about it in the break room two days later—as though being sentient and in uniform the night an alarm got tricked was something to brag about.

"Yeah," he said now, eyes aimed out the window in a way that was the opposite of bragging. "We blew that one, didn't we?"

"Hear any theories about who might have done it?"

"Well," he said. "I always thought gangbangers. Or . . . you know. Professionals."

"Seriously?"

His face flushed a little. "Not from here," he said. "Obviously."

"What makes you think that?"

"The way they got into and out of the place so fast," he said. "I mean, I was on patrol that night. I was no more than five minutes away from the CVS when I got the call and by the time I showed up . . ."

"So you're saying they knew what they wanted and went for it."

"Right. In and out. They took just pills and the money out of the pharmacy cash register. Didn't bother with any of the other cash registers, ignored the regular merchandise. Didn't really mess things up that much, other than breaking the lock on the back door."

Pearl watched him as he drove. She started to say more, then stopped, then started again, daring herself to speak. Could she trust him with her idea? Was it even worth it? "Bobby?"

"Yeah?"

"You think maybe it could have been a kid from around here?" she said. "Or a few kids. Looking for trouble."

He shook his head vigorously. "Come on."

"Think about it. It's possible."

"Do you know any kids from around here who are looking for that kind of trouble? Because I've lived here my whole life and I sure don't."

"Yes," she said. "I do."

"Who?"

"The one who took Amy Nathanson's car."

He let out a long, harrumphing sigh. "Everybody's saying she lied about that kid. They're saying she ran Liam down herself and freaked out and made up a story."

"Who's everyone?"

"Give me a break, Pearl. Jeez. It's even on TMZ."

"*I'm* not saying it."

"Well, I am," he said. "I was there that night too, you know. I saw her come in just like you did." He actually sounded a little angry with her.

It was Pearl's turn to sigh. This was why Udel would never be a great cop. He made up his mind too quickly and he did it based on feelings, not facts. He'd rather be "right" and done than spend a moment uncertain, because uncertainty meant taking the time and energy to learn the truth. He didn't ask questions and backed away from answers, even if they were handed to him. It made her mad, that utter lack of curiosity, that laziness. "What happened to those feelings you were telling me about?" she said. "Don't you even care anymore about your poor cousin who lost his best friend? You said you were like family, the three of you. Is that no longer true?"

He stared out the window, his jaw tight. "Of course I care."

"Then why wouldn't you want to know who might have run Liam down?"

"I do want to know." He turned the corner, pulled into the Havenkill High parking lot, past the line of fire-bright maple trees. "Hell, I *do* know," he said. "It was *her* and she's gonna pay."

"Amy Nathanson says that the kid who took her purse had lots of prescription drugs that he showed her. Do you see how that might connect, Bobby?"

Udel slid into a space near the school's entrance and shifted into park, staring at Pearl the whole time.

"A big Baggie full of them," Pearl said. "Like a pharmacy. That's how she described it. She used those words. Like a pharmacy."

"She still could have been lying."

"Hell of a coincidence if she is. And the bartender at Club Halifax—"

"Where?"

"The place where Amy Nathanson played that night. She said there was a teenage boy in there with a fake ID—a jumpy kid in a black hoodie who kept going to the parking lot, where Amy had parked her Jag."

He stared at her. "The bartender said that?"

"More or less."

"She said he was wearing a black hoodie?"

"Yes. And she even remembered his name. Wade." Pearl took a breath. Udel's seat belt was off. She was about to stop him from getting out of the car, but she realized he hadn't made a move to open the door. He wasn't going anywhere. "Look," she said. "It is possible that there really was a boy, and that he was from around here. He had a big stash of pills that could easily have been taken from CVS. And he knew enough about the Kill to dump the car in it. Amy doesn't know anything about this town. Plus, she was such a basket case that night, she never would have been able to—"

"Wade," he said. "That's what the bartender told you. The kid's name was Wade? You're sure?"

"Yeah . . ."

"There's a kid in my cousin's class with that name."

"Well . . . Okay. That's interesting, Bobby. There's more than one Wade in the world, though."

"This Wade just posted some nasty shit on Liam's girlfriend's Instagram. On a post about Liam's memorial."

"He did?"

"Ryan showed me. I guess Tamara deleted the whole exchange, but he took a screen grab of the comment."

Udel dug his phone out of his pocket, called it up, and handed it to her. Pearl looked at the screen, feeling his gaze on the side of her face:

RG1999 Stay strong, Tam.

Wade.Reed She's not strong. None of you has ever been
strong. You spoiled brats. You wear grief like it's the latest
fashion. You don't care deeply enough about anything or
anyone to really feel the pain of loss. You're liars. Can't
wait for the next of you to die.

Udel said, "RG1999 is my cousin. Ryan Grant."
Pearl nodded. "He'll be here today for this assembly. Right?"
"Ryan? I think he stayed home."
"No. Wade Reed."
"He should be," Udel said. "He's a senior, just like Ryan."
Pearl said, "We should probably call the sergeant, right? And
the state detectives."
And for once Udel didn't just sit there breathing through his
mouth. He took his phone back and jabbed the station's number
into the screen. "I'll call them," he said. "I'll tell them."

PARENTS WERE ASKED to attend the special morning assembly at
the high school, and so Jackie did. She took the seat Helen had
saved for her, her gaze drifting around the packed auditorium
as Helen huddled and whispered with her poor, teary daughter.
Jackie had been to this auditorium before. The eighth graders had
held their graduation here, but it had felt like a completely different place then—full of brightness and noise and anticipation, the
kids talking too loud and whooping at each other, continuously
needing to be shushed. There had been a big sign on the back
wall, hand-painted by the kids in big swirling red letters covered
in glitter: WELCOME TO OUR FUTURE it had read. Wade had helped
paint it. Jackie was pretty sure Liam had too.

It was so different in here now. The kids were different—sniffling, heads bowed, speaking in hushed voices. Every so often, she'd hear a sob.

Jackie recognized a few faces: boys from the hospital, girls she'd seen palling around with Stacy in pictures on Helen's Facebook feed and, moving toward the front of the auditorium amid a cluster of boys, Rafe Burgess. All of them tear-stained, all of them shell-shocked. She scanned Rafe's group for Wade, then the whole audience for him, until she finally caught sight of her son toward the back of the kids' block of seats, slumped over, head down, folding into himself. From this angle, he looked like a pile of old clothes. But Jackie still recognized him. She'd know her son anywhere.

Wade was at the far end of a row, one seat away from a group of girls who were huddled over a box of Kleenex, plucking tissues and holding them softly to their crumpled faces in a way that felt almost like a ritual, a sacrament.

Wade wasn't a part of their conversation. He wasn't part of any conversation, and while this wasn't entirely unexpected, it still made Jackie sad. They'd had another nice evening together, Connor, Wade, and Jackie, even if Connor had been more quiet than usual. Wade had been so sweet and polite. He'd asked Jackie about her day, studiously avoiding her trip to Red Hook and the argument after. He'd brought his dishes up to the sink again and he'd gone to bed early. *Sleep,* Jackie had thought last night as she drifted off herself, the Xanax tightening its velvety grip and the images on Wade's phone growing more benign in her mind, more easily explained. *That's all he needs. A good night's sleep.*

Wade must have felt Jackie's gaze on him because he straightened up. He turned and looked directly at her, though for a moment it seemed as though he didn't see her. Even from this distance, she could read the expression on his face, which was strange—a sorrow that didn't seem to fit with the grief of the others. *Haunted.* Jackie raised a hand, waved at him.

His face changed. He gave her a quick wave, then turned around fast. *Maybe it wasn't me he turned to look at.* Jackie glanced at Stacy, who stood with her hands on her hips, glaring down at her mother, oblivious to her and Wade both. She remembered Stacy's coldness at the hospital, the unpleasant way she'd said Wade's name. "My mom showed him out," she had said, indifferent about how that might sound to Wade's own mother.

"Dad would understand," Stacy was saying. "You don't get it at all, but Dad does. If Dad were here—"

"Well, Dad isn't here, is he?"

First time she'd heard Helen snap at her daughter like that, ever.

"You can't take the rest of the day off," Helen said. "You can't go out with your friends. I know you're grieving. I know you're sad. But life goes on."

"Ryan got to stay home."

"I'm not Ryan's mother."

Stacy looked at Jackie as though she was noticing her for the first time. "Wade stays home from school all the time, right, Mrs. Reed?"

Jackie frowned. "What do you mean?" she said.

But Stacy was back to Helen again. "You have no heart."

"You can insult me all you want," she said, "but it is fall quarter senior year, and you can't just take the afternoon off."

"There are other things in life besides school and work and *being freakin' responsible.*"

Helen shushed her again.

"Mom, this isn't fair."

"You'd better go sit with your friends," she said. "The assembly is starting."

Stacy left in a swirl of indignation with Helen staring after her, her skin a livid pink. She gave Jackie a weak smile. "Kids," she said.

"Stacy didn't mean that, did she? About Wade ditching school?"

Helen shook her head. "She has no idea what she's talking about," she said softly.

Jackie put a hand on hers. *Maybe you should let her take the afternoon off,* she wanted to say. *How often does a kid her age lose one of her closest friends? Obviously, she's hurting.* But she didn't. Close as she was to Helen, Jackie didn't know Stacy at all. Couples here socialized with other couples and so, despite their long history together, Jackie was Helen's "work friend" now, their time together limited to that one space, to celebratory lunches after one of them made a sale or maybe the odd girls' night out. As kind as Helen was to her boys, Jackie couldn't remember the last time she'd been to Helen's house, and it had been ages since she'd laid eyes on Helen's husband, Garrett—probably not since the office Christmas party, nearly a year ago. "Stacy's wrong," she said.

"What?"

"Nobody has more heart than you do."

She sighed. "I wouldn't go that far."

Two police officers took the stage, a man and a woman. Both were quite young. The male officer's face still bore traces of acne, and when he started to speak, Jackie half expected his voice to crack like Connor's. He thanked everyone for coming, explaining why they were all there, as though that needed explaining. "For those of you who don't know me, I'm Officer Udel," he said.

"And . . . I went to this school." He took a breath. "I'm sure you all know what happened to Liam Miller, but with a tragedy like this, rumors get spread. And the truth . . ." He stopped for a moment and dragged an arm across his face. Jackie was worried he might get emotional, which was the last thing these kids needed. The last thing she needed, for that matter. A crying cop. The female officer gave him a quick, sharp look, but when he continued, his voice was calm. "From what we know, Liam Miller died a hero." He said nothing more—just let the word hang there in the over-heated air of the auditorium. *Hero.* The room went dead quiet, save for a few sniffles, and a soft sob that, Jackie realized now, had come from Stacy.

Jackie looked at Wade, motionless in his chair, and felt desperately uncomfortable. "What's going on with that cop?" she whispered to Helen. "Do you think he's okay?"

She didn't reply. Jackie longed for someone, anyone, to speak. Finally, the female officer obliged. "I'm Officer Maze," she said. Her voice was reassuringly no-nonsense, her posture straight. She said words like "ongoing investigation" and "working together with state police," and Jackie was able to breathe again.

Officer Maze urged everyone to call with any relevant information that might help police "determine what happened in the early-morning hours of October twentieth," and, for a moment, the picture on Wade's phone flashed in Jackie's mind again—raindrops on a windshield. But that didn't mean anything, she told herself. It only meant he was in a car during those hours—probably his own car, parked outside their house at night.

As Officer Maze gave the number for the tip line, Jackie pushed the image out of her thoughts. *Not relevant. It couldn't be.* She never should have seen it, never should have picked up Wade's phone. ". . . so please put this number in your phones or write it down," Officer Maze said. "If you lose the number, it is posted on the Web site for the Havenkill Police Department, as well as the Facebook page . . ."

Jackie glanced at Officer Udel looking on. He made her so nervous. She leaned over to Helen again, so as not to look at him anymore. "Have you spoken to Liam's parents?"

"I was at their home yesterday," she said, eyes trained on the stage. "He was an only child, just like Stacy. I can't even imagine."

Jackie closed her eyes for a second, that image intruding again, and when she opened them, two more people had joined the young officers onstage—a man and a woman, both in their forties or fifties. The man introduced himself as Mr. Penny, the guidance counselor, and Jackie winced, remembering that she'd called him over the weekend. How selfish of her, at a time like this. How thoughtless to take up space on his voice mail like that, asking if they could meet about her son, her living son . . .

"I'd like to introduce Dr. Klein, a psychotherapist who specializes in grief counseling and has a private practice in Rhinebeck," Mr. Penny said as the woman stepped forward to take the mic, a round, squat woman with wavy, carefully set blond hair and a soft, pleasant face. Penny was in many ways her physical opposite—angular and balding and slightly angry-looking. He seemed to tower over both Dr. Klein and the two police officers, and as the therapist started to speak and he peered out at the audience, Mr. Penny's glance landed on Jackie. For a few seconds they locked eyes. It felt as though the temperature in the room had suddenly dropped, so cold and appraising was his stare, his eyes such a piercing blue that Jackie could feel the chill of them, even from the back of the auditorium.

As Dr. Klein started to speak, Jackie focused on her soothing voice, the soft curls of her blond hair, and her dress, which was really the most comforting color—the same blue as the blanket of a newborn baby boy. "None of this is normal," Dr. Klein was saying now. "None of this should be happening. That's the first thing you should know. If you feel that you can't just go on with life and act like everything is okay, you're right in feeling that. It's not."

Stacy, who was sitting toward the back of the students' section, whipped around in her seat and stared daggers at Helen, who gave a long sigh. Jackie tried a smile. "My kid won't even look at me," she said. "So you've got that."

Helen shook her head. "He's a good person," she said quietly.

Jackie looked at her, a little surprised. "Wade?"

"He's always been sweet. Special."

Jackie felt herself smiling. Helen, always with the right thing to say. "You think so?"

"He's an artist. Artists feel things in ways the rest of us don't understand."

Jackie nodded, an image flickering in her mind: the portrait Wade had drawn of Bill's family . . . She pushed it away.

Helen's calm green eyes rested on Wade. She put a cool hand on Jackie's arm, smiled her wise, dreamy smile. "We kick ourselves, Jackie, but we're only human," she said quietly. "And we're doing the best we can."

AT THE END of her speech, Dr. Klein asked the kids to describe how they felt about Liam's death in one word. Jackie expected silence, but dozens of hands went up.

"Shaken," said one kid.

"Unfair," said another.

Dr. Klein called on Stacy. "Ripped in two," she said.

"Can you find the one word, sweetheart?"

"Crushed."

"Good."

Stacy gave her mother another withering look and then turned back around. It was starting to make Jackie angry, this seeming determination to blame Helen for everything. *So she wants you to stay in school for the day. She's your mother. Get over it.* As uncommunicative and distant as her boys could be, Jackie couldn't recall either one of them looking at her like that.

"Jackie," Helen whispered.

"Yes?"

"Do you still have your tattoo?"

It took Jackie a while to realize what she was talking about—the topic hadn't come up in all the years since she'd moved back here, after all. But then she remembered. Of course she did. Senior year in high school. The Friday before prom. Jackie, Helen, and their friend Rachel had played hooky from school and driven all the way to New York City in Rachel's car. They'd found a tattoo place on Bleecker Street and they'd all three gotten tramp stamps in honor of the Furies, which they'd been reading about in English class. "No, I got it removed," whispered Jackie, who until ten years ago had actually liked her tattoo, an ornate *M* adorned with thorny red roses to honor Megaera. "After your husband leaves you for another woman, a tattoo in honor of 'the Jealous' doesn't feel so great."

Helen winced. "Sorry."

"I'm over it."

"I still have mine," Helen said. "I miss those days."

Jackie nodded. She missed those days too. Who didn't miss the end of senior year of high school when the future felt like a perfect fresh egg, just about to crack open, and you hadn't done anything wrong that couldn't be fixed? Jackie longed for the energy she used to have back then, when no one relied on her for anything, when she had no real fears or worries, when her heart had never been broken, and everyone she ever loved was still alive. "These poor kids," Jackie said. "They'll never have days like that. Whenever they think of their senior year, they'll think of Liam and they'll feel . . ."

"Crushed."

"Yes," she said, both of them looking at Stacy, head bowed, two friends' arms around her narrow shoulders. "Crushed."

ONCE THE ASSEMBLY was over, everyone stood up. Jackie noticed several kids making their way to the parents' section. Nearby, she saw another girl she recognized from Helen's Facebook feed: tall, with shiny black hair and brown eyes. When she got closer, Jackie saw her embrace Rita, the mother of Connor's friend Jordan, Rita taking her in her arms and holding her close . . . *Must be Jordan's older sister, Tamara.*

"Poor thing," Helen said, watching her too. "Stacy told me they were thinking about getting engaged."

"What?"

"Tamara and Liam."

Tamara. Liam Miller's girlfriend. She watched Rita. Poor Rita, with her daughter going through a tragedy like that. She felt silly and selfish, obsessing over Wade's possible secret heartbreak a few days ago when this poor woman had to console a daughter whose first love was now dead.

Jackie moved away from Helen and into the crowd of students, determined now to find her son, her sensitive artist son, who felt things in ways she'd never understand. That was fine, she knew now. She only wanted to talk to him, to let him know she was here.

She found the row he'd been sitting in, but he was no longer there. Jackie scanned the group for his dyed black hair, his sad face . . . Finally, she caught sight of him standing near the opened door of the auditorium, the light from outside pouring in around him like foam from a wave. She called out to him, but he didn't seem to hear.

Jackie felt a hand on her shoulder just as she noticed the young male police officer talking to Wade, and when she turned around, she saw Mr. Penny, the guidance counselor. "Mrs. Reed?" he said. "You called me over the weekend?"

Jackie's eyes were trained on Wade and the policeman. "It's not important, Mr. Penny," she said. "I shouldn't have called." What was he saying to Wade? Why was Wade backing away?

"Mrs. Reed," Penny said, "would you mind coming to my office now?"

"I told you it isn't important." She hadn't meant to sound so harsh. "I mean," she said, "it can wait."

"No, Mrs. Reed, it can't," he said. "It concerns your son." She stopped and looked into those ice-blue eyes. Her heart dropped. "Follow me please," he said.

And so she did. She followed his weaving path through the teary students as Helen called after her. "Jackie? Honey? You want me to wait?"

She shook her head, following him out of the auditorium and down an echoing hallway, all the way to the end until they reached the office with his name on the door. When Mr. Penny opened the door, she saw the three of them standing in front of the receptionist's desk: those two officers from the assembly. And then her oldest son slumped between them, his head bowed like a prisoner's.

Fifteen

Wade wouldn't look at Jackie. She was sitting right next to him in the guidance counselor's office, with those two cops from assembly and two state police detectives. She kept saying his name and yet he wouldn't look at her. Wouldn't speak. "Wade," she said again. "Please . . ."

"Wade," Mr. Penny said. "Are you all right?"

Jackie wanted to slap Mr. Penny, with that suspicious tone of his, the way he tilted his head to the side the better to examine the state of Wade's pupils. She half expected him to ask her son how many fingers he was holding up. *He's not on drugs, you judgmental ass.* "Of course he's all right," Jackie said. "Why wouldn't he be all right?"

"Nobody's in any trouble here, ma'am," said the male state police detective. So condescending, that "ma'am." "We'd just like to ask your son a few questions. We can all go by the station, if you feel like you guys might be more comfortable there."

Right, because a police station is the most comfortable place there is. It made Jackie think of something her grandmother once told her: "Never believe anything said through a mustache."

"Wade has school today." She threw another pleading look at her silent son, feeling as though she'd stepped into one of those dreams where you can't move and you can't speak and nothing goes the way it's supposed to go. "He needs to get to class."

"It's perfectly all right for him to miss class," Mr. Penny said, "considering the circumstances."

"What circumstances?"

The female detective was saying Wade's name now, asking him to please respond, again and again. Jackie leveled her eyes at both the uniformed officers, neither one of them much older than her son—the boy officer in particular, with his acne scars and the way he'd practically cried onstage. A child. "What circumstances?" she asked him directly.

He turned away. *What a strange response.*

"Mrs. Reed," said the female detective. "A witness claims to have seen your son with the carjacking victim the night Liam Miller was killed."

Jackie blinked at her. "What?"

"That's a lie," Wade said, coming to life. He looked at Jackie. "I wasn't with anybody."

"According to the witness," the detective said, "a young man with your name and fitting your description was at Club Halifax where Aimee En had been performing . . ."

"Aimee En?" Jackie said. "The singer from the 1980s?"

". . . between six and eight PM. You want to tell us where you were during those hours if you weren't at Club Halifax?"

"He was at his SAT class. It goes on till seven PM," Jackie said.

She looked at Wade, and again he wouldn't return her gaze. "Weren't you? Wade?"

He stared at the desk. "I'm sorry, Mom," he said softly.

Jackie's face heated up. She felt dizzy. "Aimee En?" she said again. "Aimee En was the carjacking victim?" As though that were the point of the story—the celebrity tie-in to Liam Miller's death—and not the fact that her own son had been at a club when he was supposed to have been at his eighth and final SAT class, classes she'd been paying for, which was again beside the point. She stared at Wade, who was looking at her now. She had no idea what was behind those sad eyes, or if he was even sad at all, or whether the sadness was just something she read into them. *I don't know my son.*

"I was there," he said. "I was at Club Halifax."

"All right," Mustache said. He glanced at his partner and Jackie caught it, the two of them oh-so-cat-that-ate-the-canary. Probably wishing they could high-five. "You want to tell us where you went after?"

"I went home."

"Why were you there?" Jackie said, her voice rising.

"Ma'am," Mustache said. "If you don't mind—"

"Why were you at a club watching some one-hit wonder from thirty years before your time when you were supposed to be preparing for tests?"

"I don't know."

"Wade," said the female detective. "Were you still at the club when Aimee En left?"

"No."

Jackie said, "Of course you know why you were there!"

"Ma'am, *please.*"

She continued. She couldn't help it. "Were you with friends,

Wade? Did you meet anybody at this club?" She watched the side
of his face, thinking of "T." "Did you meet a girl there?"

"No."

"Then why on earth were you—"

"I just wanted to . . . to go somewhere."

"What?"

"I wanted to be where no one knows me." He turned and
looked directly at her. "Okay?"

"Let's leave that aside for now," the female detective said. "If you
could just look at this, please, Wade. We'd like to know if you can
remember posting this comment on Tamara Hayes's Instagram."

*Jordan Hayes's sister, Tamara. That black shiny hair. Those
widow's eyes and dewy lashes, Stacy's arm around her narrow
shoulders in assembly, comforting her. They'd been planning on
getting engaged, Liam and Tamara. Beautiful, sad Tamara. Tamara, whose name starts with a T . . .*

The female detective placed a printout in front of Wade: two
short Instagram comments, blown up big. "This was at the end of
a comment thread, on a post for people who wanted to pay their
respects to Liam Miller's parents. If you could just look at this
final comment here, and let us know if you did, in fact, post it."

Jackie read over Wade's shoulder. Her mouth went dry. Wade
started to answer and she squeezed his arm. "Don't answer," she said.

Mr. Penny started to say something, but she cut him off. "Is my
son under arrest?" She glared at Mustache.

"No, ma'am."

"Then we're leaving." She turned to Penny. "We're going home."

"But—"

"You said it didn't matter if he missed school so we're going
home," she said. Her grip tightened on Wade's arm, practically
lifting him off the chair. On their way out, she turned to the two

detectives. "He won't speak to you again without a lawyer," she said.

"MOM," WADE SAID as Jackie led him down the hallway, past fluorescent-lit classrooms full of students and droning teachers and turning heads. Yes, people were turning to look at them. She could *feel* it. "Mom. You're hurting me."

She realized now that she was still holding his arm very tightly, as though he might run away if she didn't. Her grip tightened.

"Mom."

They were in front of the school now, moving around the side to the parking lot. Once they reached it, Jackie stopped. He was a few inches taller than she was, but when she looked into his eyes he seemed to shrink.

"I need to talk to you, Wade."

He said nothing.

"I am going to ask you some questions, and I need you to tell me the truth, no matter what. If you can't answer me honestly, then tell me exactly that. Say, 'Mom, I can't answer that question,' and I will accept that. The one thing I can't take from you now is one more lie."

"I haven't lied to you."

"*Wade.*"

"Okay," he said softly. "I promise. No more lies."

Jackie kept her eyes on him. She was aware of a few groups of parents, moving through the parking lot, getting into cars, their heads bowed. She heard doors slamming, engines sparking to life. She noticed kids too, loitering at the edges of the lot, someone sneaking a smoke, others talking to one another in voices so thin and distant, they almost sounded like birdcalls. She felt watched, even though they probably weren't paying any attention to her. She wished she could be alone with her son, but she couldn't wait for that. She needed answers, now. "Did you steal Aimee En's car?"

"No."

"Did you run over Liam Miller?"

"No, Mom."

"Were you home when it happened?"

"No."

"Where were you?"

Wade took a long shaky breath. His eyes darted around the parking lot. "My car," he said.

Her heart sunk. *Raindrops on the windshield. Three* AM. "You were in your car?"

"No, Mom. My car. *Look at my car.*"

He started to move, but she kept hold of his arm. "Where were you that night?"

Wade yanked away from her and started to run across the lot with Jackie following. "Answer me, Wade."

"I can't answer that question," he said. "I can't answer any more questions. I shouldn't have to. You shouldn't be asking." He kept running, then came to a halt, Jackie standing next to him, next to the car she'd given him three months ago, her old car she'd presented to her son four months after his seventeenth birthday, topped with a red, oversize ribbon she'd actually found online. "You are the best, Mom," he had said, and it had made her so happy. *I raised him right,* she'd thought. *He isn't spoiled. He loves this car as much as I do.*

All four tires had been slashed. On the windshield, in red lipstick letters, someone had scrawled the name LIAM.

"Oh Wade," she said, wrapping her arm around his shoulder.

"Don't," he said, his back stiffening, pulling away like a stranger. "Don't."

Sixteen

Your nose isn't broken," Connor said to Noah when he came running up to him before first period, same way he'd always done before this weekend, as though nothing had happened. And if you didn't know better—if you just looked at Noah's goofy smile and ignored the bruise on his cheek, the shadow of dried blood on his lip, and the Band-Aid stretched over the bridge of his nose, which was still swollen a little—you'd think nothing really had happened, that the whole fight had just been a bad dream Connor was waking up from.

"Yeah," Noah said. "My mom totally overreacted."

He said it without a hint of sarcasm, which made Connor feel bad—not just for beating him up, but for every mean thought he'd ever had about Noah over the past several months, for all the pulling away he'd been doing, as though Noah's good-heartedness was something to pull away from.

"So you want to work on our science project during lunch?" Noah said. "I talked to Mrs. Briggs and she said she'd let us use the lab."

"Sure."

"What's wrong?" Noah peered at Connor's face, as though it had all his thoughts printed on it in letters too small for him to read. "Mrs. Briggs says it's okay that we broke the beaker, if that's what you're worried about . . ."

"Hey, Noah?"

"Yeah?"

"You know how you said those things about my brother?"

He cringed. "I'm sorry, dude. Mason Marx is an idiot. I don't know why I—"

"No," Connor said. "No. Listen . . . I got upset because I was scared, deep down. Like . . . maybe I don't know him as well as I think."

Noah stared at him. The bell rang announcing the start of class, but both of them just stood in the hallway, frozen, with the other kids flooding past them, Carly Daniels from their home-room telling them they'd better hurry up, class was about to start.

Finally, Noah spoke. "You're kidding, right?"

Connor pulled him aside, out of the foot traffic, a feeling like a wave pressing up against his throat, his skin, the backs of his eyeballs, the need to let something out—either tears or the truth; probably both. He heard himself talking to Noah in hushed tones that weren't his own, words he never thought he'd say. And it was like jumping off a high diving board for the first time, that strange exhilaration of wanting to turn back, but knowing you can't: "If Wade killed Liam and I knew about it, would you still be my friend?"

"I'm always your friend."

"Would you keep it a secret?"

Noah said nothing for several seconds, his face pale, the bruise on his cheek more pronounced because of it. "Dude," he said.

And it was as though that same wave was now pressing against Noah's throat, that same war raging inside of him. Torn, that was how it felt. Like actually being torn in two. "I would try to keep it a secret," he said. "But I don't know whether I could."

"You don't know?"

"Yeah, Connor. A really nice kid has been murdered, and if you told me that you knew who killed him, I don't know if I could just keep that to myself. I mean, could you?"

"This is my brother."

"That doesn't answer the question."

"You're right," he said. "It doesn't."

"Is this like . . . some kind of weird hypothetical test of loyalty? Or are you just messing with me?"

Connor wanted to say yes and change the subject, to dance away from this tearing guilt the way he had last night, when Wade had cornered him in the hall between their two rooms and asked him what was wrong, why was he so quiet, why wouldn't he look him in the eye. "Just school stuff," he'd said. "No big deal." But this was Noah, simple, easy-to-read Noah, whom he knew better than Wade, better probably than himself. The one person in the world he actually *could* look in the eye.

"We'd better go to class," Noah said.

And Connor stopped him right there, by the bank of lockers in the empty hallway. He put a hand on each of Noah's shoulders and made him promise on his mother's life not to freak out. And then he told him everything.

"Wow," SAID NOAH after Connor finished.

Connor had hoped for a little more than that, but nothing came. For a good half minute, Noah stood there, gaping at Connor, the word *wow* hanging in the air above them.

"Is that all you're going to say?"

"Well . . ."

"Wow" and "Well." Great. Why had he bothered telling Noah Weston anything? "We'd better get going . . ." he started to say.

But Noah grabbed hold of his arm, stopping him. "You didn't ever open the bag, right?"

"Right. Wade told me not to."

"So you don't even technically know it was a phone."

Connor frowned. "I'm pretty sure it was a phone, Noah."

"You don't know," he said. "Could have been anything. Weed. A pack of cigarettes. I've seen Wade smoking cigs before. Outside school. In the park too."

"Why would he want me to throw out a pack of cigarettes?"

"It could have been anything." There was a tinge of desperation in his voice, and when he smiled, it wasn't his usual goofy one and there was a strange look in his eyes too, like the first hint of fever. "Wade would never kill anybody," he said. "He'd never run over someone and drive away. You'd never help cover it up. You're my best friend, and best friends know each other and I know you wouldn't do that."

"Noah?"

"Yeah?"

"That almost sounds like a threat."

Noah cast a quick glance down the hallway, which was empty now, class having started. "Saturday was the worst day of my life."

"I'm really sorry."

"I'm not talking about the fight," Noah said. "I'm talking about when my mom told me I couldn't hang out with you anymore."

"Oh."

"And if what you're saying about Wade is true . . ." He took a breath. "If it was what's-her-name's phone in that bag, and if he had it because he stole her car and killed Liam with it. If that's really the truth . . ."

"You won't be allowed to hang out with me?"

He shook his head. "No," he said. "It's worse than that. I'll have to tell the cops."

"You will?"

"And if you aren't with me on that, we probably won't ever talk to each other again. Right?"

Connor swallowed hard.

"I want things to stay normal."

"Me too, Noah."

"Good. So let's just agree that it probably wasn't what's-her-name's phone."

Connor exhaled. "Okay," he said. "Agreed."

"We'd better go to class. We are so late, man. She's gonna kill us."

Noah was right. It could have been weed or cigarettes in the bag, or it could have been some other random phone Wade wanted to get rid of. Wade could have had entirely innocent reasons for coming into Connor's room after three in the morning, drenched from the storm outside, dripping rain on Connor's floor, and making him promise not to tell anyone, ever.

But none of those excuses made Connor feel normal. They made him feel as though something unstoppable had already started—an avalanche, with boulders and ice and fifty-foot waves of snow, capable of destroying Connor's family, the school, the entire town. And the only reason why they weren't all buried yet, the only reason why Noah was able to feel normal about things, was that the two of them were standing at the foot of the mountain, with their backs turned.

TYPICAL HOW THEY scattered at the sight of a uniform—the group of kids clustered at the edge of the parking lot, watching Wade Reed and his mother bowed over his vandalized car and snickering. Some had their phones raised. Pearl and Udel had been on their way to the parking lot anyway when the pointless call had come in from Romero back at the station, alerting them to a 10–21 B that was literally thirty feet away and telling them Wade's mother, also thirty feet away, had called it in.

And so the first thing Pearl had done was to head straight toward the kids—a group of skinny little white boys in Nike warm-up jackets and joggers, obviously from the middle school next door. "Can anybody here tell me if they saw . . ." she started, but they dispersed before she could finish the sentence, a frightened flock of pigeons.

She took off after the kids and caught up with three of them on the sidewalk that ran between the high school and the middle school, barely breaking a sweat. They stared up at her, these three idiots, breathing hard, clearly terrified. "Never run from a police officer," Pearl said.

"We're sorry," said the tallest of them, who was a couple of inches shorter than Pearl, his voice higher than hers. Adolescence had not so much as grazed these boys. "We just got scared. It was dumb of us."

"Yep. Extremely dumb."

"We'll never do anything like that again."

"How about ditching school? You plan on doing that again?"

"No, ma'am," the boy said solemnly. His hair was pale and soft as a baby's and his ears stuck straight out from his head. Not much of a spokesperson. But he was talking, at least, which was more than could be said for his companions. "Today's just weird," he said. "You know."

Pearl nodded. "You came to the high school to pay your respects?"

"Um."

She knew what that "um" meant. This dork had been holding up his phone. "Did you guys see who did that to Wade Reed's car?"

"No. It had already happened when we got there."

Pearl said, "Let's see what you got on tape."

"Huh?"

"I saw you. Give it."

He handed over the phone. As Pearl opened the kid's videos, one of his friends made a whimpering noise, like a kicked puppy. She looked over at him and saw him shaking his head dramatically at his baby-haired filmmaker buddy and she knew why. Funny how easy it was to read the minds of tween boys. "His footage is online, isn't it?" She turned back to the videographer. "You stream it?"

He nodded.

"Facebook Live?"

"It's just a couple of seconds."

She made him open his Facebook page for her. She played the footage he'd streamed live and then posted . . . about twenty seconds of the hobbled car, the lipstick scrawl on the windshield, then fifteen more of Wade and his mother running across the parking lot, making the discovery. Nothing surprising in any of it, save maybe for the callousness of the voice-over. "Check it out. He runs like a girl." What made Pearl's throat catch, though, was the comments—the sheer number of them. It had been streamed and posted just a little more than five minutes earlier, and already there were dozens. Why were these kids allowed to keep their phones on in school? She read around ten of the comments and her heart sank. She couldn't look at the page anymore.

"He posted something really mean on Liam's girlfriend's Instagram," the video kid said.

Pearl looked at him. "So you think he deserves this? All of this?"

He shrugged.

Her jaw tightened. "Give me your student IDs."

"What? Why?"

"Hand them over. I'm taking down your names, and I want the names of your friends who ran away. You're all potential suspects."

"I swear we didn't do anything."

"Then there's nothing to worry about," she said. "Is there?"

After she took down all the kids' names, Pearl handed back the tall one's phone, a sickening feeling welling up inside her, a type of dread. The boy, whose name was Cody, muttered an apology. But she waved him off. "Delete the post," she said. Heading back to the parking lot, Pearl ran too fast. Her boots slammed at the pavement. A stitch worked its way into her side.

By the time she made it over to the car, Bobby was taking pictures of the slashed tires with his phone. He glanced up at her as she approached. "You get anything out of those kids?"

Pearl shrugged, avoiding Mrs. Reed's sad gaze. "Not much."

Bobby took a picture of the back end of the car and straightened up. "You can come by the station anytime and fill out a report," Bobby said to Mrs. Reed, in a voice that sounded assuring and professional—a relief to Pearl, who'd been afraid he might take out his raw feelings on Wade. He'd almost lost it a few times during the assembly, and on their way to Mr. Penny's office she'd felt as though she needed to watch him very carefully—not so much because of anything he'd said, but because of the way he looked at Wade Reed, as though he were a bug that needed to be squashed.

Those middle school kids might not have had any real reason to hate Wade. But Bobby Udel—so shaken over the death of his cousin's best friend—now seemed to believe he did. "I know him," Udel had said to her before the assembly, right after he'd gotten off the phone with Sergeant Black. "I know Wade Reed."

"We won't be coming into the station anytime soon," Mrs. Reed said. "We have no desire to go to the police station."

Bobby started to say something, but Pearl cut in. "That's fine," she said. "We've already got pictures and all the information we need, don't we, Officer Udel? If you think of anything else, you can call it in."

Bobby shot her a look.

Pearl ignored him. "We can call you a cab if you like."

"That's all right," said Mrs. Reed. "I have my car."

Wade said nothing. Pearl ventured a look at him, swallowed up in his dark clothes, staring at the pavement. She tried to imagine him grabbing Amy Nathanson's purse and pushing her to the ground, but he seemed too frail for that. Not to Bobby though. In Bobby's mind, Wade was a known car thief.

"Sergeant reminded me," Udel had told her, his face full of hate. "Two years ago, a kid stole his own mother's vehicle, took it to Red Hook. That kid was Wade Reed."

"All right then, ma'am," Pearl said. "If you need anything else, please call."

Mrs. Reed didn't respond. She just looked into Pearl's eyes and then turned away.

As Pearl headed back to the cruiser with Udel, she thought of those eyes, how very dark they were, like two endless black caves, shielded by black lashes, shades darker than her carefully combed hair. Mrs. Reed and Wade had the same eyes. It was hard to tell what was behind them, but it felt to Pearl like a world of pain.

Once she was at the wheel, Pearl turned to Udel. "She didn't press charges, did she?"

"Huh?"

"When Wade stole her car and took it to Red Hook," Pearl said. "Mrs. Reed didn't press charges."

"Oh. No. She told the sergeant it was all a misunderstanding."

Pearl nodded. "So there's no record. He was never finger-printed."

"No."

She started up the car and pulled out of the parking lot. They drove several blocks without saying a word, the only sounds in the car the engine, the crackle of the police radio, and their breathing.

"I think he did it," Udel said as they neared the station. "I think it was Wade Reed who killed Liam."

"A few hours ago, you were convinced it was Amy Nathanson."

"That was before I knew anything."

"You still don't know anything."

He turned to her, his face starting to flush. "He was at the club with the victim on the same night as the carjacking and he was repeatedly in the area where her car was parked. He posted hostile comments on Liam's girlfriend's Instagram the day Liam died. He has a history of auto theft. And he's a psychotic fuck. I know *all of that*."

"Okay," Pearl said. "But you know that it isn't enough to arrest him, right? I mean . . . I think Wind and Wacksman are working hard. But so far everything you've said—including the psychotic fuck part—none of it amounts to much without witnesses, DNA evidence of some sort, or a confession."

He turned back to the window. They were at the station now. As Pearl pulled into the parking lot in back, she watched Udel out of the corner of her eye, breathing hard, his jaw working. "I want justice," he said. "I want closure."

Closure. That word, which made her think of her brother on the phone, of her father, who apparently wanted closure now, after leaving her to grow up in the home of her mother's older sister—a hoarder, driven crazy from grief. *Closure.* What an impossible thing to want in this messy, chaotic, unfair world. And what a selfish thing, to expect it. Pearl parked the car, staring bullets at Udel. "Take a chill pill, Bobby," she said.

THE TOW TRUCK arrived quickly, and once the driver had hitched up Wade's Corolla and Jackie had filled out all the necessary paperwork and taken down the address of the mechanic, she and Wade headed back to her car. "You want to get breakfast?" she tried.

He shook his head.

"I'll just take you home, then."

He said nothing, which she took for a yes. She started up the car. Her radio was tuned to NPR, so they listened to that—the host of the local morning show interviewing the director of a production of *King Lear* up in Troy. The host's voice grated at her—the way he seemed to chuckle out the words, as though everything was one great big laugh, including tragedy. When the host said, "On the plus side, Lear makes you appreciate your own children," she couldn't take it anymore and flicked off the radio.

They drove in silence for a while until she saw it up ahead: the shrine to Liam, so big and colorful now that, from a distance, it looked like an upended parade float. Wade didn't seem to notice it. He just sat there, long limbed and gangly with his hands clasped, his legs spread, both too big and too small for the seat at the same time—this overgrown thing she'd completely lost control of. "Why did you make that terrible comment on Tamara Hayes's Instagram?"

Wade replied to the floor of the car in a voice so quiet she could barely hear it over the engine. "I deleted it right away. Somebody screenshotted it, I guess."

"Okay. But why did you post it in the first place?"

"I was angry."

"Why?"

She pulled up to the red light and stared at him, that dyed hair flopping in his face, those pale, clasped hands. He smelled of cigarette smoke and weed and everything else he never told her about. "Why?" she said again.

"*I don't know,*" he yelled, loud and sudden as a bomb going off. "*I don't know why I fucking feel anything so stop fucking asking me!*" He put his head in his hands and she kept driving, her heart hammering into her ribs, hands shaking on the wheel, waiting for an apology that didn't come. He scared her. Her own boy scared her. It was the most awful feeling she'd ever had.

Jackie stayed quiet for the rest of the drive home. So did Wade. As he opened the door and got out of the car, Jackie thought, *Lawyer. I have to find a lawyer.* She picked up her phone and started to tap in Helen's number, thinking about Helen's husband, Garrett—calm and steady and a lawyer, a good one. But then she heard the slam of her front door and thought of everything that had happened in the past few days. All of it. She put the phone down and cried.

Seventeen

From the Facebook page of Cody Lerner, aged thirteen. Early comments posted under a video, streamed live from the parking lot at Havenkill High School at 9:00 AM on Monday, October 22.

👍 5 shares; 490 people like this

Brittany Thomas Wait who is that freak?

Ben Lee Murderer

Jack Klein He killed Liam Miller. He was on meth.

Ben Lee Bath salts

Sarah Amanda He does run like a girl lol

Mason Marx fag

Ben Lee Somebody should run *him* over

Dylan Rogers He worships the devil. My cousin goes to the high school and she told me she saw him sacrifice a dog.

Brittany Thomas HE SACRIFICED A DOG?

Dylan Rogers Yep

Mason Marx I heard cat but maybe a dog too.

Eric Jones He was creepin on Liam's girlfriend. He sent her a dick pic.

Brittany Thomas Why did he kill Liam? Was he jealous?

Eric Jones He's crazy. Nobody can figure out what goes on in the brain of a crazy person.

Christa Parker My mom says we have to lock the doors now. We live a block from where Liam got hit. She doesn't think our neighborhood is safe anymore. That's *his* fault.

Mason Marx I'd cut more than his tires.

Brittany Thomas He looks like a perv.

Dylan Rogers he should fry in the chair

Mason Marx I'd waste him myself #GoodGuyWithAGun

Brittany Thomas Who is he??????

Hailey Adams MURDERER

Maddie Riley His name is Wade. He's Connor Reed's brother.

Close to three hundred messages followed. The post was ultimately removed after Wade Reed's mother, Jacqueline, reported it as abusive.

Eighteen

Mason Marx was short and squat, with mean little pig eyes and the personality of bad cheese. He hadn't even gotten his voice change yet, but a lot of kids thought he was hot shit—especially the younger ones. Mason's dad was a big-time record producer who worked in the city and only came up on weekends, and so he was superrich, with a mansion outside of town that had an infinity pool and a screening room, a professional recording studio, and an arsenal of high-tech guns straight out of James Bond. That house was Mason Marx's only redeeming quality, but it worked for him. He had a little group of buddies—seventh graders who would follow him around, agreeing with everything he said and laughing at all his lame jokes. For the school talent show last year, Mason had tried to rap like Jay Z and it was literally the stupidest thing Connor had ever heard, but he'd still gotten a standing ovation.

Mason and Connor didn't have any classes together, mainly because Mason was in all the dumb-kid classes and Connor was in the smart ones, so they rarely crossed paths. But when Noah and Connor tried to get in line at the cafeteria, Mason and his brigade of asshats power walked up to Connor and stood in front of him with crossed arms, not letting him pass.

Noah smiled at them, because Noah smiled at everybody. "What's up, guys?" he said.

But Mason ignored him. His eyes stayed fixed on Connor. "Saw your brother today."

Great. That was just what Connor needed, especially now. More cat-sacrifice stories. He stared straight back into Mason's nasty eyes, because that's what he'd learned to do with kids who mocked his brother. Don't back down. Don't act embarrassed. Act like they're the ones who should be ashamed and wait for them to walk away. "Saw your mother last night," he said.

One of Mason's friends gasped.

"Oh boy," Noah whispered.

But Mason kept staring at Connor, breathing through his nose like a bull. Connor started to feel a little nervous. It wasn't Mason's size—he was bigger than Connor, but in a slow, lumbering way. Connor could probably take him in a fight, but what made him uneasy was the look in his eyes, as if he knew something. Mason licked his lips. "I saw your brother," he said again. "Video of your brother."

"What?"

"You can't hear me?" Mason gave his shoulder a push. "Or are you just a retard?"

"Are you a Satan-worshipper like your brother?" It was one of Mason's buddies who said that, a spiky-haired little dork who looked like an elf.

Connor said, "What video?"

"Yeah," Noah said. "What video?"

"He knows," Mason said.

"No I don't," Connor said, confusion turning to anger.

Mason pushed Connor again. And this time Connor pushed back, hard enough to make him stumble. "It's on, bitch," Mason said.

And then Coach Grady, the gym teacher, came barreling up to the two of them. "You boys cut it out or I'm taking you to the principal's office." He said it too loudly. By now, a group had gathered around them. Grady glared at Mason, then at Connor, as though he was actually trying to figure out who had been in the wrong. "We have a zero tolerance policy here for bullying," he said. "I shouldn't have to tell you that."

"Sorry, coach." Mason Marx nodded at his pathetic crew and the three of them left, the little pointy one purposely bumping into Connor.

Noah started talking fast. "We weren't doing anything, coach, I swear. We were just standing here."

"I saw pushing," Coach Grady said.

Noah said something about Connor's hand "bumping into" Mason's shoulder "by accident," which was about as pathetic an excuse as anything, but that's not what Connor was thinking about. When he'd left, Mason had grabbed Connor's arm when the coach wasn't looking. He'd whispered in his ear. "Your brother's a murderer," he had said. "He killed Liam Miller and everybody knows it."

As they were getting their food, Connor felt eyes on him, dozens of them. Across the cafeteria, he saw Jordan staring straight at him. *A friendly face. Thank God.* But when he smiled and raised a hand, Jordan didn't wave back.

"There's Jordan," Noah said, and started to head toward his table.

Jordan picked up his tray. He left the cafeteria without looking at either one of them.

"What's up with him?" Noah said. But Connor knew. It was the avalanche, closing in.

"AREN'T THEY INVESTIGATING Aimee En?" Helen said. "I mean, honestly. I couldn't imagine any of our kids doing that, least of all Wade. That whole story of hers sounds made-up to me."

They were back at the office, for which Jackie was glad—a reason to be out of the house, the dead quiet of it with Connor still at school and Wade locked in his room, Jackie listening hard for the rustlings within it, just to make sure he was alive. Without asking, she'd made him a grilled cheddar cheese sandwich—his favorite. She'd put it on a plate with a pickle slice and some potato chips and a note that read "I believe in you" and left it on the kitchen table because she wanted to believe in him. She needed to. "I assume they are looking into Aimee En," she said. "They're looking into everything."

"I am so sorry about Wade's car, honey."

"So do you think Garrett can represent him? I'm hoping it doesn't come to that. But if the cops want to question him again."

Helen's phone rang. She held up a finger and answered it—a potential client. Jackie knew before Helen said very much because she was speaking to the caller in her professional voice, smoother and slower than the one she used in real life, the voice of an on-air shrink from a radio call-in program. After she finished the call, Helen turned to Jackie. "He's not a defense lawyer."

"I know that. I'd just rather have someone I can trust."

Helen exhaled. "I'm sure he'll be able to," she said. "But I don't think it will be necessary."

"I hope not."

"Look," Helen said. "I know this is tough, but you're in the worst of it now. The truth will come out soon, and you'll look back on today and think, *Thank God that's over.* I know that, Jackie. I know it with all my heart."

"Why?"

"Because life only gives us as much as we can take."

Jackie looked at Helen, her coiffed, cared-for hair, her skin dewy and unlined even at their age from regular facials in the city and so very little stress. In youth and in adulthood, Helen had been blessed with a happy family, a lovely home, friends who adored and supported her. She'd never had to worry about money, never lost a loved one. Hell, she'd never even broken up with anyone, and so of course she believed in something as simple and childlike as the fairness of life. *Ask someone living on the street if they've only gotten what they can take. Ask Sheila and Chris Miller.*

Jackie was annoyed with Helen, who seemed to sense it. She turned back to her keyboard, began clicking away. "We used to listen to Aimee En," she said.

"Yep."

"Remember those racy songs of hers? Those outfits she wore in her music videos? The drug busts? She's no angel."

Jackie bit her lip. She remembered Stacy's face at the assembly, that look she'd given a mother who believed life had a way of working out the way it should, that good always won in the end, that grief was not worth missing school over and only temporary, even if it crushed you. "Please talk to Garrett," she said.

THE MILLERS' HOUSE was huge, palatial even. It reminded Amy of a mansion she'd been to in Holmby Hills once back in the day—the home of a music-industry exec whose name she could no longer remember. She and Vic had gone to a party there as guests of Rodney Bingenheimer on an L.A. night when the hot Santa Ana winds kicked up her short skirt as she stood on the doorstep, a night that now seemed like centuries ago, a different lifetime.

Amy had been invited here. Sheila Miller had contacted her via Facebook Messenger last night, giving her the address and asking her to *please stop by tomorrow if it isn't too much trouble.* (So very polite, these people with old money.) Amy had said yes, of course, arranging for Jacinta and settling on a time before hopping into her rental car. But on the whole ride over she'd felt this terrible apprehension, as though the invitation were a trap. And even now, she couldn't quite shake that feeling. She knew what people were saying about her. She'd read TMZ, and she was sure Sheila had too. Who didn't read TMZ? Her knees weakened, just thinking about those comments, the idea of Sheila reading them and taking them to heart.

Amy hesitated before pressing the doorbell. She considered making a run for it and messaging Sheila some excuse—a sudden cold, an issue with Vic—before she noticed the security cameras aimed at her and realized that the visit was already documented. There was no turning back.

She made herself push the bell and heard footsteps approaching, a female voice saying "One minute" that she assumed belonged to the housekeeper. But the woman who opened the door was Sheila, no housekeeper in sight. Amy recognized her from the pictures on her Facebook page, for she and Sheila were Facebook friends now, privy to each other's memories, the musings of each other's friends. *Whoever is responsible for your dear son's death, I hope he or she is brought to justice,* someone had posted on Sheila's wall today. And in the comments, someone else had responded simply: *She.*

Amy cringed. She told herself to stop thinking.

Sheila Miller looked so different in tragedy than she did in the glorious pictures on her Facebook page. Her chiseled, patrician features seemed gaunt in person, free of makeup or filter or a summer tan. Her highlighted hair was dull and unwashed, and though she wore jeans with a flattering cut and an expensive-looking cashmere sweater in a lush royal blue, it all seemed like something she'd thrown on moments ago—a last-ditch effort to look "presentable."

"Thank you for coming," Sheila said.

Amy hugged Sheila. She smelled too heavily of lily of the valley—perfume thrown on quickly rather than carefully applied. And she seemed more to lean into the hug than reciprocate it. "I'm sorry," Amy said into Sheila's neck. "I'm so, so, sorry."

"I know," she said, once she pulled away. "For some reason, it makes me feel a little better, just meeting you in person."

"I'm glad."

"Come with me."

They were standing in a great room with wooden floors and a crystal chandelier over their heads. The floors gleamed furiously and smelled of pine. There had to be a housekeeper around here somewhere, Amy decided. Sheila couldn't be keeping this clean all by herself, especially in her grief.

She followed Sheila down a hallway and into a parlor—a room with antique furniture and red silk wallpaper that looked as though it had been plucked from another era. Sheila sat on a straight-backed chair with clawed feet and gestured at a love seat, also in red silk and adorned with two adorable needlepoint pillows. She told Amy to make herself comfortable. "Chris is napping right now, I'm afraid," Sheila said. "But I know he sends his best."

There was a coffee table of dark polished wood with a marble top, a tray of cookies at the center next to a teapot, two white china cups, and a stack of linen napkins the same blue as Sheila's sweater. Amy sat down, her gaze traveling from Sheila's haggard face to the small, cold fireplace, the framed photos on the mantel—almost all of them of Liam. "He was your only child," Amy said.

Sheila nodded. "Would you like a cookie?"

"No thank you," Amy said, that uneasiness again creeping through her. She started to ask why Sheila had contacted her— the one question she hadn't wanted to ask, as it almost sounded accusing—but then Sheila spoke.

"People have been telling me they think you did it."

Amy's heart dropped. "Excuse me?"

"A lot of people," she said. "My friends. They think you ran over Liam and drove away. Just yesterday, a very close friend of mine was saying that you probably panicked and, knowing you'd be arrested for a hit-and-run, drove your car into the Kill to get rid of any traces of Liam that may have been on it. Blood. Tissue." She pushed a lock of hair behind her ear, an odd smile crossing her face. "Can you believe someone actually said that to me?"

"No," Amy said quietly. "That's a thoughtless thing to say."

"They say you were probably drunk, that you walked all the way from the Kill to the police station, and it was that long walk in the cold and rain that sobered you up."

Amy's cheeks heated up. She knew they were flushing red and she hated herself for that, the way her body was betraying her. Last night, she'd driven to the shrine and knelt at it and begged Liam's forgiveness. In preparation for today, she'd let herself sob it out, the horror of that night, the guilt, until there was nothing left inside her. She had hoped it would stay that way. "I wasn't drunk," Amy said, which sounded evasive. She tried again. "When I wrote you about what happened, I was telling the truth."

Sheila plucked one of the cookies from the tray—a powdery little thing that looked like a puff of smoke. She brought it to her lips and took the tiniest of bites, then carefully spread out one of the linen napkins and placed the cookie on top—a painfully slow ritual that seemed to have nothing to do with eating. "I asked you here because I wanted to look you in the eye," she said. "When I look people in the eye, I can always tell whether they're lying."

Amy nodded, unsure of what to say next.

Sheila poured tea into the two cups and handed one to Amy, who raised it to her lips, the cool white china unexpectedly soothing. The tea was delicious and tasted of gingerbread, and Amy had the fleeting, shameful thought that maybe Sheila was drugging her. "I'm not a liar," she said, her voice shaking slightly. "I wasn't drunk, and I would never, ever drive away after hitting your son or anyone."

"Tell me how it happened again."

"I was driving home from my gig—"

"No," she said. "No, please. Just the part with Liam."

Amy took another sip of tea and found Sheila's eyes with her own. She didn't want to be here. She hated being asked to relive that night, especially that part of that night. But Sheila Miller's grief trumped her own discomfort. It trumped everything, really. For all Amy had lost in her life, she'd never had a child to lose, and sharing a room with Sheila Miller, she felt grateful for that. "Liam came from out of nowhere," she said. "I was on the pavement— the carjacker had pushed me. I had been yelling and screaming and I thought no one would come, but there he was. He was calling out to the boy driving. He was yelling at him to stop. I think he knew him. I feel like he must have. But whether he knew him or not, his bravery was beyond my comprehension."

Sheila put her cup down. She wiped a tear from her eye.

"He ran for the car, Sheila. I was on the pavement, and he rushed right at it, waving his arms."

"Oh . . ."

"He was trying to save me, to save my car. He was willing to risk his own life in order to do a good deed for a stranger."

"He was a good boy." Sheila said it almost like a question.

"He was exceptional. He was a hero." Tears sprung into Amy's eyes. She wiped her face, her hand now streaked black from mascara, but she left the stains for fear of staining a lovely linen napkin, her stained hand blurring in front of her eyes from more tears, a flood of them.

Sheila stood up. She moved over to where Amy was sitting. Amy stood up too—another strange, shameful idea entering in her mind that Sheila was about to slap her across the face. But that didn't happen. Sheila took Amy in her arms and the two of them hugged each other for quite some time, the first and last women to see Liam Miller alive, Amy staining Sheila's beautiful sweater with her black, guilty tears. *If I hadn't played that gig. If I hadn't gone home with that couple . . .*

When they finally pulled apart, Sheila took a breath. "I didn't even know Liam was out that night," she said.

"You didn't?"

"I'd thought he was at home in bed, right up until we got the call from the hospital. As much as my heart's been broken by this, I've been so angry at him too. Furious at him for sneaking out. Do you know what I mean? I keep scolding him in my mind. I keep saying, 'See what happens when you go out walking at night?' He didn't even take his car."

Amy wasn't sure where she was going with this, but she nodded anyway. Sheila had an odd look in her eyes, as though something behind them had come undone. "But now, after hearing this story, I think maybe it was a calling. Like . . . he knew someone was in trouble, and so he was just pulled there, by an unseen force."

Amy had seen the same look in Vic's eyes when his mother passed away. "She keeps sending me signs," he'd said. And the "signs" had been everywhere: stray pennies, birds on the ledge outside their bedroom window, an unexpected rain shower. In his mind, everything was significant.

This type of thing happened with many people, she had heard—a type of temporary insanity in response to grief. A very specific type of magical thinking, though she hadn't been close enough to her own parents to experience it herself. Amy put a hand on Sheila's shoulder, and for a few seconds, she felt as though she were talking to Vic—not when his mother had passed away, for that was years ago, when he was all there otherwise and he was still deep down a self-absorbed jerk. No, she felt as though she were talking to the Vic of today, that poor, weak creature, undeserving of a single negative thought. Guilt tugged at her again, but she yanked herself away. Sheila's feelings were more important. "I think you're right," she said.

Sheila asked if she could stay for dinner, and Amy said yes. Of course she did.

CONNOR DIDN'T KNOW how he would have gotten through the rest of the day without Noah. And even with Noah by his side throughout all his classes telling him nothing was wrong, that people were just acting weird since Liam's death, that was all, Connor felt strange. Paranoid, as though the whole rest of the school were in on some awful secret—even the teachers—and it was printed out in a bubble above his head. That was the way everyone was looking at him, anyway. And as much as Noah tried to tell him otherwise, he knew he wasn't imagining it.

He was riding home on his bike when he saw Liam's shrine, so big and bright now it was noticeable from blocks away. Connor's impulse was to avoid it, but where did that impulse come from? He could hear Mason Marx in his mind again, back in the cafeteria, the skin-crawl of Mason's breath in his ear. *Your brother's a murderer.* And even as he pedaled, his knees felt weak. What if it was true? he wondered. *No, it can't be true. No way is Wade what Mason says he is. Stop thinking that way.*

Stop thinking.

As he neared the shrine, Connor saw Jordan Hayes standing on the street corner, taking pictures of it with his phone. His heart sank. He'd seen Jordan a few times today—in math class, gym. He'd also passed him in the hallway. And each time, Jordan had responded to him in the same bizarre way—looking directly at him, and then through him, as though he wasn't there at all. Jordan had even said hi to Noah once, without giving Connor so much as a nod.

Once he was within a block of the shrine, Connor's plan was to turn up Flower and take the back roads to his house, to do it before Jordan put down his phone and saw him coming. But his legs kept pumping the pedals, handlebars aimed straight ahead, his brain telling him to face the music, whatever that was supposed to mean. But still. Confronting Jordan had to feel better than the way he was feeling right now. At least he'd have answers, right?

"Hey," he called out.

Jordan didn't say anything, didn't even turn to Connor until he
was inches away and there was no avoiding him and even then,
the look he gave him, it was as if Connor was something his dog
had just thrown up.

"What the hell is your deal, Jordan?"

Jordan started to get back on his bike, but Connor grabbed the
handlebar. "This isn't fair," he said. "We're friends. Why are you
acting so weird?"

Jordan exhaled hard. He glanced up and down the street. "You
know why," he said. "You've got to know why."

"Is it because of what Mason Marx is saying? He's full of crap.
You know that."

"I don't care about Mason Marx." He started to get on his bike
again, but Connor wouldn't let go of the handlebar. "Get away
from me."

Connor's heart pounded. "Just tell me what's going on," he
said. "Please."

Jordan peered at him. "You seriously don't know," he said.
"You're not just shitting me?"

"Don't know what?"

Jordan whispered something under his breath, something
Connor couldn't quite hear, but he didn't want to ask him to re-
peat it. "Don't know what?" Connor said again, his voice more
pleading than he wanted it to be.

Jordan started messing with his phone. "If I show you, will you
leave me alone?"

"Show me what?"

"You have to promise."

"Fine," Connor said. "Whatever. Fine."

Jordan handed him the phone: a screenshot glowered at him.
A series of direct messages on Tamara Hayes's Instagram. "My

sister sent these to me and my parents and all her friends," Jordan said as Connor stared at the screen. "Everybody's seen it now. He's in trouble. Wade. She's blocked him and reported him and she's never gonna unblock him. No matter what you say."

Connor scrolled down the screen, his eyes dry and itchy from not blinking. Message after message after message. All from Wade's Instagram. Each one of them in all caps. Angrier and angrier, and yet Tamara hadn't answered a single one, and so it wasn't her fault. Nothing could have caused it other than Wade's own anger, building on itself until it turned to rage. *HATE YOU . . . THE FUCK IS YOUR PROBLEM . . . GET WHAT YOU DESERVE . . . DIE.*

Connor could feel Jordan watching him as he read. *None of this sounds like him,* he wanted to say. *These couldn't have been sent by Wade.* But he didn't know that, not anymore. He tried to let the words blur, the ugliness of them, focusing instead on the times the messages had been sent. But in many ways, that was even worse. All had been sent around noontime, a minute apart at the most. *SHOW THAT SHIT TO PEOPLE AND THINK YOU CAN GET AWAY WITH IT YOU FUCKING BITCH . . .*

"Someone trashed your brother's car," Jordan said. "He took it out on Tamara."

"*Why?*"

"Because he's batshit."

Connor's head was swimming. He couldn't think. This all felt like a weird dream he was stuck in, one of those dreams he used to have when he was little where he was trapped in a room with a monster—that razor-toothed, drooling alien from the movie Wade had let him watch without Mom knowing—and the teeth were edging closer, snapping open and shut and Connor couldn't move a muscle.

"Tamara was the one who always stuck up for Wade with Liam and Ryan and those guys," Jordan said. "She told them all they should give Wade a chance, because I was friends with you."

"Was?"

"When Liam got killed, all her friends were saying Wade Reed did it. He must have done it. And she said no way. Both she and I said no way would Wade do that. He's weird but not in a dangerous way and he isn't a murderer. That's what both of us were telling everybody."

"They were all saying that?"

"Why do you think I was doing that whole investigation thing, Connor? Why do you think I was at the scene of the crime in the freezing cold and listening in to the cops and trying to find evidence against . . . gangstas or what's-her-face with the weird hair or anybody but Wade? For extra credit? For my freakin' *health*?"

Connor stared at him.

"Give me back my phone."

Connor did. "Do you think he did it? You really think Wade killed Liam?"

Jordan looked away. He got on his bike. "My mom says I can't be friends with you anymore."

What does somebody say to that? There's nothing anybody can say.

"Why did Wade have to go and do that?" Jordan said, very quietly. "Why did he have to be so mean to my sister?" And then he rode away.

CONNOR PEDALED THE rest of the way home, his mind numb, the cold air the only thing keeping his legs moving, that movement the only thing keeping him upright. He thought of the phone in the plastic bag again, and Wade in his room late at night, wet from the storm. He thought of Wade's car stopped outside Liam's house just yesterday and the way he'd stared it down—staring down a bunch of mourners, revving his engine at them—and how very strange Wade had become in the past few months especially. He tried to think about last night and the night before, the nice, normal dinner conversations he and Mom had been having with Wade, but that didn't prove anything. It just made him feel worse.

Sometimes when he finished his homework but Mom thought he was still working on it, Connor would go onto Reddit and read the crime threads. He'd read one once about a serial killer called John Wayne Gacy, who had a job and a family and dressed as a clown at kids' birthday parties. Someone had posted an article on the thread. It was all about sociopaths, how many people knew them as personable and kind, but that was only because they were so adept at mimicking that behavior. They were like robots, really, able to program themselves to act a certain way, but without the emotions to back up those actions. Without a conscience.

By the time he reached his home, his head was throbbing and he wanted to throw up. His mom's car wasn't outside and neither was Wade's, and he felt a moment of relief—at least he'd be alone. Until he remembered that of course Wade's car wasn't there. It had been trashed by someone who blamed him for Liam's death.

Connor got off his bike and started to wheel it toward the front door, feeling more alone than he'd ever felt in his life. His only friend now was Noah, and Noah would only stay his friend if he didn't talk about Wade.

He took out his phone and debated texting Noah anyway, asking him if he wanted to play video games, but then he wondered if maybe Jordan had shown Noah those direct messages too. *What the hell were you thinking, Wade? If you're going to be a sociopath, why can't you be a good one?*

Anger and fear battled it out in Connor's mind as he headed up the walkway, and then he heard a car pull up on the road behind him, a man's voice calling out his name. Connor turned and saw a police car and fear won. Big time.

"Hey there, young man. Is your name Connor?" The officer said it through his open window, a smile on his face that did nothing to calm his nerves. He was young and strong-looking. Like a college football player or something, only in a uniform. All Connor could think of was the cop who had shown up at their front door on Saturday morning. The gun in his holster.

Connor wished his mom was home. "Yeah," he said.

"Great," said the cop, his smile growing so wide, Connor could see all his teeth. "I'm Officer Udel with the Havenkill Police. Can I talk to you for a few minutes, please?"

Nineteen

From the Facebook page of Liam Miller.

Ryan Grant ▶ Liam Miller

October 22 at 3:00 AM

You were just in my dream. We were in Rhinecliff at the train station because we were going to go to the city, and all of a sudden you jumped onto the tracks and started running. I said, "Liam, don't do that. You'll die." But you just laughed. "I can't die," you said. And you just kept running. I saw the train rushing at you and I tried to yell, to warn you, but no sound came out. I was frozen.

And then the train turned into a giant shark and it opened its big toothy mouth and swallowed you whole. I yelled myself awake. Well, barely awake. I'm still half asleep and I feel like I'm trapped in the dream. Because I am. There are some things you never wake up from.

If I die tonight, will I see you, Liam? Will you be waiting in a shaft of light, like in the movies, telling me not to be afraid, telling me how death is some special place where you can be young forever—and how this is fair, what happened to you, that there is meaning and a reason? Or am I just typing words on a screen that don't mean anything at all? I'm scared that's true. I'm so scared, Liam.

PS Right before I woke up, the shark's eye turned back into a train window. I saw the face of the conductor.

This post was deleted fifty seconds later. Though he'd posted on social media that he planned on going to the assembly in the morning, Ryan Grant was marked absent from school that day.

Twenty

Pearl was at Club Halifax, halfway through her first Scotch, when her phone buzzed. She glanced at the screen: *S'up?* Paul. She smiled a little, the alcohol warming her cheeks, unwinding the knots at the back of her neck. *Most persistent one-night stand ever.* But really her mind was elsewhere. Leaving the station at the end of her shift, she'd met Liam Miller's closest friends.

There had been three of them standing in the front room with Udel—two big, strapping boys obviously from the football team and a leaner, class-president type, all of them with shaved heads, like soldiers from the same regiment. "They did it after school," Udel had explained. "In memory of Liam. A lot of the senior guys did."

Udel had rested a hand on the class president's shoulder, but Pearl hadn't recognized him as his cousin until he introduced him. Ryan Grant looked so different at the station than he had that night at the pool, and it wasn't just for the lack of his dark, wavy hair. "It was Ryan's idea," he said, his cousin cringing at the attention. "Tonsure. Shaving the head as a sign of mourning. It's a Hindu thing. He learned about it in AP religion class, right, buddy?"

"Yeah." Ryan didn't seem to recognize Pearl either, and so Pearl had just left it that way and said nice to meet you—a do-over of sorts.

"What were you guys here for?" she'd asked.

Again, it had been Udel who'd spoken for all three of them. "Questioning," he had said. "They came in to talk with the detectives. They want to do anything they can to help Liam. It was their idea."

There had been something in his tone Pearl didn't like—a spiked-up, coercive quality that made her miss the lazy Bobby Udel of yore. *If it was their idea*, she had wanted to ask, *why are you doing all the talking?*

A wind kicked up outside the bar, which reminded Pearl of the gusts that had hit the station when she was shaking hands with the boys, a sudden barrage of wind like back talk from the sky, the thin walls whistling from it. She glanced at Paul's text again. Maybe another storm was starting. She should get home before it became too tough to drive. Get home and in bed.

She thought about texting Paul back. What harm could it do, really, when he'd offered her nothing but douchy *S'up* texts since he'd left her apartment? Maybe the specialness of their postcoital conversation had all been in her mind, with Pearl projecting depth into it because she hardly ever had decent conversations with anyone. She could barely remember what he'd said to her anyway. It couldn't have been as good as the sex.

She typed: *Hey.* Sent it.

Back at the station, Ryan Grant's eyes had been tear-bruised and vacant, his jaw slack, the rosiness drained out of his cheeks. Such a handsome kid and obviously popular, but his most noticeable

feature had been his sadness. In that way, he may as well have been
Wade Reed. Pearl finished the rest of her whiskey, hanging on to
the burn of it. Joy sauntered over with the bottle. "Thinking cop
thoughts?"

"Kind of," said Pearl, who had never told Joy she was a cop.
Apparently, she hadn't needed to.

Joy said, "You want a refill?"

Pearl glanced at her texts. Paul hadn't answered yet. He'd most
likely moved on. "Yeah, thanks so much." She said it as though
she were a guest in Joy's house and didn't have to pay for the
drink. She really needed to find herself some actual friends.

Joy poured Pearl a long one and peered up and down the
bar needlessly. Again, the place was practically empty. A trio of
middle-aged Hudson Valley good ol' boys in hunting jackets sat at
one end of the bar, a hipster couple at the other, all five of them
nursing draft beers. How did this place even stay open?

Joy said, "You're from Havenkill, aren't you?"

Pearl looked at her. "How did you know that?"

"Aimee En," she said. "I follow local news on social media, and
she and that poor kid have been all over my Twitter feed since
this morning."

"She's famous again," Pearl said.

"Tons of pictures of her from back in the day, right next to the
ones where they're dragging her car out of the Kill and she's crying." Joy smirked. "She's bigger than the Psychedelic Furs cover
band now."

"I don't think this is the kind of publicity she was hoping for."

"You didn't see her set," she said. "The woman is thirsty."

Pearl looked at her.

"So did she run over that boy and lie about it?"

"You're asking me?"

"You're a cop. You know."

Pearl raised the glass to her lips. "I'm a uniformed cop from Havenkill. I get cats out of trees." She took a long swallow.

"You were asking me about her," Joy said, "and that boy who was at her show. Obviously, you were investigating."

"Your memory is too good."

"It happened last night. And I wasn't drunk."

"I really don't know anything," Pearl said. It was the truth. Pearl thought of Wade, how close to certain she'd been that he'd staked out Amy's car and followed her. But after meeting him in person, she wasn't so sure anymore. It was hard to explain. The boy Amy described had been actively looking for trouble, but Wade Reed wasn't that type of boy. He was someone whom trouble found and pounced on without his asking for it. Pearl was certain of that, because when it comes to being that type of unfortunate person, it takes one to know one.

"I used to work in Poughkeepsie," Pearl said. "A lot more challenging there for a uniformed cop."

"Is that why you moved to Havenkill?"

It was the obvious question. After all, who wouldn't prefer rescuing cats from trees to patrolling a town with a population of just thirty thousand yet one of the highest crime rates in the country? Still, Pearl found it irritating, not just because it supposed something of her that wasn't true, but also because it made her remember a whole bunch of things she didn't want to: The stares in the women's locker room. The way her partner went completely silent on her, even during long stakeouts, as though he were on strike. The envelope taped to her locker, containing a Mother's Day card and a bullet. Good investigators in Poughkeepsie, she'd give them that, though whoever had spread the news had gotten her age wrong at the time of the murder.

When her partner finally confronted her about it, he was convinced she'd been a teen and had shot her mother dead because she wouldn't allow her to date an older man. Juicier story, she supposed.

"No," Pearl said. "That wasn't why I moved."

Joy nodded slowly. She was a good enough bartender to stop asking questions.

One of the hipsters asked her for a refill, and so Joy headed over to the end of the bar, leaving Pearl alone. She checked her phone. Still nothing from Paul. She was disappointed, and she hated herself for that. Later, she'd go onto her hookup app and look for another douchebag—hopefully one who had no ability to speak.

She took another swallow of her drink, and then Joy was back. "Somebody tweeted that you guys are getting close to making an arrest."

Pearl shook her head, thinking, *We'd better not be.* "Whoever tweeted that is wrong."

"If it's between Amy and that Wade kid, I'd put my money on her."

"It isn't."

Joy started to walk away again. Pearl took another swallow but realized she no longer felt like drinking alone. "Wait," she said. "Why?"

"Because I know boys. And that kid didn't fix his driver's license like that because he wanted to get drunk and steal a car."

"Why did he do it then?"

"He was in love. He was all excited about meeting some girl in this place, and it wasn't Aimee En." She plucked her phone out of her pocket, glanced at the screen. "He was in love," she said again. "It was obvious."

"Well, nothing's really obvious," Pearl said. "We all think we can read other people's thoughts and they can't read ours. Because we're all so much more complicated than the rest of the world. Please. The truth is, nobody knows anybody."

"Beg to differ. I knew you were a cop the minute you walked in."

Pearl rolled her eyes. "That was just a good guess."

"And what about Aimee En?" Joy said it to her screen. "What did I say about her?"

"You said she's thirsty."

Joy held her phone out. "This is the latest picture on her Twitter feed."

Pearl looked at it: a selfie, taken with an exhausted-looking blonde in an expensive sweater. Amy had used a filter so thick, the photo looked as though it had been taken underwater, but after a few seconds, Pearl recognized the blond woman from pool-hopping night. She read the accompanying tweet: *With my beautiful soul sister, Sheila Miller. Tragedy has brought us together. #darkestbeforedawn #heroine #blessed.*

"So?" Joy said. "What do you think?"

Pearl shook her head, her suspicions of Amy coming back to life, blooming. "I think that you're a good judge of character," she said.

CELIA RILEY, WHOSE youngest daughter, Maddie, was in Connor's class, was a relatively new client of Jackie's, a seller. They'd met in early September, at one of the monthly Women's Networking Breakfasts held at Brighton's Café on Orchard, and they'd hit it off instantly, with Celia telling Jackie she couldn't think of a better agent to put her house on the market. Jackie had given Celia's house the once-over and liked what she saw: a modern ranch with hardwood floors and a sparkling new kitchen that included an enormous marble-topped island, a Sub-Zero fridge, and a gourmet gas range. Together, they'd decided not much work was needed at all. Celia and her husband, Greg, took out a loan to spruce up their two and a half bathrooms anyway, and once that was complete, Jackie had scheduled an open house, set to take place Saturday. So when she saw Celia's number on the caller ID screen of her private line at work, it wasn't unexpected. "Looking forward?"

"Hi, Jackie," Celia said.

Jackie didn't like the tone in her voice.

"Listen. I'm really sorry, but Greg and I have decided to switch agents."

Jackie's heart sank. "What?" She'd already had signs made, taken out an ad in the local paper. The open house was on the home page of the Potter Bloom Web site. "If there's any problem you guys have with the way I'm handling your listing, I'd be happy to talk things over."

"It's nothing against you. You've been wonderful. We just don't think it's going to work out, you know, what with everything going on."

"Excuse me?"

"Maddie showed us a few things online."

Jackie's heart sank. "What do you mean?" she asked. But she knew. Maybe not specifics, but she didn't need specifics after this morning. "You're doing this because of Wade."

"I wish you and your sons the very best." Celia said it in a way that made Jackie feel as though she were sinking into quicksand with the whole world standing around her, watching and pointing and doing nothing to help. "You are in my thoughts and prayers."

"Wade didn't do anything wrong. He would never hurt anyone. He's being attacked unfairly. He's just a *boy*."

Jackie paused to catch her breath and realized the line was dead. Celia had hung up, taking her thoughts and prayers along with her. "Great." Jackie hung up the phone. She put her head in her hands and rubbed her eyes, wishing she were alone, just so she could scream. When she lifted her head, Jackie noticed a strange silence in the room, the feel of people watching her.

"It's okay, honey," Helen said.

But when she looked around the office, Jackie saw that it wasn't okay at all. The two other agents on floor time today were a usually genial retired couple named Marty and Beth. Both sat at their desks, watching her with narrowed eyes. Jackie recalled how they hadn't greeted her when they'd come in to work the way they usually did, how they'd directed their hellos to Helen, rather than herself. She said, "What are you both looking at?"

Beth spotted something fascinating through the window. Marty busied himself with his cell phone.

"Amazing," she said. And then Jackie heard her own name— her boss, Zane Bloom, standing outside of his office, asking her to come in.

Jackie got up and walked across the room, her face burning, each click of her heels on the wood floor echoing. Zane gave her a pained smile as he ushered her in and closed the door behind her. Not a good sign. Zane never closed his door.

Jackie started to sit down, but Zane held up a hand. "Listen, sweetheart," he said. "This doesn't have to be a long conversation. I just think it would be best for you to take a couple of days off."

She stared at him—the slight tremor in his upper lip, the dabs of sweat just above his tortoiseshell glasses. Zane was not a confrontational guy. He never had been in her ten years of knowing him, and so this wasn't easy for him, she could tell. And if anything, that only made her more furious, the idea that he'd had to push himself to be so blatantly unfair. "Can I ask why?"

"You know how people get in this town."

She said, "I do now."

"I've been getting phone calls, Jackie. Concerned citizens. Someone said Wade's been questioned by the police."

"Who said that?"

"People. Lots of them."

"You can't give me names," she said. "You're giving them anonymity, even though I've worked here for more than ten years."

"It doesn't matter who they are. What matters is, we're a business and we cater to the community. I can't have this type of disruption. I've started hearing from reporters."

"Reporters?" Her eyes widened. "Reporters have been calling you about me?"

"About your son, yes. And about you."

"My God." Jackie shook her head. She wanted to say more, but she couldn't find the words.

"You understand, don't you, Jackie?" He moved back toward the door and opened it. "You've got to understand."

It sounded like an order: *You've got to understand. There's no other choice.* And Jackie supposed there wasn't, not really. She moved back through the office and to her desk, the back of her neck sweat-slicked, determined not to look at Marty or Beth as she passed.

How things had changed since Liam Miller's death. Since this morning even, when Jackie had gotten dressed and driven to Wade's school, hoping she would see Sheila and Chris Miller at the assembly so that she might pay her respects.

"Everything okay?" Helen whispered.

Jackie still couldn't speak. There was only one personal item on her desk: a framed photograph of Connor and Wade, taken five years ago at the Potter Bloom picnic, both of them sun-dappled and laughing, their arms around Zane Bloom's golden retriever. The picture had been sitting there since it was taken—a fixture. For years, Jackie hadn't paid it much attention, but now it seemed to mock her. Those two happy faces, unaware of what they would grow up to be.

When did Wade lose those dimples?

Jackie picked up the photograph and dropped it in her purse.

"No," Helen said.

"You want to walk me to my car?"

"You're not leaving here."

"Just for a few days." Jackie kept her voice smooth and forced a cheery smile, well aware of Marty and Beth. "Just a little break. Walk with me."

Helen waited until they were outside to speak. "It's like the entire world has gone insane." She started to say more, but Jackie stopped her.

"I need Garrett now."

"You don't. This will blow over. It has to. This is ridiculous."

Jackie looked at Helen, at the pink sky behind her—another perfect autumn sunset easing in. She thought of Wade this afternoon, how unresponsive he'd been with the police, the way he'd yelled at her, that anger.

"Wade didn't do it," Helen said. "That's just a fact. The facts will win."

Jackie looked at her, that calm certainty in those pretty, even features, that stubborn kindness. Wade had always liked Helen. He'd always been able to talk to her. When he was younger, Jackie had even suspected he had a bit of a crush on her, and it was easy to see why. Helen looked at you like this and you saw the world the way she did and it was lovely. Unless, that is, you knew better. "He was out that night," Jackie said.

"What?"

"The same night Liam was hit, Wade was out. He admitted it to me, but he refused to say where he was."

Helen started shaking her head. "That doesn't mean anything. There were lots of people out that night. Heck, I was out that night at some point. We ran out of milk and—"

"He was out, Helen, at that exact hour. He threw his wet clothes in the dryer and dried them, and he never does that. I looked at his phone and found a photograph, taken from the inside of a car, around the same time Liam was hit."

Helen blinked. "You looked at his phone?" she said, which of course was beside the point, but Jackie understood. She said nothing for a while, watching Helen sort it out in her mind.

"Helen," she said finally. "We need a lawyer."

"You go home. I'll call Garrett," she said. "I'll call him right away."

CONNOR STAYED OFF his phone. He ignored his Facebook, Instagram, and Snapchat—easy to do, considering any messages he was getting today were probably ones he didn't want to see. After the cop left and he went into his house, Connor did his math homework, drew Magic Marker charts on big pieces of white poster board for his and Noah's science project; then he went into the den and played Minecraft for more than an hour, even though Minecraft had been boring him lately—anything he could do to forget what he'd seen today, what he now knew.

It was hard to concentrate on the game, though. He couldn't forget. In fact, Connor couldn't stop thinking of that stream of direct messages Jordan had shown him and of his brother down the hallway, behind his closed bedroom door, thinking his weird angry thoughts without ever coming out or even making a sound. Wade, who had made Connor promise to forget Friday night had ever happened, who expected loyalty from him without giving so much as an explanation in return. *Think about it*, Connor told himself. Wade might very well have killed Liam Miller. And he was ruining Connor's life. He didn't deserve that type of loyalty.

When he couldn't take it any longer, Connor got up from the couch. He headed down the hallway to his brother's room, that anger rushing through him, lava in his veins. He pounded on Wade's door.

"Just a second," Wade said.

He answered at least ten seconds later, rubbing his eyes. "I didn't know you were home."

"It's like five PM," Connor said. "Why wouldn't I be home?"

"I fell asleep."

"Oh."

"You hear about my car?"

"Yeah," Connor said, anger rising again. "I heard about your car."

"Sucks."

"Why did you go psycho, Wade?"

Wade frowned. "What are you talking about?"

"Tamara Hayes."

"You mean that one comment on her Instagram? I deleted it like five seconds later."

"Not one comment," Connor said. "A rant. A messed-up, insane, psycho-killer direct message rant that may as well have come from Michael Myers. You're lucky she didn't call the cops on you."

"What?"

"Why did you do it, Wade? Why do you do any of the shit you do? Do you have any idea how hard my life is because of you? Jordan was one of my best friends, but you went and you fucked that up just like you fuck up everything."

"What are you talking about?"

"I don't have any friends because of you!"

"I didn't do anything!"

Connor stared at him.

"I didn't send any direct messages to Tamara," he said. "I've been asleep since I got home." Wade's eyes were clear, unblinking and so obviously confused . . . Connor's stomach dropped.

"Someone sent Tamara a bunch of weird-assed messages from your Instagram."

"Why would somebody do that?" Wade said. "Everybody likes Tamara."

"To make you look bad," Connor said slowly. "To make everybody hate you."

"Whatever," he said.

"You don't care?"

"My tires got slashed today. I got called into Penny's office and questioned by cops. There was so much fucking hate speech on my Facebook page, I wound up shutting the whole page down. This shit with Tamara is just more of the same."

Connor took a step closer. He watched his face. "Why does everybody think you killed Liam?"

"I don't know."

"Where were you that night?"

Wade gave Connor a long look—half evasive, half pissed at him for asking. Then he cocked his head to one side, as though he wasn't sure how to play it. "I don't need to tell anybody where I was," he said, finally. "If other people want to believe shit about me, that isn't my problem. It's theirs."

He headed for the kitchen, and Connor followed him, guilt tugging at him so hard his chest felt constricted. He could barely breathe. Before coming into the house, he'd gotten into the front seat of the cop car. He'd told Officer Udel about Wade in his room in the middle of the night. He'd told him about the bag Wade had left in Connor's closet, how he'd thrown it out at the Lukoil station, how he was 99 percent sure that it had contained a phone.

"You've been super-helpful, Connor," Officer Udel had said. "You've done us a great service."

"I was so mad earlier when I found my car," Wade said. "I felt like I wanted to break things. But then I realized something. If I freak out, if I break things, then they win."

On the kitchen counter was an uneaten grilled cheese sandwich, chips, a wedge of pickle. Wade took the plate to the kitchen table, sat down, and took a bite. "Lunch note," he said, pointing to a folded-up piece of notebook paper. "Remember how Mom used to put those in our lunch boxes all the time?"

Connor nodded, a lump in his throat. He watched Wade open the note, watched him place it on the table, smiling a little but not saying anything.

The note read: "I believe in you."

Twenty-One

Pearl's morning didn't start out well. Yanked out of a death-like sleep, she realized she wasn't at home and panicked at first, taking several seconds to figure out where she was. Then she saw the neon Labatt's sign on the wall and Paul's Celtic-tattooed arm across her chest and knew where she was, which was worse.

The Labatt's sign had come from a bar and grill in Paul's college town. He'd worked there busing tables while studying for his premed degree, but then the bar had closed down and his scholarship money had dried up, and he'd been forced to drop out. Paul had taken the sign the day the bar closed, to remind him of everything that might have been, and the fact that Pearl knew all this about him was absolutely pathetic. Responding to his late-night text was one thing. Driving to his apartment and having sex with him was another. But talking to him afterward, sleeping with him in his bed and staying past dawn . . . Pearl cringed. *What is wrong with me?*

Carefully, she lifted Paul's arm off and slid out from under the covers, determined not to rouse him. But as alertness settled in, she realized what had woken her up in the first place—her phone vibrating beneath her pillow. By the time she managed to grab hold of it, Paul was awake asking, "What's going on?" And whoever had called had gone to voice mail.

"Sssh. Go back to sleep." She glanced at the clock on Paul's nightstand. It was 6:00 AM. She slipped the phone from under the pillow, wide awake now, heart beating faster. Calls that came at 6:00 AM were rarely calls you looked forward to taking.

"Was it your brother calling?" Paul said. "Oh man. I hope your dad is okay . . ."

Pearl closed her eyes. *Great. I told him about all that too.* She sat on the edge of the bed and waited for the phone to vibrate in her hand with the new voice message. The room still smelled of the incense Paul had burned last night, and the floor was littered with about a dozen spent sticks, discarded clothes, and empty beer bottles and . . . was that Paul's high school yearbook? *Jesus.*

Pearl looked at the screen. It wasn't her father's number and she was relieved, though she wasn't sure why she cared so much. "It's the station," she said.

"I thought you didn't have work today."

"So did I."

Paul moved next to her and kissed her cheek. "You think you'll have time for breakfast?"

"Don't know till I listen to the message."

Paul told her he was going to make some eggs and toast anyway, and she could have some "to stay or to go. Your call."

His place was just one room—convertible futon at one end, kitchen at the other. Pearl watched his naked body as he moved toward the kitchen. She couldn't help but admire the view. How she wished he'd say or do something to annoy her. She didn't mind anything about him right now—not even the Celtic tattoo. It had been a mistake, coming here.

Pearl had had one serious relationship in her life, back when she was in the police academy, and that hadn't ended well—a guy her year named Lawrence who had claimed he wasn't upset at all by her "backstory" as he so charmingly called it. But he had been. "I can't help it," Lawrence had admitted one night. "When I'm with you, I feel like I have to sleep with one eye open." He'd cheated on her, of course. From her experience, guys were always looking for an excuse to cheat, and she apparently came equipped with one. She was a bad seed, damaged goods. And if she tried to keep that "backstory" of hers hidden, it would rise up and bite her, the way it had in Poughkeepsie, so she couldn't win. It was best to stay single, to meet her needs and move on quickly, keeping her head down.

Paul was cracking eggs now. "Enjoying the show?"

Pearl smiled, though she didn't want to. "Conceited."

She clicked on her voice mail, and the automated voice announced the 6:00 AM call, followed by another voice. Her back stiffened. It was Sergeant Black, doing his documentary-voice-over impression. "There is a mandatory meeting for all local and state police officers this morning at seven thirty AM," he said in those deep, serious tones. "It concerns information obtained this morning in the Liam Miller case."

"Everything okay?" said Paul, who was watching her now.

"It is now," Pearl said. "But I have a feeling it's not going to be."

"I THINK I know what this is about." Pearl said it to Romero, who stood next to her in the crowded conference room.

"Yeah, me too," he said—the big clue being the large monitor that had been set up on the far wall. "I guess the state lab must've bumped Liam's phone to the front of the line."

Wind and Wacksman stood in front of the monitor, whispering, and Wind held a remote. Pearl watched as Sergeant Black entered the room with Bobby Udel at his shoulder, Bobby abuzz with some idea he was trying to get across.

"We'll open it up for discussion later," the sergeant told Bobby in a gentle but firm voice Pearl could hear all the way from the back of the room. Bobby's face flushed. He headed into the group of uniformed officers; the room was more packed than usual. Pearl even noticed a few cops she didn't know but whom she vaguely recognized from the Kill, all of them holding broad-brimmed hats in their hands. State troopers.

"Hey," Bobby Udel said when he reached Pearl and Romero.

"You seem awfully awake," said Pearl, and indeed, Bobby was shot full of extra energy, bouncing on the balls of his feet, every ounce of his attention directed at the front of the room, that monitor.

"I am," he said. "You bet I am."

It bothered her, like everything else about Bobby Udel had been bothering her lately. Yes, his favorite cousin had lost his best friend, and traumatic events made people behave strangely. Pearl got all of that. What she didn't get was this bizarre impatience of his, this thirst for closure. She could see it in the way his eyes had gleamed as he introduced Pearl to Ryan and his friends yesterday, the way he'd grasped Ryan's shoulder—not comforting him at all, but prodding him to speak. *Well, you're going to get your closure now, Bobby. It's on that screen.*

Pearl took a step away from Bobby. She glanced at Romero, whose eyes were on the monitor too. "What do you think we're gonna see up there?" he said.

Pearl thought about the two suspects she knew of: a woman who could barely speak without lying and a boy who barely spoke. "I'm going with headlights," she said.

By now, the sergeant, Wind, and Wacksman were up front in their designated positions, all three of them shushing everybody until the room was silent.

"Thanks for coming, everybody," said Sergeant Black. "I know many of you aren't scheduled for today, but the detectives and I thought it imperative you get this briefing."

Romero raised his eyebrows. "*Imperative.* He's using big words again."

Pearl had a strange feeling, that sense you get when you're just on the brink of learning something you aren't sure you want to know. In a way, she wished she could grab onto time and freeze it this way. But it all kept moving: Wind readying the monitor, the sergeant speaking in his newscaster's monotone, Bobby Udel bouncing next to her, aching to dive in.

"There will be a press conference outside the station following this meeting," the sergeant said. "Local and state news have been invited, as well as some national outlets—cable TV, places like that. Detectives Wind and Wacksman will be speaking. The rest of us will stand behind them, remaining silent. Understood?"

"A press conference," Romero whispered. "Jesus. What the hell press comes to Havenkill?"

Bobby raised his hand, but the sergeant went on with his prepared speech.

"Two days ago, Liam Miller's cell phone was sent to a state lab for JTAG testing," he said. "They were able to recover the contents of the phone." He looked around the room. "Those contents included film taken the night of the carjacking. It was one of many video files on the young man's phone that day, but the others were taken much earlier, on Friday rather than the early hours of Saturday, when Liam was at school."

"We've downloaded all information from Liam's phone, pertinent to the case and otherwise," Kendall Wind said. "If you'd like to take a look at any or all of it, please talk to Detective Wacksman, Sergeant Black, or myself. But right now, we're going to show you the video taken that night. It lasts just thirty seconds. I'd like to ask everyone to stay quiet throughout, as there is audio as well."

The sergeant hit the lights. Wind pressed the remote. Pearl stopped breathing. *And so it begins.*

An image appeared on the screen, a fuzzy image of moving figures, the flare of a streetlight, a car . . . Pearl could make out Amy's rainbow hair, her shiny vinyl jacket. The image grew sharper: Amy grabbing at a taller figure, all in black, trying to yank something out of his hands. Pearl exhaled, that pent-up air spilling out of her. *Amy was telling the truth.* Until now, she hadn't quite realized how shocking that concept was to her.

Pearl peered at the screen. She saw the tall figure push Amy aside and make for the car, her gleaming green Jaguar, light bouncing off the silver grille as Amy fell to the concrete.

"Help!" she yelled. "Help me, please!"

Amy's story, exactly as she had told it.

Romero leaned in, his lips close to Pearl's ear. "I just lost three separate bets."

The black-clad figure got into the car and slammed the door shut. Pearl struggled to make out his facial features, but on a phone and from this distance both his face and Amy's were flesh-colored globs.

The camera moved closer, bouncing up and down with the

filmmaker's joggy steps. Liam started to yell. "Stop!" Pearl heard. "Stop. No! Wait! Stop, wait!"

And then the camera flew, the images on the screen careening. You could hear the screech of tires, and then the streetlight was in view—the long metal stretch of it spinning almost gracefully before everything went to black.

"Did you hear that?" Bobby whispered. "Did you hear what Liam yelled?"

Pearl said nothing. She shook her head, wishing he'd just go away.

"Liam called him by name," Bobby whispered. "He said, 'Stop, Wade.'"

"He said *wait*," Pearl said, her cheeks growing hot. "As in, *wait* before you jump to conclusions and ruin another kid's life."

Bobby stared at her, jaw working, a look in his eyes that actually frightened her a little. "I'm not jumping to conclusions," he said. "I know the truth. I've known it from the start."

"How do you—"

"I know this town."

"As you can see," Kendall Wind was saying, "Ms. Nathanson was, exactly as she told us, a victim of violent crime. We will step up our efforts to investigate it as such. Anyone with any knowledge of the crime or suggestions as to how we might go forward is encouraged to talk with Sergeant Black, Detective Wacksman, or myself. Are there any questions?"

There were a few questions—mainly about scheduling, shift changes, added responsibilities as a result of the stepped-up investigation. Sergeant Black assigned a few other Havenkill cops to the local tip line, and Detective Wacksman went over specifics of exactly what would be said during the press conference. Somewhere in there, Pearl stopped listening and focused on Bobby, moving up through the group, to the front of the room. "Udel told me he knows things about the case," she whispered to Romero. "What do you think he knows?"

Romero shrugged. "More than I do, clearly."

The meeting broke up, everybody readying for the press conference, Romero heading off to the locker room to "make sure the hair's camera-ready."

Pearl stayed where she was. She kept her eyes on Bobby as he pulled Wind aside and spoke to her. She waited for the dismissive gesture from the detective, the curt nod followed by the fast escape, but it never came. Wind remained still as he spoke to her, leaning in, nodding every so often with her hands clasped at her chest, as though in prayer.

"DON'T YOU HAVE work today?" Connor said.

Jackie shook her head and served him another pancake, a few more strips of bacon. "I'm just taking some days off," she said. "I figured since Wade's car is in the shop and the weather's getting too cold for bikes, you guys might need me around for rides."

"You're taking off work to give us rides?" Connor said.

Jackie took a swallow from her cup of coffee. "You have a problem with that?" It was an old deflecting trick, answering a question with a question. And it seemed to work.

"I guess not."

"Go get your brother," Jackie said. "We're going to be late for school."

Wade had spent most of last night in his room, and she'd let him. He was hiding from her and Connor, Jackie was certain. But in truth she was hiding from Wade as well. She'd phoned Helen last night, left a message on her voice mail asking if she'd spoken to Garrett and when Wade and she could meet with him, the idea being to let Wade know she'd hired a lawyer once she had a game plan she could explain. The way he'd exploded in the car yesterday was understandable, once you took a step back. His car had been vandalized. He'd been intimidated by suspicious police. And that horrible live-feed post she'd had to report to Facebook . . . The whole world seemed to be ganging up on Wade, everything spiraling beyond his control. Who wouldn't explode, given that situation? Who wouldn't want to hide?

Jackie had hoped Garrett might help her see things more clearly, show her from a legal perspective how this situation could play out with an ending that didn't feel so dire so she could have some hope to pass on to her son. But Helen had never called back. Wade had stayed in his room. Jackie had even brought him his dinner in there. She hoped he'd eaten it.

"Mom?"

Jackie looked up. Connor and Wade were both standing in the kitchen, Connor carrying a couple of big pieces of poster board, Wade looming behind his little brother like a shadow he couldn't escape.

"Noah's mom's giving me a ride to school." Connor tapped the poster board with his index finger. "We're doing our science project at school and need to set everything up in the lab."

"Okay, honey."

He headed out of the house fast. Jackie looked at Wade. "You sure you want to go to school?" she said.

He nodded.

They walked out to the car in silence, Jackie allowing herself the faintest tinge of satisfaction over Connor. Yes, his excuse had been a lame one. She could have taken him and his poster board to school just as easily as Cindy Weston could, but the takeaway here was this: Noah and Connor were friends again. Despite the fact that Connor had bloodied his nose, the boys had smoothed things over on their own. Cindy was giving Connor rides and they were back at work on their science project, good as new.

If only the world worked like friendships between thirteen-year-old boys.

On the ride to school, Jackie turned on NPR, determined not to force Wade into conversation, though she did steal a few quick looks at him as she drove. His hair was still slightly damp from his shower this morning, and he was wearing the blue Shetland sweater that Jackie had given him for Christmas last year, her favorite. She loved him so much it hurt.

They were nearing the school. Wade asked to be let out a block away, the way he used to when he was younger. Jackie pulled over, dread creeping up on her again. She couldn't help it—just one block away from the school parking lot and all the memories that now came with it: Wade's defaced car; that horrible live feed of the two of them discovering it. *Those comments* . . . What was in store for Wade today? It had been twenty-four hours since the police had marched him into the guidance counselor's office in front of most of the student body. Twenty-four hours for word of it to spread and distort and grow into a monster. If someone had done that to Wade's car back then, what would they do to him now?

Before he got out, Wade leaned over. He gave her a kiss on the cheek, taking her by surprise. "It will be okay, Mom," he said.

Her heart swelled. "I know it will."

But as he closed the door behind him, Jackie was nearly overcome by the urge to pull him back into the car, to strap him in and drive far away and never come back to this town again.

During Jackie's drive home, NPR shifted from national to local news. She turned it up, waiting for the weather as she drove down Orchard, watching the gloomy day go by, the browning leaves. In just a few days, fall had peaked and now it was all downhill, the wind and rain accelerating the decay. Quite a few of the trees were near bare already.

The radio announcer was starting in on the weather now—something about another rainstorm. But Jackie wasn't sure whether it was the forecast for Dutchess County or across the river in the Catskills. She gripped the wheel, unable to focus.

What she wanted to do was save the day, to swoop in and make Wade's life normal again. She wished she could paste the leaves back on the trees and turn back time, turn it all the way back to before the divorce, because that's when the bad seed had been planted in her son and he'd stopped trusting everyone, including himself. If she had to do it over, she would have insisted on joint custody, or at least enforced visitation. She would have ensured the boys saw their father regularly, that Bill was there for them, whether he wanted to be or not.

But would she really do that? Jackie refused to admit it even to herself, but the truth was, she'd gone along with Bill's abandonment of his sons without trying to fight it, without even complaining. And she knew why. In the darkest part of her heart, Jackie had wanted Wade and Connor to resent Bill just as much as she did. Full custody for her; full love for her too. Bill a villain. Jackie a self-sacrificing hero. She'd let Bill get away with so much and she'd deprived her boys of a father, just so she could be that to them. And even now, with Wade so broken and in so much trouble, Jackie wasn't sure she'd be able to trade that in.

The radio announcer said Liam Miller's name and Jackie almost drove off the road. She turned up the volume. ". . . at a press conference in front of the Havenkill station early this morning, police spoke of 'stepped-up efforts' to find the carjacker," the announcer said. "And now in Hudson Valley weather . . ."

Jackie gritted her teeth. *Why wasn't I listening?* And then her phone rang. She picked it up to the sound of her son's voice. "Hi, Mom, it's Wade."

"Hi, honey. Why aren't you in class? Is everything okay?"

"I don't know. I'm at the police station." He laughed a little. A frightened laugh. "Can you come meet me here, please?"

Twenty-Two

Riding to school in the back of Noah's mom's car, Connor felt uncomfortable. The backseat was small, and since the trunk was filled up, Connor had to share the cramped space with the poster board charts for the science project. They were resting on his lap at a weird angle so that Noah's mom could see out the back window, with the tops of both boards pressing into his forehead. But it was the silence that was the most awkward part. On a regular day, Cindy was one of those moms who was always trying to make conversation, tossing out questions about classes and vacation plans and even how you felt about the weather. But today, she said nothing. Every so often, she'd glance at Connor in the rearview, this look in her eyes as if she'd been assigned to kidnap him and her boss kept asking her to make sure he hadn't escaped.

Maybe she hasn't gotten over the whole nose-punching thing. That was possible, Connor supposed, though he doubted it. Noah had insisted his mom had forgiven him, and Noah didn't lie about anything.

More likely, this had to do with Wade, that video of him in the parking lot, not to mention all the stuff everybody was claiming he'd said to Tamara. It had already cost Connor forty Facebook friends since yesterday morning and made him stop checking his private messages. *Your brother's crazy, you must be crazy too.* That was their thinking. And when he tried to defend Wade, to let them know that he hadn't sent those messages and that his Instagram had been hacked, that only made it worse. *Are you a Satanist too? Do you and Wade sacrifice cats together?* Somebody had seriously posted those questions on his Facebook wall.

He was sure Cindy had seen every post, read every comment. The only way Noah was allowed to have a Facebook page was if Cindy friended everyone on his list. She followed everybody on his Instagram too. She was always watching.

Cindy was watching Connor now, those eyes in the rearview trained on him, shooting lasers, with the radio turned off and Noah stuck in his own world, preparing for a Spanish test by listening to exercises on his headphones. Connor wanted to look out the window, but the poster boards were leaned against it, so he watched the back of Noah's head, listening to the buzz coming out of his headphones, barely audible, like ants speaking Spanish.

School seemed as though it were a thousand miles away. Connor's phone, which usually vibrated nonstop during morning rides like this with texts and messages, was silent. He slipped it out of his pocket, put it on his lap, and checked it. No texts. Nothing on Facebook Messenger, which was understandable; he hardly had any FB friends left.

If they only knew . . . In this quiet car, it was easy to think back to what he had done the previous afternoon, how he had betrayed his brother. Feeling the engine rumbling beneath him, he remembered that Officer Udel's car had been running too, how he'd sat in the front seat with him, staring at all the machinery on the dashboard, the thick plastic divider that blocked off the backseat. "It's like a spaceship in here isn't it?" Officer Udel had said. He'd shown him all the equipment, what it did, as though Connor were six years old or something.

Up close, Officer Udel had looked so much younger, practically the same age as Wade, and as he spoke to him in that calm voice, showing him all the stuff in the cop car, a part of Connor had wished Officer Udel was his brother instead of Wade—especially at that moment, right after Jordan had announced they could no longer be friends. That initial fear he'd felt when Officer Udel had called out to him had turned into anger again, anger at Wade.

"I know you're a good kid," Udel had said. "You aren't anything like your brother." And that had done it. Connor had spilled everything.

Maybe it wasn't important. Maybe they'd soon find Aimee En's phone somewhere else, in the possession of some gangbanger. Or better yet, maybe Aimee would confess to the crime herself.

His Instagram said he had one message, and his mind shifted back and forth as to whether or not he should click on it. It was probably some nasty homemade meme: a scared cat saying, "Get away from me, Wade."

But after more silence, Connor's boredom won out. He clicked on his Instagram, then on his direct messages. He only had one, and it was from Jordan, sent just a few minutes ago. Connor's spirits lifted a little.

"You okay back there, Connor?" Cindy said it as though she'd just discovered that he was in the car.

"I'm fine."

He clicked on the message. No words, no pictures. Just a link to a video that had been posted on YouTube.

"You feeling stuffy? Want me to turn down the heat?"

Now she decides to talk. "I'm fine, thanks." Connor stuck his earbuds in and clicked on the link.

The video was labeled *Recovered Footage from Liam Miller's Phone.* It had been posted less than fifteen minutes ago, and already it had more than 1,800 views. He didn't bother with the comments, just tapped the link, thinking *please, please, please* with all his heart. *Please let this be proof that Wade is innocent . . .*

He watched it twice, then three times. He couldn't make out faces. The Jaguar's headlights were on, and there was also the streetlight, but Rainbow Hair and her attacker were both in the shadows. He watched it all the way through to when the footage got shaky and everything spun around and the image died. He listened to Liam's cries, the last sounds he made as a conscious living person, but he tried not to think about that. He needed to concentrate on facts. *Is the guy in the hoodie Wade's height? What is Liam yelling as he runs at the car? Is that "Wait"? Or is it . . .*

Connor closed his eyes, collecting himself. He left Instagram and shoved his phone in his pocket. For the rest of the ride to school, he watched the back of Noah's head as he listened to his Spanish tape, nodding like an old lady, oblivious to everything around him. Connor envied Noah for it, that lack of curiosity.

The school loomed in front of them. As Cindy pulled into the parking lot, Connor noticed Mason Marx, talking with his idiot friends by the back door. *Have they seen this video?*

"Have a great day, sweetie," Cindy said to Noah.

"We're here already?"

"Yep. Good luck on your Spanish test."

Connor said, "Thank you for the ride."

Cindy gave him a pitying look. "No problem, Connor. Have a nice day."

Noah slammed his door shut, and Mason Marx and his friends turned and glared at them, Mason crossing his arms over his chest like a bouncer. As he maneuvered out of the car with his poster board charts, Connor imagined making a new one: "People Who Think My Brother Is Guilty." A chart with a red line, ever rising.

HELEN HAD NEVER called Garrett, which was strange. But he was kind and professional over the phone with Jackie, explaining he'd worked late the previous night anyway, and Helen never liked to bother him at work.

"But this is work," Jackie said. "It's a job for you."

"Good point. When can you get to the police station?"

"In about five minutes?"

"My office is two minutes from the station. I'll be out front when you get there."

True to his word, Garrett was waiting—dapper in a charcoal-gray suit and a blue silk tie that played up his eyes. He shook Jackie's hand with a firm grip and a serious expression, and for several seconds Jackie just stood there, taking in the situation, her ears ringing. *I am meeting a lawyer outside a police station. My son is inside.* She was normally the type of person who became calm and resourceful in times of panic, but in the past, those times of panic had been the kind that a mother might expect—a high fever, an arm broken playing soccer, a fall from a tree, requiring stitches. Not an arrest. Was that what this was? Had Wade been arrested?

"Are you okay?" Garrett said.

She realized she was trembling. She couldn't get her breath to slow down. "I'm fine," she said. "Let's do this."

He put a hand on her arm. "Jackie."

"Yes."

"Do me a favor and look up and down this street."

She frowned. "Why?"

"Humor me."

Jackie did.

"Sidewalks are more or less empty, right?"

"Yes."

"You hear anybody shouting questions at you?"

She shook her head.

"So there are no reporters. Focus on that, okay? This may feel out of control to you, but it's not. We can have our say, get Wade out of there, and most people won't know he was ever even questioned."

"You're right." Jackie took a deep breath. "Thank you."

"Save the thank-yous till you've gotten my bill." He gave her a smile, a practiced wink. "Lawyer humor. Gotta love it."

"I do?"

He laughed. "Listen, Jackie," he said. "I've known Sergeant Black for years. I handled his and his wife's wills. He's a nice, reasonable guy."

"What about those detectives?" she said. "Do you know them?"

Garrett put a hand on her shoulder. "I don't," he said. "But I know you. And I know your kids. And so I can tell you with certainty that everything is going to be okay."

Jackie thought, *You actually don't know my kids at all.* But she didn't say it. He was opening the door for her now. As he followed her into the station, Jackie thought about what a gentleman Garrett was, and how lucky Helen was to be married to a kind man like him.

WADE WAS NOT wearing handcuffs. This was a relief for Jackie, who had prepared for the worst. After Garrett introduced her to Sergeant Black (who did indeed seem nice and reasonable—he even apologized to Jackie for interrupting her day), the sergeant led the two of them down a hallway and into a conference room, where Wade was sitting at one end of the table, alone, his head down, back slumped.

"Wade?" Jackie said.

He looked up and smiled and Jackie stepped back. She saw him at two years old, at six, at twelve. It was the same lopsided smile, a smile that changed his whole face. He hardly ever smiled these days, and so when he did, it was a shock to the system. "Mom," he said. "I'm so glad you're here." And then his eyes found Garrett and the smile disappeared.

"Hey there, Wade. Not sure you remember me . . ."

"Sure I do," he said in a small voice. "Mr. Davies."

"Garrett's fine." He moved toward the conference room door and closed it. "Mr. Davies is my dad."

"Why are you here?"

"Your mom called me. I'm going to be acting as your lawyer, if that's okay with you."

None of them said anything for what felt like an uncomfortably long time. Then finally, Wade said, "I've been alone in here since I called you, Mom. Nobody has explained anything to me."

"I spoke to the sergeant and there's really nothing to be afraid of," Garrett said. "The detectives have some new information they wanted to ask you about. Probably nothing. The big thing is, they now have video of the incident. Very fuzzy video. You apparently fit the description of the carjacker. But so do a ton of boys."

"So why do I need a lawyer?"

Jackie stepped forward. "It's for our protection. I didn't like the tone of those detectives back at school, and Garrett knows how the system works, what questions you should and shouldn't answer. With him by your side instead of just me, they'll know they can't mess with you."

"That's right," Garrett said. "Your mom is smart." He winked at him, just as he'd winked at Jackie outside, but it didn't seem to put Wade at ease.

Wade kept his eyes on Jackie, as though Garrett wasn't even in the room. "Why would they want to mess with me?"

That's a good question. Jackie found it encouraging, that confusion. *He is innocent. And he's acting that way.*

"Why is there a video camera in here?" Wade said, and Jackie noticed it for the first time, set up on a tripod, at the far end of the room.

She turned to Garrett. "Any idea?" she said, trying to keep her voice calm.

"Procedure."

"Really?"

There was a soft knock on the door, and then Detective Wind's voice, asking, "Are you ready?"

Garrett replied, "Yes," though Jackie didn't feel ready at all.

DETECTIVE WIND SEEMED to be handling the questioning this time. She sat across the table from Wade, hands clasped in front of her, while Wacksman sat at the end of the table, leaning back as though to give them some space.

Jackie was glad for that. She liked Wind better than Wacksman. She seemed more professional, less patronizing. And besides, Jackie could not stand that mustache. Her eyes were drawn to it whenever Wacksman spoke, so thick and luxuriant she couldn't help but imagine him grooming it, using a tiny tortoiseshell comb and a rack of imported oils as though it were a pet.

Wade sat between Jackie and Garrett for the questioning. Jackie could feel him leaning into her, his discomfort palpable, even as Wind asked him simple questions: his name, age, school, number of siblings; questions Jackie imagined were designed to put him at ease. Wind asked him what his hobbies were and he said, "Drawing, I guess."

"And your favorite subject in school?"

"Umm . . . English?"

"Do you have any friends, Wade?" she asked in the same conversational tone. Jackie cringed.

Wade glanced at Garrett, then stared at his hands. "Not really."

"How would you describe your little brother?"

"My brother?"

"Yes."

"He's thirteen. His name is Connor."

"Okay," she said. "Would you say you guys get along?"

"Sure."

"So, he's your friend, right?"

Wade squinted at her. "He's thirteen. He's my brother."

"Do you talk a lot?"

"We used to. When we were younger. But not so much now, I guess."

"How would you describe his personality?"

"He's a nice kid."

"Would you describe him as trustworthy?"

Jackie frowned. This was getting a bit strange. She cast a long glance at Garrett, but he regarded the detective mildly, as though this was a perfectly normal line of questioning.

Wade said, "Yes."

"He's not a liar?"

Wade shifted in his seat. "No," he said. "Connor isn't a liar."

"Listen," Jackie said. "If you're wondering where Connor was at the time of the hit-and-run—"

Garrett held a hand up, saying her name softly. "I don't think the detective is trying to imply that Connor had anything to do with what happened to Liam." He looked at Wind. "Are you?"

"I just want to establish that Wade gets along with his brother. They haven't had any big fights lately. Connor isn't a liar, and would have no reason to lie about him."

"Oh God," Wade whispered. "Oh my God."

Jackie turned to him. "What's wrong?"

He shook his head slowly.

Wind continued. "So if I said to you that Connor claims you came into his room at around three in the morning on October twentieth, wet from the rainstorm outside . . ."

"I can't believe this."

Jackie's eyes widened. "Is this true?"

Wind pressed on. "If Connor said you gave him a bag and asked him to dispose of it . . ."

"Jesus."

". . . and in that bag was a phone, much like the one missing from Amy Nathanson's bag . . ."

"Connor told you all of that?" Wade said, his voice rising and cracking. *"Connor told you?"*

"Wade," Garrett said. "Wade, you don't need to answer."

Wade whispered, "I cannot believe he would do this to me."

"Wade," said Garrett. He looked at Wind. "We're going to need a minute."

"No we're not," Wade said. "I want to go home." He turned and looked straight at the video camera. *"I want to go home."*

"Whose phone was it, Wade, if it wasn't Amy Nathanson's? Whose phone did you ask your brother to dispose of the morning of the hit-and-run?"

Garrett said, "*We are going to need a minute.*" More firmly this time.

Wind looked at Wacksman and then nodded. "We're happy to give you all the time you want." The two of them got up and left the room.

Garrett held up a hand. Then he stood up, switched off the video recorder, and unplugged it for good measure. Wade put his head down on the table and closed his eyes, as though someone had pulled the plug on him as well.

Jackie watched him for a while, unable to speak. Both her sons. Connor and Wade. Keeping so much from her.

Garrett's face changed. It looked harder now with all the good-will drained out of it, his eyes like slate, the sparkle gone. "Wade," he said. "Where were you on the night of the incident?"

But Wade didn't move, didn't speak.

"Why were you in your brother's room? Where had you come from? Why did you ask him to get rid of a phone?"

Still nothing.

"If you can't at least meet me halfway, I can't help you."

"I don't want your help, Mr. Davies," Wade said.

"It's Garrett, and whether you want my help or not, you need it, buddy."

"*I'm not your buddy and I don't need your help!*"

Garrett let out a long sigh. He looked at Jackie. "I don't think this is going to work out."

"But," she said. "But . . . what are we going to do with no lawyer?"

"There are lots of lawyers out there," he said. "I'll ask around."

He picked up his coat, and went quietly through the door, turning briefly before he closed it. "You should tell Bill about this. He's a lawyer and he's also the boy's father. It's the least he could do."

After he shut the door behind him, Jackie stood staring at it. "Nice parting shot," she said.

Wade didn't lift his head. His eyes stayed closed and he remained completely still, so still that Jackie could believe that he had actually fallen asleep. She took the seat next to him again, a feeling of calm coming over her, that warm-blanket feeling that usually happens after a good cry. She ran a hand through her son's messy hair and felt moisture on his skin. Tears. She put an arm around his shoulders, which were shaking, ever so slightly. She rested her head on his.

"I know you didn't do it," she said.

She knew he didn't. As many secrets as he was keeping from her, Jackie knew this much about Wade: he would never run someone down and leave him there to die. But he wouldn't respond to questions, wouldn't cooperate with a lawyer. Wouldn't meet her halfway. Even now, he couldn't give her the satisfaction of nodding his head, and so here she was, cleaning up after Wade as usual. *He left a phone with his brother and asked him to throw it out. Why?*

Jackie thought about phones, all the information they held: pictures, videos, texts. And how much you could find out about a person if you knew their pin number . . .

Wade's phone. She pulled away from him and saw the edge of the phone poking out of his jacket pocket. She remembered picking it up from the floor of his room when it was plugged into its charger, the feel of it in her hand as she'd scrolled through his pictures. Had it felt slightly different than it had days earlier, just a little bit heavier than when she'd picked it up and read that text from "T"? And the sound of that text tone. *Like a bomb going off . . .*

Jackie slipped her own phone out of her pocket. Texted *Hello* to Wade's number. Sent it.

The phone in Wade's pocket made a soft dinging sound.

Wade sat up. Slipped his phone out of his pocket. Looked at the screen. "Mom?"

A lighter, thinner phone with a different text tone. "It was a different phone," she whispered.

Wade looked at her, his face red and tear-streaked. "What are you talking about?"

"The other day. In the kitchen. Your phone. It had an explosion for a text tone."

His eyes went big. "I don't know what you mean," he said. But he did. It was obvious. When it came to lying, teenagers were just children, and that's what Wade was. A child, lying. Trying to protect a burner phone. Secret texts from some girl who clearly didn't want to be seen with him.

"You had a different phone," she whispered. "You talked to 'T' on it. You wanted to keep it private."

"What?"

"Does 'T' have a boyfriend? Is that why?"

"No. No, you don't even know what you're talking about."

"I'm going to get them back in here," Jackie said. "You can tell the truth."

Wade stared at her, his face changing, fear sparking in his eyes. "No."

"Just tell them about the burner phone. Tell them it was a girl. Tell them this is all about a girl and they'll let you go."

"I wasn't with a girl."

Jackie moved toward him. "Wade, please."

She put her hand on his shoulder. He swatted her away. "I *mean* it. You have no idea what you're talking about, and I'm not going to tell them that. I *won't*."

"Wade, please. Wherever you were, it's an alibi. Protecting some girl from her boyfriend is not worth going to jail for."

There was another knock on the door. Jackie and Wade froze, staring into each other's eyes.

"You can come in," Wade said.

Jackie held her breath.

Watching both of them carefully, Kendall Wind and Alex Wacksman walked into the room and took their seats at the table.

"Everything okay?" Wind said it to Wade.

He was composed now, sitting up straight in his chair, face wiped free of tears. "I want to leave," he said.

"Excuse me?"

"I want to go home now." He looked at Wind. "It was just an old phone I found in the school parking lot. I told Connor to throw it out because I was scared someone would think I stole it."

"Where were you at three in the morning of October twentieth?"

"I was walking in the rain." His voice was as dry as sand. "I was alone."

Wade stood up. So did Jackie, though she was yearning to speak, the words pressing up inside her. *It was a girl. He was with a girl that night.* But her words were worth nothing, and, really, neither were his.

The only words that mattered were the words of that girl.

"Don't you want to help out, son?" Wacksman was saying. "I mean, Liam Miller was one of your classmates. I'm sure you want to help us find out who murdered him?"

"I told you everything I know."

Wacksman and Wind looked at each other. "All right," Wind said. "We'll be in touch."

Wade moved toward the door, and Jackie followed. *I'm going to find that girl,* she thought.

Twenty-Three

The following are selected comments from the Reddit subgroup True Crime Discussion, under a post begun on October 22, titled: "Upstate New York Teen Dies from Injuries in Aimee En Hit-and-Run."

Magpie22

Just devastating that Liam Miller died. My niece knows him from church camp and says he was one of the nicest people she ever met. At least he died a hero.

Ted4041

Okay, guys. I said this on yesterday's thread. No disrespect, but this whole story is super-hinky to me. I'm a New Yorker, and I've been to Havenkill. No way is it a place where carjackings routinely—or ever—happen. This story feels like one of those "shaggy-haired stranger" tales (i.e. Diane Downs, Susan Smith). Anybody know much about Aimee En?

Savannahgirl

I thought the same thing so I did some research. Aimee En was busted for co-

caine possession in 1997. She's also got a couple DUIs under her belt, plus driving with a suspended license. Here's a link to an archived LA Times *article about the cocaine bust: (link to article)* Dead Enz Lead Singer Aimee En Arrested; Pop Star Faces up to Seven Years

Marciamarciamarcia

Looks like she copped a plea. Fine and rehab. Check out this People *mag story from 2004: (link to article)* Where Are They Now: Aimee En's Sweet, Sober Life

Ted4041

Can anybody find anything written about her in the past decade? I can't . . .

MissMystery

Am I the only one who feels sorry for Aimee En? Looks like she was trying to make a comeback, she finally gets a gig, and then this happens. She is sober, so wasn't driving drunk. If she did hit that boy, what was he doing out so late to begin with? It was probably very dark, with few streetlights. Those who don't wear reflective clothing take their lives into their hands.

Savannahgirl

I get what you're saying but let's not shame the deceased for not wearing reflective clothing.

Ted4041

Did you miss the part about her three past DUIs? Sober people fall off the wagon and get into car accidents/hit-and-runs.

MissMystery

She could be telling the truth, tho. I saw an FBI profiler on ID once, and he was saying that a lot of times, the weirdest stories are the ones that turn out to be true. Keep in mind, Diane Downs's "shaggy-haired stranger" story was actually very plausible!

MissMystery

Lookee here! I was right! (Link to AP story) Breaking News: Footage from Hit-and-Run Teen's Phone Exonerates Aimee En

Savannahgirl

Whoa sorry @MissMystery!

MissMystery

Apology accepted @Savannahgirl ☺

Ted4041

Just watched the footage. Anybody else feel like Liam Miller knew the carjacker? Not sure why, but there was something about the way he called out to him that felt familiar.

Savannahgirl

Could be a fellow athlete. The way he pushed Aimee En to the ground looked a little like a football move.

MissMystery

Wondering if they've done a clean sweep of that street corner. She could have drawn blood during that struggle outside the car. Anybody else see him rub his arm after tangling with her?

Savannahgirl

Who is the attacker???? I've been following this case from the beginning, and I'm wondering about his motivation. I'm also wondering why nobody else came to help. Looks like there were houses around. You mean to tell me not one person even called 911?

Magpie22

Bystander effect.

Ted4041

Just saw on Twitter that they were questioning a local kid.

Magpie22

I saw that too. No name released yet. He's a minor, so they're keeping things quiet until an arrest is made, but I hear through the grapevine that he's a Satanist. A known animal torturer.

ConnorR

HE'S NOT A SATANIST!!!

Magpie22

Whoa, dude, watch the caps.

MissMystery

@ConnorR do you know the suspect?

Magpie22

Are you the suspect?

Ted4041

crickets

Magpie22

Methinks we've been invaded by a troll. A very young one. Anyway . . . more info. Suspect was in the same class as Liam. Rumor has it he was selling pills. And Liam was threatening to turn him in.

Ted4041

A drug-dealing animal torturer? Sounds like a winner.

Magpie22

Yep.

Savannahgirl

Wow. The weirdest things happen in small towns.

From the Facebook page of the Havenkill Police Department. Posted on October 23 at 11:00 AM.

URGENT REQUEST

A carjacking/hit-and-run took place on Shale Street near Orchard at approximately 3 AM on Saturday, October 20. The video posted below was taken from the phone of the victim, a 17-year-old white male. Anyone with any FACTUAL, SERIOUS, AND PERTINENT information is encouraged to call the tip line, listed below.

45K views; 1.5K shares

Twenty-Four

Happy kid, huh?" said Kendall Wind.

Pearl nodded.

The two of them were in the evidence room, in front of a glowing laptop, Wind showing Pearl the content of Liam Miller's cell phone at Pearl's request. Already, Pearl had looked at some of the texts and scrolled through his pics, but what had really interested her was his collection of videos. Pearl maybe had four videos on her phone, all of them dirty and better off deleted. Liam's phone, on the other hand, held close to a hundred of them, arranged into folders that he'd named and alphabetized. It struck her as unusually organized for anyone, let alone a teenage boy, and it made her think about the type of person he might have grown up to be, had he been allowed to grow up. There was a folder called Tamara, consisting mostly of sappy, romantic messages from his girlfriend, as well as older, smaller folders with other girls' names, still more videos named for proms, vacations, stays in summer camps. Such a short life, yet so painstakingly archived.

Most of the larger folders contained downloads—movies,
music videos, viral stuff, grouped and placed in folders according to artist or genre. Pearl had asked which folder Liam's final
video had been in. Unlike all the others, this one had initials
for a name: "SL." What could that stand for? Wind had opened
it for her—a folder of just three videos. They were looking at
the oldest, taken the previous March. At the start of it, Liam's
face filled the screen, laughter overtaking him, his smile huge
and open, eyes scrunched into crescents. Happy. Hence Wind's
comment.

"Any sound?" Pearl said.

"No," Wind said. "But there's quite a punch line."

As Liam continued to laugh silently, the camera panned up to
reveal a night sky, then panned back down, the person behind it
taking shaky steps back, until Liam's surroundings were revealed.
He was in the town graveyard, leaning against a tombstone.

"Kind of chilling, isn't it?" Wind said. "Considering what happened to him?"

Pearl nodded, but she was more interested in the beer bottle
in Liam's hand. "Cemetery's closed at night," she said. "It's illegal
for him to be there."

Wind shrugged. "He's a teenage boy," she said. "*Was.* Nobody's
saying he was a saint."

"Actually . . ." Pearl started, then stopped. She couldn't go
down this road, not with one of her superiors—a state detective
who was doing her a favor by letting her see this footage. But she
couldn't help but think it. *Everybody is saying he was a saint.* At
least three GoFundMes had been started in Liam Miller's name
since his death, one of them to raise money to build a statue of
him. People all over social media were eulogizing Liam, calling
him brave and golden-hearted and wise beyond his years. Not to

mention the shrine. An actual shrine at the spot where Liam was killed, and now it spanned half a block. It was affecting traffic. Yet somehow, this video was more touching than any of that—Liam laughing his ass off on someone's grandpa's grave, high as a kite, breaking rules. Human.

Liam smashed the bottle against the tombstone, breaking it into a thousand shards. Pearl jumped back. *Okay. That wasn't quite so touching.*

"I heard yesterday morning wasn't your first school assembly," Wind said.

"Huh?" Pearl closed the video and let the cursor hover over the next one, taken in August.

"You've had more contact with the high school kids than just that morning."

"Oh. Right," Pearl said. "Yeah, I did safety assemblies at the middle and high schools last May."

"Did you have any contact with Wade Reed during those assemblies?"

Pearl's hand stilled on the mouse. "I don't think he asked any questions," she said. "Or if he did, I don't remember him."

"Hmmm . . . Okay."

"Why?"

"Not that big a deal. Just looking for a baseline."

Pearl looked at her.

"He seemed a little out of it when we were questioning him back at the school," she said. "I'm wondering if that's a recent thing or if he's been at it for a while."

"Out of it?"

"Drugged up. A little belligerent. Come on. Even the guidance counselor was looking at his pupils. You didn't notice?"

"No," Pearl said. "I thought he just seemed scared."

"That's helpful."

Pearl wasn't sure if she was being sarcastic or not.

"I mean it," Wind said. "Ever since I found out Amy was telling the truth, I've lost all faith in my own powers of perception."

"Well, for what it's worth, I've gone back and forth on Amy myself," Pearl said. "I think anybody would. She doesn't come across as the world's most reliable narrator."

Wind smiled, tapped her fingernail against the next video. "This one has sound," she said, and opened it, the laptop filling with a tanned Liam in his bathing suit, bouncing on a diving board against a twilit, pink-spiked sky. "Watch me!" he said. "Watch."

And who could help but watch as this shining boy jumped off the board, touching his fingers to his toes and then arching into a perfect dive, straight as a spear, the blue water accepting him without so much as a splash?

"*Awesome*," said the voice behind the camera. And then Liam emerged from the water, thumbs first and then wrists and arms and then finally, the reveal of his smiling face, spitting water at the camera. Pearl took note of the pool's pink Mexican tiles and male laughter in the background and how Liam's blue eyes matched the blue of the chlorinated water. "Man," she whispered. Pearl knew those voices. She knew that pool. She knew exactly what was going to happen next.

"*Cops!*"

"Pool-hopping night," Pearl said.

"Huh?"

"Ed Tally and I went to that house on a call from one of the neighbors. The owners were out of town, and those boys broke in and used the pool. Liam and three of his friends. Two of them ran away." She turned to Wind. "Bobby Udel's cousin Ryan Grant was the one taking the video."

Wind paused the video. "Bobby never told me that."

Pearl looked at her, taking note of the way she'd said his first name, the familiarity of her tone. "Maybe Bobby never knew about it," she said. "He wasn't on duty that night, and I doubt it's something Ryan would want to brag about, especially to his cop cousin."

"We spoke to Ryan yesterday."

"How did he seem?"

"Sweet," she said. "And broken. He really wanted to help."

"And did he?"

She breathed in sharply. "Liam texted him two hours before the incident. Ryan was asleep. He was taking the SATs the following day, so he'd gone to bed early. He said he didn't even see the text until after the SATs. He found out what had happened to Liam, then he saw it."

"Did he show it to you?"

Wind nodded.

"What did it say?"

"*S'up.*"

Pearl gave her a sad smile. "Too bad we can't plan the last things we say to our friends."

"Yep." Wind hit play. On-screen, Liam's smile dropped away. His eyes focused on something beyond the camera and went wide with terror. "He was looking at me at that point," Pearl said. "Oh my gosh," said Liam. And then the screen went black.

"Did you arrest those boys?"

"No. Just gave them a talking-to." Pearl's gaze returned to the laptop screen. "What do you think this folder is about? Just three videos in it. 'SL.' What do you think that means?"

Wind shrugged. "Summer Lovin'?"

"He's breaking the law in two of the three."

"And he's a hero in the third," Wind said. "Maybe this is his adventure folder."

Pearl nodded. "That makes sense," she said. Though a feeling nagged at her, like a puzzle missing one piece.

"Funny. I bet Liam thought he'd add hundreds of videos to that folder." Wind closed out of the file and shut down the laptop. "Actually, that isn't funny at all."

There was a knock on the door, and Wind opened it to her partner as Pearl kept staring at the dark screen, thinking. "Wade Reed's mother is here," Wacksman said. "She's brought a lawyer."

"I'm ready."

Pearl turned around and followed them both out of the room, locking the door behind her.

She had to pass the conference room on her way out, and as she did, she cast a quick glance through the open door at Wade Reed looking up at his mother, dark eyes big with hope. "Mom. I'm so glad you're here."

Maybe this terrified kid really had pushed Amy to the ground, stolen her car in the middle of the night, and run over one of his classmates with it. Maybe the detectives knew something Pearl didn't know about Wade, something that justified carting him in here at the start of a school day and subjecting him to this. But right now, Pearl wished she'd never said his name out loud to Bobby Udel. And when she walked out the side door and into the parking lot and saw the small cluster of curiosity seekers that had formed in front of the station aiming phones at the door, some clutching bulky cameras, she wished she could will Wade and his mother somewhere far away from this town.

Her next shift was a patrol—the usually peaceful area between the park and the schools. As she slipped into a cruiser,

Pearl's mind returned to that folder. *What does "SL" mean? Why did he group those three videos together? There were plenty of other folders with outdoor activities in them. Why did he open this one to film a carjacking?* Pearl sighed. For all she knew, "SL" did stand for Summer Lovin' and he'd randomly opened it in his haste to save the day. But she couldn't help but wonder if there wasn't more to it than that. When a folder contains the last video of someone's life, it should also hold answers.

BY THE TIME Jackie and Wade left the police station, it was late morning, close to lunchtime. Jackie offered again to let him take the rest of the day off, figuring he might jump at the chance to avoid his classmates and hole up in his room. But Wade insisted on going back to school. "I'm going to flunk out if I keep missing classes," he said.

When he pushed open the door, someone shouted, "There he is!" and they came at Jackie and Wade like a wave—cameras flashing, phones held high, his name hollered like an obscenity. Jackie blinked, stumbled back. She grabbed for her son's arm and put him behind her, shielding him with her body. Where had they all come from? How had they found out?

"Wade! That's him. That's Wade Reed!"

"Did you kill Liam Miller?"

"Have you been arrested, Wade?"

"Have you always hated Aimee En?"

"What did they say to you in questioning?"

Jackie's face felt cold, the flashes like ice in her eyes. Behind her, Wade was stock-still. She heard him say, "What's going on?" and her back straightened, her hands became fists. "Leave him alone!" Her voice was lower and louder than she'd expected. A growl. "What's wrong with all of you? *He's just a kid.*"

She took Wade to the parking lot, shielding him from the cameras with her body until they reached the car, where they were safe. Reporters—was that what they were? Or were they bloggers? True-crime addicts? Fans of murder? What reporter would wait outside a police station where no one was being arrested, just to get a shot of an underage boy? *Fans of murder. Ghouls.*

Jackie could still hear their shouts through the closed car window. Wade's name, bleated over and over in a way that brought to mind zombie movies. She started up the car and felt the heaviness of Wade's breathing.

Passing the reporters, bloggers, murder fans, whatever the hell they were, these wastes of skin, Jackie nearly put up her middle finger. But that would have made too good a shot, and so she opted instead to stare out her window and pretend they didn't exist. *How dare you*, she thought. *How dare you.*

Wade was shaking. She wanted to talk to him but waited to speak until she was a few blocks away from the police station and she could no longer see puffy jackets in the rearview.

"I don't want to scare you," she said. "But this is only going to get worse."

"What do you mean?"

She kept her voice calm, even. "Your name's been all over the net. Someone tipped them off that you would be here," she said. "People are against you, honey. They are actually out to get you, but we can fix this if you meet me halfway."

"What do you mean?"

"Tell me where you were the night Liam was run down."

"You asked me that back at school," Wade said quietly. "You asked me, and you said that if I wanted to, I could say, 'I can't answer that question.' You said that would be a good enough answer. That it's better than a lie."

"It could save your life," she said. "It could save you from getting arrested."

"Do you want me to lie to you, Mom?"

Jackie stopped at a traffic light. "Wade."

"Because seriously, that's like . . . that's the only option here.
You either believe in me, or you don't."

"I do."

"Okay," he said. "Good."

"But, Wade . . ."

"What?"

"Me believing in you. That can't save you."

He turned away from her and looked out the window, but before he did, she saw the fear in his eyes. The light turned green.
They drove in silence until they were a block away from school and
then Jackie pulled to the curb and Wade opened the door—a do-
over of this morning. Only this time, Wade didn't kiss her good-
bye. "See you tonight, Mom." He said it with his back turned. She
knew he didn't want her to see his face.

CONNOR WAS TWENTY minutes into English class before he listened to a word Ms. Chastain said (a town's name, Maycomb)
and realized he hadn't done last night's reading assignment. He
hoped she wouldn't call on him—for obvious reasons, but also for
emotional ones. He kept thinking of that expression: "under the
microscope," how he'd probably heard it a million times in his
life, but never really understood what it meant until now. For all
of today, he'd felt exactly that way—isolated and watched at the
same time, powerless as a germ on a slide.

In homeroom and science, Noah had been by his side, and so
he'd been able to ignore the stares, the purposeful bumps in the
hallway as they hurried between classes, the stage whispers about

Wade and murder and devil worship. If he paid attention only
to Noah and his teachers, most of his teachers anyway, Connor
could pretend things were normal. But now he was on his own.
Please don't call on me. As it was, Connor could feel most every
eye in the classroom on him, even as he sat at his desk quiet and
still, his own gaze aimed at his opened book, not a thing about
him moving other than his thoughts.

Ms. Chastain must have asked a question, because Julia Feeney,
the biggest kiss-ass in the class and the only person in the room
who didn't seem focused on Connor, was working her center
seat in the front row, lifting out of her chair, as though her per-
manently raised hand had a thousand helium balloons attached
to it.

Connor's phone buzzed in his jacket pocket. It had to be Noah.
He was the only one who'd been texting Connor since the whole
Wade/Tamara thing. His hand moved to the phone.

Ms. Chastain said, "What do you think, Connor?"

The hand dropped. "Um . . ." His face flushed. "I'm sorry. I . . .
uh . . . I didn't hear the first part."

Someone snickered. Connor heard whispers but couldn't make
out words. Ms. Chastain said, "Boo Radley," and he felt as though
he were underwater, people talking above the surface. He stared
at her. What was that? An expression? A name?

"I'm asking about the emotional meaning," she said patiently.
"What does that mean to you, the idea of living a life like Boo
Radley, being trapped in your own home?"

Connor swallowed. *Nothing,* he wanted to say. Connor felt
trapped in his own skin, his own family, his own life, and he
wished so badly he could say it without getting into trouble. *It
means nothing to me.* He hadn't started the book yet, true. But

right now, being locked in a house sounded like a party. "I don't know," he said.

"Why do Scout, Jem, and Dill dare each other to touch Boo Radley's house?"

"I don't know."

"Why is Boo Radley an outcast?"

He exhaled. "I don't know who Boo Radley is."

He heard someone snicker again but Ms. Chastain didn't seem to notice. "You don't know?"

"I . . . uh . . . wasn't feeling great last night."

Disappointment pinched up her features. "So you didn't do the assignment."

Connor almost felt like laughing. What was wrong with her? Did she have no idea what had been going on in this town over the past forty-eight hours? *Do you care about anything in the world besides this one stupid class?* Or maybe she knew everything about Wade. Maybe she thought all of it was true, even the devil-worshipping stuff, and she was asking Connor questions about outcasts for a reason. "I've got a bad stomachache," Connor said. "Can I go to the nurse?"

She didn't say anything for several seconds, and he felt his face burn deeper, redder.

"All right, Connor." It felt like an insult, the way she called him by name.

Connor stood up. He walked toward the back of the classroom, his sneakers squeaking on the wood floors, everyone staring at his face, his clothes, the back of his head, each eyeball a gun scope, trained on him.

Once he was outside the door and walking down the empty hall to the nurse's office, Connor could finally breathe again. He couldn't stand it, this constant shame. He blamed Wade. This was Wade's fault. Whether or not he was guilty of killing Liam, people believed he was guilty. That was what mattered, and that was all on him.

THE NURSE GAVE Connor a paper cup full of ginger ale and some saltines wrapped in plastic. She took his temperature, and since he didn't have one, she told him to lie down on the bed until he felt better. Connor couldn't imagine ever feeling better, but he did lie down on the bed, which had a screen set up in front of it for privacy. This was as alone as he was going to be all day.

Connor patted his jacket pocket, the buttoned one, just to make sure it was still there—the drawing he'd stolen out of Wade's room last night, when everyone in the house had been sound asleep. He'd slipped it from beneath Wade's bed as he snored and brought it back to his room. Afraid that Arnie might wake up and make noise if he turned the lights on, Connor had gotten under the covers with the picture, shined the flashlight from his phone on it: a front and back view of a girl, the face the faintest outline but the body more detailed than he'd ever imagined it would be. Connor had been fascinated. Transfixed as he'd been as a little kid, watching Wade draw pictures of spaceships.

Wade hadn't copied a picture from a Web site or magazine, Connor could tell. Those pictures were always Photoshopped. In this one, there were freckles and scars and even a tattoo. It was as though Wade had mapped out every inch of this girl's body, so he could keep it all with him, in his memory.

Connor had planned to put it under Wade's bed before he woke up, but he'd fallen asleep under the covers with the drawing and slept through his alarm. He'd folded it up and shoved it into his pocket just to hide it, but now he couldn't imagine ever returning it to Wade, not with the fold marks. Connor finished the rest of the ginger ale, then touched his pocket again, the paper rectangle under the thin cloth. *What would Noah think if he saw this?* Connor wondered, which made him remember the text message from English class. He pulled his phone out of his other pocket and opened his texts.

"Connor?" the nurse said from behind the screen. "You want me to call your mom?"

"No thanks." Connor stared at the text. It was from a number he'd never seen: *Your brother is sick and evil,* it read. *Your whole family should die.* "I'll be fine," he said.

Twenty-Five

From Aimee En's Facebook fan page.

October 23 at 2:00 PM

Hello, all. In the early hours of Saturday morning, I was the victim of a carjacking. A young hero by the name of Liam Miller attempted to help me and save my car, but was run down by the car thief, which led to his death. As I aid in the police investigation, I've become friends with Liam's parents, Sheila and Chris Miller. They are kind, spiritual people, just as remarkable as their son. For those of you who don't know Liam, I've posted pictures below, so that you might get a better sense of this very special human being.

A star football player for his high school team, the Havenkill Ravens, Liam was also on the honor roll, student council president, and before this tragic accident, he was excited that he'd gotten a part in the chorus of the school musical, *Les Misérables*. Sheila also tells me that he played the guitar and sang—a rock star in the making. I wish I could have heard his beautiful angel's voice. I can't stand the fact that it has been silenced forever.

On October 29 at the Red Door Tavern in Havenkill, I will be paying tribute to Liam Miller, his music, his voice. For the Love of Liam: A Benefit Concert will take place from 6–9 PM. Proceeds will go toward a football scholarship in Liam's name—a project that has been in the works since his untimely death. It is a concert for all ages. Children are welcome. Tickets can be purchased by clicking on the link, listed below.

This page has received 7,000 new likes.

Twenty-Six

Parking her rental car across the street from the Havenkill police station, Amy felt like a newer, cleaner version of herself. Her lipstick perfect, she wore a navy vintage dress with white polka dots and a bright red crinoline that matched her lips. And her hair was adorable. This morning, she'd left Vic with Jacinta and driven to a lovely salon in Rhinebeck, where she'd had it snipped into a sleek bob and colored sunset red. No more of that rainbow crap. She was Amy 2.0 now, with a just-announced concert that was already sold out and close to ten thousand new likes on her Facebook page. Even more satisfying, the state detectives were finally treating her like the victim she was. "I hope you don't mind, but Officer Maze is on patrol so she won't be there during your questioning," Detective Kendall "call me Kendall" Wind had said over the phone. *I hope you don't mind.* Did Amy say she was a *victim*? Make that *survivor.*

And it was all because of Liam Miller's video. Interesting that while he had been unable to save Baby, Sheila's son had saved Amy's image and possibly her life. Already, she'd gotten a call from someone with the *New York Times*. She'd done a phoner with him, and set up a photo shoot. And she knew that was just the beginning. She would have to look around for a publicist because there would be more newspaper interviews, talk show appearances, and then, almost certainly, a record deal. Amy would manage her fame better this time around, now that she was older, wiser, soberer. She'd milk it and keep the cream, rather than the white powder like before.

If she held out for a good deal and invested it well, Amy would be able to hire a whole staff to take care of Vic. They could move into a larger home—a stately mansion like the Millers' but with a whole wing for Vic's junk, a team of housekeepers and landscapers to take care of the rest of it. They could live like royalty—or at least like human beings.

There was a group of people milling around by the police station door, some of them holding expensive-looking cameras. Amy headed straight for them. Though they clearly didn't recognize her right away, Amy cut such a striking figure that many looked twice. One shouted, "Are you Aimee En?" And when she said yes, they all set upon her, begging for autographs and pictures. In her youth, Amy had often been difficult with fans—a combination of her punk diva image and too much cocaine. But she was gracious now. Could have been Sheila Miller rubbing off on her, come to think of it, for Sheila Miller was the most gracious woman she'd ever met. But whether it was due to Sheila's influence, or whether it was simply out of gratitude, Amy signed notebooks and rare vintage Dead Enz vinyls and even arms. She made pleasant conversation and posed for pictures, and gave quotes to the ones who identified themselves as reporters. She behaved not like a has-been but like a true celebrity—the type who would live on through fans' heartwarming stories. Like George Michael. Or, actually, like Liam Miller.

Once she'd posed for her last photo, Amy headed into the police station, where a pretty young thing introduced himself to her as Officer Romero, and led her back to the conference room, where the two detectives sat at the table, across from Sergeant Black. They all shook hands with her, Sergeant Black complimenting her new hair.

"How are you holding up?" Kendall Wind said.

"I'm fine, Kendall," Amy said, relishing the detective's first name. "Well . . . as fine as can be expected."

The sergeant produced a manila folder and set it on the table. "We'd just like you to look through these pictures," he said. "Let us know if any of them look like the young man who attacked you."

Amy nodded. There weren't that many pictures in the folder—maybe twenty. Most of them were mug shots. Some could have easily been class pictures, but something about them seemed mug-shot-like too: the hardness in these boys' eyes, not a single one of them smiling. Quite a gallery, though none of them jumped out at her immediately.

"Keep in mind, some of these pictures are several months old," Kendall said. "Try to look past things like hair color, keep in mind that he could have gained or lost weight."

"Right," Amy said. But this was harder than she'd thought it would be. A few of them she was able to rule out right away: one with a snake tattoo on his face, another with a Cro-Magnon forehead and unusually deep-set eyes. But the rest . . . "Do you have alternate pictures?" she said. "Profile shots?"

Wind said, "Take your time," which wasn't an answer and in fact rather patronizing. Amy glanced up from the folder, prepared for a scowl, but instead she got a smile. Amy had never seen Kendall Wind smile before, and it was surprising how much the smile changed her face, softened it. Her gaze dropped to the pictures, to the half dozen she'd separated from the rest, thinking they might be possibilities. "It would help if I could see their teeth," she said, the image flashing through her mind, the boy approaching her car. "He was smiling."

"Just try to imagine," Wacksman said, fanning out the six pictures in front of her, those grave faces. "It helps to focus on the eyes."

She nodded, her gaze drawn to the photo his hand was resting on. Those eyes, black as caves. His face was pale, as that boy's had been, walking toward her car in the glow of the streetlight, that white, sweat-sleeked forehead. That smile as he shook the bag. "You interested?"

And she'd opened her window, the cold air biting her skin. "What have you got?"

"Everything you want, beautiful. Everything you need."

That smile. The way the dark eyes had crinkled at the corners, the mouth forming that word. *Beautiful.* Amy's breath caught. "It's him." She tapped the picture with a bright red nail, her garnet ring glittering. "I'm almost positive."

She looked up. Wind was smiling again, along with Wacksman; Black too. "Great job," she said.

Amy smiled back, basking in the young detective's admiration.

PEARL HADN'T EXPECTED to see him. It was early afternoon, and he was supposed to be in school. But when she did see Ryan Grant, she knew she had to take action. The streets surrounding the middle and high schools were mortuary-quiet, the way they almost always were when school was in session but even more

so now, as though Liam's death had added an extra layer of still-
ness. She'd been patrolling the streets for close to an hour on this
cloudless, crisp day, her radio silent, the park like a movie set,
the half-bare trees motionless props. As she slowly drove past,
she saw one woman pushing a stroller along the cement path
that ran down the center of the park, another walking a golden
retriever on the autumn-brown grass. Pearl was about to turn
and make another loop around the schools when she noticed
his shaved head in her rearview, his athlete's stride. She made a
snap decision, circling around the park, pulling up behind Ryan
Grant as he started along the cement path. She gave him a few
quick bleats of the siren, so as to get his attention without scaring
him too much. Ryan spun around. His expression shifted from
mild annoyance to surprise when he saw Pearl behind the wheel.
Must have assumed it was Bobby, she thought, which then made
her wonder how often Bobby followed Ryan in his squad car.

Pearl opened the window. "Can I talk to you for a few seconds?"

"I just needed to get some air," Ryan said. "I'm going right back
to school, I swear."

"Hey, I'm not going to tell on you."

Ryan stayed quiet, his arms hanging at his sides. His face was
flushed, his fingers quivering, though Pearl couldn't tell whether
that was due to nerves or the cold. It was gloves-and-jacket
weather, and he was wearing neither, just a sweatshirt, and the
shaved head couldn't have helped. The tips of his ears were red.
She worried about frostbite.

"How do I know you won't tell?" he said.

"I could have told Bobby about how you and Liam broke into
the Schwartzes' house, and I didn't."

"I thought maybe you didn't remember me."

"Oh no, I remembered."

"Okay."

"So obviously I'm not going to tell your teachers you cut class." Ryan gave her a weak smile. "Thanks."

Pearl unlocked the passenger-side door. "Get in." She said it like an order. "Warm up."

He opened the door and slid into the front seat, dragging the cold air in with him. He blew on his fingers and clasped his hands between his knees and sniffled, his shoulders shaking.

"Amazing how much things can change in a few hours," Pearl said.

His back stiffened. "Huh?"

"It was warmer this morning."

"Oh," he said. "Right."

Ryan wouldn't look at her. Pearl studied his profile, the tension in it. Back at the police academy, she'd taken a course called verbal judo, which was just a catchy name for questioning techniques. When talking to anyone—witness, suspect, suicide threat—reading body language was key, and the idea was finding a way to balance it. If the subject was keyed up, for instance, your aim was to calm him down. If he was calm and cocky, you wanted to scare him a little. But Ryan was hard to read. Plus, he wasn't a suspect or a witness or a suicide threat. He was a kid who had slept through the last text his best friend would ever send. How do you get information out of that kid? Pearl had no idea, so she just asked him flat out. "Would you happen to know what 'SL' stands for?"

"Umm . . . Am I supposed to?"

She watched his face, and then his hands grasping each other. "Liam had a folder of videos in his phone," she said.

"He had tons of folders," he said. "He'd been collecting videos for years."

"Right," she said. "But this folder had only three videos in it. And one of them was of the carjacking. The folder was called 'SL.'"

"Oh, okay," he said. "But how would I know what that means?"

"Because you shot one of the videos," she said.

"I did?"

"Liam's dive. The Schwartzes' pool. You were holding his phone and taking the video."

"Oh. Right."

"The other one was Liam drinking in the cemetery."

He looked at her blankly. She pressed on. "So you understand, right? This tiny folder, just three videos in it. In two of them Liam's misbehaving. Then the third . . . You ever do that thing in school where your teacher gives you three different-looking pictures and you try and figure out what they all have in common?" She forced out a laugh. "I guess that's more something you do in kindergarten."

"Yeah."

"Anyway . . ."

"Uh-huh?"

"'SL.' What do you think? Is it a club or something? You have a friend with those initials?"

"I don't think so." He shifted around so he was facing the window again, shoulders slumped, shrinking into the seat. Pearl watched him, waiting for him to say more, but he stayed silent. She wished she could read his thoughts.

"I'm just asking," she said, "because we're trying to figure out who killed Liam. And I know you want to help."

Ryan turned to her. His eyes were bloodshot, his face pale. He looked as though he hadn't slept in days and maybe he hadn't. As sad as he'd looked at the police station, there was something else in his eyes now—anger and exhaustion and something that burned. "You guys know who killed Liam," he said. "Bobby knows. Everybody knows who killed Liam."

She stared at him. "Do you, Ryan? Do you know?"

His eyes clouded. "Doesn't matter. He's gone. He died a hero. And now he's dead and nothing will ever be like it was, ever again."

"I agree with all of that," she said, slowly, "except the part about it not mattering."

A tear slipped down his cheek. "May I leave the car now, please?"

"Yes, of course," Pearl said. "Just wait one sec." She pulled a Kleenex out of the box she kept in the front seat, handed it to him, along with a business card. It had her name on it, plus the number of the Havenkill Police. She'd written her cell phone number as well. She kept a few of them around like that. She knew the sergeant wasn't a fan of her giving out personal information, but this was Havenkill, and a lot of people would rather call a cell phone than a police station, especially kids. "Call me if you hear anything," she said. "Or if you just want to talk."

Another tear fell down his cheek, and he swatted at it with the Kleenex. Then he opened the door and walked back down the path and into the park, Pearl watching him until she couldn't see him anymore. *He knows what 'SL' is. He just doesn't want to say.*

Pearl pulled away from the curb. She drove in silence for a few blocks, an image in her mind—Ryan and Liam sitting next to each other at the Schwartzes' pool as they waited for their parents to show up, exchanging a quick look, a smile . . .

Nothing will ever be like it was, Pearl thought. And then her radio sprung to life, Sergeant Black summoning her to the high school to assist in searching a student's locker.

THE STUDENT WAS Wade Reed. Pearl hurried down the hallway to the principal's office, weaving through throngs of students just leaving class, many following her out of curiosity and milling outside the office, straining to hear what was going on. And there was much going on, much to hear. *"I didn't do anything!"* from behind the principal's closed door, hoarse and angry. *"This isn't fair!"*

She opened the door to find Udel and Tally on either side of Wade, gripping him by the shoulders as he thrashed about, Sergeant Black standing in front of them, telling him to calm down. "Listen," he kept saying, "Listen to me. If there's nothing in your locker, then there's nothing to worry about."

"You aren't allowed to look in my locker." Wade looked directly at Pearl. "He isn't, is he? Doesn't he need a warrant?"

"He doesn't need a warrant," said the principal, a tall, balding man in horn-rimmed glasses. "Your locker is technically considered school property, not private property." He looked at the sergeant. "Am I right?"

"Yep."

"Let go of me," Wade said.

"Take it easy." It was Tally, and he looked irritated. Udel, on the other hand, looked flat-out angry, his grip too tight on Wade's arm, his face twisted up and red.

"Let's all try and be calm," said Pearl, more to Udel than anyone else.

Tally and Udel led Wade out of the office, Pearl filing in behind the sergeant. "What's this about?" she whispered.

"We got a call on the tip line."

As they passed, the throng in the hallway went silent. Though Pearl did hear whispers: "Murderer . . ." "Crazy . . ." "Worships the devil . . ."

She kept her eyes on the back of Wade's hanging head, his frail neck and narrow shoulders, submitting to the grip on them, falling into it, with Tally and Udel practically holding him up. "Don't drag your feet," Tally said.

When they finally reached Wade's locker, which was on the bottom row, Sergeant Black said, "Officer Maze," and so she slipped thin evidence gloves out of her pocket, put them on and knelt down to open the locker. As the principal read off the combination, Wade kept saying, "Please," and "No," and "This isn't fair," over and over, to the point where Pearl thought maybe she'd been too kind to him, maybe he did have something to hide. When she turned the lock to the final number and opened it, the first thing she saw was a stack of sketches. And when she put her hand on them, Wade made a noise as though he'd been punched in the stomach.

"What's in there?" someone said behind her, which made her notice they had an audience. "Back up, please," she said to a girl leaning over her shoulder, so close she could feel her breath. "Please step away." She flipped through the sketches—five nudes, all of the same woman, her face erased in each. Pearl looked up at Wade. His face was red.

"Please," he whispered.

"Who's that?" a girl said.

"Probably one of his victims," said another.

"Perv," replied a boy's deepening voice.

Pearl glanced up at the principal, who said nothing.

"Be quiet," Pearl said to the boy. "If you are going to stay here, you aren't allowed to say or *think* a goddamned word."

The principal frowned at her, and Pearl went back to the locker. She wasn't quite sure where that had come from, but honestly, she didn't care. She had no tolerance for name-calling from these rich little bastards, one of whom had no doubt slashed Wade's tires.

She lifted a stack of books out of the locker, and noticed the glint of a plastic bag, wedged into the back corner, under several sheets of lined paper. She lifted it out. *Oh, Wade,* she thought. *Why . . .*

There were more than a dozen pill bottles inside. Alprazolam, hydrocodone, clonazepam. Clorazepate, chlordiazepoxide. Pain pills and benzos, just as Amy had described. "Like a pharmacy," she'd said. And indeed, each bottle bore a prescription label, each with a different name, each label from CVS. She looked up at Wade.

He stared at the bag, his jaw dropped open. "No," he whispered.

Pearl handed it to the sergeant.

"Bingo," said Udel.

Tally said, "I'm afraid we're going to have to take you in."

Wade's voice came back. "That isn't mine!" he shouted. "I swear to God! I've never seen those before!"

He struggled to get away, but Tally and Udel held him back.

"Anything else in there, Officer Maze?" the sergeant said.

But Pearl couldn't answer right away. She felt cold and motionless—frozen, down to her blood.

"Officer Maze?"

It had been placed beneath the bag of pills and now it sparkled out at her—a ring, adorned with a yellow citrine heart. She plucked it out of the locker and held it up, high enough for Wade to see.

"What is that?" the sergeant said.

Pearl turned to Sergeant Black, putting Wade behind her. "This is Amy Nathanson's ring," she said. "She lost it when she was fighting with the carjacker."

FIND THE GIRL, Jackie told herself. *Find the girl,* as she arrived home, headed straight down the hall and pushed open Wade's closed door, without thinking about it, his privacy no longer important, not now with his whole life at stake and Wade too dumb or too in love or too much of both to understand that.

As ever, the room was a mess. The first thing she noticed was that the dress shirt she'd folded and placed on his bed two days ago had been unbuttoned, turned inside out, and tossed to the floor. She checked the pocket, but the box was no longer in it. Wade had gotten rid of the *T* necklace—proof that he was still thinking about her. He'd disposed of evidence of her as recently as yesterday. It made Jackie even firmer in her belief that Wade had been with her, or at least he'd been trying to be with her, the night Liam had been killed. *Find the girl.*

There had to be more evidence.

Wade's phone was gone, but his laptop was on his unmade bed. Jackie yanked it off the bed, flipped it open, went to Google, and opened his search history. He clearly hadn't erased it in a long time. Jackie saw searches for figures and events from seventeenth-century history, a course he'd taken last year, SparkNotes for books that had been required summer reading, porn . . . Jackie ignored that. She skimmed the list and found nothing helpful, though his most recent search choked her up: *art scholarships + college.*

Jackie exhaled. She opened up his e-mail—most all of it junk, college and pharmaceutical spam in equal measures. She saw several assignments from his SAT prep teacher, all of them unopened, and gritted her teeth. *Don't get angry. Don't get distracted. Find the girl.* She looked for his Facebook icon, but it was no longer on his desktop. And when she went onto Facebook and logged on as herself, her heart dropped. He'd deleted his account. Who could blame him, what with that awful video from the parking lot, those cruel, hateful comments? She folded up the laptop, thinking, *What now . . . where to go now . . .* and spotted three spiral notebooks stacked up under his bed. Had he been keeping journals? She went for them, hoping with all her heart that he had.

They weren't journals. They were notebooks for classes. And they weren't even from this year. Jackie wanted to punch a wall. *Great.* But she opened the most recent one anyway—an English notebook from the previous spring—just to see his handwriting. Wade had always had the most beautiful handwriting.

Jackie ran her hand down the page, losing herself in the carefully formed block letters, the pristine *O*'s and the sharp-edged *A*'s. It was the handwriting of an artist, an architect, each letter perfect and complete. The notebook was from last April, around the same time he'd texted with Rafe Burgess about English assignments, Jackie remembered, and really the last time he'd seemed to truly care about a class. Mrs. Crawford. That was the teacher's name. He used to talk about her. Well, as much as Wade ever talked about anyone.

She flipped the page, reading his words. "Creative Writing assignment: Imagine yourself in the same situation as the Count of Monte Cristo . . . Spark word: Revenge . . ." Jackie looked at the date at the top of the page: "April 2," and wished it could pull her back in time. Had he known the girl then, before the Summer of Odd Jobs? Had she been in this English class as he took notes? Jackie flipped another page, her eyes starting to blur and burn, her throat clenching up. What was she expecting out of a class notebook? What was wrong with her?

She flipped to the very last page: "Spark word: Devotion." Jackie's gaze shifted from his notes to a doodle on the inside of the cardboard notebook cover. A girl's face in profile, the faintest of sketches. Below it, one word, written with a calligrapher's care: "Tristesse."

Jackie read it and reread it—*tristesse*, the French word meaning "sadness," but Wade had no interest in languages. He'd flunked Spanish last year.

Tristesse.

Jackie closed the notebook. She placed all three of them back under the bed. A spark had ignited within her, the slightest hint of hope. And if she could only breathe on it, if she could turn it into a flame and then a raging fire . . . *Tristesse*, French for sadness, began with the letter *T*. It also happened to be Stacy Davies's full first name.

JACKIE HAD NO idea what Helen's work schedule was like this week, but when she arrived at Helen's house, she saw her car outside and took it as proof that the tide was turning. She could save Wade.

She only had to ring Helen's doorbell once too, before her friend answered the door wearing sweats and no makeup or contacts, her hair tied up in a ponytail, squinting at her from behind cute coed glasses. "Oh Jackie," she said. "I'm so sorry about the communication breakdown. I did call Garrett, but his secretary apparently never gave him the message and—"

"It's okay," Jackie said. "Can I come in, please?"

"Sure, honey, sure." She stepped aside.

Jackie hadn't been in Helen's house since the boys were little, and it had been remodeled completely since then: polished wood floors, an enormous abstract statue in sleek pink marble, a colorful, expensive-looking throw rug that made her think of that Iggy Pop song she and Helen and Rachel used to sing in high school:

"Here comes my Chinese rug . . ." It was like walking through a familiar door into a completely new house, and it took her a few minutes to get her bearings.

"Hey, how did everything work out at the police station? I haven't had a chance to speak to Garrett."

"He's not taking the case."

Helen's face fell. *"Why?"*

"It doesn't matter," she said. "Look. Stacy's been hostile to Wade."

"She has? I'm sorry. She can be so thoughtless. I'll get her to apologize."

"No," Jackie said. "No, honey, that isn't why I'm telling you."

Helen frowned at her. "Come on into the living room."

Jackie followed her through to a room with beamed ceilings, Mexican tile floors, a bright bay window, and a buttery leather couch. Helen sat down on the couch and motioned for Jackie to do the same. "Can I get you anything?" she said.

Jackie was starting to get frustrated. "I just need you to listen to me."

"Okay . . ."

"I think Stacy has been hostile to Wade because there's been something going on between them."

"What?"

"Helen, I think Wade is in love with Stacy and she doesn't feel the same anymore. I think he's been with her in the past, and he was with her the night Liam was killed and for some bizarre reason he's refusing to tell anyone."

"What?"

"Maybe she's just embarrassed. I know how all the kids feel about him. But you have to tell her to let it go. Talk to the police. This is my son's life, Helen . . . He refuses to say a word."

Helen stared at her, concern flooding her features. "Honey, Stacy wasn't with Wade that night. She was here. Home. Sleeping."

"Are you sure?"

"She had SATs the next morning. Ryan Grant picked her up and took her there. They've been seeing each other, sort of. Stacy doesn't hang out with Wade."

"You saw her in the morning," Jackie said, very slowly. "But did you see her in the middle of the night?"

"Well, no. Of course not . . ."

"We don't know what our kids do in the middle of the night, Helen. Trust me. They have these entire lives we know nothing about."

"Jackie. You're scaring me." Helen stared at her, and for a moment, Jackie could see herself how her friend did, how little sense she was making, how scant and sad her evidence was.

"He wrote her name in his book," she said weakly. "He wrote 'Tristesse.'"

"Okay . . ."

"I'm sorry," Jackie said. "I . . . I think I'm grasping at straws. Not thinking things through."

"That's understandable."

"Can I use your bathroom?"

Helen nodded, directing her to a room across a narrow hall-way. Jackie splashed cold water in her face and leaned over the sleek sink, cool tiles under her palms. *It will be okay,* she told herself. *Everything is going to be all right.* She straightened up and looked at her reflection—the circles under her eyes, the sunken cheeks, the stress and lack of sleep turning her into a mirror image of her oldest son . . .

"Oh my God," she whispered, her gaze shifting from her own face to the bathroom wall behind her.

"Are you okay in there, honey?" Helen called out.

"Yes," Jackie said, taking it all in: The big mirror. The pale pink walls. The framed black-and-white photograph of the Eiffel Tower. "Wade was in this house in May!" she called out.

"What?"

Jackie opened the door. "He was in here, Helen. He took a picture in this bathroom."

"I'm telling you he's never been with—"

"You need to talk to Stacy." Jackie's phone buzzed in her pocket. She plucked it out and glanced at the number on the screen—a number she didn't recognize. She answered it.

"Mrs. Reed, this is Sergeant Black calling."

"Oh, I'm so glad you called."

But he kept on as if she hadn't said anything at all. "I'm sorry to tell you this, but your son Wade is at the county jail." He hurled words at her: auto theft, manslaughter.

"What's going on?" Helen said.

As Sergeant Black continued speaking, Jackie focused on their images in the mirror, hers and Helen's, the Eiffel Tower between them. The photo had been taken back in May. Stacy wasn't even in it. It proved nothing, other than the unsettling fact that her son had been in this house, possibly without Stacy even knowing it. "Wade is under arrest," she said.

"Oh my God. Oh my God, Jackie."

Black was giving her directions to the county jail when she stopped listening altogether. She let go of everything—the phone, her hopes, her mind—and collapsed onto Helen's bathroom floor.

Twenty-Seven

From the secret Facebook group "RIP Liam."

October 22 at 12:00 PM

Thank you all so much for reaching out to Chris and me during this time. I know that many of you feel powerless to help us. I've heard this a lot. But please know that your thoughts and prayers and especially your stories of Liam have done more for us than you will ever know.

There's no guidebook for losing one's child. That's a good thing. If there were, it would make the loss of a child something common, and Chris and I wouldn't wish this experience on anyone.

But your stories have shown us what an impact Liam made on this earth during the very brief time he was here. He made his friends laugh; he helped them get through tough times. He taught them to enjoy life and that anything could be an adventure. There are many young people who told me how much he meant to them, as well as grown-ups who still remember what a sweet little boy he was. His third-grade teacher, Mrs. Epstein, gave me a poem he wrote in her class that she's kept to this day. The poem is called "Always Be Kind."

I can't tell you how much all of your memories mean to Chris and me. If you can, though, I'd like you to do one more thing for us: Please remember Liam always. Especially the young people. After you graduate high school and go out into the world and figure out who you really are, keep him in your thoughts. Hold him in your hearts. Take him along for the ride.

With love,

Sheila Miller

👍 95 people like this

October 22 at 5:00 PM

Liam has been cremated. For those interested, there will be a memorial service tomorrow, October 23, at St. Gregory's Church at 5:30 pm. We look forward to seeing as many of you as possible.

With gratitude,

Sheila and Chris Miller

Twenty-Eight

It was strange how quickly you could grow to love another person if you opened your heart and allowed it to happen. Amy had known Sheila Miller barely a day, and their paths had crossed under the most terrible of circumstances, but Amy now considered her one of her closest confidantes. They reached out to each other. They clung to each other. They gave each other strength. Over the past twenty-four hours, in person but especially during their many phone conversations, Amy had probably shared deeper thoughts with Sheila than she'd ever shared with anyone, even Vic. It made her realize how lonely and lacking her life had been before, and as she stood waiting to see Sheila and her husband in the long reception line at St. Gregory's Church at Liam's memorial service, hugging fellow mourners, signing memorial programs and, yes, telling them *that* story again and again, Amy felt so much gratitude for Sheila, her best friend. She couldn't see her soon enough.

Chris too, of course. Chris was a dear. But to be honest, she hadn't had that much contact with Chris. He'd spent most

of the time locked up in his room sleeping as Sheila and Amy
gabbed in person or on their phones, sharing everything from
stories from their youths to philosophical beliefs to recipes,
both of them terrified of silence, both fighting it off as their
men lay unconscious. The last time they'd spoken, it had been
three in the morning. "You're the only person I know I can call
at this hour," Sheila had said. "My other friends might pretend
they don't mind. But with you I know it's real."

Amy was reaching the front of the line, where Sheila and Chris
stood, Chris in a dark suit with sad, drugged eyes, Sheila in a
black sheath that hung on her, her weight loss obvious. Amy wore
a black dress too, a satin shift from the 1950s with a high collar,
but seeing the Millers she felt inappropriate, too fat and festive
for the occasion.

"It's so wonderful to see you," Sheila said, throwing her frail
arms around Amy and pulling her close. Amy inhaled her lily of
the valley scent, a touch of spring on this cold day, and her awkward feelings faded.

She gave Chris a quick hug. He smelled of cigarettes. "I heard
they arrested someone," Chris said—as many words as she'd
heard out of him since they'd met.

Amy nodded, eager to answer. "It was based on my ID," she
said. "They showed me pictures of a bunch of suspects, but I
picked him out immediately."

"Good." Chris had a direct, honest gaze that probably served
him well in business. Cerulean eyes, much like his son's. "He'll be
brought to justice."

The minister smiled at them on his way up the pulpit steps.
"If you could all please take your seats," he said as he made himself comfortable behind the lectern, tapping the microphone and

clearing his throat. The reception line broke into bits and started to fill the pews.

Most everybody here was in couples or families. Amy thought about Vic. He'd been more out of sorts than usual today, wishing her good luck at her Whisky gig, his mind back in L.A. Part of it was that she'd been gone so often lately, but there was more to his confusion, she knew. She needed to bring him to the doctor soon to adjust his meds. But that would mean taking him out in a car that wasn't Baby, and she wasn't sure how he'd survive that or even if he would. Turning to find a seat, she felt a shot of panic. But Sheila grabbed hold of her hand. Her grip was firm and cool. "No, no, no," said Sheila, who had lost everything that life had to lose and still had it in her to reassure a lonely woman. "No, Amy. You are sitting with us."

JACKIE HAD LOST fifty friends on Facebook. An odd thing to be thinking about while coming out of a panic attack, but that was the first rational thought she had as the dizziness started to lift and she felt that heavy wetness over her closed eyes—a cold compress, soft hands patting her face, a voice, Helen's voice, saying, "Honey, are you okay . . ." Fifty friends, some of them clients from years ago, others whom she'd known since high school. She'd noticed it back in Wade's room, when she'd logged on to her page from his computer, but at the time she'd been too blinded by hope to care. *How petty. They hear a few rumors and they run . . .*

But it was more than rumors now. Her son had been arrested, charged with auto theft and manslaughter. Was that what the sergeant had said to her over the phone? And also . . . God . . . something about drugs . . . Her mind was still fuzzy, the dizzy feeling threatening to return. She needed a Xanax. Had she remembered to put the bottle in her purse before leaving the house? Could she take half of one and still drive to the county jail?

"Can you hear me, Jackie?" Helen said.

She pulled the compress from her eyes. "I didn't pass out," she said, a little embarrassed in spite of everything. "It was a panic attack. I've . . . I've had them and they feel like fainting, but they're not."

Helen stroked her hair. She was too close to her face. "You'll be okay, sweetheart."

"I have to get to the jail."

"It's okay. I've called someone."

"I need a lawyer."

"I got you one," she said. "He's on his way. He actually happened to be nearby, in Rhinebeck, so he should be here soon."

Helen handed her a glass of water. Jackie gulped it. She'd never felt so thirsty in her life. She pulled herself up to her feet and saw her reflection in the mirror—blotchy skin, mascara streaks on her face. A true sight. She peered at herself, noticing again the Eiffel Tower picture in the mirror behind her.

"Stacy might know something," Jackie said. Her voice sounded thin and distant, as though it were coming from somewhere else. She hadn't completely recovered. She could hear her own pulse. She needed to sit down again, but she fought it. She forced the words out. "I know it's a long shot, but if you could please just talk to Stacy . . . Even if she wasn't with Wade that night, he cares for her. I know that. She might know something that could help him."

Helen put a hand on her shoulder. "Jackie, I need to tell you who I called."

Jackie blinked at Helen. Why was she ignoring everything she was saying?

A buzz interrupted Jackie's thoughts—a loud, alarm-like thing that cut through the fog in her brain.

"That's the doorbell," said Helen. "Look, Jackie. I called Bill."

"You . . . Wait. What?"

"He's going to be Wade's lawyer. He wants to be Wade's lawyer. It's the least he could do."

"You called Bill?" She could hear her pulse again.

"Are you going to be okay?"

"That's an interesting question."

The doorbell exploded again. "Don't be mad at me," Helen said. Then she ran to get it.

Jackie struggled to her feet. She was very thirsty. She went to the sink and put her lips to the faucet and sucked down cold water until she felt alert, almost normal. She wiped the mascara off with a tissue, splashed water in her face, dabbed at it with a towel. *Bill. She called Bill.*

She heard voices coming from the entryway. A man's voice saying, "Is she all right?" Bill's voice. She wasn't upset. Helen had been right to call him. Wade needed a lawyer, and Bill was as good a lawyer as he was a bad father to his sons. Well, maybe not that good. But he was well connected. After nearly twenty years of practicing in this area, he knew the judges, the cops. Everyone.

"Jackie?" Bill was in the living room now, saying her name for the first time in person in she didn't know how long, probably since he'd taken Wade to that Yankees game.

She left the bathroom. Bill was standing next to Helen. His hair had gone gray. He wore an expensive-looking suit and a trench coat that hung at his sides. And he looked older. So much older. "I'm sorry," he said.

AMY SAT NEXT to Sheila as the minister spoke. He started out by describing the many summers Liam had served as a counselor at church camp, how he'd carved walking sticks for the young campers and taught them to swim. Amy found the stories heartwarming and sweet—more memories for Sheila to treasure. But when he launched into his own interpretation of Isaiah 57:1, talking about how "good men often die before their time and for good reason," she tuned out what he was saying. Amy was never a great fan of organized religion, but she found it particularly cruel when it insisted that everything—no matter how awful— was a part of God's master plan. Isaiah would have you believe that God had taken Liam in order to protect him from the evil in the natural world. But what did that say about Liam's parents? Shouldn't they be the ones protecting him rather than some power-mad, micromanaging *deus ex machina* who couldn't trust two perfectly decent people enough to let them do their job? To Amy, there was far more comfort in chaos, and she wanted to tell Sheila as much. But Sheila was nodding slowly, listening to the words. *We all take comfort from wherever we can find it.*

Amy started paying attention again when the minister announced Liam's best friend, Ryan Grant, and a boy emerged from a group of kids that was sitting a few rows back. He was tall and wore a letterman's jacket and khaki pants, his head shaved bald. "He did that for Liam," Sheila whispered. "All the boys shaved their heads for him."

"Why?"

"I really don't know. Probably so they could feel like they did something."

The boy pulled a crumpled piece of paper from his jacket pocket. He spread it in front of him, hands shaking, and when he spoke, his voice was barely audible, even from the front row where Amy and the Millers sat.

"This is a letter Liam sent me from camp, the summer between seventh and eighth grade. Liam and I loved Camp Arcady. At that point, we'd been going there together every summer for three years, but my grandma was sick, and my parents said we had to go and visit her. Being a selfish thirteen-year-old kid, the only thing I could think about was missing camp. I was really upset."

Ryan dragged a hand across his eyes. The minister tried to hand him a Kleenex but he waved it away. "Anyway," Ryan said. "They don't let you text from Camp Arcady unless it's an emergency. They make you write letters. Liam sent me this letter when he was away, and I've kept it ever since . . ."

He grasped the lectern for several seconds, as though he was trying to stay steady on his feet. There was an uncomfortable silence, a few people coughing to fill the void, until finally he began to read. "'Dear Doofus,'" he said. "'Camp sucks. It won't stop raining and they got all new counselors and every one of them is mean. All we do all day is clean toilets, except when they give us a break and make us peel potatoes. With a butter knife.'"

Ryan paused. There was a hum of soft, polite laughter, Sheila and Chris included, of course. They were kind people, and this boy was so clearly struggling. His back straightened slightly but his head stayed down, the crown so pale and vulnerable from the shave.

He continued. "'None of our friends are here. Just a bunch of big, mean girls who keep beating me up. And I can't hit back because they're girls. I tried telling on them, but the counselor socked me in the eye. She was a girl too.'" More laughter, louder this time. "'The food sucks too, by the way. Nothing but vegan stuff. When they remember to feed us.'" Louder laughter. A few kids applauded. Ryan smiled at the paper, and when he started to read again, his voice was louder, more confident. And slightly familiar to Amy. "'Are you feeling like you dodged a bullet, dude? Good. All that stuff I told you was a lie. Except the part where I said: Camp sucks. It does. But only because you aren't here.'" He cleared his throat and looked out at the crowd for the briefest of moments. Amy caught sight of Ryan's eyes, his dark, glittering eyes, which seemed familiar too. She tried to imagine him with hair, with a black hoodie, a bag of pills in his hand . . . *No. You're being crazy.* "'Your friend, Liam,'" Ryan read, and Amy pushed the thought away. It wasn't possible, and when he walked up to Sheila and Chris, hugging them both, she decided she had definitely been seeing things; her mind had been playing tricks on her. She'd picked the right boy back at the station. She knew that face. And the way the detectives had looked at her, as though she'd given them the correct answer . . .

"Ryan's parents are the nicest people," Sheila whispered as the minister returned, and Ryan went back to the pews, a couple coming forward, the woman wrapping him in her arms. "I'll have to introduce you later."

Amy said nothing, Sheila's whisper a breeze on her neck as the room grew airless. She started to sweat. For there was Ryan's father in his expensive suit. His shaved head. His diamond earring glittering, even at a distance. *I'm a big fan* . . . There was his young, plump wife with her luxuriant hair, hugging her son, a son she'd never mentioned that night Amy had spent with them at their lovely Tudor home, though Amy had walked by a boy's room at one point during the four hours she'd spent there. Opened the door thinking it was a bathroom. Sports pennants on the wall, a neatly made bed. Empty. At the time, Amy had assumed they had a son who was off at boarding school, or college.

Twenty-Nine

Posted on the secret Facebook group "RIP Liam."

October 23 at 8:00 PM

Thank you all so much for coming to our memorial for Liam. It is lovely to know that Liam had so many caring classmates, teachers, and even former camp counselors who showed up for what was a very special evening. Chris and I count all of you as our extended family. We'd like to offer special thanks to Father Charlie from St. Gregory's for putting on such a lovely service, to the church auxiliary for the delicious treats at the reception, as well as Tamara Hayes, Ryan Grant, and Stacy Davies for their heartfelt, deeply moving speeches about Liam. Liam chose mature and admirable young men and women to be his closest friends—this is very clear. Kids, your parents should be proud. I would also like to thank Amy Nathanson, aka Aimee En, for joining in the memorial. While she had to leave before it was over due to an emergency at home, she did want me to remind you all of her benefit concert on the 29th. (See the link below.)

As I get through the end of another day, my heart is full, as
I never thought possible. As hard as I know the future will be,
Chris and I will cherish this night, and all of you, always. At the
reception, a few of you asked me about that poem Liam wrote for
Mrs. Epstein's class.

Here it is:

"Always Be Kind"
By Liam Miller, Age 8

If you meet up with a grizzly
With really big claws
Or a shark in the ocean
Who looks just like Jaws
If a scary bank robber
Points a gun in your face
Or a bully says "you loser"
And makes you feel out of place
Don't be hurtful or mean
That will make you bad as them.
Be kind! Join the nice team!
Kindness wins in the end

Thirty

Bill knew his way around the county judicial system, Jackie had to give him that. Before they even took off for the jail, he'd arranged to have Wade brought to the courthouse, where, after a speedy hearing, he got him released on his own recognizance. Jackie had expected Wade to be angry at the sight of his father, but as he was brought into the courtroom, wrists cuffed, Wade looked more shell-shocked than anything else. And watching him, Jackie felt the same. As Bill spoke to the judge, she recalled a dream she'd had the previous night: Wade and herself, standing at Liam's shrine. They'd come to pay their respects, but before long, they discovered the shrine was dangerous—not only inhospitable to them, but a living, breathing, growing thing. In the dream, Jackie had watched helplessly as the shrine swelled around Wade and drowned him, bouquets of flowers squirming over him like snakes, trophies bashing at him, stuffed animals suffocating him with Mylar balloons, the whole awful colorful mass gathering into a wave and pulling him under . . . She closed her eyes, forced the memory from her mind. Made herself look at Wade again. The handcuffs couldn't come off soon enough.

Once Wade was released, they got into their two separate cars. "You need directions to our place?" Jackie said.

Bill shook his head. "I remember."

Wade didn't speak at all in the car. When they were about halfway home, Jackie said, "Your father wanted to represent you. I know it's strange, but I think he'll do a good job."

Wade shrugged. He didn't reply, didn't open his mouth. They drove the rest of the way home in the dark of early evening, neither one of them speaking. Jackie tried to remember what little she knew about the booking process for prisoners; then, after remembering, tried to forget it. When they pulled into their driveway, Bill's car was outside. He'd actually beaten them there, always a fast driver. Jackie thought of him inside the house, with Connor, how awkward that must be. She got out of the car quickly, then opened Wade's door. "I believe in you," she told him. "We're going to beat this."

"You shouldn't," Wade said.

"What?"

"You shouldn't believe in me."

He got out of the car, and she followed him up the driveway. Walking along the short path that led to the front door, Jackie had the strangest feeling of being watched. She looked up and down the street, and ushered Wade inside fast, knowing that it wasn't just a feeling. They would be watched for a while.

CONNOR DIDN'T WANT to open the door. He was scared in his own house. More scared than he'd ever been, anywhere. He'd toughed it out through school, ignoring the stares from the other kids, sticking close to good old oblivious Noah for the rest of the day and trying not to think about that text he'd received, who had sent it. *Your whole family should die . . .*

And then, as he and Noah were heading to the parking lot, one of Mason Marx's loser friends had shoved him in the hallway—the dorky elf with the spiky hair. "Your perv Satanist brother got arrested today," he'd said, smirking. "They found drugs and kiddie porn in his locker."

Connor had shoved him right back, and Noah had called him an asshole and a liar. But he still had a sinking feeling, the avalanche barreling closer. And then, about an hour after Noah's mom had dropped him home, just as he was starting to lose himself in Minecraft, Mom had texted him telling him Wade really had been arrested. Connor had thought again of that avalanche. *Brace yourself. It's here.*

Connor had purposely stayed off social media, but that didn't do much to alleviate this creeping sense of panic. He had to get his brain off whatever was going on with Wade's arrest. The more he thought about it, the more worried he got—not so much for him or even for Wade, but for Mom. She had anxiety issues. Connor knew that for a fact—he'd seen the pills in her nightstand. Xanax. What if the stress of Wade's arrest got to be too much for her and she had a heart attack? He hadn't been able to get that thought out of his mind—Mom on a stretcher in the back of an ambulance. He knew he had to catch up on *To Kill a Mockingbird* for English, and so he'd tried to do that, but the words just danced and blurred on the page, none of it making any sense to him, the panic bearing down.

About twenty minutes ago, Mom had texted him again. And while he was relieved she was still okay, the text itself had disturbed him even more: *On our way back from the courthouse. Wade released. We will have a trial date soon. DON'T WORRY. Dad is on the case. He will prove Wade's innocence.*

Connor had stared at the text thinking, *Dad? Seriously?* And then someone had driven by their house, horn blaring, tires shrieking, a group of people yelling out of a car window: *"Murderer!"* Connor could hear them, all the way from the kitchen.

What is happening?

And now the doorbell. Connor didn't want to answer it. He wanted to run to his room and hide under the covers, stay there until he could wake up from this nightmare.

The doorbell rang again. He put his book down and turned around so he could see the window next to the front door. A man was standing there. He could see his outline in the porch light— tall, wearing a suit and an opened trench coat. Could be a cop, or maybe a vigilante out to get Wade. Could be a contract killer, or Slenderman. Anybody. Connor's heart pounded. The suit rang the bell again, pounded on the door. "Connor?" he said. "Are you in there?"

Okay. I'm pretty sure Slenderman wouldn't know my name. Connor moved toward the door. "Yeah?" His voice cracked.

"Open up. It's your dad."

Wow. Mom wasn't kidding. Connor opened the door slowly. He looked up at the man's face. Connor hadn't seen his dad since he was three years old probably. And outside of a few super-old photos in the scrapbook under her bed, Mom didn't keep any pictures of him around the house either.

"Hi," said the man. His eyes were the same color as Connor's, and he kind of had Wade's bone structure.

"You're my dad?"

He winced. "Use the term as loosely as you want," he said. "I know I haven't been very good at it."

Connor's shoulders relaxed. He backed up and let the guy in, made sure the door was locked behind him. "You want some frozen pizza?"

"You're not mad at me?"

"Not really," Connor said. "I don't even know you."

Connor heard footsteps coming up the walk, the front door opening, then Wade and Mom coming in together.

"Hey," Connor said.

Mom's cheeks looked gaunt, sunken in, her dark eyes tired and bloodshot, just like Wade's did so much of the time. But she went to Connor fast, and when she hugged him, there was strength in it. "Don't worry," Mom said. "We're gonna get through this."

"Your mother's right," Dad said. "From what I've seen so far, I think we can win this case."

Connor didn't say anything. Over Mom's shoulder, he could see Wade watching him with his eyes like metal spikes. *What's wrong with you?* he wanted to say. But he had a feeling he might know . . .

Mom pulled away. "You really think we can win, Bill?"

He nodded. "Look, I'm not exactly F. Lee Bailey, but I can see the holes. Yes, Nathanson ID'd him, but that was days after, in a situation where she was obviously trying to give those cops the answer that they wanted. And the stuff they found in the locker . . . Locker combinations aren't exactly private information. The principal has a copy of all of them, not to mention Wade's friends—"

Wade interrupted him. "I want to plead guilty."

Mom stared at him. "Honey, what are you talking about?"

Wade's eyes were on Dad. "I did it," he said. "I stole that

woman's car and I killed Liam with it. I saw him coming toward me, and rather than stop, I ran him down. Then I drove the car into the Kill."

Dad said, "I don't think you're thinking this through."

"Why?" Wade said. "You don't think a son of yours would do something like that?"

Connor's gaze went to Mom, her mouth opening and closing.

"You don't want people finding out we're . . . uh . . . related?"

"Wade."

"I got news for you, asshole. If there's anybody on this planet whose son would grow up to be a murderer, it's *you*."

"Wade, *please*," Mom said.

Connor said, "Stop it. You're hurting Mom."

"Don't even talk to me, Connor. You told the police about the bag. You promised you wouldn't tell, and you did. You're a liar. You betrayed me."

Connor felt as though he'd been kicked in the gut. "I didn't . . ." His voice cracked. "I didn't mean to . . ."

"Wade," Mom said. "What phone did you ask Connor to throw out? We can help you if you just tell us the truth."

"It was Aimee En's phone."

Dad moved toward Wade. "I know that isn't true."

"You don't know a damn thing. You don't even know *me*."

"I know I messed up your life. Take it out on me. Hate me. You have every right. But please don't take it out on yourself."

Wade looked at him, his face softening slightly. "You should go back to your family."

Mom started to say something, but an explosion cut into her words, the breathtaking crash of glass breaking.

Wade then burst out the front door, and Dad took off after him, yelling at him to wait.

"Oh my God," Mom said. "Oh my God." On her knees, next to a pile of shattered glass—the big window by the front door. Connor went to her and knelt beside her. "Look at this," she whispered. There was a big rock on the floor. Someone had thrown it through the window. Letters painted in red on the top: DIE SCUM.

"Look at this."

He put his arm around her. *Mom. Poor Mom. She doesn't deserve this. She didn't do anything wrong.* He heard shouting outside— Wade's voice and their father's, then tires screeching away from the curb. He looked at the rock again, the red letters, anger sparking inside him, heating up in his veins. He picked it up and went running outside, yelling louder than he'd ever yelled before, his own voice scraping the back of his throat, *"Leave my family alone!"*

"Get back inside, Connor," Connor's father said. His father, a complete stranger, telling him what to do.

In the bushes along the side of his house, Connor heard a rustling. He whirled toward it, raised the rock over his head with both hands, and hurled it at the sound. It didn't go very far, landing on the grass, just a few feet away.

"I mean it, Connor," his stranger-father said, but the last part was drowned out by a deafening crack. It shook Connor's body, like a train smashing into it. *A live wire,* he thought. *I stepped on a live wire.* Which made no sense at all.

And then he couldn't move. *What is happening to me . . .*

Connor heard his mother scream and only then did he feel the stiff grass against the side of his face, the copper taste in his mouth and the chill, the awful blast of it, as though he'd never be warm again.

"I KNOW PEOPLE," Udel was saying over a mouthful of pork lo mein. "I mean, I don't have a psychology degree or anything, but

I knew Wade Reed was a bad dude the first time we questioned him." They were parked on Orchard and Flower after stopping at the one Chinese place in town, grabbing dinner in the middle of a patrol. After Wade had been booked, the sergeant had given Pearl, Udel, and Tally the option of taking the rest of the day off, and while Pearl had said she'd be glad to work another shift, she hadn't thought Udel would be part of the deal.

Pearl bit into an egg roll. "I didn't see it," she said. "He seemed kind of lost to me. But not bad."

He slurped up more noodles, shaking his head. "No. He's a bad, bad dude."

"And you know because . . ."

"I know people. I study them until I can figure out how they tick."

Pearl rolled her eyes. She took a swallow of Diet Coke, wishing it was beer. "Gotcha, inspector."

"You laugh, Maze, but I probably know you better than you know yourself."

Pearl took another swallow, thinking, *Forget beer. Bleach.*

Udel started to say something else but was cut off by the radio: Tally on dispatch telling them of a 10–72 on 291 Maple Street.

"At that address?" Udel replied as he started up the car and pulled away from the curb.

"Outside. On the lawn. Suspect running from the scene."

Pearl looked at him. They both knew that address. They'd learned it this afternoon. "Wade Reed's house," she said.

They arrived at the house in minutes. She saw a woman crouched over, a man with a phone in his hand, a pool of blood. *Wade,* she thought. But then she caught sight of the shooting victim and her heart dropped.

"Over there!" the man with the phone shouted. He pointed at a house across the street. "The shots came from over there! I saw someone running."

Pearl took off. She raced across the street and around the back of the house with Udel somewhere behind her, she didn't know, didn't care. The backyard was small, with a neatly trimmed lawn, an aboveground pool. She saw a shadow inside the house, a light going on. "Turn on your lights please!" she shouted. "Ma'am! Sir! This is the police. Please turn on your outdoor lights!"

Someone must have heard her because in an instant the backyard was flooded with light, and Pearl caught sight of a husky figure, tearing across the back of the lawn into the woods.

"Stop!" she called out. "Police!"

She headed after him, weaving around trees until she was just a few feet away from him—a short, burly man dressed all in black. He slowed down. He was in bad shape. Pearl was so close she could hear his labored breathing as he stumbled into a clearing, still moving. She could see the gun in his hand. A big, sleek semiautomatic. She had hers out of her holster, the first time she'd ever drawn on the job, and she didn't want to use it. "Stop! Drop your gun!" she yelled out. "I can see you."

He stopped. Breathing hard. Pearl kept her weapon trained on him. "Drop the gun," she said again.

He dropped it.

Pearl exhaled. She could sense Udel next to her now, reaching for his gun. "Don't," Pearl whispered. She kept her eyes on the man. His thick, short legs. His Nike sneakers. "Put your hands in the air, and turn around slowly."

He did as he was told. When the man turned around, it took Pearl a few seconds to register that he wasn't a man at all. He was just a boy, apple-cheeked and sweating, tears streaming down his face. "I didn't mean to do it," he said, once he finally caught his breath. "It's my dad's gun. I just wanted to scare them."

"Scare who?" Pearl said.

"Connor and Wade."

"Why?"

"I don't know." He was crying now. "I don't know. I don't know."

"What's your name?" said Pearl. "How old are you?"

"I'm thirteen years old," he said. "My name is Mason Marx."

Thirty-One

"I'm so cold, Mom," Connor said through trembling lips. Jackie kept her gaze on his face, not the blood. She knelt over him in the grass and pulled off her coat and threw it over his body, and then his own coat, which she'd somehow grabbed out of the closet before running outside. *Keep him warm. He's just cold, that's all. Just cold outside.*

"I'm here," she whispered. "Dad and I are here."

"Dad," he said.

"I know, right? Weird."

Bill was on the phone now, talking to 911. "Yes, still awake," he was saying. "He's my son."

Jackie found herself thinking back to Helen—the privileged, rosy way she looked at things. "Life only gives us as much as we can take," she had said. How ridiculous she'd found those words at the time, how maddening. But now she found herself hanging on to them with everything she had. She pressed the coats to Connor's chest, trying to stanch the bleeding. Stroked his matted hair and looked into his scared blue eyes. *This is all that I can take. No more. Please.*

"Someone shot me," Connor said.

Jackie nodded. "But you're going to be okay."

His eyelids fluttered. "You sure?"

"Of course I am."

"I'm tired, Mom."

Keep him awake, Jackie told herself. *Keep talking.* She arranged the coats around Connor and talked to him in a low voice, saying anything that came to her mind, just to keep those blue eyes focused, opened. "You know, honey, I heard it might rain again. I heard it on the radio, earlier today, but you know, I wasn't sure whether it was the Catskills forecast or ours. NPR can be so confusing, all those detailed weather reports for such a large area. The way they do them at once."

"Mom," said Connor. "You're, like, babbling about the weather. Which is . . . sorta weird."

A tear spilled down Jackie's cheek. She smiled at him. "You're a funny kid, you know that?" she said.

"I'm sorry."

"For what?"

"Running outside. Tell Dad I'm sorry I ran outside." Jackie touched his forehead with the back of her hand. He was so cold.

"Oh thank God," Bill said. Jackie heard sirens. She looked up and saw a police car screeching to the curb, Bill shouting at them, pointing across the street. She didn't look. Instead, she kept her hand on Connor's forehead, her gaze on his face, that milk-pale skin, so very like he used to look in his crib, when he was a baby. "You stay awake now," she said, thinking of opposites, reverse lullabies. "You stay awake now, kiddo."

She wasn't sure how much time passed before the ambulance

pulled up. It could have been seconds or hours, it didn't matter, the way time was running, each fragment of each second suspended and hovering, Jackie's heartbeat ticking like a clock. "You think it will rain?" she said to Connor as two paramedics lifted him onto a stretcher and hooked him up to an IV. "I think it will rain so hard that the roof will leak, and we'll put out buckets and make hot cocoa and listen to the patter."

"That sounds nice, Mom."

Jackie was allowed to ride in the ambulance. Bill followed behind. As they sped to the hospital, the younger of the paramedics turned to her—a guy with sparkly eyes, a fish tattoo on his neck. "He'll be fine," he said. "I've seen a lot worse than this."

Jackie wasn't sure whether or not he was lying. She thought he might be.

AMY DIDN'T SHARE a bed with Vic. She couldn't, as he slept fitfully on rubber sheets and often had accidents. But she did sleep next to him, in a cot with wheels that she pulled right up against the hospital bed, so close their faces were nearly touching. It usually helped her get to sleep, listening to the sound of his breathing, his heavy snores. But not tonight. She was meeting that *New York Times* reporter for lunch tomorrow, and she was nervous. She kept running different outfits through her mind, pairing vintage dresses with lipstick and shoes . . . Should she go conservative or sexy or a little of both? She wasn't sure. Maybe pants were a better way to go, though Amy hardly ever wore pants. Palazzos, maybe. She had a lovely pair of orange palazzos.

Amy's brain was a mess. She'd taken two of Vic's Ambien at least an hour ago, but they weren't doing any good. Her mind kept sparking up and wandering and she didn't like where it went. The Grants' Tudor home. She'd gotten to know so much of it: their four-poster bed and their kitchen table, the mirrored wall in the dining room and the staircase, right in the middle of that long staircase, with Amy's own songs blasting over the stereo, unstifled moans and clothes flying and lamps tipping over, no one the least concerned about making noise because they were the only ones in the house. Ryan hadn't been home.

Amy shut her eyes tight. Tears seeped out of the corners. *It was a coincidence. It had to be.* Ryan was probably sleeping over at a friend's that night, maybe partying with some girls. Ryan was popular, while Wade Reed was a loner, an angry young man. She'd read online somewhere that he worshipped the devil. And besides, they'd found Amy's ring in his locker. Sergeant Black had told her. Her yellow citrine ring.

It was Wade who ran Liam down. Not Ryan. Ryan was Liam's best friend. It didn't even make sense.

Amy began to relax, the Ambien finally getting to her, spreading over her body like a heated blanket. Vic started snoring and the rich hum filled the bedroom, the life in it lulling her to sleep.

She'd never have to think of the Grants again. She'd never have to mention them to the police or to anyone. Wade had killed Liam Miller, not their son. The Tudor mansion could be forgotten, as though it had never happened at all. *And Vic, my sweet Vic, will never find out . . .*

Drifting off to sleep, Amy thought of orange palazzos. Orange palazzos and pale pink ballet flats, a low-cut silk blouse. Oh, and the red patent-leather clutch she'd bought from Etsy a few weeks ago, the one that matched her lipstick and made her look like a dream.

PEARL WAS STANDING in the middle of a field with her gun drawn, a hooded figure in front of her. "*Stop,*" she said to the figure.

"Freeze." The figure was Death, and if she shot it, everyone who ever died would come back to life. Including her mother. *"Hold still,"* Pearl said.

But Death wouldn't cooperate. Its hooded cloak billowed up into a wave, then shrank down into a black hoodie. Pearl pulled back her safety and pulled the trigger and shot Death in the head, blood spewing out, a crimson arc. But when it turned around, Pearl saw that it wasn't Death at all. It was her mother, bleeding everywhere. Pearl was wearing the black cloak. Pearl was Death.

Mason Marx marched out onto the field, carrying two cymbals. *"Wake up,"* he said. He crashed the cymbals together and Pearl woke up out of the dream to a different ringing sound. A text message. Pearl sat up in bed, switched the light on. According to the clock on her wall, it was 2:00 AM.

She took a breath as the last of the dream left her. Mason Marx. That doomed kid. No matter what happened to Connor Reed, Mason Marx would never be free of this night. He would feel it in nightmares always, the explosion of the gun in his hands, a boy his own age dropping to the grass, all that blood, because of him. It wasn't something you could ever recover from, no matter how much therapy you went to. Pearl knew that, and she had been a lot younger than Mason, her memory of it cloudier . . .

Pearl checked her texts. Now that she was more awake, she realized the text had probably been from Paul. He had been working tonight, just like she was. He had been the one to take Connor to the hospital. She'd FaceTimed with him, after Connor had gone into the ER. He'd been so scared for this kid, and though it usually wasn't like Pearl to comfort a man, it wasn't like most men to seek comfort from her either. And so she'd comforted Paul, as best she could. "You're the only one I can talk to," he had said.

"You're the only one who understands." Paul, whose last name Pearl still didn't know.

She opened her texts, and sure enough there was one from Paul, unread, though he'd sent it not at two but at one. She held her breath. Closed her eyes and hoped in a way that felt almost like praying, and Pearl never prayed. *Please,* she thought. *Please, please, please.*

Then she read the text: *The kid's gonna be okay!!!!* ☺ ☺ ☺

Pearl's heart swelled. She felt herself smiling so hard her face hurt, tears seeping out of the corners of her eyes. An emotion she wasn't sure she'd ever felt before. *Overjoyed.* That's what she felt. She ran her fingertip over the exclamation points, those stupid, corny smiley faces. She texted Paul: *If you're still awake, come over. Key under the mat. Leave your shoes outside the door.*

After she sent it, she checked the 2:00 AM text. It was from a number she wasn't familiar with, and it said, simply: *SL = Side Life.*

There was an attachment. A video. And as Pearl watched it, the sappy happiness drained out of her, the overjoy replaced by a different feeling: stronger, grimmer, and more familiar. It was the feeling of that last puzzle piece sliding into place.

SHE WATCHED THE video one more time before calling the number it had come from, her mind running through the videos she'd seen, on Liam Miller's phone and from this number, ticking off the crimes: *Defacing a grave, breaking into private property, a purse theft, a carjacking. The CVS robbery.*

A male voice answered.

"Ryan," Pearl said.

"Yes."

"I watched the video. I saw you and Liam in CVS."

He said nothing. She could hear his shaky breathing.

She kept going. "You were daring each other to do bad things. It was getting worse and worse."

"Yes."

"Are there others on your phone?"

"Yes."

"What kind?"

"Nothing violent."

"Okay . . ."

"Drug stuff. Graffiti. We slashed the tires on a UPS truck . . . We held up a gas station in Fishkill, but we just pretended we had a gun."

"Why?"

"I don't know. We were bored. Our whole lives, everything was so easy." He took a breath, and Pearl thought of the CVS video: All that smashed glass. The two of them all in black, holding handfuls of pills, laughing like crows. "We weren't hurting anybody," Ryan said. "We just wanted to see what it was like."

"To see what *what* was like?"

"Being in danger."

Pearl exhaled. "It was you in the black hoodie. You and Liam planned it. It wasn't Wade. It was you."

His breathing grew heavier. She heard him sob. "I didn't mean to kill him," he said. "He wanted in the car and I hit the accelerator instead of the brake . . . He was my best friend."

"Bobby knew about this?"

"Yes. I mean . . . I told him the next day."

"He covered it up?"

"Yes. He made me put that stuff in Wade's locker—the pills and the ring. He made me bully Wade's friend Rafe Burgess into giving me the combination. His Instagram password too. Bobby sent those awful texts to Tamara from it. I didn't do that. I never would say those things to a girl, I swear."

Pearl took a deep breath. She thought of Udel, back in the car with her, bragging about how he could read people. Sucking down lo mein when he'd just watched an innocent kid get processed, cavity searched, humiliated. She thought about Bobby just a few hours ago, saying he was going to "sleep real well" tonight, after they'd brought Mason in, after Connor had been rushed to the hospital. Couldn't wait to "get some shut-eye," he'd said, with all these lives ruined and all that knowledge in his head.

"I didn't know what to do," Ryan was saying. "I was scared. I didn't want to tell my parents. I pushed her car into the Kill and stayed out all night. The next morning I went to Bobby's. He told me he would help. He said every story needs a hero and a villain. And if we played it his way, Liam could be a hero."

Pearl gripped the phone. Pathetic, lazy-assed Bobby Udel, who thought of this town as a book he'd read before. Making up lies. Destroying lives, just to get the ending he wanted. "Ryan."

"Yes."

"You know who the real villain is here."

Ryan took a deep breath. She could almost feel him trembling. "I do," he said, finally. "I do."

Thirty-Two

A deleted text exchange between Ryan Grant and Liam Miller from the cell phone of Ryan Grant, October 20, 1:00 AM.

You awake?

S'up?

They kicked me out again.

Srsly?

They have "company."

Ugh who?

Don't tell anybody, okay?

I never tell anybody. It's so gross, man. Your parents. WTF is wrong with them?

Right? Anyway, this one is a singer. They met her at a club. She's got a sweet ride. A Jag. Looking at it right now.

You're outside your house?

I'm in my car. Sneak out. I'll pick you up. I've got a plan for SL. Jack the car. Steal her stuff. It'll be easy.

No way!

I was asleep. They kicked me out of the house. She deserves it.

I don't know dude. My parents think I'm asleep.

Come on. Be a friend. Help me get her. They'll never find out. I promise.

OK.

Any pills left?

Lots.

Good. Bring em.

Thirty-Three

"Good thing you got my broad shoulders," Dad said.

It still felt weird, thinking of him as Dad, but after tonight it felt even weirder not to think of him that way. He was here with Mom, after all. He'd come to the hospital. Wade wasn't here. Not that Connor wanted him here. "Where's Wade?"

"He's home, honey," said Mom. "I texted him you'll be fine. He's very relieved."

Connor rolled his eyes. It hurt. He had a headache, and he felt groggy and weak. He'd just come out of surgery. They'd removed the bullet from his shoulder, transfused him full of blood. "Good as new," the doctor had said. "You'll be in a sling for a few weeks though. With a cool cast for all your friends to sign."

All my friends, Connor thought now, picturing a plain white cast, with Noah's lone signature, again Wade's fault. If it weren't for Wade, Connor would have lots of friends, not to mention an intact shoulder and a nonbroken front window and a mom that didn't look the way his mom did right now—gray-skinned and hollow-cheeked, a person eaten alive by worry.

"I'm so happy, honey," Mom said. Connor felt like crying.

"I'm really tired, guys," he said, his voice cracking. "I think it's the drugs."

Dad nodded. "I should probably be getting home anyway. It's after two in the morning." He ruffled Connor's hair. "See you soon, buddy."

"Really?"

"Yes. I promise. I'll be here tomorrow."

"Weird," Connor said. "But good."

"Right?" Mom kissed him on the cheek. She squeezed his hand. "Thank you," she whispered, but not to him, or Dad, or anybody in the room. "Get some rest, sweetheart."

After Mom and Dad left, Connor stared at the ceiling, remembering back to when he was a little kid, finding that romance novel manuscript Mom had written, deep in her desk drawer. Wade had read some scenes aloud to Connor—stuff about the British countryside in the 1800s, a lonely lady landowner and the ghost of a duke. Connor couldn't remember the details, but he could remember how he had felt, hearing all those big words, that detailed story, as though there was this whole other part of Mom that they'd never seen before, this secret skill of hers, like a superpower. It had made him proud. But now it felt as if that part of her was gone, along with every other part of her that didn't have to do with worrying about Wade.

Connor closed his eyes and tried to sleep, sounds filling his mind: The smashing window. Gunshot cracks. Wade's tires screeching away from the curb, leaving his family behind.

WADE HADN'T ANSWERED any of Jackie's texts. She'd lied to Connor because she didn't want him to worry, but now she was hoping against hope that he'd gone home and to bed. After she'd sent her latest text, saying Connor had come out of surgery and that he was going to be all right, she'd used the GPS program she'd downloaded last year but had never used and tried to find Wade that way. But it hadn't worked. He'd turned off his phone. One step ahead of her. She turned her Facebook notifications back on, even though Wade had taken his page down. Maybe someone would see him and contact her on Messenger. Some friend she didn't know about. The only hope she had.

"Look," Bill was saying, "if you need me to stop by the house and see if he's back, I can."

Jackie pictured Wade, waking up from a deep sleep to find his father standing over him. "No, no. I'll go. Soon as I get Connor situated. You get back to your girls."

"Jackie."

"Yes?"

A look crossed his face—regret mixed with something else, something Jackie had to turn away from. "Everything will be okay."

She knew that wasn't what he'd wanted to say. All these years apart, Jackie could still read Bill's mind, and she was grateful to him for keeping his thoughts to himself. "I know it will," she said quietly. "Life only gives us as much as we can take."

BOBBY UDEL STILL lived with his parents. Pearl probably shouldn't have visibly reacted to that information, but when Ryan Grant told her, she still rolled her eyes.

"Tough guy," Tally said, taking the words right out of her mouth.

They were in the parking lot of Havenkill High School, where Ryan had been waiting, Pearl having woken up half the Haven-kill Force, including Sergeant Black, for backup. Not one of them had complained, but Pearl wasn't surprised. They were all solid guys. Bobby Udel was the only one who might have raised a fuss about being woken up in the middle of the night to go to a high school parking lot and tape-record a kid's confession. And he was at home with Mom and Dad, sleeping off his lies.

"He says it saves him money," Ryan said. "I actually feel bad for his mom and dad." He was braced against his Jeep, shivering in the cold. His hands were cuffed behind his back—protocol, but he didn't seem to mind. He'd come with a written-out confession and subjected himself to the sergeant's interview, answering every question fully. There was freedom in admitting one's guilt, in having no more left to hide. And Ryan seemed as relaxed and free as Pearl had ever seen him, his shoulders no longer slumped from the weight of all those secrets.

"Do you have anything else you want to add?" Sergeant Black said, tape recorder still running.

Ryan nodded. "Yes," he said, his stubbled head sparkling in the parking lot light, his eyes glowing in shadows. "Liam was trying to stop me from taking the car. He changed his mind about stealing it. That was why he ran at me. He wanted to do the right thing."

He looked at Pearl. She met his shadowy gaze and said nothing.

"He was a hero," Ryan said.

The sergeant nodded. Turned the tape recorder off. Then they all got in their cars and headed off to get the villain.

THE HOSPITAL WAS far from crowded. Gunfire or not, this was still Havenkill, and so Connor wound up with a room of his own in the pediatric wing, two nurses moving him there shortly after Bill left. Jackie followed the gurney as they wheeled him down the hall to the elevators, holding Connor's bag of bloody clothes. His coat too, as though somehow he'd need it there. "He's a strong boy," said one of the nurses as they lifted Connor into the bed. "He'll do great." She said it as though it were something out of a script, but Jackie was thankful anyway. Connor was sound asleep, so she knew it was for her benefit.

As the nurses were leaving the room, Jackie's phone chimed. *Wade*, she thought, her spirits lifting. But when she checked the screen, she saw Helen's name. She slipped into the hallway and answered fast. "Helen? Why are you awake? Is everything okay?"

"I'm fine. Just didn't take my Ambien," she said, though her voice sounded frail, the psychologist-calm sucked out of it. "Honey, I went onto Facebook. Someone posted about gunshots on Maple. They thought . . . one of your boys might . . ."

"Connor."

"Oh my God."

"No, no. Connor's going to be fine . . . I'm at the hospital now and—"

"I'm coming."

"What?"

"I'm joining you. I'm your friend. It's the least I can do."

"Wait. Helen. Can you please check on Wade?"

"Wade?"

"Just . . . Before you come to the hospital, drive to my house and see if his car's outside. Okay?"

She exhaled, a deep, draining sigh. "Yeah," she said. "Yes. Of course."

After she hung up, Jackie went back into Connor's room. It was painted a cheery yellow, balloons dancing across one of the walls. She listened to her son's deep breathing as she put the bag down for a moment, thinking about laundry. How on earth was she supposed to get out bloodstains that thick? Maybe Helen would know.

Jackie sat down on the chair across from her son's hospital bed, draped his coat over her lap. She slipped her hand into the pocket and removed Connor's phone in its Minecraft-themed cover, the battery long dead. The other pocket was full of gum wrappers, a business card from a game store, ficus leaves from his science project—artifacts from before tonight, before this past weekend, a happier time. *Why can't someone let us know when things are going to get worse, so at least we can enjoy the before?* Jackie's eyes clouded with tears. She cupped the ficus leaves in her hands, inhaling the scent of them, glad only for the fact that her son was asleep, that she was alone in this room, no one around to see her doing something this ridiculous.

The breast pocket was buttoned closed—odd for Connor, who even on the coldest days had to be held down and forced to zip up his jackets. Jackie unbuttoned it and removed what was inside. A piece of paper, carefully folded. She unfolded it, saw the sketch marks. A drawing of Wade's. She could tell his work anywhere, the carefulness of it, those graceful lines . . .

She unfolded the drawing all the way and looked closely at it. Her breath left her.

And when Helen showed up ten minutes later with bottles of water and a bag of apples, all she could do was hand her the drawing, then watch silently as Helen's mouth opened and closed, trying to form an excuse that didn't exist.

BOBBY UDEL'S PARENTS' home was a quiet little ranch house much like Wade Reed's, with a neat lawn illuminated by garden lights, a row of rosebushes under the windows, dutifully trimmed back for the fall.

Ryan had called Bobby. Told him he was coming over. "There's complications, man," he'd said. "You have to help me. Meet me outside your house in ten minutes."

"It can't wait till tomorrow?" Bobby had said over the speakerphone in a whining voice that made Pearl want to break glass. Pearl had driven over in Ryan's car, Tally in the backseat, Ryan still cuffed, in case he suddenly changed his mind. Romero, Sergeant Black, and an older cop named McHugh had all taken cruisers and parked blocks away, out of the house's line of view, lights killed, radios on, guns loaded.

In theory, this was overkill. But Bobby Udel was so easily underestimated, it was better to be safe. Pearl clicked on the dome light, tapped Bobby's number into Ryan's phone, and put the speaker on. Waited.

Bobby answered fast. "Dude. Text. Don't call. You know my mom is a light sleeper."

"Whatever," Ryan said. "I'm outside."

"You getting smart with me?" There was a threat in Bobby's voice. A menace. Pearl glanced at Ryan, the hint of fear in his eyes.

"No. Sorry, man."

Pearl and Tally slipped out of the car, guns drawn. They helped Ryan out and onto the sidewalk. "Wait," Ryan said. "I almost forgot. My sweatshirt pocket. Left side."

Pearl and Tally looked at each other. Tally removed a Baggie from Ryan's pocket. Held it up. Inside was an iPhone, the case encrusted in fake rubies that matched Amy Nathanson's lipstick. "Evidence," Ryan said. "It's got my fingerprints all over it. Bobby's too."

"WHOA, WHOA, WAIT," Bobby said once he saw Tally and Pearl on either side of Ryan, and heard Tally reading him his rights. "You're shitting me, right? This is some kind of joke?"

"No joke," Pearl said. "You framed an innocent kid for manslaughter. You had stolen prescription drugs planted in his locker. You also sent harassing messages to a young girl from his Instagram account . . ."

"Did Ryan tell you that?"

Ryan looked at him. "You know it's true."

Tally said, "I'm not even going to start on you covering up the CVS break-in. What kind of horseshit is that?"

"I can't believe this. At my parents' house. We've been so good to you, Ryan. My whole family."

"Let's go, big guy," Tally said flatly. "As they say in the movies, the jig is up."

Bobby was wearing boxers. A Giants T-shirt. And, as Pearl saw now, he held a gun in his right hand. "He's carrying," she said.

Tally said, "Jesus, Bobby."

"Drop it," Pearl said.

Bobby didn't drop the gun. His eyes darted from Tally to Ryan to Pearl. "Get the fuck off my mom's doorstep."

"Hold up, hold up," Tally said.

Pearl slipped her gun out of her holster, but he was too fast. Within seconds, she felt the barrel of Bobby's gun pressed against her forehead.

Ryan breathed in sharply.

She was aware of Tally unholstering his weapon and aiming it at Bobby, of the cars down the street pulling up, doors slamming, everything moving in slow motion, a type of strange, sad choreography. "Put the gun down, Bobby!" shouted the sergeant behind her. "Drop it and raise your hands."

"Bobby," Ryan said. "Please."

Bobby kept his eyes locked on Pearl's. She felt almost as though she could see into them, through them, into the cold dullness of his mind. "All my life I've been taking care of you, Ryan. Every single fuckup, every crappy grade I've helped you hide from your parents. Every time I've covered your sorry, spoiled rich ass and this is what I get. You team up with *her*. Do you even know who she is?" His eyes flickered at Tally. "Do you know who she is, Ed?"

"She's a police officer," Tally said slowly, carefully. "You don't want to do this."

"She's a murderer." Dabs of sweat on his upper lip. A sheen of it on his forehead and those eyes like the gun barrel, cold on her skin. "I have friends in Poughkeepsie. They told me. She killed her own mother."

Pearl felt something deep within her snap in two. She was aware of Ryan's shallow breathing, of Tally shifting on his feet, both hearing those words, not knowing what to do with them. The truth hurt. It always would. The way it hung in the air, changing everything. Pearl felt it in the weight of her own gun in her hand, in the metal at her forehead: the knowledge of what she was.

It doesn't matter who shoots first, said the voice in Pearl's head. *He's done anyway. And you've been done since you were three.* "You were right, Bobby. You do know everything about me," she said. Then she fired her gun at his foot, ready for him to pull the trigger.

"I DIDN'T WANT to hurt my family," Helen said. "I thought for sure the truth would come out about who really ran Liam over, without Wade or me having to . . . I mean . . ."

They'd moved from Connor's room into the waiting room,

Jackie wanting Helen nowhere near either of her sons, even her younger one, even sound asleep. The drawing was on the table, spread out atop a *Nickelodeon Magazine*—naked Helen, front and rear views, with her C-section scar, the tattoo on her lower back, *T* for the Fury Tisiphone, every inch of her middle-aged body, faithfully re-created by Jackie's son.

Helen had been doing most of the talking. All of it, actually. Ever since she'd arrived, Jackie had said one word to her, the only word she could get out: "*Why?*"

"It was a mistake," Helen was saying now. "Stacy had invited him and stood him up. Back in April. He really did have a crush on her, and she can be so cruel that way, and I just . . . I tried to make him feel better. I didn't intend for anything to happen, but . . . Jackie, I'm weaker than you know."

The name in Wade's notebook. "Tristesse." Written back in April. The girl's profile. Stacy's profile. It all made sense.

"I was lonely myself. I still am. Garrett's never around, and Stacy's more interested in her friends. And that loneliness was something the two of us had in common. Something he understood."

Jackie found her voice again. "You were lonely together. You and my son."

"It was only a few times."

"You gave him a burner phone."

"It was the summer. I was crazy. Midlife crisis. He's an artist. Like no one I've ever known and he drew me, Jackie. He drew me so beautifully."

Jackie stared at her. Perfect Helen, with her pretty, lineless face and her psychologist's voice, her yoga breathing and her kind, giving nature. Helen, who believed so deeply in the fairness of life, that everybody only got out of it as much as they could take . . . Funny how you can be friends with someone for more than thirty years but never truly know them until they slip up. *Teenagers are terrible at keeping secrets, Helen. You ought to know that. You're the mother of one.*

"We just went for a ride that night," Helen was saying. "That's all. I was trying to tell him it was over. I'd been trying to tell him for weeks. For the sake of my family, I said. He wouldn't listen. He bought me a necklace and wanted to run away with me and he kept trying to see me, even in the hospital. Stacy was right there . . ." Her voice trailed off, Jackie's eyes pinning her. Silencing her. "I'm sorry," she said. The only thing she could say.

Jackie stood up. "Tell the police," she said. She walked out of the waiting room and headed back down the hall to Connor's room, leaving Helen to find her own way out.

Jackie watched Connor sleep for a few moments, his slow breaths calming her, when she heard her phone ping. Her first thought was, *A text from Wade.* But then it pinged again, and again, and she realized it wasn't a text at all. It was her Facebook notifications. *Please let this be about Wade. Please let him be safe, with a friend.*

She clicked on the icon, but when she opened up the app, she saw that it wasn't Facebook Messenger that was pinging. It was people liking her post. "I didn't post anything." She said it out loud, to her sleeping son.

She checked her page, and saw that someone had posted as her at 2:45 AM. Just about fifteen minutes ago. She read the first line:

By the time you read this, I'll be dead.

She read the rest quickly, thinking, *No. No please. It isn't fair. This can't be happening,* with the night caving in all around her, her entire world falling apart. With shaking hands, she reached into her purse, fumbled around, looking for her bottle of Xanax.

It was gone. She moved into the hallway, headed for the elevator. *Think, think, think,* she told herself as she pushed at the buttons, getting off at the first floor, running out of the building, through the grounds toward the parking lot, pushing toward her car. *There's a clue in there about where he is. There's got to be a clue.* But what she saw in her mind was the Eiffel Tower, the black-and-white one from the picture in Helen's bathroom. She saw it crumbling, collapsing into itself, leaving only a pile of dust.

Thirty-Four

Wade closed his eyes. He inhaled the scent of the old cabin—mold and cedar and a deep earthy smell, like being buried alive. He liked it here. It reminded him of the safety cones in his room and the dead birds and glittering rocks he liked to take pictures of—things nobody else would ever notice, but that made them more special to him.

Helen was like that in a way. She'd complain about it all the time, how no one ever noticed her, not Stacy or Garrett or the people she worked with. Even guys on the street. She'd talk about how they looked right through her, as though she were a ghost. Helen called it the "middle-aged vanishing act." Or "disappearing before one's time." But he'd never met an older person who cared about it as much as she did. "You're the only one who sees me, Wade," she'd once said. As though that was his best quality. Maybe it was.

What she would never know was that he hadn't seen her either. Not at first. And even as he tried to force Helen's image into his mind, it was Stacy's that kept coming to him, Stacy last spring, in the park after school, that smile of hers, cigarette smoke curling from her lips and the perfume she wore that smelled of vanilla. "You're the only one who listens to me, Wade."

For three weeks, Stacy Davies had met with him in secret. She'd told him her hopes and her darkest fears and her real name, which meant "sadness." She'd told him he was unlike anyone she'd ever known, and she'd said that like it was a good thing and she'd made him think maybe this town wasn't as shitty as he'd thought and she'd kissed him. Just once. But it had all been a lie. Those three weeks had started on a dare and ended with a video of that one stupid kiss, posted on a message thread that included practically every kid at Havenkill. Kissing sounds behind his back in the hallways; laughter that made his face burn. Stares and grins and attention that felt never-ending. And the one to dare Stacy. The kid who'd said, "Let's mess with Reed." That kid had been Liam Miller.

Helen didn't know that. She didn't know any of it when Wade had shown up at her house looking for Stacy, unable to stop shaking. She'd comforted him out of her own loneliness, and when that comforting took a turn, Wade had thought, *Good*. Because he could think of no better way to hurt Stacy.

Of course, that plan had failed, like every other plan of Wade's. He was still mad at Stacy. He'd die mad at her, but he couldn't bring himself to hurt her. And he could never hurt Helen.

Wade's arms and legs felt heavy and pointless. He'd taken Mom's entire bottle of Xanax, swallowing a few at a time to keep from throwing up. Washed them down with a beer he'd bought from the Lukoil—the only place where they didn't laugh at his fake ID. When he started to feel sleepy, he posted his note on Facebook, trying to think of his orange cones, of his dead birds, of Helen rather than Stacy or Mom. He didn't want to think of Mom right now, what his death might do to her. He wished she hadn't worked so hard to get him to tell the truth.

Wade had picked this place to take the pills because it was a special place to him. He'd come here with Helen before. He'd taken Connor here when he was a little kid. His friends too, back when he had them—though they'd mostly thought of it as a place to party. These days, Wade came here alone, whenever he needed to calm his mind.

What kept bringing him back was the ghost—the girl who had come here to slit her throat. The official story was that she had slaughtered her entire family, but Wade thought that she was probably like him—a kid accused of something horrible but unable to tell the truth about it. That's when you kill yourself: when you aren't allowed something as basic as honesty.

Wade rested his head against the wall, his phone next to him. He was getting really tired now, with a weird headache, like lead weights on his eyes, and little white sparks when he closed them. He lay down on the floor and crossed his hands over his chest and tried to think of nothing.

But he kept seeing the ghost. The deeper he slipped into the dream, the clearer he saw her, the falsely accused murderer draped in a gauze shroud, her pale face splashed with her own blood. She spoke to him.

"Why did you do it?"

"Same reason you did."

"Nope. That's wrong."

"What do you mean?"

"I did it because I lost my family. You have one. A good one. They're looking for you."

"Oh . . ."

"Whatever your reason is, I bet it's a dumb one."

"Hey, that isn't fair."

"You're a dumb guy, you know. You notice shit like candy wrappers because you think that makes you an artist. But you don't pay any attention to people who love you."

Wade's hands scraped the wooden floor, his fingernails digging into it, trying to stay awake. *This is wrong,* he thought. *This is stupid. I shouldn't have done this. I shouldn't . . .*

"You also feel way too fucking sorry for yourself."

His breathing slowing, blackness closing in, Wade thought of bad decisions, how he kept making them, over and over again. *I like my family. I like the Kill. I like drawing and breathing, but I got rid of all of that.*

Wade drifted down further, darkness curling around him like black water, Wade sinking into it, lights glowing on the surface. At one point, he could have sworn he felt cool hands on his face, Mom's voice saying his name. *Just a dream,* he thought, letting go. *My last dream.* He knew he would haunt this place forever.

Epilogue

Two weeks later

Pearl had visited Wade and Connor Reed in the hospital. Wade, who had been naive enough to attempt suicide with low-dose Xanax, had given his mother, police, and paramedics plenty of time to find him. But it had been his brother who had saved the day. Called at the hospital by a frantic Jackie Reed and roused from a deep sleep, Connor had been alert enough listening to Wade's suicide note to pick out one line: *I'm all alone here right now, unless you count the ghost lol.* "That's the shack by the Kill," he'd told Jackie over the phone. "It's haunted." A detective in the making. Finding those clues.

The afternoon Pearl had visited them, Wade was just about to be released. Connor still needed another week, but the two boys were sharing a room. By then Bobby Udel, who was in a different wing of the hospital recovering from his gunshot wound, had been charged with conspiracy, obstruction of justice, official misconduct, and attempted murder, and word had gotten out about

Ryan Grant's confession too. Everyone in town and in the world at large wanted to apologize to the Reeds, and as a result, the boys' hospital room was filled with flowers, stuffed animals, Mylar balloons—a shrine to the living. Neither one of them seemed very comfortable with it. But Jackie Reed, who greeted Pearl along with the boys' father, Bill, said, "You can't stop people from caring."

Pearl had stopped by the hospital to tell Wade that the Havenkill PD had chipped in to pay for new tires for his car, at which he'd asked his mom, "You think my car will make it to California?"

Jackie and the boys were leaving Havenkill, despite their newfound celebrity, the GoFundMes in Wade's name, the song Aimee En had written for Wade—"Sensitive Boy"—to be released on a major label next month.

"So why are you leaving?" Pearl had asked.

Wade had looked at her with those black, sad, survivor's eyes. "Why stay?"

Pearl envied that in Wade—the simple ability to leave the past behind. She didn't have it, not yet. Which was why she'd finally buckled under and called her brother and arranged to see her dying father, whose name was Milton. Milton Maze.

She'd never referred to him by name or even thought of him by name, and so, sitting in Paul's car, on their way up to Albany, she'd wondered aloud what she should call him. "Milton? Mr. Maze?"

"What about Dad?" Paul said, proving for the millionth time how very different he and Pearl were.

"No. Not Dad."

"Pops?"

"Stop it."

Milton Maze lived in a white two-story row house, wedged in between two very similar-looking row houses, one yellow, the other blue, a few blocks from Albany Med. There were some cars parked out front—the place had no garage—and so Pearl wondered which of the cars belonged to her brother, just to have something to wonder about that didn't terrify her as they walked to the door.

"The roof didn't cave in," Paul said. He was talking about the roof at the Havenkill police station, which, despite some very stormy weather, had remained intact long enough for the big move into the double-wide. He'd pointed that fact out a few times, whenever Pearl had expressed doubts over seeing her father. *The roof didn't cave in. See? You aren't as doomed as you think.*

"Paul."

"Yeah?"

"I'm still working out of a trailer. I can't turn around without bumping into another cop and whenever we bust someone who isn't, uh, hygienic, the whole place reeks for days."

"Meaning . . ."

"Meaning nothing. Meaning there is no meaning behind the station's noncollapsing roof. Much as you may want there to be."

Paul smiled at the sidewalk. "I like you," he said.

JAMES WAS WAITING for them—a tall twenty-three-year-old with Pearl's curly dark hair and gray eyes. "Wow," he said, when he met her. Nothing more. They hugged, very awkwardly. Paul shook his hand. And then James took Pearl upstairs to Milton's room and left her there, as much of a stranger as he'd always been, nothing really changed at all.

Inside Milton Maze's bedroom, Pearl's breath caught. She

wasn't sure what she was expecting to find on the other side of the door. Her memories of her father were so vague, but they all involved a tall figure standing over her, turning away. She imagined an angry shadow in the bed, so when she walked into the room and saw a frail, white-haired man with watery eyes, she was surprised enough to move closer. The sun shone through the shaded window, the air too close—medicinal and slightly stale.

"Pearl." His voice sounded like snow crunching, and Pearl felt outside of herself, as though she were watching the moment as a movie.

He held out his hand. She reluctantly took it. It was soft and dry, his fingernails clean. Well cared for, for a dying man. He smelled of medicine and soap, and he smiled at her. It made her feel strange.

She heard herself speak. "I shot a man a couple of weeks ago."

His smile dropped away.

"Second person I've ever shot. It was in the line of duty and he had a gun drawn on me. When I shot him, I figured he'd shoot me too . . . that he might kill me, considering where his gun was aimed. I closed my eyes. I waited for it. But when I opened them, he was down. A couple other officers tackled him."

Pearl's father watched her with bloodshot eyes, silvery from cataracts. She wasn't quite sure whether he could see her at all. "My gun was aimed at his foot, his at my head. But I was the one who fired. Can you believe that?"

"How did you feel," he said, "knowing you were going to stay alive?"

"Surprised," Pearl said quietly. "Disappointed, maybe."

"I'm sorry."

"Don't be. It's just the way I am."

"No," he said. "It's the way I made you."

Pearl let go of his hand.

There was a pitcher of water and a stack of cups on the nightstand. He motioned to it. She poured him a cupful and he took a few long, greedy gulps. "She'd been cheating on me," he said finally, as though coming up for air. "I'd just found out. I was mad, but couldn't . . . I couldn't say it. I knew if I said it, she'd leave me. Take you kids with her. You were on the floor, playing with my shoes. You always liked to play with my shoes."

He motioned to the water again. Pearl poured him another cupful and waited for him to drink it, a ritual that was already getting to her. She didn't know why she was waiting. She wasn't sure she wanted to be here.

"She was putting her makeup on. The safe was under the desk and it was open. It was right next to my shoes." He took another swallow. "I saw you pick up the gun. I was standing in the doorway."

"I don't need to hear any more."

"You picked it up and you pointed it. Just like you'd seen me do at the shooting range."

"Please stop."

"You pointed it at her. I could have kept you from doing it but I didn't. I stayed in the doorway. I turned my back until I heard the shot."

An image flashed in Pearl's mind. Something she'd seen in nightmares. The heavy thing dropping out of her hand. Her ears ringing. A woman in a black dress, falling onto a pale pink carpet, pooling blood. And Pearl, all alone, looking for her dad . . .

"I waited. I didn't come in the room right away. I watched her fall, and I watched you, this little girl . . ." Milton Maze's face was red. Tears trickled down his cheeks. "I was glad it had happened."

Pearl stared at him. She knew what she was supposed to say: *I forgive you.* But she couldn't do it. Her mouth wouldn't form the words.

"I couldn't look at you after. It's why I left you at your aunt Ruth's. I couldn't look at you, Pearl, without remembering what kind of monster I am."

Pearl took a step back from the bed; the smell was getting to her: soap and medicine and sweat and death; the words were getting to her too. What did he want from her? What did he expect? "Thank you for telling me." She couldn't say any more than that. She put Milton Maze behind her, swallowing tears, knowing she'd never see him again.

Walking back to his car, Paul turned to her. "So what did you call him?" he said. "Milton? Milty? Mr. Maze?"

Pearl grabbed Paul's hand more tightly than usual. She kissed him on the cheek. *The roof didn't cave in. Maybe it never will.* "What the hell is your last name?" she said.

Six weeks later

Jackie was at the wheel when they crossed the California border, Wade's car hitched to the bumper, Death Valley spreading out in front of them like some strange, lifeless planet. Connor was asleep in the backseat and Wade was next to her, eyes closed, headphones jammed into his ears. She tapped him on the shoulder, and his eyes opened, taking it all in. "Welcome to Mars," Jackie said.

"Wow." He grabbed his phone out of his pocket and started taking pictures.

It was about as much conversation as they'd had during this trip, Jackie and Wade, with Connor only slightly chattier. But she found comfort now in these silences, the nodding of their heads as they listened to their music, the sound of their breathing. It was all she needed—the two of them, alive.

Yesterday morning, she'd gotten an e-mail from Helen. A long letter detailing her divorce that ended, *I hope you can find it in your heart to forgive me.*

Such a strange expression—as though the heart were a messy closet you dug around in, forgiveness stashed in some long-forgotten shoe box. Jackie felt sorry for Helen. She might forgive her, maybe write her back someday. But for now, she had a rental in the valley to settle into, two boys to acclimate to new schools, a real estate job to start, a half-finished manuscript to complete. So many new things to begin that the idea of looking back on anything seemed unappealing and remote.

"Mom," said Wade. "Let me take your picture."

Jackie turned to her oldest son. He held up his phone, the desert sun shining on his floppy, two-toned hair. She'd forgotten how oddly bright California was.

"Don't look so serious," he said.

Jackie flashed him a smile, not so much posing but watching him: a young man, heading into his future. Connor snored in the backseat, growing older by the second, and Jackie wanted to hold this moment in her hands, to keep it with her always.

Acknowledgments

Tremendous thanks to Sergeant Peter Dunn of the Rhinebeck Police Department, Lee Lofland, and cybersecurity and digital forensic expert Josh Moulin for answering all my police-related questions. Thanks also to Sergeant Dunn for his hospitality in allowing me to tour the Rhinebeck station.

As ever, I am so grateful to my wonderful and insightful agent, Deborah Schneider, and the ever-organized Cathy Gleason, as well as the amazing team at William Morrow, including Liate Stehlik, Priyanka Krishnan, and my truly brilliant editor, Lyssa Keusch. Thanks so much also to the great Selina Walker and Sonny Marr at Penguin Random House UK.

Thanks and hugs to so many good friends, including Sharon Breslau for letting me know how a Realtor thinks; James Conrad and Jackie Kellachan of my all-time favorite bookstore, the Golden Notebook; and, for their support and advice, Chas Cerulli and James (again), Jamie and Doug Barthel, Paul Leone,

Wendy Corsi Staub . . . and of course my beloved FLs who always make it nice.

Finally, but not least, thank you to my in-laws, Sheldon and Marilyn Gaylin, and my mother, Beverly LeBov Sloane, for much-needed emotional support. And of course, Mike and Marissa Gaylin, without whom the roof would cave in.

P.S.

Insights,
Interviews
& More . . .

Meet Alison Gaylin

Franco Vogt

ALISON GAYLIN is the author of the Edgar-nominated thriller *Hide Your Eyes* and its sequel *You Kill Me*, the stand-alone Edgar-nominated *What Remains of Me*, and the Brenna Spector series: *And She Was* (winner of the Shamus Award), *Into the Dark*, and the Edgar-nominated *Stay With Me*. A graduate of Northwestern University and Columbia University's Graduate School of Journalism, she lives with her husband and daughter in Woodstock, New York. ∽

"We're the Guinea Pigs"

There was a time, back in the days when MySpace was first becoming a thing, that I took little notice of social media. To my mind, it was a fad, possibly worthwhile as a marketing tool for my books, but still destined to go the way of the CB radio. Did I worry about its potential effect on my then six-year-old daughter? Not even for a second. The Disney shows she watched—with their emphasis on over-the-top materialism and outsmarting grown-ups—seemed like a far more pressing concern.

It's more than a decade later, and obviously things have changed. Like *If I Die Tonight*'s Jackie Reed, I think a lot about my teenager's online activity. And while I have many conflicting feelings about it, the overwhelming one is a type of helplessness. Yes, I've friended her on Facebook. I follow her on Instagram. Yet I'm aware that she probably has other accounts I don't know about (every kid does) and probably spends more time on them than she lets on (again, every kid does), which means that every day I lose her to an alternate world with its own set of dramas and dangers—a world that I'm far less familiar with, and within which I feel ill-equipped to keep her safe.

I'm not alone. According to a Pew research poll conducted in 2015, 92 percent of teens reported going online daily, including 24 percent who claimed to be communicating on the internet "almost constantly." And their moms and dads ▶

"We're the Guinea Pigs" *(continued)*

are worried about it. The 2017 C.S. Mott Children's Hospital National Poll on Children's Health found internet safety topping such issues as teen pregnancy, child abuse, and suicide as a primary concern among parents.

It's no wonder it's such a prevalent fear: as well as we think we know our teenagers, the fact is, they all long to escape us. It's not our fault. It's simple biology, that desire for independence. And the internet is, as it turns out, an incredibly effective getaway car.

Especially considering that we aren't all that adept at hopping in and taking the wheel. As a good friend of mine put it (in a Facebook message of all things): "When it comes to social media, we're the guinea pigs." Raising a teen is tough enough when you're dealing with issues that have been around for generations . . . dating or driving, for instance, or even drinking and drugs. But as my friend pointed out, we know about all those things because we've lived through them. Never having known what it's like to have posted the wrong picture in the wrong place, to have fallen prey to cyberbullying or catfishing or revenge porn or any number of newly named horrors that didn't even exist when we were teens, we are uniquely unqualified to help our kids navigate their way around them now.

And we tend to be dangerously slow on the uptake.

Preparing to write this piece, I posted on Facebook, asking parents of teens for stories having to do with "social media impacting your child's life in some unforeseen way."

Almost immediately, I received close to two dozen private messages, the stories ranging from shocking to surprisingly sweet to borderline tragic. There was the dad who discovered the private message thread in which his son desperately attempted to counsel a suicidal friend. There was another man, shocked to learn that his stepdaughter had put out feelers over Snapchat to purchase illegal prescription drugs, and had begun corresponding with a stranger about it. There was a woman who learned that her son, treated cruelly by girls at school, had secretly joined an online "men's rights" group. Yet another mother found out that her daughter was being bullied over Instagram without ever telling her about it, while a stepdad was delighted to learn that his wife's young teen daughter had learned sign language, on her own, via YouTube.

In every incident—from cyberbullying to sign language—the parent happened on their child's online life long after it had begun. And that seems part and parcel of this brave, new, confusing world that our kids have settled into. We are always, *always* the last to know.

What can any of us do to keep our children safe in the internet age? For me, the answer is to be as vigilant as I can in real life. I pay attention to her moods, ask questions about her life and try to ▶

"We're the Guinea Pigs" *(continued)*

know as many of her friends as I can. My husband and I have warned her of the dangers of the internet, and we've let her know that if she ever runs into trouble, we're here.

It's not perfect. But then again, when it comes to parenting, is there ever a perfect answer? Haven't all of us been disappointed in them, in ourselves, at least once?

We do what we can. Everything we can. And we trust them. ∾

Fake News

It was a small headline in a local newspaper from a nearby town. And for those new to the area and those who didn't have children, it was not terribly memorable:

Local Teen Victim of a Hit-and-Run Accident.

In the weeks that followed, though, the story took hold and spun wildly, as small-town news stories so often do. The boy hit by the car died, and another local teen emerged as a suspect and was later arrested. Because of their ages, both of their names were kept out of the paper. But that didn't stop everyone—particularly the young people—from embellishing the story. As days and weeks went by, the hit-and-run was said to have been gang-related, drug-related, a purse-snatching gone wrong, the inevitable culmination of a years-long vendetta between the two boys who, as it turned out, were from rival schools.

Outside of them being from rival schools, none of it was true, of course. But in a way, it didn't matter. Those spinning the various stories were younger kids, friends of my daughter who had never met either boy but who suffered from that nagging, yearning boredom so specific to kids growing up in small towns.

It was fake news, complete with a hero, a villain, and various conspiracy ▶

Fake News *(continued)*

narratives. And with the help of social media, it became something to follow, to believe in and swear by, to whisper about and post about and comment on incessantly, inaccurately . . . until the next bit of dark gossip took hold and spread.

Though the hit-and-run took place a few years ago, I am still haunted by the thought of both boys, of their mothers trying to learn the real truth, even as their children were transformed into characters in an ongoing gossip-fueled narrative, their humanity disappearing as their bleak shared story took on a life of its own.

I GREW UP in the suburbs of Los Angeles and went to college in the Chicago area, after which I moved to New York City for graduate school and wound up staying for several years. But when my husband and I settled down and had a child, it was in a small town, two and a half hours north of New York City—one of many lovely, idyllic hamlets on the banks of the Hudson River or nearby, with historic buildings and public squares and populations smaller than that of most universities. In many ways, my town is a wonderful place to raise a family—the streets are safe, the cost of living is low, the public school is a good one, and the pace is slower, less cutthroat than it is in the city.

But as many good things as there are to be had in a small town, so many of them—the slow pace, the familiarity, the utter *safety* of it all—can also make it a breeding ground for malicious gossip, especially when something, or *someone*, happens to threaten that fragile status quo. It's been going on since the beginning of time. Think of the Salem witch trials, McCarthy-era finger-pointing, or, more recently, the persecution of the three bullied goth teenagers from Arkansas known as the West Memphis Three, who were imprisoned for a series of brutal child murders until documentary filmmakers found the evidence that ultimately freed them. The early rape conviction of *Making a Murderer*'s Steven Avery (which was later overturned) arguably stemmed from the disdain the citizens of Manitowoc County felt for Avery and his odd-duck family, all of them clearly outsiders in their pleasant little community.

We all believe what we want to believe, and in a small town, those beliefs catch on and spread like fire, especially in the era of social media. Nothing is vetted on Facebook, Instagram, or Twitter, yet a false post or comment is all too often taken at face value and repeated and repeated until it becomes an accepted fact.

It doesn't take something as devastating as a murder to get the rumor mill churning, but tragedy does send it into overdrive. Perhaps it's the desire to make sense out of the senseless, to restore that fragile idea of order by naming a villain, painting ▶

Fake News *(continued)*

him as truly evil, and punishing him for it as quickly as possible.

But motivations and people are rarely as simple as we'd like to believe. And my heart still aches for those boys involved in the hit-and-run, whose truths most of us will never know. That memory—particularly the anguish I believe their mothers must have felt—was what inspired me to write *If I Die Tonight*. It was my attempt to explore the way real lives can be swallowed up by the driving, dangerous need to tell stories, to punish those who disturb us, to "make sense of things." ∾

Five Big Books Set in Small Towns

If I Die Tonight is the first book I've ever written set in a small, fictional town, but I've been a fan of them for years. The setting, so often charming and idyllic, can also be tense, claustrophobic, a breeding ground for bad behavior and dark, desperate thoughts. Throw in the fictional element and the town itself becomes another multifaceted character. From *To Kill a Mockingbird*'s Maycomb to *Absalom, Absalom*'s Jefferson (located in Yoknapatawpha County, which is actually mapped out in the book) these towns have made an indelible impression on me over the years—while the fictional locales in these five books have had a more recent impact.

The Fever
by Megan Abbott

Bathed in mist and built around a toxic lake, Abbott's Dryden is spooky to begin with. But when the girls of Dryden High start experiencing bizarre unexplained seizures, it gets downright horrifying. As any Salem witch could tell you, small towns are ripe for outbreaks of hysteria, and Abbott exploits this memorably in her chilling tale. ▶

Five Big Books Set in Small Towns *(continued)*

Sunburn
by Laura Lippman

Lippman ventures from her familiar territory of Baltimore, setting this 90s noir tale in the depressed village of Belleville. With descriptions so vivid you feel like you're walking its dusty streets, Lippman creates a territory ripe for desperation and daydreams—the perfect place for her characters to lie low, think big . . . and fall deeply and dangerously in love.

Still Life
by Louise Penny

Penny's first book introduces the lovely fictional town of Three Pines, explaining that the only reason anyone locks their doors there is "to prevent neighbors from dropping off baskets of zucchini at harvest time." With all that charm, the Quebec-area town proves to be a particularly intriguing spot to set a mystery, in the same way a bright smile can belie the shockingly unpleasant thoughts behind it.

The Virgin of Small Plains
by Nancy Pickard

Corruption and sin roil beneath the surface of the eponymous Kansas town in this quietly suspenseful book, which shifts back and forth between 2004 and seventeen years earlier. With the grave of the "virgin" attracting visitors from all over, many of whom view it as some type of healing shrine, Small Plains gains a strange notoriety as years pass. But it's the town's many dark secrets that will define it for readers.

Blame
by Jeff Abbott

Abbott's Lakehaven is more of a suburb, but the rumor-mongering, backstabbing, and secret-keeping that go on within its jurisdiction are the classic attributes of a fictional small town. Add in the fact that the book's heroine suffers from amnesia—and may or may not have done something terrible during the period she doesn't remember—and the feeling of isolation is so pervasive it's terrifying. ∽

Discover great authors, exclusive offers, and more at hc.com.